THE SOUTH BAY SERIES

THE UNEXPECTED GUESTS

A Novel

Ruth F. Stevens

Black Rose Writing | Texas

This is a work of fiction. Names, characters, businesses, places, events, and incidents are either the products of the author's imagination or used in a fictitious manner. Any resemblance to actual persons, living or dead, or actual events is purely coincidental.

ISBN: 978-1-68513-534-8
LIBRARY OF CONGRESS CONTROL NUMBER: 2024941037
PUBLISHED BY BLACK ROSE WRITING
www.blackrosewriting.com

Printed in the United States of America
Suggested Retail Price (SRP) $23.95

The Unexpected Guests is printed in Book Antiqua

*As a planet-friendly publisher, Black Rose Writing does its best to eliminate unnecessary waste to reduce paper usage and energy costs, while never compromising the reading experience. As a result, the final word count vs. page count may not meet common expectations.

Cover art by Jamie Ponchak
Photograph courtesy of Richard Ruthsatz

PRAISE FOR
THE SOUTH BAY SERIES

THE UNEXPECTED GUESTS

"Whether she's warming your heart or tearing it apart, Stevens delivers a compellingly realistic look at how our demons haunt us until we face them . . . and how we can come out the other side into love and joy."
–Pamela Taylor, author of the *Second Son Chronicles*

"A witty novel about love, family, friendship, and starting over. The characters are endearing and heartbreaking as they maneuver through new love, complex relationships and the bonds that bind them together."
–Tricia Hopper Zacher, author of *Many a Sudden Change*

"Just five sentences in, Ruth F. Stevens' *The Unexpected Guests* had all my senses alert to the mutually exclusive hopes and anxieties of Margaret, an editor with more talent than she realizes and an eagerness to connect with Charlie; and Charlie, a well-known author, secretly worried about his career and wanting nothing to do with Margaret. Hint by artful hint, Stevens pulled me into the backstory and the here-and-now of these two, and I was hooked.

Soon I found myself deeply engaged with a supporting cast of intertwined characters: Sunny, bankrupted when she left work to care for her ill mother; Gwendolyn, Margaret's havoc-wreaking mother with a secret fear; Henry, Margaret's unrepentant ex-husband; and Michael, Margaret's fractious son. Some of these I rooted for. Others I wanted to boo off the stage. But as Stevens skillfully revealed more about each character, who to cheer and who to boo grew unclear. Many authors would struggle to pull off this complicated choreography, but Stevens excels.

At the novel's highly satisfying end, not everyone has achieved full redemption—life doesn't work that way—but all the characters stay in my mind, and I'm looking forward to reading Stevens' next offering."
–Marsha Jacobson, author of *The Wrong Calamity*

"With her latest novel, *The Unexpected Guests,* author Ruth F. Stevens demonstrates her mastery of clean and clear prose that draws readers into the lives of its characters from multiple points of view. The narrative is tender, but it is through the nuanced portrayals of the three protagonists where this book truly shines. Perhaps most notable is Stevens' handling of the elderly matriarch, whose bizarre antics are by turn disquieting, heartwarming, and disarmingly funny. Through deft dialogue and a keen eye for detail, Stevens invites her readers to connect with the emotions, the struggles, and the ever-present wit of each of her characters.

The Unexpected Guests is a novel that navigates the complexities of the human experience with sensitivity and grace, offering us a glimpse into a world that always feels authentic."
–Erica Karlin, co-author of *The Sipping Sisterhood Series* and contributor to *Shakespeare & Company, Paris*

"Reading *The Unexpected Guests* is like hanging out with a delightful group of friends. Stevens's writing is fluid, lovely and enjoyable to read. She brings us a cast of characters who face everyday challenges, and a few who face more sinister issues related to their health and well-being. Chances are, you'll relate to one or more of them as you see your life reflected in theirs."
–S.M. Stevens, award-winning author of *The Wallace House of Pain*

"In *The Unexpected Guests*, Ruth F. Stevens portrays a cast of middle-aged and older characters in a fresh, memorable, and realistic light. Sunny, an attractive woman in her early 40s, is haunted by memories of her abusive father as she makes bad choices about men, self-medicates with alcohol and drugs, and fails to prepare for her future. Having worked with child abuse victims for years, I've known many women like Sunny. I'm all too familiar with the painful long-term consequences they suffer daily.

Sunny's story is told in alternating POV with two other main characters—Charlie, a novelist grappling with writer's block, and Gwendolyn, a widow in denial about aging. All three are fighting their personal demons as their lives intertwine and relationships grow more frazzled. Despite the serious issues the characters face, their story abounds with humorous encounters and funny dialogue. Author Stevens likes to write stories that make readers laugh and cry, and *The Unexpected Guests* succeeds on both levels."

–Mary Jo Hazard, retired marriage family therapist and author of *Stillwater*, a coming-of-age novel

"Just when Margaret and Charlie finally resolve their complicated feelings for each other and decide to share a home, houseguests upend their personal lives. Stevens builds complex characters who face difficult decisions—and her trademark twists and turns have the reader flipping pages to find out what happens next."

–Cam Torrens, award-winning author of the *Tyler Zahn* series

MY YEAR OF CASUAL ACQUAINTANCES (PREQUEL)

2023 CIBA Somerset Awards: Semi-finalist
Literary Contemporary Fiction

"When Ruth F. Stevens writes about gray divorce and second chances, you'll believe anything is possible. An optimistic novel about looking for the best in everyone, including ourselves."
–Indies Today **5-star review**

"Touching, polished story of a woman embracing growth, post-divorce… This is a lovely story of finding yourself later in life."
–BookLife **Editor's Pick**

"I appreciated Ruth's immersive prose, the witty first-person narrative, and the excellent editorial work. I highly recommend it to those readers who prefer character-driven novels with compelling protagonists."
–Readers' Favorite **5-star review**

"A humorous journey of heartfelt connections that will keep you turning the pages and rooting for reinvention."
–Sublime Book Review

"A fun, entertaining novel! I can't imagine anyone who wouldn't enjoy this book as much as I did."
–Leslie A. Rasmussen, award-winning author of *After Happily Ever After* **and** *The Stories We Cannot Tell*

"Recommended for memorable characters, sun-drenched settings and a fast-paced storyline."
–Gail Ward Olmsted, bestselling author of the *Miranda Quinn Legal Twist* series

"A multi-layered, enjoyable read. I can't get enough of the intelligent contemporary way this author writes, holding nothing back, bringing in just enough humor to balance the serious themes."
–Paulette Mahurin, international bestselling author of *The Seven Year Dress*

"Stevens is clearly an observer of people, with wonderful insight into how they act and the quirks that make them unique."
-Anna Daugherty, award-winning author of *Outside of Grace*

"The characters are three-dimensional and rise off the page."
–Marisa Rae Dondlinger, author of *Come And Get Me* and *Open*

For Jake, Luciana, Lucas, and Nicolas . . .
and my extended family of relatives and friends.

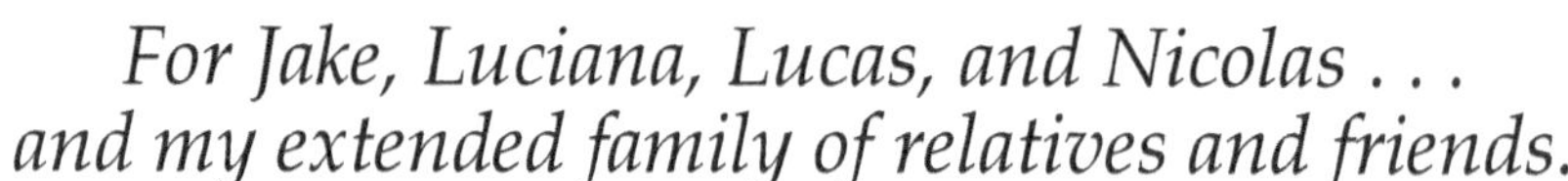

*"Sometimes . . . you find your true family with the people who start
out as unexpected guests and end up changing your life."*

THE UNEXPECTED GUESTS

CHAPTER 1

Have a drink. Eat dinner. Break up with her.

As Margaret opened the door, Charlie reminded himself to stay on track with his game plan. She'd told him she was serving lasagna, and mouth-watering aromas enveloped him as he entered the cozy waterfront apartment. On the coffee table, a bottle of champagne nestled in an ice bucket, its stainless-steel surface glistening with beads of condensation. The eating and drinking portions of the evening were already a fait accompli.

Margaret looked good – *too* good – in jeans and a clingy red cashmere V-neck sweater, her soft brown curls falling to her shoulders. The breaking up part of the agenda might not be so easy. "Break up" was probably the wrong term, considering they'd barely seen each other during the past six months. Their relationship had been a whirlwind affair – only one short, passionate month. Charlie had fallen for Margaret – fallen hard; but she'd broken things off without warning last June, and the rejection wounded him to the core. But now she'd asked him to dinner, making no secret of the fact that reconciliation was her goal.

"Charlie. I'm glad you came." Her face lit up with a welcoming smile.

"Hi, Margaret. I thought you might like to serve this with dinner." He thrust a package toward her – a bottle of wine inside a knitted Christmas gift bag with candy cane striping, tied at the top with a red ribbon from which a pair of jingle bells dangled. All at once the bag appeared silly, embarrassing even. But he was glad he'd brought it. If nothing else, it created a physical wedge between them, a barrier that kept them from touching or kissing.

"Thank you," she said. "Do I need to chill this?"

"No, it's a red. Sangiovese." He had to stop himself from adding *your favorite*. He mustn't sound nostalgic. It might encourage her. She motioned for him to sit on the couch as she popped the cork on the champagne bottle and picked up a pair of crystal flutes, filling each glass with the bubbly liquid. Champagne seemed inappropriate, yet he couldn't accuse Margaret of a social faux pas in choosing it. She had no way of knowing he'd come on a mission of closure, not celebration.

In the December darkness, Margaret's place felt warmer and more intimate than he'd remembered. The recessed lights were dimmed. Candles flickered on the dining table. In the distance, looking out beyond the sliding door that led to the balcony, he could see Christmas lights twinkling from the masts of sailboats docked in King Harbor in Los Angeles's South Bay area. The effect was charming. She'd set the stage for a romantic evening. Her texted invitation was clear on that point.

> **Margaret**
> You gave Nomi a second chance. Now, how about me? One chance, please, to show you how things have changed. How I have changed. Dinner at my place next Friday, 7 p.m.?

Though Margaret was not a writer of fiction like Charlie, she edited a technical journal, and the woman knew how to turn a phrase. The words *second chance* echoed the title of Charlie's newest novel, about a woman named Nomi who sought forgiveness after cruelly driving away her husband. In the end, the husband took her back. Margaret (who had never been cruel, merely honest) wanted from Charlie the same consideration he'd granted his own protagonist – another chance to make things right. But it was too late for that.

This wasn't the first time in the past few months that Margaret had been in contact. In early November, she'd recruited him to visit a fan named Vincent at a senior home where she volunteered. He suspected Margaret had an ulterior motive in inviting him, though he only saw her for a few minutes during his hurried visit. Then she'd turned up at one of Charlie's book signing events. The dinner invitation soon followed. Perhaps he should have turned her down, but he'd decided to meet face-to-face and explain why he couldn't pick up where they left off six months ago. That was the plan – to let her down gently but firmly and close the door on their relationship once and for all.

•   •   •

"That was scrumptious," he said, laying his fork across the empty plate.

"Beginner's luck. I've never made it before." Margaret laughed softly, her dark gaze warm and inviting. The delicious white lasagna – his favorite – told Charlie how much effort she'd made to please him.

He was struck, as always, by how young she seemed for a woman of fifty. It wasn't just the candlelight benefiting her; her skin was smooth, her cheekbones pronounced, her hair natural, her expression animated. No one would ever call Margaret gorgeous, but she had an aura about her that Charlie found more alluring than any classic expression of feminine beauty.

Dammit. He shouldn't have come.

"I can't pretend cooking has become a new passion. But I've been changing a lot of things about my life."

Here we go. Over champagne and dinner, they'd confined their conversation to safe topics. They spoke at length about the early success of *Second Chance,* published the week prior to Thanksgiving. They discussed their friend Sunny Ericsson; he learned from Margaret that she was planning to move back from the San Francisco area. And they lamented that the holiday season was always so hectic.

But Margaret was pivoting to a more serious subject. This would be the perfect time for him to segue into his rehearsed remarks. *I'm glad you've made positive changes, Margaret, but I can't be part of your life going forward. When you broke things off, I had an extremely tough time.*

Perhaps the worst part had been the effect on his writing. *Second Chance* was already being prepared for publication when Margaret gave him the bad news. Charlie was trying to build momentum on a new manuscript back then, but after their breakup he had frozen in his tracks – unable to write, unable to focus. This had never happened to him before, not even when Bet died of a stroke over four years earlier. Back then, work had been a soothing balm, a way to escape the traumatic shock of his wife's sudden death.

After enduring a much graver loss, why did he fall apart over Margaret? It made no sense. He'd given up trying to puzzle it out, concluding only that he was better off staying unattached. He couldn't risk letting another romantic rejection disrupt his success as an author after so many years of disciplined work. There was far too much at stake. But he didn't share this with Margaret. Instead, he said, "Why don't we step outside for some fresh air?"

"Great idea. It's stuffy in here."

Out on the balcony, they gazed down at the distant marina. "Do you hear that?" Margaret asked, cupping one hand to her ear.

"Carolers," said Charlie. "I hear them, but I don't see them."

"They're way down on the docks, but the wind is blowing the sound toward us." It was a chilly evening by California standards, cold enough for them to see their breath. Margaret shivered. If Charlie was being a gentleman, he'd offer his jacket or put an arm around her. But no. There'd be none of that.

"It's colder than I realized," Charlie said. "Maybe we should go back indoors."

"Listen to us — it's too hot, it's too cold," she said, trying to diffuse the awkwardness.

On the way in from the balcony, Charlie stumbled lightly over a rawhide dog bone. "You have a dog?" he asked as they took their seats back at the dining table.

"Petey. Do you remember him? He's the Wheaten terrier who was with me at the senior home."

Charlie thought back on his meeting with Vincent, a kindly old gentleman who knew all of Charlie's novels. How nervous Charlie had been that day, seeing Margaret for the first time in months. She'd seemed tongue-tied as well, and he recalled the way Vincent tried to build them both up, singing each one's praises to the other. Charlie felt equally nervous tonight, as though his entire career depended on breaking free of Margaret's spell. And perhaps, indeed, it did.

He then recalled the handsome terrier lying by Vincent's wheelchair, doing his job as a therapy dog. "I remember Petey. But I didn't know he lived with you."

"Long story, but I have him on a sort of shared custody basis with his original owner. She's moving to New Jersey sometime in January, and then Petey will be with me full-time."

"Ah. And how is Vincent doing?"

"He—Vincent died," she said, looking down at her uncleared dinner plate and tracing the rim with one finger.

"Oh, no."

"He had a serious heart attack a couple of weeks after you met him. When I visited him at the hospital, they'd moved him out of the ICU, and he seemed to be recovering. But he didn't make it."

"I'm sorry to hear that. I could see you two were good friends."

"At the hospital that day, he talked about you."

"He did?"

"Yes. He told me how much it meant for him to meet you." Margaret glanced up, tears filling her eyes. She looked so vulnerable, he half-wanted to slip his arms around her. Why did he feel this confusing urge to hold her when he'd come here to push her away?

"Thank you for telling me that. So sad."

"Yes . . . well . . . can I pour you another glass of wine? We've only half-finished the Sangiovese, which was perfect with the dinner, by the way."

Charlie shook his head. "Thanks, but no more wine for me."

"Coffee? Espresso? I've got regular or decaf."

He should do it now – tell her why he couldn't be part of her life. "No, I—to tell you the truth, I'm exhausted. This book launch has taken it out of me. I'll be heading home now."

She responded without missing a beat. "Wow, when we talked about the holiday madness, I wasn't even thinking how the marketing campaign for the book has added a whole extra layer of pressure for you."

"Yes, it has."

"Maybe we—we can get together when things aren't so crazed."

Charlie coughed into the crook of his elbow. He didn't need to cough, he was buying time to come up with a response. *I know you want to pick up where we left off, and I'm flattered by your interest – but I can't do this again. I came tonight to tell you in person. That's* what flashed through his brain, but the words that came out were, "I don't know. It looks like things are going to stay busy for a long time." He stood and retreated toward the door. "Thank you for dinner."

There was no mistaking Margaret's look of defeat as she lowered her guard, her shoulders slumping and the corners of her mouth turning down as if yanked by a strong gravitational force. For a moment, Charlie feared she was going to cry. She looked beautiful in her sadness, and he suddenly felt a hollow ache of loss in his own heart. Straightening her back, Margaret stood and let out a slow breath, recovering her composure. "You're welcome."

"Goodnight." He tipped his head in a formal nod.

"Goodbye, Charlie."

•   •   •

On the short drive home, Charlie replayed all the moments this evening when he'd failed to confront the situation, all the things he should have said but didn't. When Margaret had ended their affair, she at least had the courage to tell him face-to-face. She'd explained, with kindness and candor, why she couldn't continue to see him. Charlie wanted more from her than she was willing or able to give at that point in her life. She needed time alone after the demise of a long marriage to Henry, her unfaithful husband. The news had stung, but he couldn't fault the delivery, which was direct and forthright yet caring.

And how did he respond tonight? With spineless avoidance and lame excuses about being too tired, too busy. Now that it was over, Charlie felt no relief or resolution – only an overwhelming sense of self-reproach.

Schmuck. Dickhead. Coward!

CHAPTER 2

Back home at 10:15 p.m., Charlie poured himself a scotch, a rare impulse. The squeaking of the liquor cabinet door, the clinking of glass as he pulled out a tumbler, the clattering of the whiskey bottle on the counter – every sound echoed in the high-ceilinged living room, hollow and empty. He sank into the deep sofa and rearranged the throw pillows his late wife Bet had once custom-ordered in a dozen sizes and patterns, but he couldn't get comfortable. He lit a fire, but a chill lingered despite the crackling logs.

What was the point of an *Architectural Digest*-worthy house that oozed good taste when he couldn't even relax in it? The Spanish-style villa felt cold and unwelcoming after the warmth of Margaret's modest, jewel-box apartment. He sipped on his whiskey, forcing it down like a dose of foul-tasting medicine, but it didn't heal what ailed him.

Eyeing his cellphone, at 11:00 p.m. he moved into the den and turned on the television. He needed something clever and funny as a distraction. A *Seinfeld* rerun had just begun. Perfect. When he'd started traveling the country on book tours, Charlie tuned to sitcoms on the in-flight entertainment systems to pass the time. Tonight, the first show he watched was that classic episode where George pretends to be a marine biologist to impress a date. But the next three shows were a blur – Charlie was hard-pressed to recall even a single funny line. His mind drifted back to the night he and Margaret sat in this same spot last June, shoulders and thighs touching as they laughed over reruns of *Curb Your Enthusiasm*. He shook his head as though trying to erase the image from his mind.

Turning off the downstairs lights, Charlie noted it was a few minutes past 1:00 a.m. on the antique clock in the front hall, the one his publisher had given him to commemorate the first time he topped the *New York Times* best-seller list. He really should get to bed, but he still felt antsy. He headed upstairs to the yoga and meditation area he'd created in the second-floor foyer, next to a small balcony filled with flowering plants. Colored spotlights illuminated the plants at night, creating a floral light show. Margaret had admired the display last summer. Would she like the red and green spotlights and large poinsettias he'd added to the mix of greenery for the holidays? *Stop it,* he commanded himself.

Charlie stretched out his lean, six-foot frame on the yoga mat. Though his practice had taught him both to meditate and to visualize, the images forming in his head right now weren't helpful. He recalled lying here with Margaret, their bodies entwined. So real was the feeling of her warm skin, the scent of her hair, and the sound of her soft breathing, Charlie had to sit up abruptly and open his eyes to reassure himself she was not really there. *You're an experienced yogi, you can do better than this.* Reclining and closing his eyes once again, he focused on deep breathing for the next half hour.

Picking up his phone again, Charlie scrolled for messages – even while asking himself, who would text at 1:35 a.m.? Time to pack it in. He brushed his teeth in the master bathroom without even bothering to turn on the light, then climbed into the king bed and pulled the cool covers up to his chin. Lying on his back, he resumed the breathing exercises.

Charlie glanced at Bet's old alarm clock on the bedside table. It was their first digital clock, and she'd complained that it looked like something you'd see in a railway station. The display had just progressed from 2:00 to 2:01 a.m. when Charlie flunked meditation for the second time that night, unwanted thoughts creeping back into his consciousness. This was when he replayed his parting words with Margaret. He had said "goodnight." But she responded with "goodbye." Of course, his actions informed her he'd accepted the invitation only to tell her this. And yet he lacked the balls to speak this one simple word. *She* had been the one to say it, to accept the finality of their meeting. But that's what he'd wanted her to do. So his mission had been successful after all . . . hadn't it?

A dull ache built slowly in the side of his head. Scotch was a bad idea. Charlie flung the covers off and padded back to the bathroom, this time turning on the overhead light in search of Tylenol. The wall clock (who the hell even has a clock in the bathroom?) said 2:10 a.m. Glancing in the mirror as he swallowed the pills, Charlie noted that his gray eyes were rimmed in red. He found the bottle of eye drops, washed his hands, and leaned into the mirror to apply the solution. Despite the growing presence of silver strands in his thick, dark hair, Charlie usually thought he looked good for fifty-three. But tonight he did not admire the face scowling back at him as he blinked and wiped away the excess liquid around his eyes.

He got back into bed, though sleep continued to elude him. Abandoning all hope of mind control, he allowed himself to revisit the events of the evening. The scene replaying most often was Margaret's face in that moment she lost control, that desolate look of loss and disappointment. He cringed at the recollection, hating that he'd caused her such pain – because he knew the hurt ran deep, despite her courage at concealing it. As his resolve weakened, he reminded himself again that after their breakup, getting back in the groove with his writing had been a hard-won battle. He should not, *must* not surrender now to sentimental thoughts.

The bedside clock said exactly 3:12 a.m. when Charlie conceded he was still in love with engineering journal editor Margaret Meyer.

Goddammit.

His realization led to fantasies of sex. This was not emotionally overwrought make-up sex, or cold and dispassionate revenge sex. No. Theirs was the best possible form of intimacy – tender, solicitous, joyful. In his mind, he parted Margaret's lips with a probing kiss, parted her smooth thighs with a gentle thrust. Allowing his writer's imagination to engage fully, he spun an elaborate tale of their lovemaking. Once the fantasy took hold, the notion that it might never happen seemed far more unbearable than the possibility Margaret might reject him again someday. More unbearable, even, than the possibility his writer's block might return if she did so.

At 4:30 a.m., abandoning any hope of sleep, he devised a plan for reconciliation. Armed with flowers, he would knock on Margaret's door in the morning and sweep her into his embrace. He mentally rehearsed several versions of what would follow, all of them physically gratifying.

With the first light of morning, Charlie went down to the kitchen. The scotch and the sleeplessness had given him a jittery stomach, so he fixed himself a mug of plain tea and a slice of dry toast. He noticed that the timer on the microwave said 6:34 a.m., but the hands on the wall clock pointed to 6:40. Why have so many damn clocks when they only confused him?

Deciding that 8:00 a.m. presented the first civilized opportunity to disturb another adult on a Saturday morning, Charlie waited impatiently for the hour to arrive and checked his phone every five minutes or so, as if this constant monitoring would somehow accelerate time. Between phone checks, he busied himself with mundane tasks: sorting through yesterday's mail, taking out the trash, wiping down the countertops. When the time arrived at last, his hands trembled as he scrolled his contact list for Margaret's cell.

The call went straight to voicemail. He remembered she used to find it sexy when he imitated Cary Grant. Should he use his Cary Grant voice now? No, bad idea. He hung up without leaving a message. He called again every fifteen minutes, hoping for a different result, but she did not answer.

He waited until 9:00 a.m. to try texting instead.

Charlie

I'm so sorry about last night. I was an idiot, and it was inexcusable. Now I am the one asking for a second chance. Please, can we talk?

Still no response. Should he keep texting every half an hour or so? No, he already seemed too much like a stalker. Charlie took a seat at the kitchen island and opened the morning paper, but his eyelids descended like heavy curtains. He was cradling his head on crossed arms, half-asleep, the smell of newsprint in his nostrils, when the text chime on his phone startled him into wakefulness at 10:25 a.m. He sat up with a jolt.

Finally! Margaret. Her reply was brief.

Margaret

Had my phone off. Been trying to sleep. OK.

Charlie

OK what?

Margaret

OK, let's talk.

His pulse quickening, Charlie contemplated what flowers would be best and where to stop along the way to buy them. Roses. Red roses. Sure, they were the clichéd flowers of romance, but sometimes a sentimental gesture could send a potent message.

Charlie
May I come over?

> **Margaret**
> No. Call me.

He took a deep breath and punched a finger into the phone to redial her number.

"Hello, Charlie." Her tone was flat, unrevealing.

"Good morning. Actually, it's not a very good morning, is it?"

"I've had better."

"Look, I expect you're wondering why I came to dinner last night, if only to behave like such an asshole?"

"That question did cross my mind, yes."

He figured he deserved that, though he'd hoped for a warmer response.

"I'd meant to be direct with you, the way you were with me in June. My intentions were good, my follow-through was not."

"What was it you intended to be direct about?"

"I—I wanted to explain things. Our breakup kind of derailed me. In both the personal and the professional sense. It took a long time to get myself back on track." He heard a sigh at the other end, but she didn't speak. Charlie continued, "You know I've been immersed in work for the *Second Chance* book tour, but the important thing is I've been writing again too. I'm not caught up yet, but I'm getting there. I need to keep my eye on the ball.

No distractions. No complications. And especially, no risks. I'm scared of another derailment."

"That's the reason for your reluctance?"

"Pretty much, yes."

"So it's not that you're angry with me? Or you've plain lost interest?"

"No, Margaret—no. I told myself I'd moved on, that I didn't want to get involved with you, or *anyone*. But seeing you last night . . . it brought back a lot of old feelings."

"I see." She sighed again. "After I read your first book, *Change/Of Course* . . ."

"What about it?" Charlie's debut novel had been a work of magical realism about teenaged siblings, a boy and girl imbued with special powers.

"I listened to an interview you did on NPR. You said it was necessary to suspend disbelief in order to embrace the idea that these kids had superpowers. You claimed it was the only way readers could jump into the story. That phrase stuck with me – *jump into the story*."

"I remember the interview, but how does that relate to us?"

"You and I need to suspend distrust, Charlie. We need to stop worrying about who's gonna hurt who. Every time I've tried to reach out to you, it's been clear you're afraid to trust me."

"Six months ago, you weren't ready for a relationship. That isn't such a long time. To be fair, how do I know you won't get cold feet again?"

"It feels more like six years than six months. I told you, a lot of things have changed since June."

"I *do* want to hear about that. Even though I didn't act that way last night."

"But even though I've changed, I can't promise I won't hurt you again. And I can't promise I won't die." *Like Bet.*

"So, if we both suspend distrust, what then?" Charlie asked.

"Then . . . we can jump into the story."

He smiled for the first time that day. "What if we agree to erase last night? Start over as if it never happened?"

"You mean you'll show up at my place at seven tonight and we'll eat lasagna again?"

"Oh, I don't think I could wait that long. How about now?"

She paused before answering. "I'm a little fuzzy from lack of sleep. Give me time for a cup of coffee."

•   •   •

When Margaret opened the door for him, Charlie's eyes had to adjust to the semi-darkness of the apartment. The blinds were closed, blocking out the late morning light. She was in gym shorts and a cropped t-shirt that exposed her midriff. No bra. Maybe this was the outfit she'd worn to bed? Even in the dim light, he could see she looked tired around the eyes. His gaze drifted down to the firm flesh of her bare middle, which he desperately wanted to kiss.

And so he did. This elicited a sharp gasp of surprise from Margaret. She flung her arms around his neck, and the two of them found one another's mouths, kissing hungrily. He couldn't say later which one led the other into the bedroom, which one set the pace as they made love in harmony, a well-orchestrated duo. Afterward, they lay facing each other and grinning like a pair of jewel thieves who'd pulled off a heist.

Margaret sat up in the bed and tilted her head toward the ceiling, gazing upward with her hands in prayer pose. "Vincent, I hope you're watching." He gave her a puzzled look. "When I saw him at the hospital the week before he died, Vincent said something else that I didn't share with you last night."

"Which was . . . ?"

"He thought we would make a nice couple. In fact, he encouraged me to chase after you."

"Which you did."

"Shamelessly."

"And it's a good thing too."

"Yes, it is." She smiled, leaning in for a hug.

He spent the rest of the day in her bed. They spoke little, preferring to bask in the knowledge they'd crossed a barrier that had blocked their way forward. They kissed often. They smiled at each other and laughed for no reason. Around two o'clock, Margaret went to the kitchen and returned with bowls of reheated lasagna, which they devoured while sitting propped on pillows.

Margaret's cell buzzed. "Hi, Sunny. Really? Great. Yes . . . sure . . . I'd love a tour sometime. Oh, I see. Whenever you're ready." She smiled at Charlie as she put down the phone. "It's a done deal. Sunny's opening a day spa here. Her cousin Eleanor just signed the lease."

"Good for Sunny," he said, winding his arms around her. "I know she missed LA."

They made love again. And finally, they slept – dreamlessly, for hours, nestled together like spoons. Charlie awoke wondering, would he later regret allowing an amorous impulse to win out over his puritanical work ethic? Possibly. But right now, that didn't matter. Right now, life seemed just about perfect. Except he'd forgotten to buy the roses.

•   •   •

He spent as much time with Margaret that week as their busy schedules allowed. Next thing they knew, Christmas loomed ahead.

Major holidays were tough to navigate for any new couple, and he and Margaret were no different. Should they spend Christmas together? Interact with one another's families? Exchange gifts? They confronted these issues head-on without tension or conflict.

"My mother is flying out from New York," said Margaret.

"I'm spending the holiday with my cousin and his wife in San Luis Obispo. I plan to stay there and go wine tasting with them after Christmas."

"That sounds more fun than hanging out with Mum." Her eyes rolled heavenward.

"Will I get to meet her?"

"She's only staying four days."

"Why such a quick visit?"

Margaret groaned. "Well, it appears Mum has a new love interest, but there's another woman in the picture. Mum doesn't want to stay away from New York for too long."

"Wait—your mother is how old?"

"Seventy-eight."

"And she's in a love triangle? That sounds intriguing."

"It is. Though intrigue is not the quality you want in a septuagenarian mother."

He smiled. "It sounds like Mum and I won't cross paths, though."

"Just as well."

"You're afraid she won't like me?"

"*Au contraire*, I'm afraid she'll try to steal you away."

"Thanks, but I'm not into the cougar scene. Anyway, I thought she was hot and heavy with the guy back home."

"A little thing like that wouldn't stop Mum. She could split her time between you in LA and the old dude in New York. You could write a book about it."

"I could call it *Bicoastal*." He and Margaret laughed. This was the title of his novel on a similar topic, his biggest commercial success. It later became a popular film.

"I'm joking, of course. But as for the idea of you and Mum meeting, it seems like it's a bit—"

"Too soon?"

"Yes. Too soon." She gave an apologetic shrug.

Charlie raised the dicey question of whether to give each other presents.

Margaret furrowed her brow. "Hmm, the dreaded gift exchange." She made a "tsk, tsk" sound. "That's tricky territory for two people in a new relationship."

"Like tiptoeing around landmines," said Charlie.

"Or worse. I mean, suppose I gave you a dried fruit and nut holiday platter, and you presented me with—I don't know—"

"Diamond earrings?"

Margaret nodded. "Great example. Imagine how awkward that would be."

"Tough to say who'd be more embarrassed."

"It's a toss-up."

"So . . . no Christmas gifts this year," Charlie said.

"Too soon," said Margaret.

"Too soon."

•   •   •

The night before Charlie left for his cousin's, Margaret slept over. Waking early, he tiptoed out to the yoga alcove and began doing cat-cow stretches with eyes closed. While in a swayback cow pose, Charlie didn't hear Margaret approach and was startled when she climbed on top of him, legs astride. "Giddy-up." She gave him a light tap on the butt.

"Can't you tell? I'm a cow, not a horse."

"No, you're definitely a horse. You're my Charlie horse."

He smiled at her. "Charlie horse, eh? That's clever."

"I'm known for my razor-sharp wit," she said.

"Yes, you remind me of someone."

"Old-school or contemporary? Are we talking Dorothy Parker . . . or Tina Fey?"

He considered this. "Winston Churchill, more like."

She burst out laughing and dismounted, sitting cross-legged on the floor to face him. "I love you, Charlie horse," she said. His eyebrows shot up in surprise. Blushing, she clapped one hand over her mouth like a schoolgirl who'd been caught speaking out of turn. "Oops," she said, cheeks reddening even more. "Too soon?"

Charlie took her face in both hands and gazed at her happily. "No, my love. Not too soon."

CHAPTER 3

In the fifteen months since they'd so blissfully reunited, Charlie had never seen Margaret this nervous.

She stood across from him at the kitchen island, bobbing on her toes as she jotted notes on a scratchpad. "Make up bed in guesthouse – check. Fill fridge with bottled waters and snacks – check. Put clean towels in guest bath – damn, I need to do that." He heard an intake of breath as she scribbled another note. "Flowers! I'll buy daffodils for Mum's bedside table. But I'd better wait till tomorrow, don't you think? Daffodils have a shelf life of about six seconds." She was talking much faster than normal. "Aaaarghh!" she added in her best pirate voice. "Give me strength to power through this."

"Why are you so apprehensive about your mother's visit?" he asked, chomping into his toast. A few crumbs dropped to the floor, and Petey bounded over to lick them up. Charlie stroked the terrier's back.

"I'm not apprehensive. I'm annoyed."

"Wait a minute. Gwendolyn hasn't even arrived, and you're already annoyed with her?"

"I've learned over the years, if I get excited when Mum comes to visit, the reality never lives up to the anticipation. I end up disappointed and hurt. So if I decide ahead of time that she's going to grate on my nerves, no more disappointment."

Charlie laughed. "Maybe things will be different this trip. It's been a long time since she's come to California."

"Over two years," she agreed. As it turned out, Gwendolyn had to cancel her visit a year ago December. She'd been sidelined with flu or something – Charlie couldn't remember the details. And this past Christmas, a visit was impossible because moving boxes occupied every square inch of Margaret's apartment. But at long last, the notorious Mum was due to arrive.

"Let me come with you tomorrow to pick her up at the airport."

"Oh, she insisted on renting a car. 'I'll find my own way, Margy dear,'" said Margaret, imitating an English accent. She pronounced the nickname with a hard "g" as in margarita.

"I suppose we should be glad she's so independent."

"Independent, yet needy." Margaret sighed. "I hope I've planned enough activities to keep her happy."

"The two of you could spend the whole week gabbing and still not catch up after all this time."

Margaret nodded. "It's true. When I visited New York last fall, between my work and everything else, Mum and I hardly found time to talk." She walked over to him, massaged his shoulders for a moment, then kissed his head. "Thanks for letting her come. She'll love this place."

"You don't need to thank me. This is your house too." He grinned, then looked down at the dog. "You too, boy." It was March, two months since Margaret and Petey had become part of his household. He thought back to the day she'd agreed to move in here.

•   •   •

For months, she'd been searching for a house to rent or buy for herself and Petey. Her cozy apartment was not ideal for pets, and Margaret wanted a yard for her young grandson Benny's visits. But nothing measured up. One place was too small, another too dark, another on a busy street with no sidewalks.

Finally, one day Charlie told Margaret he'd found the perfect house for her. "I'm taking you there myself," he said. They got in the car, and he drove to his own house.

"Did you forget something?" Margaret had asked, oblivious to why he'd stopped.

"No, I didn't." He turned to her, smiled, and raised one arm in a dramatic flourish. "*This* . . . is your perfect house."

She sat in the car, silent, looking out across the front lawn. He couldn't read her expression. Then she reached over and hugged him. "You're right. This *is* perfect for me and Petey. And Benny." Then she pulled back and looked him in the eye, her brow furrowing with mock concern. "But Charlie . . . where will *you* live?"

And so it was decided. The only remaining topic of debate involved Margaret's workplace. She wanted to rent office space for her longtime job as editor-in-chief of the engineering journal called *Powder World*. Charlie made it a point to thumb through every issue, but it was like trying to read Arabic. Lots of incomprehensible stuff about powdered ingredients used to manufacture chemicals and food products and such (though *not* gunpowder or explosives, as Charlie had feared). The publication was headquartered in New York, but Margaret had always worked remotely. She assured Charlie that Robert, her boss, would cover the leasing expense. "You need privacy for your writing," Margaret said.

"My office is on the first floor. I'll turn the second-floor den into an office for you. We'll each have our own space." The conversion was easy. Charlie brought in a computer desk and chair, installed LED lighting for the workspace, and removed a side table to make room for Margaret's filing cabinets. The sofa bed and television remained so the room could still serve as a den or guestroom as well.

He knew Margaret didn't want to encroach too heavily on what she still regarded as "his" space. But she was rarely in his way. Between the job, her workout routine at Seaside Fitness, her visits with Benny, and therapy dog rounds with Petey at local nursing homes, she was constantly on the go.

By the end of each afternoon, Charlie couldn't wait to greet her with an embrace, pour them both a glass of wine, and discuss their day. He felt happier than he had since—well, since long before Bet's death, to be honest with himself. Charlie had loved his wife, but Bet was never an easy person. She'd always been fragile, moody, and quick to become frazzled by the most mundane tasks. By comparison, Margaret was steady and self-sufficient, a calm lake after the stormy seas of Elizabeth. But there was clearly one thing that rocked Margaret's boat – her relations with her family.

•   •   •

Shortly after Margaret bustled upstairs to find a set of matched towels worthy of Mum, Charlie's cellphone buzzed with a call from his agent. "Morning, Kathleen."

"Good morning."

"Did you hear from her yet?"

"Debra? Yes."

"And?" He took a deep breath. Debra was his editor at Scranton Publishing, and she'd had his new manuscript for a few weeks.

"No news yet – more of a heads-up. She's almost done reading, and she'll be back to us soon with her feedback."

"How soon?"

"Before the end of next week."

"All right." He heaved an audible sigh.

"You okay?" Kathleen asked.

"Yeah, I guess. You know, even after all these years, waiting to hear from my editor still puts me on edge. But I *love* revisions. Whatever she comes back with, it'll be fine, right?"

"Sure, Charlie. It—it'll be fine." Charlie thought he detected a note of false cheer as she signed off with, "Later."

"What's the news from your editor?" Margaret asked as she descended the stairs. The stack of towels she carried could accommodate an entire family, let alone a single guest.

"Debra will finish reading next week."

"She'll think it's brilliant, like all your work." Margaret gave him a confident grin. He smiled back, but the expression was forced. Though her comment was meant to reassure him, it heightened his apprehension instead.

His nerves were likely a product of anticipation, not anxiety. Or so he told himself. Charlie tried to push aside his doubts, focusing instead on the tasks that would follow Debra's notes. He'd pore through her comments and edits, discuss them with her in detail, then settle down to the challenge of rewriting. The first draft of a novel was the most agonizing – especially those early chapters, when the blank computer screen mocked him with its emptiness, challenging him to fill the pages with something that held value and meaning.

But for rewriting, Charlie had to apply a different skill set. Rewriting was like rearranging the pieces of a jigsaw puzzle until they fell into place, fitting together to form a perfect picture. He found it stimulating, gratifying, even fun.

"I forgot to mention, I'm going to surprise my mother with a gift card for a treatment package at Sunny's spa. That's right up Mum's alley," said Margaret. "I better text Sunny right now."

Charlie was curious to see what Gwendolyn was like after all this buildup, and he expected there'd be some entertainment value in watching the mother and daughter spar. It would be the perfect distraction while he awaited Debra's critique.

Then he remembered the parting comment from his agent. Kathleen had assured him everything would be fine, but she'd stumbled over the words – leaving him with a nagging feeling that maybe it wouldn't.

CHAPTER 4

Though Sunny was usually delighted to see her best friend, Margaret couldn't have picked a worse moment to walk into the Village Canyon Day Spa.

Mrs. Darling, a new customer who was anything *but* a darling, had ended her massage early and stomped out to the lobby, fully dressed, to express her displeasure over the music piped into the treatment room. "Joni Mitchell? The Mamas and the Papas? The Byrds? Who ever heard of music like that in a spa?" Mrs. Darling whined.

Sunny, who as spa director had hand-picked every playlist, tried to hide her consternation. "This is Laurel Canyon music. It's the theme of the spa. But we stick to the mellowest tracks."

"Mellow, my ass . . ." Mrs. Darling squinted at Sunny's name badge and hissed, "*Miss Ericsson.* I want harps. Chimes. Pan flutes. How can anyone be expected to relax in this place?" Sunny suspected it was a rhetorical question.

Margaret stood awkwardly by the entrance. "Looks like I came at a bad time. I'll stop back for the gift card when I finish my workout."

"The gift card — oh, sorry. I'll bring it to you at the club later."

After Margaret gave a thumbs-up and made a hasty retreat, Mrs. Darling resumed her tirade. "My back is more in knots than it was when I got here. I'm not paying for this."

"I'm sorry you didn't enjoy your experience," Sunny said.

"I don't understand this canyon theme crap. I mean, what's the point of it?" She gestured toward the mural behind the front lobby desk, an enormous photo montage covering the wall. Designed by Sunny herself, it depicted the mountainous terrain, unique homes, and winding roads of the Laurel Canyon neighborhood in the Hollywood Hills. Interspersed with these scenic images were headshots of the famous musicians who made up the local counterculture. Before Sunny could respond, Mrs. Darling turned away from the colorful tableau and stormed out.

Now it was the therapist's turn to dump on Sunny. Fiona marched up and splayed her hands on the granite countertop in a confrontational pose. "I shouldn't have to put up with this shit. I hope you're not blaming me for what happened."

"Of course not."

"This was supposed to be a two-hour treatment," said Fiona. "Now my whole afternoon's shot."

"Don't worry," Sunny said, "I'll make sure you get a twenty percent tip. And you can enjoy the afternoon off." Fiona appeared to brighten at this. As a salaried employee, she wouldn't lose any portion of the unpaid treatment fee. The spa would have to absorb it all.

Sunny winced at the thought. Business had been off this year, alarmingly slow in fact. And many of the customers were still using holiday gift certificates, so the bookings weren't generating new revenues. Last year – their first in operation – fell short of projections, and Eleanor had warned that she couldn't keep the place afloat indefinitely.

Sunny sank into her desk chair and swiveled around to view the underappreciated mural, her pride and joy. If she'd been born thirty years earlier, she would've fit right in with the artistic and free-spirited young Laurel Canyon crowd. She loved soaking up the music, culture, and history of that celebrated time and place. When her cousin Eleanor bought the spa last year, and Sunny moved back from northern California to manage it, she dreamed up her unique thematic concept.

Sunny reached into the front desk drawer for her bottle of CBD tincture. Dispensing a few drops into a spoon, she stuck it under her tongue. It had a small amount of THC mixed in with medical cannabis – not enough to make her stoned, but hopefully enough to take the edge off after this unpleasant episode.

Sunny put down the dosing spoon and leaned forward, burying her head in both hands. Suppose all the customers turned into Mrs. Darlings? At that rate, the spa wouldn't last long, and then what? When Sunny tried to look into her future, she saw no road map – only a blank page.

•   •   •

Seaside Fitness overlooked the harbor. Though the indoor workout areas were modest, it had a two-level water view deck, a sparkling Olympic size pool and jacuzzi, and a smaller kiddie pool. Sunny descended to the lower deck in search of Margaret, who sat in a lounge chair sipping from her water bottle.

"Sunny, I thought a spa was supposed to be a place of tranquility. What the hell did I walk in on today?"

"Look up 'tough customer' in the dictionary, you'll find Mrs. Darling's picture. Anyway, I think you caught the gist of it." Sunny changed the subject. "No hip hop class today?"

"Nah, I did a little strength training. Not nearly as fun, but important. Now I'm taking a break before I finish arranging the guesthouse and walk Petey." Margaret's Wheaten terrier lived for his "walkies."

"I'm not feeling all that motivated myself." Sunny dropped wearily onto the chair next to Margaret's.

"That woman was a bitch on wheels. Don't let her get to you."

"It's not that. I'm worried about the spa."

"I thought business was decent."

Sunny shrugged. "Not really. We missed our sales goal for last year. And it's gone from bad to worse since New Year's, with no sign of improvement."

"What does Eleanor have to say about it?"

"She's concerned."

"I'll bet the two of you can cook up a plan to drum up new business," said Margaret. "You and your cousin are a good team."

Sunny knew she should listen to Margaret, who was eight years older and a good deal wiser. Whenever her friend calmed her anxiety, she never did it in a patronizing way. Margaret had been a trusted confidante from the time they'd met a couple of years ago. Sunny was going through a rough patch then, but Margaret never judged or dissed her. Lots of other women wouldn't have been so generous.

"How are things with Todd?" Margaret asked.

Todd was Sunny's boyfriend – a retread, like Charlie. They too had broken up but gotten back together after some hesitation on Sunny's part. "What if he dumps me again?" she'd said at the time, discussing her reluctance with Margaret.

"I didn't know he dumped you. I thought he moved for a new job."

"It was a bit of both," said Sunny. "The job was in Orange County. You don't have to end a relationship because you're moving fifty miles. My life was a mess back then. He wanted an excuse to get away from my problems."

Margaret, a believer in second chances, had encouraged her friend to give Todd another go. And here they were, three months into it. "Todd and I are okay. We see each other a few times a week. He's coming for dinner tonight. But we're not batshit crazy about each other like you and Charlie." She hoped Margaret didn't hear the edge in her voice.

"Oh, is that what we are?" Margaret bit her lower lip as if trying to stifle a shit-eating grin.

Sunny would grin too, in her place. Renowned author Charles Kittredge was a catch. When she'd first met him at Seaside Fitness, a year after his wife died, Sunny would've dated him in a heartbeat. This was a secret she kept carefully hidden.

Almost on cue, Charlie strolled out to the deck. "How are things?" he asked Sunny.

"Better. Your girlfriend has been reminding me that the glass isn't half empty, it's half full." *Then again, Margaret's cup runneth over.* Sunny chastised herself for the envious thought. If only she had Margaret's self-confidence and a man like Charlie (or the *actual* Charlie). If only she had children as her older sister Julia did. If only she were prettier, like half the women at this gym. *If only.*

Once Margaret had complimented her, saying, "You have eyes the color of emeralds and hair that matches your name. Who wouldn't kill for that?" But Sunny's feelings of inadequacy persisted. She disliked the straw-like flatness of her hair; the slim-hipped, small-breasted, coltish shape of her long body; and the fact that, at age forty-two, she was still trying to figure out her life.

"Glad I could help with the attitude adjustment," said Margaret. "Mum arrives tomorrow. After a couple of days with her, I'll be crying on *your* shoulder."

"It'll be fun to meet your mother," said Sunny.

"Oh, yeah, Mum's a lot of fun – if she's not *your* mother. Anyway, I suppose I can tolerate her for seven days."

Sunny laughed. "That reminds me, here's her gift card." Reaching into her bag, she handed her friend an envelope.

"I'd better get to yoga class," said Charlie. "See you later."

He bent down to kiss Margaret on the lips and she hooked one arm around his neck, pulling him in like a fisherman reeling in a catch. Did they have to linger in the kiss quite so long? Sadness welled up within Sunny at this reminder of what she was missing. But she didn't let them see it. "Enough, you two. Get a room." She smiled bravely and wagged a finger at them.

Charlie laughed, waved at Sunny, and headed indoors. Sunny turned to Margaret. "I rest my case."

"Huh?"

"Batshit crazy."

•   •   •

Sunny stopped for Mediterranean takeout on the way home. She'd offered to fix baked chicken and rice, but Todd had said, "Let's do the kebab place instead. Okay, babe? Save you from having to cook. I'll bring wine." Considerate of him, but she had a feeling her boyfriend preferred restaurant food to her home cooking.

She carried the food upstairs to the second-floor condo she rented from an elderly couple from Beverly Hills. It was close to the water, three blocks from the apartment building where Margaret used to live, but it was one of the less desirable units. The cramped studio had a sliver of ocean view from a balcony about the size of a typical hotel room terrace. But the condo faced a park and had cooling ocean breezes, so she had no cause for complaint.

Sunny turned on the oven to low and stashed the food on the center rack. It was almost seven, and Todd should arrive any minute. She considered mixing a drink but decided on a little weed instead. As she walked out to the balcony and lit a joint, her cellphone rang. Caller ID flashed the words "The Bramwell," which Sunny recognized as the new boutique hotel in the harbor-front area. Most likely a promotional message, but maybe it was a business call being forwarded from the spa. "Good evening. Village Canyon Day Spa," Sunny said in her professional voice.

"Hi, this is Zoe Patrick, manager of The Bramwell. Glad I reached you. I wasn't sure you'd still be open."

"What can I do for you?" Sunny sat on a deck chair. Zoe explained the hotel was too small for an in-house spa, so they wanted to partner with an independent spa in the area. In return for exclusivity, the spa would be expected to provide discounted services and priority scheduling.

A surge of adrenaline coursing through her, Sunny dropped the joint. It landed on top of her shoe. She retrieved it and snuffed it out in an ashtray. "We'd be very interested in that, of course."

"Our restaurant manager is a customer of yours, and she said it's a great little place. By the way, she loves that you don't play the usual insipid spa music."

"She does?" Sunny's back straightened. "That's nice to hear."

"This will be a competitive bid, so you'll be up against one or two other facilities," Zoe said. She discussed the details of the proposal she would need from Sunny before signing off.

Sunny's mind teemed with ideas as she contemplated the call. She would bundle together special packages of services available only to Bramwell guests. A new hair and nail salon was opening soon in a big building down the block. Perhaps she could bring them in on the partnership. She'd build in incentives for the hotel's referrals: complimentary passes, free treatment upgrades, tiered pricing based on how many customers they sent.

Sunny smiled broadly and pumped a fist in the air. This might be just the shot in the arm the Village Canyon Day Spa needed. She could do this. Going forward, she mustn't be so quick to resign herself to defeat. Maybe it wasn't her karma to suffer disappointment and failure forever. No, the time had come for good things to happen.

Standing up, she re-lit the joint and leaned against the balcony railing, taking a toke in the darkness. The strong cannabis filled her lungs, burning and soothing at the same time. She gazed down at the park, deserted except for a white-haired man walking a beagle along the path, softly lit by antique-style streetlamps.

Sunny coughed a little and then breathed in the salty air, still warm for a March evening. Snuffing out the joint once more, she made a mental note that she was low on supplies. Time for a trip to the dispensary. She used cannabis almost every day, but that didn't make her a drug addict, did it? It comforted her to know it was there when she needed it.

She went back into the crowded space that served as living and dining room, kitchen, and bedroom. Glancing at her phone, Sunny was surprised to see it was seven-thirty. She shot a text to Todd.

Sunny
Where are you? Everything OK?

Todd
Tied up with something. Be there soon.

But by the time Todd arrived, it was eight-thirty. The dinner had dried out from too much time in the oven, and Sunny had stuffed herself on crackers. "Hey, babe, sorry to be late. I went for a drink with the guys." Todd gave her a quick kiss, and she could taste beer — and something stronger, she thought — on his breath. His dark brown eyes looked bloodshot, and his dimpled cheeks were flushed.

Using his free hand, he raked back his dirty blond hair, darkened from perspiration around the forehead and neck.

Though he looked pretty wasted, Todd maintained the boyish air of a surfer who still thought he was twenty years old rather than forty. He extended a bouquet to her with the other hand. Half a dozen small roses in a green and white wrapper. She knew they'd come from one of those vendors who worked the intersection along Vermont and Pacific Coast Highway. "Thought you might like these," he said.

"Thanks. I'll put them in water." She noticed they were already wilting. Sunny stuck the roses in a vase and, while in the kitchen area, grabbed a Malbec from the cupboard since Todd had not brought the promised wine. Sipping the Malbec and chewing their way through the dried-out kebabs, Sunny shared the good news about the hotel opportunity.

"That's great." Todd raised a glass and flashed a grin at her. He did have a cute smile. "I had a good week myself. I landed a nice equipment order from that new manufacturing plant out in Brea. Six figures."

"Congratulations." Sunny raised her wine glass.

They ate in silence for a few minutes. "Mind if I turn on the Laker game?" Todd reached for the remote before Sunny could answer. Another one of those rhetorical questions. CNN came on. A reporter was talking about a rare blizzard in the deep South, another result of climate change.

"I want to see this," said Sunny.

But after a minute, Todd stabbed the remote again, switching to the basketball game. "Enough. It's nothing to do with us." Feeling mellow and buzzed from the glass of vino on top of the weed, Sunny was in no position to argue.

Todd stayed the night with her on the queen-sized foldout sofa. The sex was a little clumsy, perhaps the result of their inebriation, but Sunny didn't much care. She liked the warmth of his body against hers, the rhythmic sound of his breathing when he fell asleep moments after they'd finished. She got up to pee, wincing as she banged her shin on the corner of the bed frame en route to the bathroom.

Sunny had an inconsiderate boyfriend who tried to buy her off with flowers that were past their sell-by date, a job that held promise but stressed her out every day, and a studio so small she was forever bumping into things. But two years ago, she had no boyfriend, no job, and not even a roof over her head – unless you counted the roof of her old Toyota Corolla, which had served as her only home for months. If only she could convince herself that Margaret was right: She'd come a long way since then. The glass was getting fuller all the time.

CHAPTER 5

Gwendolyn waved her martini glass in the air and announced, "I'm ready for a top-up, Margy." They sat together in Charlie's (and now Margy's) living room on a couch so massive that Gwendolyn's stylishly clad feet dangled a few inches from the floor.

Margy didn't look like she was in any hurry to fulfill the drink request. She relaxed into the deep sofa, her unruly brown curls fanning out against the seatback. Gwendolyn reflected her daughter would still look naturally youthful twenty-five years from now. It was in the genes. Gwendolyn had treated herself to a little Botox here and a little collagen there – and colored and styled her ash-blond hair tastefully – but she still looked damned good without stooping to full-on plastic surgery. Margy furrowed her brow. "Mum, it's only four-thirty."

Honestly. She'd barely arrived, and her daughter was already acting judgy about the drinking. "Don't forget I'm on East Coast time," Gwendolyn said in self-defense, putting down her glass. A book on the end table caught her eye. She examined the cover, then flipped the book over and gaped at the author photo on the back of the dust jacket. Also on the table was a framed picture of the same man, his arm around Margy. "What on earth? . . . This is your boyfriend?"

Margy nodded. "I told you his name was Charles Kittredge."

"You never told me he was *the* Charles Kittredge. I read one of his books, some time ago."

"*Bicoastal?*"

"Yes. I understand he wrote a sequel. Is this it?"

"It is."

"Well, Margy, I'm speechless. Gobsmacked, for that matter. And darling, he's a looker. Positively *luscious.*" She could hear her own English accent growing more pronounced. This happened whenever she became excited, even sixty years after moving from London to New York as a teenager.

"I don't know . . . can a man be luscious?"

Gwendolyn observed the sexy gaze, the aquiline nose, the full head of nearly black hair. "This one can. But I'm very cross with you for not telling me this months ago. I would've had such fun sharing it with the people in New York."

"Yes, I pictured you broadcasting it from an electronic billboard in Times Square. That's exactly why I *didn't* tell you." Gwendolyn conjured up a hurt look, and Margy relented. "The truth is, I didn't want to get you all excited until I knew for sure that things would work out between Charlie and me. I—I guess I didn't want to jinx it."

"So when do I get to meet this Greek god?"

"Soon. He's at yoga class. Charlie asked me to apologize that he wasn't here to greet you, but he thought the two of us should have some alone time first."

"So he's handsome, famous, *and* considerate." Gwendolyn reached for her cell. "My turn to show off." She scrolled through her photos and located her favorite picture of Sam before handing the phone to Margy.

Her daughter nodded in approval. "Oh, he's cute. He's got a twinkle in his eye. How old is he?"

"Seventy-nine. Same as me."

"And the same age Daddy lived to be. But Sam looks way more vigorous."

Gwendolyn lifted a well-manicured hand and raked the fingers through her sleek hair. "Your father didn't age well his last ten years." She sighed. Edward, her husband, had been sixteen years her senior, and the age gap seemed even wider as his health failed. Sam reminded her a little of Edward – both men had enjoyed successful careers and shared a passion for all things cultural. But Sam was more like her, witty and sociable, whereas Edward had been shy, even withdrawn. Fifteen years ago, he'd left her a widow at sixty-four.

"Are you really moving into Sam's place?" Margy asked.

"Oh, yes. Parkside Gardens is marvelous – except for being on the Upper West Side." Sam had roared when she echoed Woody Allen's complaint that the West Side got all the bad weather. Gwendolyn, who owned a fashionable pied-à-terre half a block off Fifth Avenue in the eighties, was a confirmed East Side snob. "I have masses of friends at the Gardens," she told Margy, "and there are always parties and cultural outings. The dining room is excellent too."

"Sounds ideal. And if the food lives up to Gwendolyn Meyer standards, that's saying a lot," said Margy.

Gwendolyn smiled. "Sam has one of the largest apartments in the independent living wing, and it's beautifully appointed." He had lived there with his wife until her death three years earlier, she explained. "Soon, the two of us will live in sin like you and your novelist. But it's been such a brutal winter, I can't think about a move until the weather warms up."

"I—I should've told you sooner who Charlie was. Sorry, Mum."

"That's all right, dear. I've been keeping a little secret as well."

"Oh?" Margy's eyes widened.

"Yes. Remember why I didn't come out here for Christmas?"

"Of course. I was getting ready to move."

"No, I mean the previous Christmas," Gwendolyn said.

"When you came down with the flu?"

She nodded at her daughter. "I didn't actually have the flu. I'm not proud of it, but I feigned an illness so I could stay home."

Margy shook her head. "Why would you do that?"

"Well, I told you that when I first met Sam, I had a rival for his affection. Phyllis. She lived at Parkside Gardens too, so she had a geographic advantage over me and I worried it was giving her the inside track."

"I remember that's why you booked such a short trip . . ." said Margy slowly, "but why cancel altogether?"

"You wouldn't believe the way she was sinking her claws into him as I got ready to leave. She droned on about the New Year's celebration at Parkside Gardens and how happy she was to have Sam as her date. It was sickening." Gwendolyn recalled how she'd bridled at the vision of Sam and Phyllis together, all decked out for the champagne gala, while she and Margy watched the ball drop in Times Square on her daughter's little TV. "I couldn't leave him in her clutches, Margy, I just couldn't. But I was afraid if I told you the truth, you'd be upset about the last-minute change in plans."

Margy appeared to consider this. "So, you decided instead to let me worry about your health. The flu outbreak was bad last winter, Mum. I was very concerned." Her eyes narrowed into suspicious slits. "What about the other times I invited you? Were all your excuses invented?"

Gwendolyn shrugged. "That little apartment of yours sounded so dreary. I didn't fancy us packed into two tiny rooms like passengers in steerage."

"So here we are in a lovely big house, and we're bickering anyway." Margy punctuated this with a sigh and looked again at the picture on Gwendolyn's phone. "I see a woman's hand on Sam's arm. Is that your rival?"

"Yes. I cropped her out of the photo." Gwendolyn gave a malevolent smirk.

"Whatever happened to Phyllis?"

She thrust her martini glass in Margy's direction. "If you want to hear that story, darling, you will definitely need to top me up first."

•   •   •

New Year's Eve. She was dancing cheek-to-cheek with Sam, and it was pure heaven. *I was wise to stay in New York,* she thought as she breathed in his spicy cologne. She loved how Sam didn't exhibit any icky, old-man traits, like stooped posture or stubble or sagging jowls. He was always impeccably shaven, with chiseled features and wiry gray hair that was short but still thick. His cheek against hers felt rough, but in a good way – *manly,* Gwendolyn thought. And he looked so distinguished in his fitted tux.

Phyllis cut in on them and glowered at Gwendolyn before turning a fawning smile on Sam. Her hair, dyed a dark brown, shoe-polish shade, had been teased into a fussy coif for the formal event. Now Gwendolyn's rival was the one cheek-to-cheek with Sam. Infuriating. To arouse his jealousy, Gwendolyn summoned up her best seductive powers to flirt with a tall, husky fellow with a shiny dome for a head. But Sam barely gave her a sideways glance as she danced with the bald-headed man.

The whole evening, in fact, he seemed unaware that his two female companions considered themselves rivals. Perhaps he didn't want to offend either her or Phyllis by playing favorites. How could he be so nonchalant, so unwilling to assert a preference? Gwendolyn was certain that Sam Rosenthal, retired senior partner in a leading Manhattan law firm, hadn't catapulted to the top of the New York legal profession by acting wishy-washy.

•   •   •

The rest of that winter, they continued on like the three musketeers, to Gwendolyn's mounting chagrin. Occasionally, she invited Sam to her place for dinner or to the theater when she had an extra ticket. It was their only one-on-one time. Whenever Sam initiated plans, it was always to some group activity at Parkside Gardens, and *she* was there.

One day, the musketeers had agreed to meet at MOMA to see a special sculpture exhibit, but Phyllis showed up alone. "Sam had a legal emergency and had to meet with a client. He's so dedicated to his pro bono work. I try to be as understanding as possible."

Since his retirement, Sam had been a tireless volunteer for a legal aid firm. But what bothered Gwendolyn as much as Sam's absence was the intimate tone Phyllis used, as though she were the devoted mate and Gwendolyn an interloper. And dammit, now she'd be stuck with the bloody woman all afternoon. Sure enough, as the day wore on, Phyllis became more and more irksome, interjecting comments like, "Over cocktails last night, Sam said . . ." or "I couldn't agree more with Sam about . . ." Once, she even had the unmitigated gall to refer to him as "my Sam."

Her Sam? Honestly. The whole situation had taken a discouraging turn. Gwendolyn despaired that the competition for Sam might be a lost cause. She wept in her bed that night and pondered whether she should give up the good fight. She was still contemplating her exit strategy when, three nights later, Phyllis died in her sleep at the age of eighty-one.

Not a moment too soon.

•   •   •

"Once Phyllis was out of the way, it was smooth sailing," Gwendolyn told her daughter, triumphant. "In fact, her death was so sudden, the shock brought Sam and me instantly closer."

Margy pulled a face. "You're saying it's *good* that another human being died because it served your romantic purposes?"

"Your words, not mine. I will say this, though – Phyllis was conniving and two-faced. She was not a nice person, Margy. And tacky, to boot. She thought *The Lion King* was the best Broadway musical ever. Can you believe it?"

At this, Margy burst into laughter. "Mum, you are incorrigible."

"There's a lesson to be learned here," said Gwendolyn. "Growing old is no fun, but it holds one advantage. If you're competing with another woman for a man's affection, you don't need to outdress her or outsmart her or outperform her in bed." Margy wrinkled her nose as if remarking *"ew"* to this last comment. "Sometimes," Gwendolyn concluded, "all you need to do is outlive her."

•   •   •

"Why didn't Sam come with you? I'm dying to meet him, pardon the expression."

"I begged him to, but he said this should be a mother-daughter trip." Gwendolyn suspected Sam's volunteer commitments were his real reason for staying in New York. Phyllis has been right about his dedication. "When I told him you had a swimming pool, and a lovely deck, he encouraged me to have a nice long escape from the wretched New York weather." She raised the martini glass and sipped the velvety liquid. "Here's to two weeks in the sunshine."

Margy leaned in towards her. "Two weeks? I—I thought you were staying one week."

"I changed my mind. I told you. At least, I thought I did . . ." Her voice trailed off uncertainly, and Margy looked as though she were trying not to cry. Gwendolyn squeezed her daughter's hand. "We'll have a fabulous time." Then she said, in her most cheerful voice, "What's on the agenda?"

"Tomorrow, I'm taking you to lunch at a new harborside restaurant. But first I'd like to do my hip-hop class at Seaside Fitness. You could use the gym while I'm dancing or take a walk if you prefer."

Gwendolyn nodded. "A walk sounds good."

"And Saturday afternoon we've got the thing at Michael's."

"What thing?" asked Gwendolyn.

"You know, the barbecue I told you about?"

"Oh . . . right. Remind me who's coming. Besides us, of course, and Michael and Heidi."

Margy looked confused. "Heidi? Do you mean *Heather*, Michael's wife? Mum, you really need to remember the name of your only grandson's wife."

Gwendolyn felt her cheeks grow warm. "Don't start, Margy. You know I'm terrible with names."

"You won't believe how much your great-grandson has grown."

"Benny?" Gwendolyn hoped she had that one right. "I should think so. He wasn't much more than a toddler last time I saw him."

Margy ticked off the remaining names on her fingers. "Sunny, a friend of ours. I think she's bringing her boyfriend. And I'm told Henry and Alice will stop by for part of the time."

Gwendolyn clapped her hands in delight. "It will be lovely to see Henry again. But I thought you and your ex weren't speaking? And who's this Alice?"

Margy groaned. "You know – the woman he ditched me for after twenty-eight years of marriage? As for your other question, Henry and I aren't best buds, but we're civil at family gatherings. It's been easier dealing with him and Alice now that I'm part of a couple too."

Her daughter went on to describe more plans for her stay: a Jackson Pollock exhibit at some downtown museum, a Philharmonic concert at Disney Hall with that young chap Dudamel conducting, and a treatment package for Gwendolyn at a spa managed by this Sunny person who was coming to Michael's thing. Margy said, "I've arranged for some time off from work while you're here, Mum, but no way can I take two weeks." The girl sounded a tad put upon.

Now she regretted not lobbying harder to bring Sam out to LA to keep her company. He would've loved Disney Hall. This was the first time she'd left him, and she already missed his reassuring presence. Sam was the real deal. Even more than his distinguished looks, she relished his sharp mind, his animated way of speaking to her about the arts and his legal work, and the unaccustomed thumping of her heart when she was about to see him.

Sharing the rest of her life with Sam would be a gift – but a gift that she could wait for a little longer. What was a couple of weeks, after all? She'd be back in New York before she knew it.

CHAPTER 6

"What can I get you, Gramma Gwen?" asked her grandson. "Iced tea? Sparkling water?" They'd arrived a little late at Michael's thing. It took Gwendolyn longer these days to put on her face.

"A mimosa would be perfect but go light on the orange juice. The sugar is bad for me." Giving Michael a sly wink, she added, "I adore day drinking."

Michael responded with a smile that looked insincere. Maybe he found it unbecoming for his seventy-nine-year-old grandmother to be guzzling mimosas? Poor dear Michael. He was a nice young man, earnest and hard-working, but rather humorless. He had the same pouty lips and dark, deep-set eyes as Henry, her ex-son-in-law, but he lacked the Schuyler extroverted spirit.

As her great-grandson Benny skipped across the back patio, Gwendolyn marveled at how much he'd grown and how his wispy blond curls had morphed into little-boy hair: thicker, darker, straighter. But he still had his signature cowlick. Gwendolyn had brought him the gift of a stuffed dolphin, his favorite sea animal, which she presented now. To her surprise, Benny gave her a stern look as she handed him the festively wrapped package. "It's bad to wrap presents, Gramma Gwen," he said with authority. "You're wasting trees."

"He's worried about the planet," Michael explained.

"Worried about the planet? Good heavens," said Gwendolyn. "The boy is five years old."

"Five and a *half*," Benny said.

"You'd be amazed by what he understands and absorbs," said Heather, a touch of pride in her voice. "We watched a documentary about climate change in the rainforest and he's been talking about it ever since. Don't worry, Benny. We'll recycle the paper." To Gwendolyn's relief, Benny broke into a grin as he hugged the cuddly dolphin and handed the offending gift wrap to his mother.

Charlie had just regaled the group with his impression of Cary Grant. "Do Bill Clinton for us," said Margy.

"Now, Hillary, I'm not a performing seal," he said in a raspy Southern twang that perfectly captured the former president. A ripple of laughter followed. The man was a spot-on mimic.

A tall blonde approached Gwendolyn to say hello. "Hi, Mrs. Meyer. I'm Sunny, and this is my friend Todd." The man by her side had dirty blond hair and a flushed complexion. "I wanted to meet you, and Heather was nice enough to let us crash your family party."

"When Sunny offered to bake her famous brownies, it clinched the deal," Heather said with a laugh, tossing her head of brown curls that resembled Margy's.

"Sunny, you didn't add any, uh, secret ingredients to your brownie recipe this time, I hope?" Margy gave her friend a concerned look.

Sunny laughed and waved her off. "No, I promise."

Gwendolyn sensed they were leaving her out of a joke. She hid her annoyance. Then Sunny said, "I'll look forward to you visiting my spa. I hope the gift card was a nice surprise."

"The spa is fantastic," Heather chimed in. "I'm a regular there, so I get to see Sunny all the time. An added bonus." She blew a kiss in Sunny's direction.

"It sounds marvelous." Gwendolyn was far more interested in beauty than brownies. "What about you, Margy? Are you a regular too?"

Margy dropped her eyes. "I get there when I can."

Questionable. Even though Margy was a good-looking woman, she was clueless about the fine points of feminine pampering. Gwendolyn doubted her daughter spent more than thirty seconds a day on her makeup. "What do I get with this gift card?" Gwendolyn asked Sunny, her expertly penciled eyebrows arching upward.

"Margaret gave you the Canyon Triple Play," Sunny said. "A massage, a facial, and an exfoliation body scrub."

Gwendolyn pressed her manicured hands together, delighted. "Lovely. When?"

"Any day you like," said Sunny. "We're wide open." She heaved a sigh.

"Maybe I'll wait till closer to the end of my stay, so I'll have something special to look forward to. Margy, thank you again. But it's not Mother's Day or my birthday. What's the occasion?"

"The occasion is having you here." Her daughter raised her glass.

I'll bet she wants to get me out of her hair for half a day. But Gwendolyn, too, lifted her glass and rewarded Margy with a grateful smile.

•   •   •

Fifteen minutes later, Heather was passing around bite-sized stuffed mushrooms and cheese puffs as Michael grilled chicken and ribs on the elaborate built-in barbecue. The basting sauce smelled sweet and tantalizing. Gwendolyn wasn't much of a meat eater, but she supposed a little chicken wouldn't hurt her.

Somebody else had arrived at the party, a dumpy-looking woman with long gray hair, a round face, and a broad, dimpled smile. Gwendolyn sized her up and muttered to Margy, *sotto voce,* "Who invited Mama Cass?"

The new guest wore a long floral print dress (it looked like a granny dress—did they still make those?), multiple strands of beads that cascaded down her ample chest, and multi-colored bangles on both wrists. She had a pasty complexion and dull, chapped lips that stood in stark contrast to her colorful garb. She was a mess – and an overdressed mess at that. Who wore such an outfit to a backyard barbecue?

"That—" said Margy, leaning in close to Gwendolyn, " —is Alice Hanley. Henry's girlfriend."

Henry had trailed in behind Alice, stopping to admire his grandson Benny's new dolphin. He wheeled around and extended his arms. "Gwen-Gwen," he said in his friendly, booming salesman's voice. She'd nearly forgotten his pet name for her. "You look incredible. Absolutely incredible. You haven't aged ten minutes since I last saw you . . . what, three years ago?"

Not since you divorced my daughter. Gwendolyn reached out to give Henry an affectionate hug. No matter what had happened between him and Margy, she'd always be fond of the man.

"This is my—my—this is Alice," he said, stumbling over the introduction. Gwendolyn wondered, what was the proper etiquette for a man introducing his girlfriend to his ex-mother-in-law? His blue sports jacket looked a little tight around the middle. Clearly, Henry and Alice weren't missing any meals.

"I am *so* excited to meet you," said Alice, squeezing her hand so hard that Gwendolyn's rings cut a little into her flesh. Alice had the warm, sonorous voice of a radio announcer. She prolonged the painful handshake, pumping her arm with an excess of enthusiasm. "Henry has talked about you with such *fondness.*" She spoke the last word with exaggerated emotion and then paused to catch her breath, as if the overblown handshake had drained all her energy.

"How nice." Gwendolyn contorted her features into a frozen smile. She was shocked — *shocked* — by Alice. Margy had warned her that Henry's new love was "no beauty," but Gwendolyn was not prepared for this. Though Margy might not be a paragon of glitz and glamour, she was Miss America next to this woman.

"We're only here for a short visit," said Alice. "We're not eating." As she said this, she swiped a few cheese puffs from the passing hors d'oeuvres tray and popped them into her mouth in rapid succession.

"Alice and I have an engagement party to get to, over at the country club," said Henry. "The daughter of one my golfing buddies is tying the knot." That explained how they were dressed, at least.

"But Henry couldn't pass up the chance to see you, Gwen-Gwen." Alice practically crooned.

Gwendolyn's face hurt from the strain of simulating good cheer. "Can you excuse me for a minute? The loo is calling." Her mouth inverted into a scowl as she walked away. It was one thing for Henry to use the pet name, quite another for Alice to appropriate it.

When Gwendolyn returned a few minutes later, the men were gathered around the barbecue, talking shop as Michael finished grilling the meat. She watched Alice sneak a brownie from the dessert table, then a second brownie.

"Business at Schuyler Enterprises has been crazy-busy," Henry said to the group. "Last fall we acquired a contracting firm that specializes in green cleaning services. You know, environmentally friendly stuff. They've got certified teams all over the country. It's a good fit with our other businesses because they serve the same markets – commercial, institutional, that sort of thing. "

"It's been keeping us on our toes," added Michael, who had worked for his father in the family business since graduating from college seven years ago. "They also rent out facility cleaning equipment. Dad put me in charge of the rental business, on top of all my other stuff."

"Yeah, I'm a tough taskmaster." Henry clapped his son on the back. "Michael's doing great, really great. We're all going gangbusters. Gotta expand the staff."

None of this surprised Gwendolyn, who had always admired Henry's business acumen.

Todd, looking even more red-faced than before, drained his beer can and reached into the cooler to crack another one open. He struck Gwendolyn as one of those men who'd been a big hit with the girls in his youth – a dreamboat, even – and who clung to that image of his former self even though he was now going to seed.

"I've been working in sales and marketing my whole career." Todd spoke so loudly it startled her. He informed Henry how his experience in industrial equipment sales had prepared him for any challenge. She wondered, was the man angling for a job? The volume of his voice kept increasing. Gwendolyn watched Sunny frown and give Todd's arm a tug, as if urging him to tone it down. Then the girl turned toward Charlie, who had joined the group. Something in Sunny's face went dreamy when she looked at him.

"Are you doing a lot of traveling with the new business venture?" Charlie asked Henry.

"You bet. Michael and I are both on the road a lot. Alice here is supposed to focus on inside sales, but she can't resist tagging along with me to the more interesting destinations."

"Like San Francisco," said Alice with a giggle. "I canceled a week's worth of medical appointments to go with Henry. That city has the *best* restaurants. And the bakeries . . . oh, my word, they're to die for."

"The truth of it is, Alice will find any excuse not to go to the doctor," said Henry, giving her shoulder a squeeze. It struck Gwendolyn that Henry's girlfriend could use a doctor.

Or a weight loss clinic.

•   •   •

Back at Charlie's house, Gwendolyn sat with Margy at the kitchen island sipping mugs of red rooibos tea. After the eating and drinking indulgences of the afternoon, they'd agreed a light snack and hot tea would suffice for the evening.

Gwendolyn turned the discussion to Alice. " I can't believe you lost Henry to that train wreck of a woman. It's not only her looks. She's insufferable."

"Thanks for the vote of confidence. You must think I'm a real loser."

The girl could be so sensitive at times. "Oh, Margy, that's not what I meant." Gwendolyn intended for this to come across as an apology, but she knew she sounded irritable. She lightened her tone. "I meant, Henry must have lost his mind. I can't imagine what he sees in her."

"Sometimes the attraction between two people is a mystery. At times I wonder what the *other* women Henry cheated with were like." Gwendolyn knew Henry'd had several brief affairs while on business travel, although Margy didn't reveal this until after they separated.

"That's a stone best left unturned," Gwendolyn said. "At least there's no mystery why you're attracted to Charlie." This was true. "Or he to you," she added, eager to make reparations for her previous slight.

Margy gave her an inscrutable smile. "Are you enjoying the guesthouse?"

"I guess it's all right. Maybe a little . . . isolated."

"Isolated?"

"I'd prefer — never mind. Charlie must do very well with the writing. Though I imagine he isn't as rich as Henry, do you agree?"

"What an interesting question, Mum. Why don't I ask both men to produce a copy of their latest financial statements? You can compare them."

"Oh, all *right*," Gwendolyn said. "There's no need to be sarcastic." Margy gave her a look.

Charlie wandered into the kitchen holding an empty wine glass.

"What've you been up to?" Margy asked.

"Watching the local news. They had a report on the flu season. A lot of cases again this year, and it's going on much longer than usual, especially for older people."

"Mum? You had a flu shot, right?" asked Margy.

Gwendolyn frowned. "Of course I did. Anyway, it's one's biological age that counts, not chronological age. For me, there's a huge difference between the two." Gwendolyn had taken an online quiz that calculated her biological age to be sixty-one. She'd fudged a little on the questions about alcohol consumption, but she couldn't see how that mattered. Her daughter gave her a doubtful look which she ignored. "I think I'll have one more cup of tea."

"Let me fix it for you," said Margy.

"I can do it myself. I'm not decrepit, you know." Gwendolyn marched to the kitchen counter and set her mug on the granite with a clunk. She dropped in a fresh tea bag and poured hot water from the kettle into the cup. Charlie refilled his wine glass and left the room.

Margy was so irritating at times. If there was anything Gwendolyn couldn't stand, it was having her daughter – or anyone, for that matter – lump her together with "older people."

She had to admit, now and then she felt . . . how to describe it? Strange. Different. A fog of confusion would press down against her temples; and when it lifted, a few wispy clouds remained, obscuring little slivers of memory. But old?

No, not old. Not her.

CHAPTER 7

The call from his agent came the following Friday morning. Charlie hurried to his office to talk in privacy, passing Gwendolyn in the hallway.

"You're in a rush this morning, Charles." Gwendolyn rotated her head as he progressed down the hall. Why must she act like it was her job to monitor his movements? Her watchfulness unnerved him. Also, Charles was his public name, but he preferred friends and family to call him Charlie. He'd mentioned this to Gwendolyn, but she seemed oblivious.

He gave her a quick nod and kept walking, closing the office door behind him. "Hi, Kathleen. You heard from Debra?"

"Yes, I just got off the phone with her."

"So, what's the next step? Why don't we have her notes yet?"

She cleared her throat. "No notes."

"No notes? The manuscript was so stellar, she couldn't find a single thing to change?" Charlie chuckled at his own joke, but Kathleen didn't join in the laughter.

"Charlie, she—they—Scranton is passing on the book. They don't want it."

His pulse quickened, his cheeks grew warm. "I can rework it. If Debra explains what she doesn't like about the manuscript, I'm sure I can tweak it."

"Listen, I know this is tough to hear, but she's flat out not interested. She said, 'Aren't we all bored of Nomi by now?'"

Charlie slapped a palm on his desk. "Bored of? Did she actually say, bored *of?*"

"I'm afraid so."

"Christ almighty! Nomi is my most popular character. "Bored *of* . . . " he said again, his tone scornful, taking out all his disappointment on the misuse of a two-letter preposition. "And she calls herself an editor."

"The thing is, Nomi was your protagonist in *Bicoastal* and *Second Chance*. When we all talked about the new book, you said Nomi would launch the story and then fade into the background. You promised us the narrative would jump ahead several years and focus on her grown son." Charlie disliked how Kathleen stressed the word *promised,* implying this was all his fault for reneging on his word.

"It's true I told you that," he said. "But the characters took me to a different place."

"We need to think of where Debra's coming from. With this third novel, you've given us a thousand pages of Nomi as the main character. If *Second Chance* were selling better, maybe this would have legs as a series."

"*Second Chance* has done fine," Charlie said, then realized how defensive that sounded. He tried to be less whiny. "I mean, sales have been respectable."

"At first, yes," said Kathleen. "But they weren't sustained."

"What does the contract with Scranton say? Can you try subbing this to other publishers?"

There was a long pause. Then Kathleen said, "There are some contractual issues. Maybe we should shift our focus . . . try our hand at something new this time."

Kathleen kept saying *we* and *our* as if she and Charlie were collaborators, not agent and writer. *He* was the one who'd squandered his creativity on a book his editor claimed had no legs, *he* was the one who must find a solution. Kathleen had plenty of other authors in her stable, most of them younger and more in sync with the hot buttons of today's literary scene, like LBGTQ fiction and psychological suspense.

"Do you think I should go back to my original idea of writing about Nomi's adult son?"

"If you feel inspired to develop that story. But maybe you should take a different approach altogether. Charlie, you've got another great book in you. I know you do."

"I wish I shared your confidence."

"Look, you've had some bad news. We won't solve this on the phone. Let yourself feel disappointed, lick your wounds for a couple of days, then pick yourself up and move forward."

He sighed. "Okay. We'll talk soon."

"Of course. If you want to bounce any ideas off me, I'm here."

"Right. Thanks, Kathleen. Have a good weekend."

"You too."

Charlie closed the screen on his laptop so he wouldn't see the offending manuscript. *Disaster.* How could this have happened? His breath was coming fast as he tried to rein in the feeling of panic. So much lost time – time he could ill afford to waste at his age. Anxious to let off steam, he opened the office door and summoned the dog with a loud whistle. "Petey, how about a walk?" The terrier ran to his side, eager to explore the neighborhood.

Margaret was upstairs in her office. She'd taken a week off to spend with her mother, but this morning she needed to focus on work. Walking through the kitchen, Charlie encountered Gwendolyn reading. "We'll be back in half an hour," he said, praying she wouldn't ask to accompany him. He needed time alone to mull over the call from Kathleen.

"Don't worry about me, darling. I'm immersed in this book."

"What are you reading?"

She held up a paperback novel. The cartoonish cover showed a young woman with her hands cupping her ears and her mouth wide open in terror, like in the famous Edvard Munch painting, *The Scream*. "It's one of those unreliable narrator stories, about a girl who sneaks into her neighbors' houses and spies on them – but you're never sure who's telling the truth or what's really happening. I can't put it down. Sam can't either." Charlie noted the author's portrait on the back cover, a woman writer who looked about eighteen.

There you have it. The bitter taste of bile rose in Charlie's throat. He thought Gwendolyn and Sam would've had more sophisticated taste. But this was the sort of horseshit the public – and the publishers – were lapping up.

As he and Petey ventured out, Charlie noticed the sky now had an eerie, grayish-yellow glow, and the easterly Santa Ana wind carried a faint scent of smoke. A wildfire had broken out somewhere in the Inland Empire to the east. Usually these blazes were not a problem so early in the spring, but they'd had another dry winter in California.

Slowing his pace to save his lungs, and Petey's, from overexertion, Charlie mulled over the distressing call. He should've seen it coming. This book had given him trouble from the get-go. It all started when Margaret broke up with him, triggering that first-ever bout of writer's block. It took months to pull himself out of the creative doldrums. And when he did, it was only because he took the coward's way out.

Though he didn't admit it to Kathleen this morning, Charlie abandoned his original story concept because he wasn't up to the challenge. He tried and tried, but the results kept coming up short. Nomi, he could write about. He knew her as well as he knew himself. So he wrote a different book from the one his publisher had expected. An easier book.

But he didn't get away with it. And here he was, back to square one after almost two years. Charlie had never taken so long to complete a novel, even during the difficult months that followed Bet's death.

White ash particles now coated the bushes Petey was sniffing, so Charlie turned back and led the dog into the house just as Margaret entered the kitchen for lunch. Petey went crazy at the sight of her, as if they'd been apart since the last millennium. She hugged the dog, who stood on his hind legs and licked her face in the classic Wheaten greetin'. Charlie leaned down to kiss her cheek – then thought better of it, seeing the doggie spittle glistening on her face. He planted a kiss on the side of her curly head and then filled her in on the conditions outside.

He and Margaret took sandwiches and cold drinks into the den to watch news coverage of the fire outbreak. Gwendolyn ate her meager daily portion of yogurt and fruit at the kitchen island, still immersed in the trashy best-seller. When Charlie returned to the kitchen for an iced tea refill, she asked him what was going on.

"The Santa Ana winds are expected to keep blowing smoke and ash in our direction. That means unhealthy air quality until the fire's contained or the wind shifts. They're advising people to stay indoors, especially anyone who's immunocompromised, or –" He stopped mid-sentence.

Lowering her reading glasses, she made a face. "Or *older,* dear? Don't worry, I'll behave. Tell Margy I promise not to venture outside without a gas mask."

Margaret joined them in the kitchen. "I heard that, Mother." She unwrapped a square of dark chocolate for herself and put it on a small saucer with a few almonds, as she liked to do every afternoon. "Time for my chocolate fix. Anyone else?"

"Half a square for me, Margy. I'll save my calories for a cocktail later."

Margaret held up the chocolate to Charlie, who shook his head no.

"Sweetie, with everything going on, I forgot to ask—did you hear from your agent?" she asked.

Charlie paused. "Yes, she called a couple of hours ago."

"How exciting," said Gwendolyn. "Sometimes I still can't believe I'm staying in the home of a renowned novelist. Do tell us everything."

Charlie averted his head, wincing at Gwendolyn's comment. *Once renowned* might be more apt.

"Did you get things sorted out with Debra?" asked Margaret. "Ready to start on the next draft?"

"Uh—yes."

"So you've got your work cut out for you," said Margaret.

"I certainly do." What Charlie failed to mention – he wouldn't be writing another draft. He'd be writing a whole new book.

CHAPTER 8

The following evening, Gwendolyn received a text from her former son-in-law.

"Listen to this message from Henry," she said to the others. "*'Go to your front door, there's a surprise for the three of you.'*"

Margy looked up. "Why did he contact you?"

"You know Henry and I have always been close," said Gwendolyn. "Even after the divorce, when you two weren't speaking, he often reached out to me."

"Yes, whenever he wanted to pump you for information or use you as an intermediary." Margy's tone was derisive. Gwendolyn waved off this assertion.

"I'll go look," said Charlie.

He came back carrying a straw basket festooned with yellow and orange ribbons. Charlie handed her the basket. Inside it was a plastic food storage bag and a note, addressed to Gwen-Gwen, Margaret, and Charlie in calligraphic script.

Gwendolyn unsealed the bag first. It contained half a dozen enormous cookies – lemon cookies, from the look of it, topped with a thick layer of yellow and orange icing in a wavy design.

"Is this some sort of April Fool's joke?" asked Charlie, looking baffled.

She'd forgotten today was the first of April. Gwendolyn tore open the envelope. She read it silently, then burst into laughter.

"What?" said Margy.

"*'While stuck indoors on this smoky day, I occupied myself baking these delicious lemony treats. That's what we call lemons to lemonade. Enjoy, my friends! Love & kisses, Alice.'* Look at this—where she signed Love, she drew a little lemon in place of an o."

Margy shrieked. "Omigod, this is too funny. What are the yellow and orange wavy things?"

Charlie smiled. "Flames, I think."

"Oh, you're right. To symbolize the wildfire," said Gwendolyn, still chuckling.

"Did you know Alice has diabetes? For someone who's supposed to avoid sugar, she spends a lot of time baking," her daughter said.

"Maybe it's an outlet for her," said Charlie. "She makes sweets for others since she doesn't eat them herself."

"I wouldn't be so sure of that." Gwendolyn flashed on Alice sneaking brownies at Michael's barbecue.

"Shall we try them?" asked Charlie.

"Are you kidding? I never touch Alice's baked goods. There's enough sugar in a batch of her cookies to double my blood glucose level," said Margy.

"Or to triple the diameter of my thighs," Gwendolyn added.

"Oh, good one, Mum." Margy reached over and slapped her hand in a high-five.

Gwendolyn beamed at her daughter. This was how it went with her and Margy. Either the two of them were in cahoots, like a couple of teenage girls sneaking a cigarette behind the schoolhouse . . . or they were at each other's throats. There wasn't much middle ground.

•   •   •

Margy worked all the next morning and ate lunch at her desk, leaving Gwendolyn feeling neglected. The girl finally emerged at two o'clock to take her to Seaside Fitness. They parted company in the locker room, Margy heading to the cardio equipment room while Gwendolyn walked down the hall for Zumba class.

Back in New York, Zumba was her favorite workout. But today, the gyrations seemed faster than what she was accustomed to and the choreography more complex. The other women in the class – most of them younger even than Margy – executed the difficult moves seamlessly, laughing and whooping as they danced. Discouraged, Gwendolyn slipped out of the studio after ten minutes to stroll along the harbor-front instead. The wind had shifted this morning, sending the smoke and ash away. It was a pleasant afternoon, and the walkway wasn't too crowded, but Gwendolyn remained in a snit over the Zumba fiasco. Her daughter had said this teacher was the most popular dance instructor in the club, but what did Margy know? The woman was impossible to follow.

Also vexing was Margy's amped-up work schedule. During the first week of Gwendolyn's visit, they'd enjoyed pleasant lunches and cultural outings. But now Margy was all business again, and how was Gwendolyn supposed to amuse herself? And who knew for how long? She'd been scheduled to fly home in two days, but the airline had already canceled her flight due to a blizzard forecast to slam New York.

Charlie offered to help her rebook, but she'd said, "Oh, no, dear, it looks like you'll be stuck with me a while longer. Sam warned me that three nor'easters are lined up and are likely to hit the city over the next ten days. I'll just stay here and we'll see how it goes."

She walked for about twenty minutes before turning back toward Seaside Fitness. But when she arrived at the club, she grew confused about how to find Margy. The door she first entered led to a smaller outbuilding – some sort of children's club, apparently. She remembered that Margy sometimes took Benny there. Then she trudged up an outdoor staircase that led to the pool deck, but the entrance was blocked at the top. By the time she made her way inside the club and back to the women's locker room with the help of a front desk employee, her heart was pounding. Why, she couldn't say. She hadn't been lost, after all. Just discombobulated.

Margy was chatting with a plain but wholesome-looking woman with tightly coiffed gray hair. "Mum, there you are. This is Judith. She's the consultant I told you about, the one who helped me downsize and organize all my belongings after the divorce."

"Oh yes, of course. I remember Margy singing your praises," said Gwendolyn, who remembered nothing of the kind.

"Glad I could be of service. Her little apartment was a shithole before I got my hands on it," said Judith with a honking laugh. "Oh, crap. Pardon my French." Her potty mouth seemed at odds with her clean-cut appearance. Gwendolyn flashed her a tight smile.

"How was Zumba?" Margy asked.

"Lovely, dear," Gwendolyn lied.

"Maybe you'd like to take the class again on Wednesday?"

"Possibly," said Gwendolyn. When hell freezes over.

Fortunately, dear Henry had invited her for cocktails and dinner the following night. It would be a welcome change of pace. He'd been begging her to see his new house, which by all accounts had a panoramic view of Santa Monica Bay. Gwendolyn wasn't sure she could tolerate Alice's cloying chatter, but she supposed it was worth it to spend an evening in her former son-in-law's congenial company.

And after that, she'd have to find other ways to occupy her time until returning to New York. Whenever that day might come.

•   •   •

Sunny squinted at the computer screen as she inserted an aerial view photo of Laurel Canyon into the PowerPoint slide. No matter how many times she adjusted the size and position of the image and tried to juxtapose the text, she couldn't achieve the desired look.

Last night, she'd had the brilliant idea to create a fun, multimedia presentation for her pitch to The Bramwell management team. Instead of walking them through a dry Excel document, she'd intersperse her business proposal with Laurel Canyon music and images. Certainly, that would set her apart from the competition and wow the prospective hotel client.

A great idea in theory, but not so easy to execute. Sunny knew a little about presentation design, but she'd never had formal training. As a result, tasks that should've been completed in minutes took hours. She often regretted that she hadn't gone to design school. Her father believed art school was a waste of time, another one of her harebrained schemes. He'd insisted on liberal arts college for her with several courses in business. She'd hated the business classes, which seemed so far removed from art, her one true passion.

Hunched over her computer at the spa, Sunny labored on The Bramwell pitch for nearly a week, endlessly tweaking the presentation until it looked polished. She felt confident about the content as well. She'd bounced it off Margaret, who gave her valuable feedback as usual. Sunny followed her friend's suggestions, except for one. Margaret had said, "What other spas are you competing against? Make sure your proposal plays to your strengths and their weaknesses." A sound idea, but Zoe had not shared that information, and Sunny didn't feel comfortable asking.

The only frustrating thing (apart from her clumsiness with PowerPoint) was her failure to engage the new hair and nail place preparing to open down the block. Called the Salon DHQ, it was under construction behind a small storefront on the opposite side of the street. The salon was attached to a larger two-story building that'd sat vacant for some time. Nobody knew what was happening with the main structure, though there were rumors of a designer clothing store moving into the space.

Sunny tried three times to call the Salon DHQ's owner to propose a joint venture. The two small establishments could band together to offer a range of bundled services to The Bramwell clientele. When the owner didn't respond, she walked across the street to pay a visit. A curt building contractor informed her the owner was not on the premises. Sunny hoped to catch a glimpse inside, but visitors were forbidden from entering the building.

In the meantime, the daily business of the spa consumed little of Sunny's time. They had few customers outside of friends and family. Gwendolyn had come in two days earlier for her Triple Play treatment, and Heather had booked herself a facial that same afternoon. The current sluggish pace would not be supportable for much longer – Eleanor had been crystal clear about that. Sunny must land the hotel account, whatever it took.

To quell the mounting anxiety and the roiling in her gut, she rummaged in the desk for a cannabis vape pen she thought she'd stashed somewhere. No sign of it. She took out the bottle of CBD tincture and applied the spoon under her tongue, though she knew it wasn't potent enough to do the job.

Her cellphone buzzed. "Julia, hi." The call from her older sister was unexpected, as they seldom talked. The two had never been close. Older by a full twelve years, Julia had been out of the house from the time Sunny was a little girl, and they'd lived hundreds of miles apart as adults. "Everything all right?" Sunny asked.

"Yes, I'm okay. How about you? I was just thinking about our family because—you know, because of what day it is today."

"Right . . . um . . ." Sunny stammered, wondering what Julia was talking about.

"It's Far's birthday. He would've been ninety." *Far* was what both girls called their father. It was a traditional term for father in Sweden, from where their paternal grandparents had emigrated.

"Oh—of course." Sunny felt her cheeks flush at this unwelcome reminder of their long-deceased father. "I lost track of the date." Karl and Lilly Ericsson had been forty-seven and forty-two, respectively, when Sunny was born. Even as a young girl, Sunny sensed she was a latecomer, even an intruder, to this small family as her parents stayed on course with their daily routines, Karl as a businessman and Lilly as a high school English teacher.

"Are *you* okay?" asked Julia. "You sound funny."

"I'm a little distracted. I've been working on an important new business presentation for the spa."

"That'll keep you out of trouble," her sister said. "I was just feeling nostalgic, you know?" Truth be told, Sunny *didn't* know. Julia's relationship with Far had been different from hers. To this day, her sister had no clue how profound the differences were. What was the point in discussing it? Julia had adored Far and would likely take his side if Sunny divulged her real feelings.

Sunny's bond had been with her mother. Lilly died a few years ago from Alzheimer's; and through those last difficult years, Sunny was her loyal caregiver and financial supporter.

"Nice to hear from you, but I need to go," said Sunny. "I have a lot of work to finish up."

"One more thing. We're planning a family Zoom on my birthday. I'll let you know the time, okay?"

"Sure," Sunny said. "Talk soon." When the call ended, she tried to shake off the jittery feeling that overcame her whenever she thought about her father. She had enough on her plate without worrying about that right now.

•   •   •

Two nights later, Sunny sat on her balcony, reflecting on that afternoon's presentation and tour with The Bramwell team. She wasn't sure how to read it, but at least it was over.

Given the modest size of the spa, the facility tour took only a few minutes. Sunny thought she overheard the hotel concierge say, "Is that it?" to Zoe, but she couldn't be certain. With business so quiet, she'd arranged for Fiona to bring in friends to pose as paying customers, creating the illusion of a prosperous establishment. She now worried, irrationally, that the client might somehow be onto their ruse.

The restaurant manager – the one who'd recommended the spa to Zoe – was the most supportive, rewarding Sunny with encouraging smiles and nods as she guided her guests through the PowerPoint. But Sunny doubted she carried much clout. Zoe was the hardest one to figure out. Her comments were polite and sometimes complimentary, but she showed little warmth or enthusiasm. As the three hotel representatives prepared to leave, Zoe told Sunny, "Your presentation was the last on our schedule, so we expect to decide quickly. I'll get back to you tomorrow. Thank you for your efforts." She shook Sunny's hand briskly and departed.

Well, good to know they were last. Sunny'd always heard it was best to be last, because your proposal would be the freshest in the client's mind. Or was it best to be first and pre-empt the competition? Now she couldn't be sure.

•   •   •

She'd been too busy to get to the dispensary to replenish her cannabis supply, but she found the remains of a joint that was so short she risked burning her fingers when she lit it. Sunny took one long hit and then ground it out in the ashtray.

She didn't feel hungry but knew it was important to get some calories into her body. She'd already dropped three or four pounds from stress over The Bramwell pitch, enough to feel her pants loosening around her waist and buttocks. *That bony butt,* as Far had called it.

She pulled a can of vegetable bean soup from the cupboard and poured it into a saucepan. With a handful of crackers and a few cherry tomatoes, it would be enough. Tomorrow after work she'd stock up on cannabis *and* groceries, then cook dinner for Todd. She didn't like to eat red meat but knew Todd preferred it, so she resolved to fix him a steak and serve a nice bottle of wine. Or champagne, even. If things went according to plan, tomorrow there would be a celebration.

•   •   •

The call from Zoe came at about two o'clock the next afternoon. Sunny knew instantly from the hotel manager's tone that the news was not good. She scrunched her eyes closed and her heart thundered wildly, making a pulsating noise in her ears. So deafening was the sound, she only heard fragments of what Zoe was saying. ". . . great presentation . . . so creative . . . love the music and the theme . . . but we needed a broader menu of services . . ."

At this, Sunny's eyes widened, and she snapped to attention. "Services?" she asked. "What did the winning bidder have that we couldn't offer? If you don't mind my asking."

"Of course not. Well, let's see. It's rather a long list." Zoe paused, then said, "They have a eucalyptus room, a sauna, and indoor and outdoor hot tubs. A rooftop sundeck. A café and juice bar. A full-service beauty salon for hair, nails, and makeup. Besides the usual spa treatments. Even with all that, their bid was the lowest we received."

"I guess it's hard to argue with getting more for less," said Sunny, perplexed. She couldn't think of any place in the area that fit Zoe's description, and surely The Bramwell wouldn't shuttle its guests up to Beverly Hills or Santa Monica. "Which spa is this?"

Zoe hesitated before clearing her throat, as if embarrassed to respond. "Why, the new place that's opening down the street from you. Salon DHQ."

CHAPTER 9

Charlie leaned back in his desk chair and tried to remember how that old Joni Mitchell song went. Sunny would know the lyrics . . . something about not knowing what you've got till it's gone? Lately, he felt that way about his privacy. During the years between his wife's death and Margaret's arrival, Charlie's isolation in the house had allowed him to focus on his work unencumbered – except, of course, for that nightmarish period when he'd been so blocked. Now the distractions were taking their toll.

Every day he sat at his computer staring at the blank screen. But try as he might, Charlie couldn't come up with a single worthwhile idea. He used various writing drills to unblock himself. Though he could perform these creative exercises with flawless skill, he froze up again when he tried to get back to the real work of the new manuscript.

This morning, though, he tapped away, falling into the rhythm of the writing after the first few paragraphs. Encouraged by this surge of productivity, he printed out his work to review, hopeful he'd latched onto something at last. But after reading halfway through, Charlie hurled the pages into the recycle bin. He glared at the keyboard and yelled, "Fuck!" – as if the keys were themselves at fault for typing the wrong words.

A stroll around the grounds might help. Charlie liked to follow the perimeter of the property as he noodled a plot detail or character arc. That worked fine when he was alone at the house; but today Gwendolyn was stationed, as usual, under an umbrella in a lounge chair by the pool, reading. As he walked by, she lowered her book and observed him making his circuits, like a spectator following a tennis match. "So quiet out here in the mornings, isn't it?"

He gave a terse nod, trying not to engage.

"It's a whole different story after dark," she said. "I heard coyotes howling again in the dead of night. I feel like I'm in the middle of *Animal Kingdom* out in that guesthouse." Gwendolyn's intrusive presence did not stimulate the imagination. If anything, it sucked the creative juices out of him like a leech sucking blood.

To make matters worse, it now appeared she wouldn't be leaving any time soon, thanks to all the storms predicted for New York. One might expect such conditions in February, Gwendolyn had told them, but for April it was unprecedented. "Sam said this is climate change rearing its ugly head again."

Unfortunately, Benny was visiting when this happened, and news of the impending storms only fueled his fears about planet Earth. "Gramma Gwen can't go back to her house because the weather is too dangerous," he'd cried, the tears forming tracks down his little rosy cheeks.

Charlie had to agree with the boy. The indefinite postponement of Gwendolyn's departure was worthy of tears.

•   •   •

By the time cocktail hour rolled around, Charlie was glad for the opportunity to knock off his so-called work. Today, he and Margaret nursed glasses of chardonnay as Gwendolyn drank a cup of hot tea, informing them she was saving herself for one of

Henry's famous whiskey sours. She was due at his house in an hour.

Margaret asked Charlie, "How are the revisions?"

"They're . . . coming along. It's a bit of a slog."

"Would it help to talk about it?" she asked.

"Thanks, but no."

"You authors are always so secretive," Gwendolyn said, as though she hobnobbed regularly with a wide circle of fiction writers.

Charlie should've told the truth in the first place, the day Kathleen called to inform him Debra was passing on his book. But he'd been so stunned and embarrassed by the rejection that he allowed Margaret and Gwendolyn to believe he was starting on revisions. He hadn't lied outright – it was more like a sin of omission. But now he couldn't undo it, and the deceit was eating him up. A tangled web, indeed.

And what if this wasn't a temporary glitch? When Charle became blocked before, he hoped it was a one-and-done occurrence. But the problem had returned, worse than ever, and now he wondered if this was the new normal. Could creativity dry up permanently, like ripe fruit left in the sun too long? Did every author have a fixed allotment of books in his head, and Charlie had reached his quota? While he tortured himself with these thoughts, he watched Margaret managing her work-at-home routine with seamless efficiency.

Tonight her expressive face was bright with excitement as she described a conference with the publisher. "Robert announced plans to launch another magazine aimed at the pharmaceutical industry." She sipped her wine. "Pharma executives are, like, a subset of our current circulation, but their editorial needs are different. Lots of regulatory issues and stuff like that."

"How will that impact you?" Charlie asked.

"Robert wants me involved," said Margaret. "Not in a management position, but as editor-at-large."

"*At large?*" asked Gwendolyn. "That sounds like an escaped convict prowling in back alleys."

Charlie and Margaret laughed. "It means I'll be involved in an advisory capacity, and sometimes be assigned to special projects," she said.

"I thought you and Robert agreed a long time ago to reduce your schedule, not increase it," said Charlie, dividing the remaining chardonnay into their two glasses.

"We did, sort of – but that was when I wanted to help Heather with Benny. He's in school full time, so he doesn't need me now."

I need you now. Not wanting to sound like a clingy preschooler, Charlie said nothing.

"Anyway," Margaret said, "I'll juggle it all somehow." She smiled at him – energized, purposeful, focused.

Charlie opened another bottle of chardonnay.

•   •   •

Gwendolyn raised her teacup to her daughter in honor of the job news. She still didn't understand this editor-at-large business, but it was nice to see Margy looking so happy. Then Gwendolyn's cell buzzed on the tabletop. "It's Henry," she announced cheerfully. "No doubt calling to tell me what wine to bring to dinner." Winking at Margy, she picked up the phone. "Hello, darling. I'm counting the minutes till I see you and Alice."

"Gwen-Gwen." She thought he sounded different, more subdued than usual. "I hate to do this, but we have to cancel tonight."

She clutched one hand to her stomach as though she'd been punched in the gut. "What's going on?"

"Alice is under the weather."

"Is it a head cold or something?" Gwendolyn asked.

"No, she's complaining about pain in the jaw — or maybe the bottom teeth, she's not sure exactly. Anyhow, it's a dental problem. She doesn't want any dinner and she's lying down. If things aren't better in the morning, the best dentist in town is a golfing buddy of mine. I'm sure I can get her in right away."

"Alice is lucky you're so well connected. Be sure and call with updates, darling." Gwendolyn put down her cell and reported the conversation to Margy and Charlie. "I'm sure she'll be fine, but I don't know . . . Alice doesn't look like a woman who goes off her food."

"I can't disagree with that," said Margy.

"Henry did sound worried."

"She must be in rough shape," her daughter said. "You know Henry. Mister Positive. He likes to downplay every problem."

"How disappointing."

"That she's ill?" asked Charlie.

"That Henry's canceling our little soiree. I was so looking forward to a night out, but I guess I'll have to settle for another quiet evening in the outhouse — I mean the — the guesthouse out back." She saw Charlie open his mouth as if to say something, but he averted his eyes. Then a rather mischievous thought occurred to her about Alice. Gwendolyn giggled and covered her mouth with one hand. "I can't help wondering about the toothache . . . I suspect Alice has been eating too many of her own lemony delights. Maybe that's the source of her troubles. You know, the woman is a bit of a lemon herself." She looked at Margy expectantly, waiting for her to chuckle in amusement or give her a conspiratorial high-five. But her daughter wasn't laughing this time.

●　　　●　　　●

Charlie was making slow, lazy love to Margaret at daybreak the next morning. They were on the yoga mat in the upstairs alcove, a soft sand-colored blanket shielding them from the chill of the early morning air drifting through the open balcony door. As they moved gently together, her body felt warm and yielding to his touch. Then her rhythmic movements stopped, and he felt her limbs grow tense beneath him.

"Did you hear that?" she whispered.

"Hear what? I don't know wh—"

"Shhh," she said.

Sure enough, he heard footsteps, a creaking door, a cough. Definitely not Petey. "Oh good God, you scared the daylights out of me." Gwendolyn's voice rang out across the hall.

Margaret gasped. "We scared *you?* What are you doing in the house?"

"I couldn't sleep a wink in the guesthouse. First, I heard the coyotes again. Terribly disconcerting. Then I heard other noises before dawn, and when I went to investigate, two racoons were engaged in sexual activity out by the pool steps."

Margaret sounded livid. "Jesus. Can't you respect anyone's privacy?"

Gwendolyn ignored the reprimand. "Do you mean the raccoons or the two of you? Creatures shagging outside, creatures shagging inside . . . I must say, all this coupling is making me miss Sam."

"Mum—that's enough. I mean it."

Witnessing the terse mother-daughter exchange, Charlie looked down at the yoga mat, at Margaret's curly hair, anywhere but Gwendolyn.

"I guess I'll go back to the den and try to sleep a bit more," Gwendolyn said. "I pulled out the sofa bed. I prefer a real bed, of course, but it will do. Anyway, you couldn't expect me to keep putting up with that menagerie outside."

"You'd think we had pitched a tent for you in the middle of the wilderness." Margaret's voice was thick with irritability.

"I'm an exceptionally light sleeper, dear, as you know," Gwendolyn said. "Well, I'm off. Don't let me disturb you."

Charlie sighed into Margaret's neck as he listened to Gwendolyn close the door to the den – now Margaret's office, actually – behind her. "I guess we should go back to sleep too," he said, miserably. It seemed like he couldn't finish anything these days.

•   •   •

Charlie poured himself a second cup of coffee, still trying to avoid eye contact with Gwendolyn after the mortifying early-morning encounter.

Margaret said, "Mum, we have a problem." He wondered which problem she was referring to, as Gwendolyn cast her daughter a questioning look of wide-eyed innocence. "You've displaced me from my office," Margaret added, as if she'd heard Charlie's unspoken question.

"Darling, problem solved. We'll do a switcheroo. I'll use the den as my bedroom, you move your office into the guesthouse."

Charlie knew her idea wouldn't work, and although he hardly wanted to insert himself in this conflict, he weighed in with a subtle reminder. "I'm afraid the Wi-Fi connection in the guesthouse is spotty at best."

Gwendolyn said, "Just come into the house when you need the internet."

"No. I use the internet all day long. I have video conferences. I send emails. I — oh, why do I even bother to explain?" Margaret threw her mother an exasperated look.

"You have a flair for melodrama, darling," Gwendolyn said. "Doesn't she, Charles?"

"I don't know about that. I think your daughter is pretty terrific," said Charlie, leaning down to give Margaret a kiss. She smiled at him. Despite the warm moment, he was eager to get away from this strained atmosphere, yet reluctant to go to his office and call attention to the fact that he, at least, *had* an office.

"Petey and I are due over at the nursing home for our therapy rounds," Margaret said.

"Would you like company?" Charlie asked.

"I'd love that. But are you sure you can take the time off from writing?"

"Uh—it's okay. I'll finish the chapter later." Maybe next year, at the rate he was going.

•   •   •

As he and Margaret walked Petey around the assisted living facility, going from room to room, they chatted between visits with patients. "You've probably noticed it's not so much fun being around Mum and me when we're snippy with each other," she said.

"Yeah, better to be out of earshot. Preferably in a different county." Charlie winked.

A moon-faced woman with frizzy white hair greeted them cheerfully. "Hello, dear. Hello, Petey." She petted the dog's furry neck.

"Hi, Mrs. Taglieri," said Margaret. She gave Petey a signal, and the dog stood on his hind legs and waved his front paws. The old woman applauded.

"Is this your husband?" She grinned at them.

"This is my boyfriend, Charlie."

"Oh, my." The grin faded. "Does your husband know about this?"

"No." Margaret laughed. "I mean—I don't have a husband. It's okay, Mrs. T." Petey rolled over and played dead on command, then pawed the air in farewell. "I don't know what to do about Mum," said Margaret as they resumed their rounds.

"While conditions are so bad in New York, we can't force her to go home," Charlie said.

The next patient also seemed intrigued by Charlie's presence, barely glancing at Petey as he performed his tricks. "Aren't you the handsome one?" she asked flirtatiously. Charlie gave her a little salute as they proceeded down the hall.

Margaret continued to multi-task, issuing commands to Petey as she vented about her mother. "I know you didn't sign up for this. You thought she was staying two weeks, but now who can say? She could be with us two months."

"Two *months?*" Charlie pressed his lips into a firm line to conceal a grimace.

"Hopefully not that long," Margaret said.

"I'll call the cable company and have them install another router in the guesthouse. That'll solve the Wi-Fi problem."

Margaret seemed to contemplate this idea. "I don't know — it sounds like a lot of trouble. I can manage for now. It's sweet of you to offer, though."

He stifled the urge to gather her in his arms, not wanting to give the patients further cause for gossip. "Look," he said, "I signed up for *you,* and your mother is part of the package. She can't go home, and we can hardly stick her in a hotel. We'll make it work."

Margaret ruffled his hair. "How'd I get so lucky? Not only are you the most wonderful writer I know, you're also the most wonderful man." Charlie had to stifle another grimace, this one triggered by his conscience. He wondered if Margaret had any idea what *she* had signed up for.

CHAPTER 10

Gwendolyn eavesdropped on Margy and Charlie's discussion about writing, even though it was mind-numbing when the two of them went on like this. Today's topic was—drum roll, please—punctuation. Bloody hell.

"There's a school of thought that colons and semicolons should be avoided in fiction writing," said Charlie.

"But why?" Margaret asked.

"Because they come off looking too formal, too academic."

"What are you supposed to do, then?"

"Use an em dash. Or an en dash. Or three dots," he said.

Margy's lips turned down and her nose wrinkled in an expression that combined aversion with alarm, as if Charlie had suggested she sprinkle salt in her coffee instead of sugar. Gwendolyn suppressed a titter while wondering what an em dash was. She wouldn't recognize one if she tripped on it.

"You poor fiction writers," Margy said. "I feel for you, being reduced to an overreliance on dashes and ellipses."

"And short choppy sentences," said Charlie.

"Like that one."

"Exactly."

"Not even sentences," Margy added.

"Fragments."

The two of them burst into simultaneous laughter while Gwendolyn sat bemused. Honestly. A medically induced coma would be more stimulating than this conversation. Her phone buzzed, saving her from the dueling grammarians. She left the room to take the call.

It was Henry. He must be calling to reschedule their dinner. But without so much as a hello, he announced, "Alice is in the hospital. She had a heart attack."

"Oh, good heavens! Is she doing all right?"

"I—I don't know. She's in the ICU at South Bay Medical Center, and they've got her heavily sedated. You know the jaw pain she had last night? Turns out it was a warning sign, but she misdiagnosed it."

"Oh, dear, I'm so sorry. But I'm sure she'll be in good hands. Is there anything we can do? Should we visit her?"

"No, I'm barely allowed to visit myself. Only one person at a time, and very limited hours. She's so out of it, I don't know that it matters."

"How terrible."

"It won't be for long, I hope. South Bay has the best cardiac unit around. I'm sure she'll turn the corner soon."

Turning the corner sounded like life-or-death business to Gwendolyn, but she didn't say so. "Of course she will, darling. Of course she will."

But the daily updates from Henry grew disheartening as he dropped his upbeat salesman's tone. "The doctors think there's been damage to the heart muscle. And I'm worried about Alice's—what's that jargon they use?—her comorbidities," he said a few days after she'd been admitted. "Like hypertension and diabetes."

And obesity – though it seemed ill-advised to mention this. "At least her age should work in her favor," Gwendolyn said, trying to sound positive.

"Yes, she's only fifty." Fifty? The woman was younger than Margy. Unbelievable. Alice looked ten years older.

"Did they ever take care of her dental problem?" she asked.

"Her what? There was no dental problem, Gwen-Gwen, remember?" said Henry. "Her pain was a precursor to the heart trouble."

"Sorry, darling, I got confused for a moment."

Gwendolyn passed along the health news to her daughter and Charlie, and to Sam on their calls. It wasn't easy finding a moment to talk with Sam, given the three-hour time difference between New York and LA. But now that her stay in California had been extended, they were speaking more often. "It does my heart good to see that gorgeous smile of yours," he said during one of their FaceTime calls.

"Thank you, darling. But I must admit I hate doing video calls on a cellphone." If Sam called too early, before she'd put on her makeup, she would reject FaceTime and phone him back the old-fashioned way.

"We should use this thing called Zoom. It's best on a computer."

"You know I don't have a computer."

"Can't you use your daughter's?"

"Hmm. Her laptop is right in front of me now, but she's not here to help. I think she's gone for a walk."

"What's showing on her screen?" he asked.

"Looks like her inbox."

"Perfect." Unlike her late husband, who failed to master even the most basic computing skills, Sam was quite proficient at this sort of thing. He started a Zoom session and emailed the link to Gwendolyn's phone, instructing her to forward the email to Margy's address. Before long, they were face-to-face on the computer and Sam was teaching her how to navigate the user-friendly video conferencing platform. He advised her on the best lighting options, and on how to expand the image so it filled the screen.

"This is fabulous," said Gwendolyn, beaming at Sam from across the country. "It's like being in the same room with you. So much better than my teeny iPhone screen." They were enjoying an animated chat when Margy walked into the kitchen. "Margy, darling, say hello to Sam." Gwendolyn pulled her in close, so she'd be visible on the call.

"Very nice to meet you," Sam said with a broad smile.

Margy mumbled a response, but she wasn't smiling. "Mum, what's going on?" she asked. "I have a video staff meeting in fifteen minutes, and I need my computer back."

"No worries, I promise we'll finish up before then."

"But I need my computer now. I have documents to review before the meeting." Margy's tone was calm and even, but Gwendolyn suspected she was being polite for Sam's benefit.

"Okay, give us a few minutes to say goodbye in privacy."

Margy shook her head as if to say, "I don't believe this," and stomped out. When she returned a few minutes later, Gwendolyn flashed an apologetic smile. "Darling, I'm sure it must have been unnerving to find that I'd taken over your laptop, but I—"

"Later." Margy gave her an icy look. "I need to find a quiet place for my meeting. Not easy, ever since you moved into the room that used to be my office. I think I'll go to the den for my call, if you can manage to stay away from the TV for the next couple of hours."

"No need to move. Take the call right here if you like. I'm going for a drive."

"Where?" Margy's tone was challenging.

"None of your business." If her daughter was determined to be unpleasant, Gwendolyn would be too.

•   •   •

When Gwendolyn returned about ninety minutes later, Margy was still in the kitchen, typing on the computer. "What an ordeal." Gwendolyn plunked a shopping bag on the counter. "I had to go to three stores before I found the flavored coffee creamer that I like. They had it at the Pavilion's market." She pulled out two containers of the non-dairy creamer.

"You know, Mum, if you're out doing all this shopping, you might ask if Charlie and I need anything for the house."

"If that's the case, *you* might try giving me a list. I'm not a mind-reader." Gwendolyn turned to leave the kitchen. "I think I'll look at today's paper."

But Margy wasn't letting her off that easy. "Wait. I want to discuss what happened earlier. It is *not* okay for you to hijack my laptop for your own amusement."

"But sweetheart, Sam was teaching me how to talk on Zoom. It's marvelous, and I've learned how to use indirect lighting. It gives my skin the nicest glow, with none of that dreadful, wrinkly iPhone neck."

"Are you effing kidding me?" Her daughter threw both hands up in the air. "Go ahead, be my guest, monopolize my computer. I only rely on it for my livelihood. It's much more important for you to show off your neck to the best possible advantage."

Charlie walked in on the middle of this conversation – and to his credit, he found a solution. "I hardly use my iPad. I'll set you up on it, Gwendolyn, and you can do your Zoom sessions with Sam. But please check with Margaret first on where to take the calls, to make sure you're not disturbing her work. Her office has become like a moveable feast, and we all need to be sensitive to that."

"Thank you, love, what a perfect solution." Gwendolyn started toward Charlie to give him a grateful hug, but Margy beat her to it. Gwendolyn watched him put his arms around her daughter to administer a comforting massage—one hand on her back, the other buried in her curls.

This peace offering of the iPad gave Charlie a newly elevated stature in Gwendolyn's eyes. It had taken some time to warm up to the man. While always polite and respectful, he didn't have Henry's outgoing, hail-fellow-well-met personality. True, Charlie could be amusing when he did his celebrity impersonations, but she hadn't been treated to much of that lately.

Charlie struck Gwendolyn as a man who held something of himself back. But instinct told her he was trustworthy at the core. And clearly, he was well suited to Margy. A couple of geeks at heart, their erudite discussions were tiresome to behold – but all things considered, they were rather sweet together.

•   •   •

Gwendolyn got the news two days later.

Alice was dead.

She learned this from her grandson Michael, who sent a group text asking them to gather for an important call. "Dad is too distraught to talk," he said to the assembled trio, who were listening to his call on speakerphone. As usual, there wasn't an abundance of information. Something about another myocardial infarction, and her heart being too weak to withstand the stress.

"How is your father doing?" asked Gwendolyn.

"Terrible." Michael told them Alice's will specified there should be no funeral service or memorial gathering. Gwendolyn thought it ironic that a woman who had so craved attention and admiration in life should choose privacy in death.

After the call, Margy became hysterical. "I feel so guilty," she sobbed.

"What on earth are you talking about?" Gwendolyn asked.

"Alice was – she was always so nice, so sickeningly nice, and I never returned her kindness. Now she's dead and I can't make it up to her." She buried her face in a tissue. "I was always making nasty comments."

"Like when?" asked Charlie.

"Like when she sent over the cookies that day of the fire. Mum and I were laughing and joking at her expense."

"Margaret, listen. Alice never heard what you said about her, so what you did wasn't cruel. You were never unkind to her face," Charlie said.

Gwendolyn nodded in affirmation. "Charlie's right. Seems to me, Alice gushed effusively at everyone and everything, but you—you don't . . . *effuse.*"

"Is that even a word?" Margy sniffled a little and swiped her eyes. She and Gwendolyn glanced at Charlie simultaneously for his professional verdict, like a patient awaiting a surgeon's diagnosis.

"*Effuse* is indeed a word," Charlie said. "It's terrible she died, but let's not forget that Alice was at least in part responsible for you and Henry splitting up after a long marriage. Nobody expected you to treat her like family. She was lucky you were cordial to her at all."

But try as they might to dispel her guilt feelings, Margy burst into tears again and ran from the room.

•　　　•　　　•

"This whole episode has been so upsetting," Gwendolyn said to Sam on their next video call. "I can't bear it anymore, Sam. Maybe I should get a flight home tomorrow."

"Don't be *meshugenah.*"

"You know I don't understand when you speak Hebrew."

"Yiddish. The word means crazy. The weather is still stormy and freezing cold. You'd be miserable here, assuming you could get back at all."

"Then join me out here, darling. There's no reason you should put up with an endless winter either."

"I wish I could. I'm in the middle of a case that's going to trial next week, and I really can't leave." Sam coughed into his elbow.

"I thought you were working as a volunteer," Gwendolyn said, slightly irked.

"I am. But whether or not I'm getting paid is beside the point. Deadlines are still deadlines, and the clients depend on me for help."

Gwendolyn sighed. Listening to Sam's account of the frigid conditions in Manhattan, she concluded it would be more pleasant to remain in California. But with Margy and Charlie so immersed in their own activities, she'd have to find new ways to entertain herself. Sam interrupted their conversation with a fit of coughing.

"Are you unwell?" Gwendolyn asked, alarmed.

"No, no, I think it's something stuck in my throat."

Gwendolyn hoped this was true. "Please take good care of yourself, dear. After what happened to Alice, I feel like we're all vulnerable. Promise me you'll stay well until we find our way back to each other."

As it turned out, Sam did stay well.

And Gwendolyn stayed in California. And stayed. And stayed. And stayed.

CHAPTER 11

After The Bramwell manager phoned with the bad news, Sunny considered a relaxation massage to ease the stress. *Physician, heal thyself.* She went home early instead. Emotionally and physically drained, she'd allow herself the rest of the day to recover.

She swung by the supermarket and the dispensary to stock up. Back at the condo, as she was stashing crackers, cookies, and baking supplies in the cupboard, she pulled out a bag of assorted CBD gummies from the lower shelf to make room for the new items. She looked at the gummies with longing and reached inside the bag. *Don't do it, Sunny. You can't keep falling into that trap.*

She forced herself to pull her hand from the bag, knowing she'd be perpetually stoned if she ingested cannabis every time her anxiety level rose. Instead, she went out on her balcony with a spiral notebook and colored pencils to sketch the greenbelt below and the ocean in the distance. Drawing had a soothing effect on her.

But just as calm was descending, her phone buzzed with a call from Eleanor. Sunny could feel the familiar ache returning to her solar plexus. "Where are you?" her cousin asked. "I tried to call the spa three times and nobody picked up."

Shit. She had forgotten to turn on call forwarding. "I'm sorry, El. I've been working so hard all week on that pitch, I was wiped out. I needed a little time to recharge my batteries."

"I get that, but business will never improve if callers can't even get through to book an appointment."

"I know. It won't happen again."

"Did you hear from the hotel?" Eleanor asked.

"Yes. I—I was about to call you." Sunny related the conversation with Zoe and then said, "I think this new spa is underbidding the competition to land corporate accounts. That must be their focus." Though she didn't know this for a fact, the theory made sense.

"In that case, you need to find new ways to attract more individual customers."

"Right," said Sunny. "That's what I was thinking too."

"I want you to put together a marketing plan. And try to keep the costs within reason. We can spend a little on advertising and promotion, but I can't throw a ton of money against this."

"Of course. I understand. I'll have something for you in a few days." Sunny pulled her hair back into a ponytail and went to the sink to wash a couple of baking potatoes and prepare a green salad to go with Todd's steak. She'd be okay with just a potato and salad.

They hadn't been seeing much of each other lately. On weeknights Todd preferred to sleep at his little bungalow in Long Beach, citing important early morning conference calls. Though she'd given him a key to her condo, he hadn't reciprocated. For that matter, he never invited her to his place. Sunny didn't want to ask why. She sensed he was nervous about his job, same as she was.

Her day had gone from bad to worse. Now she had doubly disappointed her cousin by losing the hotel pitch, then leaving the spa unattended in mid-afternoon. Maybe she'd have a couple of quick hits off the vape pen before getting back to dinner prep. She sat on the couch, took a couple of deep inhales, and sat back with her eyes closed. Overwhelmed by fatigue, she slid down into a prone position on the cushions, burying her face in a throw pillow.

The next thing she knew, Todd was calling out to her. At first, she wasn't sure if she was dreaming, but the persistent cries of "Sunny. Wake up. Wake up," brought her back to consciousness. She felt a sharp tug on her ponytail. "I said, wake up." Todd swatted her on the bum. The slap wasn't hard enough to cause real pain, just a mild sting – but it frightened her. Sunny jumped off the couch and stared wide-eyed. She began to shake. "Hey — hey, babe, calm down," he said, thrusting one hand out in a peacemaking gesture. "It was only a love tap."

"You scared me," she said.

"Okay, that's cool, no big deal, right? I couldn't resist – the way you were lying, your butt was sticking up in the air and it was too tempting. Such a cute butt." Well, at least he hadn't called it a bony butt, the way Far always did.

She remembered one time, as he was putting her across his lap to spank her, he joked about it to Mother. "You know the saying, this hurts me more than it hurts you? Well, with Sunny here, that's the literal truth. Every time I smack this bony butt, my hand aches like hell." The Swedes were enlightened about child rearing, opposing any form of physical punishment, but apparently Far never got the memo.

Sunny accepted Todd's quasi-apology for the "love tap" and went to work making dinner. After they ate, Todd commandeered the remote control and found a sports channel showing replays of historic World Series games. Once again, her thoughts returned to her father, who had liked to watch baseball endlessly on TV. He tried teaching Sunny the fundamentals of the game in their backyard, but she never lived up to his expectations.

"You throw like a girl," he would say. She knew it wasn't meant to be a joke.

"But Far, I am a girl," Sunny used to respond, pulling on her blond pigtails as if to emphasize the point.

"Yeah, that's the problem. Built skinny and straight as a stick, like a little boy. But useless, like a little girl."

Sunny tried to push this recollection from her mind. "Are you spending the night?" she asked Todd.

"Can't, babe. Early call tomorrow. Next time, for sure."

It was probably for the best. She doubted she'd be good company in bed tonight.

•   •   •

She went with Margaret and Petey on a walk through Charlie's neighborhood early the next morning. "I have to come up with a marketing plan that will satisfy Eleanor," said Sunny, despondent, after bringing her friend up to speed on the events of the previous day. "I'm not sure I can do it."

"Of course you can. Let's brainstorm it right now," Margaret said. "Turn on voice memos in your phone to record this. You won't want to miss anything." Sunny marveled at her friend's ability to tackle every challenge head-on. Once their conversation got started, the ideas flowed freely. They discussed couponing programs; holiday promotions themed around Mother's Day, Father's Day, and Cinco de Mayo; and special offers to other Village businesses.

"How about a wine-and-cheese open house every Friday afternoon?" asked Margaret. "That's a nice bonus after a massage, and a good way to build community. You could even—" She was interrupted when Petey growled and strained at the leash at the sight of his mortal enemy, the German shepherd from around the corner. "Petey, whoa," said Margaret. The shepherd perked up his ears but didn't rise to the bait. After the despised neighbor dog was out of sight, they finished brainstorming.

Then Sunny said, "I've been thinking about a conversation we had a couple of years ago when we first knew each other. We talked about whether people get to have more than one life. Do you remember that?"

"I do," said Margaret. "As I recall, we both agreed multiple lives are possible. But I believe the different lives are random, and you think they're all linked."

"Yes. More like reincarnation," Sunny said. "If you lived an honorable life the last time around, you'll be born into a better life next time."

"And if you behaved poorly, you'll suffer in the next go-around," Margaret said, completing the thought. "Is that what you're thinking about your own life?"

"I don't know what to believe. I'm not stupid or lazy or completely lacking in talent," said Sunny. "So there must be something else going on here. Because no matter how hard I try to turn things around, I can't seem to catch a break."

They reached a street corner, and as they paused while a car went by, Margaret stared at her friend. "Sunny, don't give up on yourself. I refuse to believe that what's happening to you is caused by some cosmic force beyond your control."

"But what if the spa fails?"

"Then you'll do something else," Margaret said, her tone breezy, as though changing careers was as easy as finding a new lipstick color. "Preferably something you love." Sunny nodded. "What about Todd? Is he a comfort to you?"

"Not so much. Our relationship seems stalled. I don't think we're going anywhere."

"Sorry to hear. I don't know if it's much consolation, but you've always got me. And Charlie."

But I don't have Charlie, do I? What a difference that would make in my life!

Margaret continued, "And you've got Mum if you want her. In fact, she's all yours, with my blessing."

•   •   •

Heartened by her discussion with Margaret, Sunny spent the day at the spa working on her marketing plan. She bounced ideas off the therapists and a couple of customers, asking them what type of promotions they'd be most interested in. The plan was taking shape.

At home, she spent an hour on the balcony finishing a sketch. Then she logged onto the Zoom happy hour with her sister's family in Phoenix in honor of Julia's birthday.

Looking at the Hollywood Squares-style windows on her laptop screen, Sunny watched Julia and her husband Ross, and Sunny's adult niece and nephew, each paired with their spouses. The niece's adorable little daughter was poised on her lap for part of the call, giggling and chatting with a toddler's self-confidence as her fiery red curls tumbled across her forehead.

"What happened with that new business thing?" Julia asked.

"Turned out it wasn't a good fit," said Sunny. "We were relieved when we didn't get the client." Why did she always keep bad news under her vest where Julia was concerned? Well, she wasn't about to air her failure in front of the entire family.

The group chatted about work, sports, favorite television shows. Then the conversation pivoted to the crazy weather events that had been occurring all around the country. "The Earth has had good periods and bad periods for, like thousands of years," said Ross. "It's part of the natural cycle of things."

"I don't agree with you . . . What's happening lately seems unprecedented," Sunny said.

Ross snickered. "Global warming? Come on. This past winter, we had some of our coldest weather ever."

Sunny couldn't believe her brother-in-law had it so wrong. "Climate change includes all kinds of weather extremes," she said. "Hot and cold."

Ross shook his head. "Yeah, that's what you ecofreaks like to believe."

Sunny hadn't heard the term but could tell it was derogatory. The weather used to be the safest topic for polite conversation, but nowadays, it had become politicized like everything else. "If you looked at the scientific—"

"Hey, you two, cut it out. This is supposed to be a celebration," said Julia.

After the Zoom session, Sunny nuked a package of Lean Cuisine and stationed herself in front of the television for dinner. She'd finished the bottle of wine and decided against opening another, pouring herself a glass of cold water instead.

Cataloguing her activities, she decided this had been a good day. She exercised with Margaret. She made encouraging progress on the marketing plan. She worked a little on her art. And she enjoyed the virtual party with Julia's family – most of it, anyway. Maybe her karma was improving after all.

The glass is half full. For now, she would settle for that.

CHAPTER 12

The printer was on the fritz. It made ominous grinding noises and then displayed an error code Charlie couldn't find in the troubleshooting section of the manual.

Although he did all his writing on the computer, Charlie liked to print out his work to review the pages. At least, that was his habit back in the day when he actually *produced* pages. So the current printer malfunction was not of great consequence – if anything, it gave him another excuse not to be working on the book. Several days had passed since he'd even attempted to write. He hadn't planned to mention the printer until Margaret complained about her iPhone that same afternoon.

"Heather texted to say she left me a voicemail yesterday. I checked the phone and there's no sign of it, even though I got three other messages." She studied the screen. "I should've replaced this damn phone months ago. It's so outdated."

"Which version do you have?"

"The seven." Margaret sighed. "I'm way too busy to deal with this right now. At least the phone is functioning."

"That's more than I can say for my printer."

"You can proof your work online until you get it fixed. Try zooming in on the type, maybe adjust the screen brightness . . . You'll find a workaround, I'm sure." She gave him a smile of encouragement. Easy for her to say. Margaret always found a workaround. He nodded and headed back to his office. "Oh, and Charlie, did you try unplugging the printer and plugging it back in?" she called after him as he walked down the hall.

"Right."

Back at his desk, Charlie jumped onto the computer and grew absorbed in *New York Times* digital crosswords and word games. When he tired of those, he surfed YouTube for a while. He'd been spending more and more time on that site watching TED talks, sports and music videos, old movies . . . whatever. There was no end to what you might find on YouTube.

Eventually, he tried Margaret's idea about the wall plug. Moments later, the printer whirred back into action.

•   •   •

With Gwendolyn here for the foreseeable future, Charlie's office was his safe haven. If he tried to catch a little TV in the den, she'd already be tuned into *Real Housewives* or some other unwatchable garbage. If he sat at the kitchen island with a cup of coffee, she'd sidle up and park herself on the adjacent stool. Sometimes she reminded him of a bored security guard patrolling the grounds.

And then there was poor Margaret, forever searching for a quiet place to work. Charlie sometimes felt he should give her his office, since she was the one who needed it. But he couldn't do that without tipping his hand about the true status of his revisions.

Gwendolyn had just left in her rental car, going God knows where. Though he knew Margaret worried about her, Charlie welcomed any respite from the woman's relentless vigilance. Today he headed straight up to the yoga alcove. Maybe he could get in a workout while the house was quiet.

About fifteen minutes into his practice, his body inverted in *adho mukha shvanasana,* Gwendolyn's voice startled him from behind. "Is that what you call a down-dog pose?" she asked. "Maybe Petey should do it alongside."

Charlie dropped his knees to the mat and sat cross-legged. "Yes, that was downward-facing dog. Gwendolyn, I thought you'd gone out."

"Oh, I did – but I skipped lunch today, and when I started driving around, I felt peckish, so I came back for a snack."

"I see." She might try the kitchen if eating was her goal. As though reading his mind, Gwendolyn said, "I heard the strangest vibrating music, so I came up to investigate."

"Right." He sighed. Though she hadn't complained exactly, he turned off the music anyhow.

"With that hair and beard of yours, you're looking more like a yogi every day."

Charlie's hair covered most of his ears and the back of his neck, and he'd stopped shaving. The lazy work habits had carried over into his personal grooming. "Would you like to use the mat and equipment?" Charlie offered.

She made a face. "*Ew.* Lord only knows what's been happening on that mat." She winked, and Charlie cringed with embarrassment.

"Don't let me interrupt your workout," she said, having just done so. "Me, I've never been the yoga type. I should try to find a Zumba class. I didn't care for the one at Margy's gym." She turned away. "But first I'll rummage around in the kitchen and see what nibbles await there."

"Make yourself at home, Gwendolyn. Don't be shy."

"Thanks darling, that's so sweet," she said, his subtle irony lost on her. She strolled off, heels clicking on the stairs as she made her way to the kitchen. The meditative mood broken, Charlie gave up on yoga for today. It was no longer possible to visit this once-serene alcove even to do a few stretches in peace.

In bed that night, Margaret slid over and wrapped her arms around his neck. He returned the kiss she planted on his mouth.

She reached one hand down to stroke his chest hair. But as her hand slid down toward his belly, Charlie intercepted it. He raised her palm to his lips, kissing it gently.

"Sorry, love. Not tonight."

"As in, 'not tonight, I have a headache'?" she asked him, keeping her tone light.

"No headache, but I am feeling . . . tense."

Margaret stroked his cheek, running her fingers through his facial hair. "I've decided I like the beard. Very sexy."

"Thanks."

"Charlie. I don't know what's going on with Mum. She's not an easy person, but I've never known her to be this rude. Still, I don't think there's any chance she'll burst into our bedroom." Her voice was soft, sweet.

"I know. I know. But I . . . " He didn't finish the sentence. There was nothing more to say. They both understood that the printer was not the only piece of equipment malfunctioning in the Kittredge household.

•　　•　　•

"Henry is coming *here?* To visit . . . *you?*" Margaret posed these questions to Charlie over lunch the following day, as the three of them shared a salad of mixed greens, tuna, and avocado. "Bread, Mum?" Margaret asked.

"God, no. And lemon juice. No dressing."

"I didn't see how I could refuse him," said Charlie. Henry had phoned that morning. His voice sounded ragged, almost desperate. He needed to speak to someone who'd experienced what he was going through, and Charlie was a widower. "I'll have a drink with him on the patio – if you're all right with that?" He looked Margaret in the eye. "Because if not, I'll tell him no."

Margaret sighed. "Let him come. I do feel sorry for him. But I'll keep to myself in the house." He nodded and gave her a quick hug.

•　　　•　　　•

Henry arrived promptly at five with two impressive bottles of wine, a pinot noir and a chardonnay. Both hailed from a premier winery in the Santa Rita Hills area that sold exclusively by allocation to its club members. He and Henry were sipping their first glass and admiring the quality of the wine when Gwendolyn emerged.

"Henry, my poor darling," she said in greeting. "How are you holding up?"

"Not so well," he said.

"My, but you've lost weight, haven't you?"

Henry nodded. "You've always had an uncanny eye for weight gain or loss."

"Pity it's not a marketable skill," said Gwendolyn. The men chuckled at this. "That wine looks scrumptious, but I think I'll mix myself a martini," she said. "I'll join you two in a few minutes."

"Gwen-Gwen, I'll catch up with you another time," said Henry, his tone affectionate but firm. "Charlie and I have some things to discuss man-to-man."

Charlie saw a flicker of surprise in Gwendolyn's eyes, maybe even anger. But she recovered her composure. "Of course, darling." She hurried back into the house.

Well, Henry handles Gwendolyn a lot better than I do. Margaret's ex-husband rose a notch or two in Charlie's estimation.

When they'd nearly drained the chardonnay bottle, Henry asked, "Did your wife have an illness? Or did she die unexpectedly?"

"A bit of both," said Charlie. "Bet had a variety of health problems, some of which were controlled and some of which weren't. Near the end of her life, she developed atrial fibrillation. The a-fib got bad – dangerously bad."

"But they have medications for that, don't they?" asked Henry.

"Yes, and there are procedures too. But she was phobic about any form of surgery. And she didn't like the side effects from the meds, so she stopped taking them. I didn't realize that till later."

Henry reached for the open wine bottle. "If it's okay with you, I'll polish off the chard and open the pinot."

"Sure."

"Sorry to interrupt. Go on."

Charlie resumed his story. "The problem was the blood-thinner that Bet had discontinued. Without it, she was at high risk for stroke. And sure enough, that's what took her."

Henry shuddered. "Were you with her when it happened?"

"No. I returned from a book tour and found her lying on the kitchen floor. It was a massive stroke. She lived three more days in the hospital, unconscious."

"Shit," said Henry. They sat silent for a minute, continuing to drink. Henry rubbed his chin thoughtfully, as if trying to solve a puzzle. "So, if she—if your wife had taken her medications, maybe she'd be alive today?"

"Maybe she would."

Henry slapped both hands on the armrests of his chair. "Damn. It was kind of the same way with Alice."

Charlie looked up, uncomprehending. "How do you mean?"

"Denial. They were both in denial about what they needed." Henry stood, wine glass in hand, and paced. "Alice had a lot of health problems, but she ignored them. That night she complained of the toothache, she insisted on waiting until morning to see how she felt. Maybe if she'd gotten help sooner . . . " Tears streamed down his face as he poured a generous glass of pinot noir for each of them. He gave a loud snuffle and wiped a sleeve across his face. "Shouldn't she have done everything in her power to take better care of herself? And your wife too. Shouldn't she have done the same?"

Charlie felt tears stinging his own eyes. "Yes. They should have." Another silence followed as they drank. The wine had a numbing effect. "This pinot is outstanding," said Charlie. "It's kind of—I don't know. Smoky?"

"Earthy," Henry said.

"Complex for a pinot."

"Yes. So after Bet died, how did you get through it? Any pointers?" Henry asked this in a casual tone, as if seeking tips on how to improve his golf swing.

Charlie pondered his answer before replying. "Work."

"Work?"

"Yes. I know you have a successful business, and I assume it's doing well."

Henry nodded. "Never better."

"Then my advice is to immerse yourself in the work. It will take you through the darkest time . . . and eventually you'll emerge and start living again."

Henry pursed his lips as if to keep himself from crying again. "Thank you—thanks for that. Can I ask you something else?"

"Of course." It sounded like Henry had said "ash" instead of "ask." Charlie shouldn't be surprised if they were both slurring their words at this point.

"This may sound crazy, after we've been pointing our fingers at the women for not taking care of themselves, but . . . do you ever blame yourself?"

"You mean, for Bet's death?" asked Charlie. Henry nodded. "At first, I did. If only I hadn't gone on the book tour, if only I'd checked to be sure she took her meds . . . But Bet was an adult. In the end, adults make their own decisions. You can't stand over someone with a stick."

"No, you can't." Henry started squirming in his seat, as if suddenly uncomfortable. "Okay, here's the thing. If it weren't for me, Alice might still be alive today."

Charlie looked at him in disbelief. "How can you say that?"

"Her doctor told her she needed a complete cardiac workup, and she'd scheduled the appointments. But then she canceled the tests to go to San Francisco with me. I *encouraged* her to come with me. It was my idea, even. I knew how much she loved the place. If she'd stayed home, she might've gotten the medical care she needed in time."

"Maybe, but you can't rewrite the past as if—"

"Think about this," said Henry, expanding on the idea. "If Alice and I had never gotten involved, I'd still be married to Margaret. So your life would be completely different as well."

"Jesus."

"I'm sure you would have settled down with someone else, an eligible guy like you," said Henry, graciously. "Maybe you'd be with that gal Sunny. She seems nice, and she's pretty cute too."

"I don't think so," Charlie said, his tone solemn.

"You don't think she's cute?" asked Henry.

"I mean, I don't think I would be with her."

"Whatever. But when you stop to consider how many lives can change because of a single decision, a single course of action . . . it's fucked up, don't you agree?"

"Yes, Henry, I agree. It's seriously fucked up."

"Lemme ask you one more thing. When—when do you get over something like this?"

Charlie teared up again and looked at his guest with sadness. Shaking his head, he replied, "You don't."

CHAPTER 13

Henry was visiting again. It astonished Gwendolyn to witness how he and Charlie, two men who couldn't be more different, had struck up a friendship in the short time since Alice's death. To her annoyance, it was like an old boys' club to which she'd been denied admission. Only once in a blue moon did Henry invite her to share a drink with them.

Tonight he surprised her with a bottle of high-end Russian vodka in an elaborate silver gift box. "After drinking this, you'll never want to go back to Grey Goose," he said, without asking her to join them. Gwendolyn noted the price tag that had "accidentally" been left on the package. Ninety-six dollars. She smiled with pleasure, not minding that Henry had bought her off with an expensive gift.

"Oh, and I brought something else. For all of you." Henry placed another item on the patio table. It was an egg carton decorated in the pastel colors of Easter: yellow, orange, pink, and green, topped with a fussy oversized bow made from ribbons interweaving the four colors. Inside were a dozen eggshells in the same pastel hues, decorated with stick-on emojis – some with smiley faces, others with sunglasses or tongues lolling out.

Margy, who usually kept her distance when Henry was there, emerged from the house with Petey. "What's that?" she asked.

Henry gave them a sad smile. "Alice made these a few days before her heart attack. She spent hours on end decorating Easter eggs for friends and family. To be honest, I forgot all about her project until I came across these in her hobby room. I finally worked up the courage to go in there."

"Alice had a *hobby* room?" If the eggs were any sign, Gwendolyn could only imagine what tacky decorations stocked Alice's shelves. Margy shot her a complicated look. Gwendolyn could read the look well. If Alice were alive, Gwendolyn and Margy would howl over this later on. But as things stood, the posthumous gift served as a painful reminder of Henry's loss . . . and her daughter's guilty conscience.

•　　　•　　　•

Gwendolyn flossed her teeth in a counterclockwise pattern, the same way she'd been doing twice a day for the past fifty years: upper right quadrant, upper left, lower left, lower right. Monitoring the task in the bathroom mirror, she fixated on a rude shock of whitish hair above her forehead. It hadn't been colored since February. *I'm starting to resemble that old lady from "The Golden Girls."*

A new hair salon had opened across the street from the Village Canyon Spa, but she didn't know the name. The next morning, she drove over toward the spa and, after circling the neighborhood three times, she located the Salon DHQ and parked in the adjacent lot.

"You're in luck," the well-groomed young receptionist informed her. "Eliseo has just had a cancellation. You said you're looking for color?"

"Color and cut, if he has time," Gwendolyn said.

"He's just finishing up with another client. He'll be with you in about ten minutes."

Gwendolyn looked around the gleaming lobby and studied the menu of treatments. All the surfaces in the spacious entranceway – floors, countertops, even walls – looked as if they'd been polished to a high gloss. The place was far glitzier and better equipped than Sunny's offbeat little establishment. During her wait, Gwendolyn booked a massage and facial for later in the week. Margy and Sunny needn't know.

Besides, Sunny had it coming. Last week, Gwendolyn had been enjoying a Cadillac margarita at a popular Village restaurant called The Kitchen, chatting it up with a nice man at the bar, when Sunny walked in to pick up a takeout order. Gwendolyn had lifted the heavy stemmed cocktail glass with both hands and drained it to the bottom as Sunny cast a disapproving eye.

"Let me drive you home," Sunny said. "That might be safest."

"I'm perfectly fine." Gwendolyn had bristled at the insulting offer. Honestly, Sunny was such a goody-two-shoes. Worse yet, the girl reported the encounter to Margy, which led to an inevitable lecture.

The two-hour hair session with Eliseo produced mixed results. The trim was masterful; she adored the way he'd angled the cut in the front. But ash blonde was a finicky color, difficult to get right, and the end product was at least two shades darker than she liked.

This afternoon, she'd go to Zumba again. Gwendolyn had discovered the class by accident on one of her outings. They met three times a week, half a dozen or so students and a young female instructor. With time to kill before class, Gwendolyn decided on a drive around the coast, but she took a wrong turn and found herself heading inland instead. Passing a sign that said, "Welcome to Lomita," she proceeded along a dodgy commercial street lined with depressing little shops. While stopped at a traffic light, however, a corner store caught her eye, and she pulled the car over.

An old-fashioned bell chimed loudly to announce her entrance. There was no one in sight until a salesclerk emerged from behind a red curtain. A curvaceous woman of indeterminate age, she wore heavy eye makeup, purple lipstick, and a short black wig in a hairstyle that Elizabeth Taylor might have sported in the nineteen-sixties. "What can I help you with, dear?" she asked.

"Well—a wig, obviously," said Gwendolyn.

The woman walked closer and appraised Gwendolyn's head. "You have lovely hair yourself," she said, "so obviously you don't need it to cover up hair loss – unless maybe you've got a, um, medical situation?"

"No, no, nothing like that," Gwendolyn said quickly. "I would like a different style . . . and definitely a prettier color." *Something less drab than my present unfortunate shade.*

The clerk smiled. "Excellent. My favorite customers are the ones who understand what an asset a beautiful wig can be. And how rejuvenating. Let me show you a few that I think might work."

Gwendolyn must've tried on twenty wigs during the next half hour. It amazed her to see the way each one transformed her into a different person. A long, light brown wig in a feathered cut – natural hair, of course – made her look like a young woman again. She also favored a nicely styled strawberry blond hairpiece around the length of her own hair. When the clerk brought out an artificial black Elvira wig, Gwendolyn wrinkled her nose; but realizing it might be perfect for the next Parkside Gardens costume gala, she gave it a look.

What to do? She donned her favorites again, each in turn, and then tried them on one last time. She ended up buying all three.

Who knew wigs could be so expensive? Gwendolyn had expected bargain prices, given that this shop wasn't exactly on

Rodeo Drive, so it shocked her when the total tab came to nearly three thousand dollars. Well, no matter. She'd hide the receipt from Margy.

She turned on Google Maps to guide her to Zumba. Thank heavens for her smartphone. Between the directions, the camera, and the little notepad function, she kept herself on track.

The class met at a tiny dance studio close to the Village Shops, but in a less fashionable area. Despite the unimpressive surroundings, it was more to her liking than Seaside Fitness.

Most of the dancers were seniors. Fred, the only man in the class, was the life of the party. Forever cracking corny jokes, he had a wide, close-mouthed grin that crinkled his cheeks in an appealing way and gorgeous eyes that sparkled when he smiled. They were an unusual color as well – a deep blue, almost navy. She couldn't tear herself away from those eyes. The t-shirt he wore was an almost identical blue, drawing further attention to his best attribute. Thank goodness she'd gotten her gray covered, albeit badly – Fred had to be a decade younger than her.

He'd made a beeline for Gwendolyn after the last couple of classes and today, he invited her to his house for a glass of wine. She hesitated, but then she remembered all those months when Sam had been seeing Phyllis and her at the same time. Certainly, that had earned her the right to step out for a casual date.

Fred gave her the address, and when she got into her car and Googled it, she saw his home was only a block from the beach. Hmmm. Perhaps he was an eccentric, Zumba-loving millionaire. The man grew more intriguing by the minute. When she pulled up to the curb at the designated address, it was a charming old apartment building. Perhaps he owned the property? Exiting the car, she wondered how she'd find Fred, who hadn't provided an apartment number. But he stood by the entrance waiting to usher her in. They mounted an airy flight of stairs to the second floor, where he led her to an apartment toward the back of the building. Stepping inside, she was instantly dismayed by what she saw.

Fred was a hoarder. Stacks of magazines and newspapers lined the narrow hallway. In the galley kitchen, fruit flies circled a small double sink cluttered with dishes and glassware. Every available inch of counter space was jammed with empty bottles and jars, knickknacks that seemed to have no practical purpose, and dusty glass canisters filled with pastas, cereals, and grains. Fred pulled two cloudy wine glasses from a cupboard and filled them halfway with white wine from a fridge that looked like a mid-century model.

He led her to the living room where a saggy couch was the only available seating, the chairs being occupied by piles of books and clothing. Literally sinking into the sofa, they lifted their glasses in a silent toast. Gwendolyn's lips puckered at the first taste. It was the sort of wine she imagined a discount airline would serve. She tried to ignore the sourness.

Fred's mouth curved open into a smile as he raised his own glass to his lips. "Cheers." Closer to him than she'd ever been, for the first time Gwendolyn got a glimpse of . . . *his teeth.*

Fred's brownish-yellow teeth looked like they should inhabit the mouth of an old Cockney barman living around the time of the first World War – not a man with all the advanced tools of modern American dentistry at his disposal.

He told her about the oddball collection of characters in the building. Compelled to look elsewhere as Fred talked, Gwendolyn studied the small adjacent balcony. It was crammed with stackable plastic storage bins filled with God only knew what, and a glass-topped table that had likely not been Windex-ed since the Obama administration. Not surprising for a man who couldn't manage his own mouth.

Now Gwendolyn noticed that a tiny fruit fly had taken up residence in her wine glass. She observed the fly paddling in circles while she wondered why she'd ever accepted Fred's invitation. As she pondered how to extricate herself, Fred drained his glass and jumped up. "Back in a sec." After he headed for the kitchen, she emptied her wine into a planter.

When Fred returned, he brandished the half-empty wine bottle. "Top you up?"

"If only. I'm afraid I didn't realize the time," she said. "I must get home to my daughter for dinner." Making a hasty departure, she nursed fond thoughts of Sam with his stately apartment, his impeccable grooming, and his white, even smile.

•   •   •

She thought she knew the way home, but somewhere she took a wrong turn again and drove aimlessly for several minutes. Pulling over, she tried to turn on Google Maps but discovered that her phone was out of juice.

Why did the roads in Charlie's neighborhood all meander in endless curves and hairpin turns? Manhattan had spoiled her with its sensible grid of numbered streets and avenues. Finding her way around here was endlessly frustrating. Diabolical, really.

By the time she got home, Margy and Charlie were already cleaning up the dinner dishes. "Mum, where were you? I tried and tried to call you. You've been gone so long I was frantic."

"I'm sorry, darling. The battery on my phone went dead. I'm fine. And as you can see, I've had a busy day." Gwendolyn twirled around to give her daughter a preview of the new hairdo. "It's a bit dark, but I rather like the way he styled it. What do you think?"

"I think," said Margy, "you're trying to change the subject."

"I said I'm sorry. Did you save a plate for me?"

"I did. But from now on if you're not home on time, plan on getting your own dinner."

"That is ridiculous. How dare you treat me like a wayward child?"

"If you don't want to be treated like one, stop acting like one. And *please,* spare us any further unnecessary worry. It's common courtesy, Mother."

After nibbling her cold dinner, Gwendolyn toted the shopping bags upstairs to unpack her purchases. Opening the boxes, she put on the long, layered brunette hairpiece, the one that made her look so young. Surely Margy would grin admiringly. Maybe Charlie would even give her a wolf whistle. She returned downstairs. They both looked surprised, but not in a good way. Charlie turned away as if to avoid eye contact.

"Mum—what the hell?" said Margy. "Why are you acting so odd? Have you been drinking?"

"I have *not.* I had a few sips of wine, but it tasted so appalling I poured it out."

Margy shook her head. "But a wig? This isn't you."

"Who are you to say what is or isn't me? I'm the only one who knows that." Gwendolyn turned on her heel. Did *she* even know what was or wasn't her? Only then did she remember, she'd promised to Zoom with Sam at eight o'clock New York time. It was hours past that. Dammit. She phoned him straightaway. "I'm sorry to call so late."

"You know I like to watch my favorite news program this time of evening." Sam's voice was gruff. "Gwendolyn, this isn't the first time you've missed our Zoom call."

"I know, darling, Something came up."

She heard him switch off the television. "If you were in New York, we wouldn't have this problem," he said. "It's still unseasonably cold and rainy, but I think we're past the snow. Come home."

"You're right, it's time. Especially with Margy acting like the Queen of Mean. I'll do it." She poured out her heart about tonight's confrontation. "Can you believe, just because I missed dinner and didn't call, she accused me of drinking. And she threatened to send me to bed without my supper next time."

"I doubt Margy said that – and if she did, I don't blame her," said Sam. "That was rude of you. She must've been worried, like I was."

Honestly, she didn't see why a slight delay on her part should trigger a national crisis. Must everyone overreact? "Thanks for nothing. I think I'll stay in California after all," she said in a *see-what-you-made-me-do* tone.

"Gwendolyn, please—"

"No, I mean it, Sam. If I'm to endure unpleasant treatment, I might as well endure it in a sunnier climate. Please don't call me." And she hung up.

CHAPTER 14

"Here. Look at these," said Sunny. She passed her sketchbook to Todd.

He leafed through the pages. "You drew all these?"

Sunny nodded, proud of her accomplishment.

He barely spent a few seconds on each sketch. "Cool."

"So you like them?" she asked.

"Yeah, sure. But they all look kind of similar. Don't you ever draw anything else?"

Would it kill him to compliment her talent? It reminded her of Far whenever she would bring home school projects as a girl. It was never, "Good work, honey." He always zeroed in on the inadequacies. "See here, the bottom corner has come all unglued," he would say. Or, "This picture would've been prettier with more colors."

"Babe, I'm starving. Can we eat?" Without waiting for a response, Todd moved over to the small dining table. He drummed his fingertips on the straw placemat and gave her an expectant look. Far used to do the same thing when Mother was serving dinner. As Sunny was about to ladle turkey chili into a bowl, her cellphone buzzed. It was her landlady from Beverly Hills.

"Sunny. I hope I'm not catching you in the middle of dinner hour."

"That's okay, I can talk." Sunny put the pot of chili back on the stove. Todd glared at his empty bowl.

"I'm afraid I have bad news. I'll come right out and say it," the landlady continued.

"What?" Sunny's stomach clenched into a tight, burning ball.

"My husband and I need the condo back for our grandson. He landed an aerospace job in the South Bay and he's relocating from Texas. The condo is perfect for him and close to work."

"But—what am I supposed to do?" asked Sunny. She watched Todd walk to the stove to ladle out his own chili. He smacked the bowl down on the table.

"Of course, we'll give you thirty days to move out," the landlady said.

"Right." Sunny tried to process this. What next? Was she about to be homeless again?

"But if you can move earlier, we'll pay you a cash bonus as well as returning this month's rent and security. I'll outline everything in an email and send it to you right away."

Sunny turned off her cell and sank into the chair opposite Todd, who shoveled down his chili like a man who'd come off a hunger strike. "Did you hear that?" she asked.

"Only your side of the conversation. What's going on?" he said without looking up. She gave him the news.

"But what about the lease?"

Sunny heaved a sigh. "My agreement is month-to-month."

"Jesus." Todd pursed his lips and shook his head.

"This is bad," Sunny said. She spooned out a small portion of the steaming chili for herself and put a plate of cornbread on the table. But she stirred the chili round and round in the bowl, her appetite gone. "Do you have any idea how hard it is to find an affordable rental around here?"

Todd mopped up the bottom of his bowl with a square of cornbread. Still not looking at Sunny, he said, "You know, my place doesn't have enough room for two people."

Her brow wrinkled in surprise. "Who said anything about your place?"

"Nobody *yet,* but . . . if the idea of living together has crossed your mind, I've gotta say it's not a good idea."

"Todd, I'm not asking to move into your—"

"I realize you're not *asking,* but I think we shouldn't let circumstances push us into an arrangement we're not ready for."

Sunny shivered a little from nerves. "You're putting words in my mouth. I agree we shouldn't live together."

"Good. Good." His head bobbed up and down in affirmation, his relief palpable. He stood up.

"Did you want more chili?" Sunny asked.

"No, no, I should go. You've got a lot of things to work out, and . . . it'll be better for you to focus on that."

Sunny splayed both hands on the edge of the table and leaned forward. "Are you breaking up with me?"

"Now you're putting words in *my* mouth," said Todd. "Who said anything about breaking up? I just think we both need some space while you work out your issues."

"My issues. Right." Her tone was dull, emotionless. As Todd opened the front door to leave, Sunny stopped him. "The key," she said.

"Huh?"

"The condo key I gave you—I need it back. I've gotta return my keys to the owner."

"Oh, yeah." He extracted it from his key ring and handed it over. "Talk soon, babe." She didn't reply.

After Todd left, Sunny sat at the table and had a good sob-fest. She wasn't sure whether she was crying over Todd or the condo, though she guessed it had more to do with the latter than the former. Sunny thought back to the other time Todd had walked out on her, two and a half years ago. Then, like today, he'd chosen to bail when she was at a low point. Her mother had Alzheimer's, the cost of her care had depleted Sunny's own savings as well as Mother's, and then she'd lost her job on top of all that. Todd had defected to Orange County, citing the demands of his new job.

When the going gets tough, Todd gets going.

She called her sister, eager for a sympathetic ear.

"Oh, Sunny, what a drag," Julia said. "I'm sorry."

"I don't know what I'm gonna do."

"Do you want to—to stay with us for a while?" Julia asked. Sunny thought the offer sounded . . . not insincere, but half-hearted. She supposed Ross wouldn't be thrilled to have his tree-hugger sister-in-law in residence.

"Thanks, but my home and job are here."

They talked for a few more minutes. Sunny's next call was to Margaret. As expected, her friend took more of a practical approach to the problem. "You have options, Sunny. You could just stay."

"You mean, like squatter's rights?"

"Yes. It will be difficult for them to force you out as a rent-paying tenant. It could take months."

"They won't like it. They're hoping I won't even take the full thirty days to move out." Sunny explained the incentive program.

"Let's not worry whether they like it. It would buy you time."

"Yes, but at what cost to my nervous system?" Sunny said.

"What do you mean?"

Fresh tears sprang to Sunny's eyes. She stood and took a deep breath before she replied, hoping her voice would come out in something other than a tremble. "I—I haven't got the heart to fight this. I don't have it in me. I still think all the stuff happening to me may be connected somehow to past actions, maybe even past lives."

Margaret said, "Sunny, you know how I feel about you blaming karma for every bad event in your life. One of these days you'll need to—to—"

"Stand up for myself?"

"Yes."

"You may be right. But this is not the time for me to get confrontational." Then she told Margaret about Todd.

"So did you two break up?"

"There's a good question," said Sunny. "Not officially. But as far as I'm concerned, it's over." Only when she spoke the words aloud did she realize they were true.

"Jeez, I'm sorry. I feel kind of responsible."

"How so?" asked Sunny.

Margaret reminded her, "I encouraged you to get back together with Todd in the first place."

"You encouraged me to give him another chance. You didn't say I should stick with him through thick and thin. For weeks, he's been acting like an asshole and a loser. I should've given him the boot long ago."

"If that's the case, let's be glad you did," said Margaret, sounding more upbeat.

Sunny wasn't sure who did what to whom, but she appreciated Margaret crediting her with the breakup. "The last thing I need in my life is a man who reminds me of my father." As soon as she said it, she realized this was true as well.

At the other end of the line, Sunny heard a knock, then a muffled voice. Her friend said, "Mum needs me for something. I'll call you back soon, okay?"

"Sure."

About half an hour later, Margaret called. "Come live in our guesthouse."

Sunny hadn't expected this. "I thought you were using it as an office."

"I could still do that while you're at work. Anyway, I'm in the main house most of the time for the Wi-Fi connection."

"Did you . . . discuss it with Charlie?"

"Of course. He's fine with it."

Sunny's pulse quickened a little. "Tell me what he said."

"He said it was a good idea."

"Oh." Sunny fought back tears again, this time in response to her friends' kindness. "That's extremely generous, but it seems like such an imposition."

Margaret responded, "It isn't. Look, the guesthouse is small, but you'll have a lot of privacy. And it's got all the essentials – except for decent internet."

Sunny warmed to the idea. "You've gotta let me pay rent. This isn't like when you first met me, and I was unemployed and living in my car."

"Oh, I don't think Charlie would agree to that. But you can contribute to household expenses for any shared meals. And keep us supplied with wine," Margaret added.

"Wine, I might not be able to afford," said Sunny. "Rent would be cheaper." Her friend laughed.

"So it's a deal, then?"

"It's a deal," Sunny said. "I—I don't know what to say. Thank you both, so much." She let out a huge sigh of relief.

After the call, she picked up her sketchbook and a box of colored drawing chalk. Sunny didn't know what she was going to create when she touched chalk to paper. What emerged, to her surprise, was . . . a picture of Todd. This was not a portrait of a loved one, it was a caricature. His features were exaggerated, his nose bulbous, his hair plastered to his forehead. She drew his mouth in a Todd-like smirk. She colored his cheeks and nose reddish pink to accentuate the alcoholic flush. When she finished the drawing, she propped it up against a wall, backed off a few feet, and tried to view it with an objective eye. Not bad. Not bad at all.

Sunny used to limit her art projects to seascapes and nature scenes. Recently, she'd done a sketch of Petey, and Margaret had made such a fuss over it, Sunny gave the drawing to her friend. But she didn't often draw people. She was pleased with tonight's effort, given how challenging she found it to capture the essence of a human being. If you could even call Todd a human being.

With this mean-spirited thought, she poured herself a glass of wine and took a seat at the table. As she started her to-do list for the upcoming move, she considered what it would be like to live with Margaret and Gwendolyn.

And Charlie.

CHAPTER 15

Charlie entered the house with a bag of groceries balanced on one hip. He gave the kitchen door a tentative push as if fearful of what he'd find inside, half-expecting to see Margaret sprawled on the floor, dead or unconscious.

He knew this was irrational. Ever since the night he and Henry had discussed Bet's death, he kept replaying the shocking discovery of his wife on the kitchen floor after her stroke. It had happened over five years ago, but the trauma had resurfaced with raw and unwelcome freshness.

Bet had reminded him of a fragile flower, an exquisite bloom perched atop a reed-thin, precarious stalk. Her physical complaints had been numerous. But Margaret was one of the healthiest people he knew. She rarely suffered from even the trivial aches and pains that plagued most people over fifty. So Charlie couldn't comprehend this new anxiety. Maybe it was linked to his worsening writer's block.

Sure enough, Margaret was sitting as usual in an erect posture at the island barstool, poised over her laptop. Charlie dropped the groceries on the countertop and went to kiss her. "How's work?"

She sighed and leaned briefly into his shoulder. "Between *Powder World* and the launch of the new magazine, it will be a long time before my schedule gets back to normal."

"Sorry to hear that." *Not only for your sake, but mine too.*

On top of her new assignment, Margaret was short-staffed. Her associate editor was on medical leave, and her editorial assistant had resigned for another job. The resulting pressure was unrelenting. Charlie stood in awe of Margaret's coping skills, but her calm under fire cast a spotlight on his own shortcomings. The more challenged he felt to keep up with her, the more blocked he became.

"You know, it's ironic," she said. "This job used to be a cakewalk. I could polish off my duties in four hours a day, no sweat. I think this must be payback for all my years of slacking."

"Punishment for past sins?" said Charlie. "You sound like Sunny."

Margaret laughed. "Her presence here must already be rubbing off on me."

This morning he'd encountered Sunny outside the door of the guesthouse, wrapped in a flimsy robe. "I—I came out to check the weather," she said, stammering, her face pink with embarrassment as if he'd caught her naked.

Charlie thought about how his solitary domain had been invaded so quickly and by so many. Of course, he'd *wanted* Margaret to live with him, wanted it more than anything. But now he was surrounded by three women, a rambunctious forty-pound terrier, and a grief-stricken ex-husband who'd become a regular fixture around the place. And soon, Benny was coming to visit while Michael and Heather went to Colorado for a wedding.

"Why doesn't he stay at his grandfather's?" Gwendolyn had suggested. "Henry's house is nearly the size of The Bramwell, and they could keep each other company." Charlie thought this was a good idea.

But Margaret said, "Benny is traumatized over Alice's death. Michael says it will upset him to sleep in their house."

"Heavens, he tries to shield that boy from everything," Gwendolyn had said, clucking.

Charlie stashed the perishables in the fridge. "How are the revisions coming?" Margaret said. "Thoughtless of me – I haven't even asked you in days."

Thank God. "Oh . . . same old, same old," was his trite response. "Shall we watch a movie on TV tonight?"

"I don't think I have time for anything that lengthy. I need to do more work after dinner," said Margaret.

"How about I open a bottle of something nice around five o'clock and we'll share a glass of wine in the den – the two of us."

Margaret hesitated. "Sounds tempting, but Sunny and I already made plans to take Petey for a hike by the ocean." That, she had time for.

Charlie went to his computer and commanded himself to work. But when he poised his hands above the keyboard, they seized up, as if the writing paralysis had spread from his brain all the way to his fingertips. *What the hell is happening?*

He suspected why he'd grown so spooked about the writing. It wasn't enough to churn out any old book – he needed another chart-topper. Another *Bicoastal*. His career had been foundering like a swamped vessel, and it would take a masterful act to get it back on an even keel.

But what if he didn't have another best-seller in him? He couldn't bear to think of the consequences of failure, not at this stage of his life. Charlie was not a young man, but he wasn't old either. He still had years ahead of him. If his gift had deserted him forever, what then? Shaking his frozen fingers with a violent motion, he closed the laptop and hurried from his office.

Henry visited again the next night. "I need to get out of my house – it's too damn lonely. But I promise to introduce you to the subtleties of premium rye," he'd said upon inviting himself over. Charlie had regarded rye as low-end hooch guzzled by high school students, but his friend disabused him of this notion.

"Rye is *huge*," said Henry. "A good rye tastes a little spicy, a little peppery . . . not as sweet as bourbon. The premium distilleries are producing some fantastic products."

"I take it this is a premium rye," said Charlie, sipping from his shot glass. The whiskey burned a little, but the texture was velvety and pleasant. He preferred it to bourbon.

"Premium is right." Henry nodded, took a large swig from his own glass, and coughed a little. "We won't even talk about what this puppy cost me." When Henry clammed up about price, Charlie knew it must be upwards of two hundred dollars. The man loved to throw money around and was generous in sharing the bounty. It was one of the things Charlie liked about him.

Once again tonight, at Henry's instigation, the liquor-fueled conversation came around to the two women they'd lost. "Did Bet have a career? Or was she a homemaker?"

"Ha," said Charlie with a humorless laugh. "I'd have to say no to both. Bet was a writer like me, but a poet of rare talent. I felt she had the greater gift. But she didn't have the self-discipline to stick with it. She wasn't very productive through the eleven years we were married. She kept assuring me she'd start writing again soon." Charlie might as well be describing himself. He hadn't penned a single word in weeks.

"And the homemaker part?"

"Bet hated that word. She used to say no one would ever mistake her for Betty Crocker. Bet wasn't interested in keeping the house straightened up, paying bills, any of that. She could cook an amazing gourmet dinner, but only if I helped plan the menu and handled all the shopping."

"So she was more of a head-in-the-clouds type, like you'd expect a poet to be," Henry said.

"Yes. Although you might expect a poet to actually write a poem now and then." Charlie blushed, feeling disloyal to his dead wife. But it was true. "What about Alice?"

"Well, you know, she worked for me at the company. Inside sales. That's how we met."

"Was she good at her job?"

"Alice gave great phone." Henry laughed. "Everyone loved that voice of hers." Charlie recalled the melodious voice – it was memorable in part because her soft, sexy way of speaking was at odds with her sloppy earth-mother appearance.

It was Henry's turn to be disloyal. "But Alice wasn't a great one with the details. A lot of things fell through the cracks at the office. But she tried to make up for it with that can-do attitude of hers. She tried so hard. Bless her heart." He sniffled.

Charlie nodded. Can-do attitude indeed described Alice.

"Then there's Margaret. She's a woman who's good at what she does," said Henry, refilling their glasses with rye. The men had never discussed Margaret before. It was a kind of unwritten rule, but they were too drunk to care.

"Margaret gave me the impression you disapproved of her job," said Charlie.

"It's not a question of approval," Henry said. "But I always thought her skills would be put to better use in the family business. I couldn't understand why she poured so much of herself into a damned engineering journal. And for such crappy pay."

"She loves it."

"Yes." Henry shook his head, as though still unable to grasp the reality after all these years. "It's a mystery."

"What was Margaret's father like?" Charlie asked. "You knew him, right?"

"Oh, sure. Eddie died maybe – I don't know – fifteen years ago. He was a good guy, very successful, but quiet and unassuming. Gwendolyn manipulated the crap out of him."

"Did he mind that?"

"Hell, no." Henry grabbed the bottle and topped up both glasses again. "He loved having this younger, classy, attractive English wife. And Eddie gave Gwendolyn the two things she needed most in the world – money and adoration."

Charlie laughed. "Sounds like a successful arrangement."

"It was. I think they were genuinely fond of each other." The two men raised their glasses. Henry said, "Mother and daughter couldn't be more different when it comes to wealth. Margaret was never impressed with money. It's not important to her at all."

"I've noticed."

"But that job of hers, that's another story," said Henry. "I always felt she was more interested in the work than she was in me." Rattled by this observation, Charlie took a large swig of whiskey. Suddenly the night air felt damp and uninviting. He set down the glass and pulled his jacket on for warmth.

The next thing he knew, it was two o'clock in the morning. He must've dozed off in his patio chair, and he felt stiff, achy, and chilled to the bone. He vaguely recalled Henry saying goodbye but had no idea what the time had been.

Stumbling upstairs and into bed, he pulled the duvet over his neck and shoulders, grateful to nestle under the soft covers that radiated Margaret's heat. He cuddled up to her and reached one hand under her nightgown to fondle her breasts. Margaret startled awake. "Charlie! Your hand is like ice. Jesus." She turned her head to glance at the clock on the bedside table.

"Sorry," he said. "You felt so warm, I couldn't resist." He snuggled closer and nuzzled her neck, feeling romantic stirrings for the first time in weeks.

"I need to get some sleep," she said. "Six a.m. wake-up tomorrow. Early conference call with Robert." She rolled over on her side, her back to him. No matter. With all he'd had to drink, his body was probably ill-equipped to carry out the amorous commands issuing from his brain. Within seconds, he too was asleep.

When Charlie awoke the next morning, the other side of the bed was empty. He remembered Margaret mumbling something about an early call. He lay in bed, trying not to think about the hangover that was pressing into both temples. Instead he regulated his breathing and let his mind free-associate. He often had his best writing ideas lying in bed like this, first thing after waking.

But today would not be the day for Charlie's big idea, so he gave up and dragged himself out of bed. To keep his distance from Margaret, he hid in his office watching old videos of Leonard Bernstein conducting Beethoven.

He could tell she wasn't overjoyed about the middle-of-night disturbance. She looked cranky at lunchtime, and when he asked how she was doing, she said, "Tired. Exhausted." In the afternoon, he offered to bring her a cup of tea and her favorite dark chocolate. Margaret said, "Thanks, but I'm too busy, even for chocolate. We're on deadline, and I have three more articles to proof." She didn't take her eyes off the computer when she spoke to him.

"Are you mad I disturbed you last night?" Charlie asked.

"I'm just . . . super-busy," she said, her gaze still focused on the screen.

What had Henry said last night? *She was more interested in the work than she was in me.* Once again, Charlie was struck by the vast differences between Margaret and his late wife. Bet had leaned on him so much for everything. Though he'd loved Bet, it had become tedious to remain strong for her, to be the one who always had to take charge.

Life had dealt Margaret a better hand. A model of self-sufficiency, she could navigate through her days and nights without Charlie's help. And though in one sense, it was a relief for him to be freed of the heavy burden imposed by a needy spouse, Charlie was forced to admit . . . with Bet, he'd sometimes found it empowering to hold all the cards.

CHAPTER 16

Sunny stayed late at the spa, not wanting to be caught out again for ditching work early. Despite her dedication, the business continued to struggle. Her marketing campaign had accomplished no more than a glass of water spilled across the desert.

Returning home, she found Margaret sitting alone on the patio with a cup of tea. "Where is everybody?" Sunny asked.

"Charlie's playing golf with Henry."

"I didn't know Charlie was a golfer."

"He isn't. He's not a whiskey drinker either, but Henry's introducing him to all sorts of new pleasures." She stood suddenly. "Petey, no." She ran over to the dog, who was digging a hole in the far corner of the garden.

"Does it bother you?" asked Sunny. She and Margaret sat together, and Petey settled on the ground in front of them.

"Their friendship? At times, yes. But in one sense, I'm grateful Henry is providing Charlie with a distraction," Margaret said.

"From what?"

"From my unintentional neglect. Work has been crazy. It should calm down when my associate editor comes back from medical leave. In the meantime, poor Charlie is paying the price."

"What about your mother? Is she paying the price too?" asked Sunny.

"Mum is running amok, as usual. I never know what she's up to."

Sunny knew what Gwendolyn had been up to the previous day. Stepping out for a Starbucks run, she'd glimpsed the older woman emerging from the Salon DHQ. Better not to tell Margaret her mother was hanging out at the rival spa. Sunny knew Gwendolyn was still miffed that she'd ratted her out for downing the oversized margarita at The Kitchen bar. Maybe this was payback? "I've been thinking about my own mother a lot lately," Sunny said.

"That must have been rough. The Alzheimer's, I mean."

"Yes, but it wasn't all bad. I think it helped to seal off some painful memories, things that were better off forgotten."

Margaret looked surprised by this. "Like what?"

Sunny chewed on her lower lip. "Like—like the way Far treated her."

"Far?" Margaret squinted at her friend.

"Oh, sorry. That's what we called my father," explained Sunny.

"Did he cheat on your mother?"

Sunny shook her head. "I don't think so."

"Was he abusive?"

"Not physically, not to her at least." They made brief eye contact, then Sunny averted her gaze. "But Far spanked me a lot and seemed to enjoy it, I'd have to say."

"Whoa, wait. Your father used to beat you?"

Seeing the alarm in Margaret's eyes, Sunny held out one hand as if to correct the record. "Okay, 'beat' may be too severe a word. I mean, nobody ended up in the emergency room. Far used enough force to make me good and sore." She shifted uncomfortably in the chair, as if her bottom were tender right now. Then she remembered her fright when Todd had given her a playful swat.

"Oh, Sunny, I'm so sorry you had to go through that. If he didn't hit your mother, in what way did he abuse her?"

"He yelled at her a lot. Constant complaints and put-downs. He'd gripe that the roast was overcooked or there were no snacks in the pantry. He'd say, 'If you put your family first instead of school, maybe this house wouldn't be such a mess.' Stuff like that. Of course, I got criticized all the time too. Nothing I did seemed to please him."

"What does Julie say? That's your sister's name, right?"

"Julia. We've never discussed it."

"You're kidding. Why not?"

"Because . . . " Sunny hesitated. "I don't think she'd understand. She always put Far on a pedestal and vice versa." Her tone became sullen, even bitter. "Mother and I could do no right, but Julia could do no wrong in his eyes."

"Still, she must've had some idea what was going on."

"I doubt that. By the time the trouble escalated with Far, she had gone off to college."

Margaret sipped her tea silently. Then Sunny asked, "Do you . . . do you think it's wrong of me not to tell her?"

Margaret paused. "Well, that's a pretty important secret to keep from your closest living relative. At some point, it might do you good to get it out in the open."

•   •   •

After the falling-out with Todd, Sunny had spent her free time cruising a dating website to connect with someone new – trying not to compare the men to Charlie as she reviewed their profiles. Each virtual meetup proved more unsatisfactory than the last. Now that she was in the guesthouse with no internet, Sunny filled the evenings with her art instead. She experimented with various styles and different drawing and painting media. She abandoned the fluffy seascapes for more challenging portraiture: men, women, and children of all ages, even animals.

Last night she'd drawn Charlie at the golf course. In the sketch he was poised on a green, focusing on the ball as he prepared to sink a putt. She picked up the drawing to give it a fresh look in the light of day. The relaxed shoulders, the strong hands gripping the club, the snug fit of the golf shirt . . . Sunny was pleased with how these details turned out. But when she looked at the face, she now realized that the hard, thin line of Charlie's mouth was all wrong. The eyes weren't like Charlie's either – they had a disapproving coldness. And though Charlie sported a full head of hair, she had drawn this face with a receding hairline that looked more like —

She dropped the sketchpad as if it were scorching her hands. *Why didn't I see this before? I've drawn my father. Add the thinning reddish brown hair and I've nailed him.* She looked down at her artwork, disbelieving, and yanked the page from the sketchbook. She crumpled it up and hurled it in the recycle bin, then sank into a chair and tried to calm her frazzled nerves. She thought back to what Margaret had said yesterday. Perhaps Sunny *should* open up to Julia about her painful relationship with Far.

Just not yet.

•   •   •

Gwendolyn saw Fred heading her way with a purposeful walk after Zumba, and she feared that a drinks invitation was afoot. Determined to avoid another tête-à-tête in his revolting apartment, she made an announcement to the group. "Listen up, people. Why don't we organize a happy hour, starting after the next class? It'll be fun. We can take turns hosting." As she said this, she wondered how she'd make good on the offer herself.

"We can meet at my place for starters," a woman named Lainie offered. Cheerful and feisty, she had become Gwendolyn's favorite. "But how will this work?"

"It'll be strictly BYO—everyone supplies his or her own adult beverage of choice and an optional snack to share." Gwendolyn was in party-planning mode, a role she'd always cherished.

Two days later, they crowded into Lainie's cramped living room a few miles from the studio. "Look what I snagged at Tar-*jhay*," announced Fred, pulling a three-pack of different flavored Pringles from a shopping bag. Everyone but Gwendolyn tittered. She found it irritating the way people were so amused by the faux-French pronunciation of Target.

"I love that store," said the host. "I buy all my groceries there."

As they continued with this tedious topic, Gwendolyn's mind wandered. She couldn't help thinking back fondly on the spirited discussions she and Sam had enjoyed with the sophisticated Manhattanites at Parkside Gardens. Not to mention the higher-quality libations at the New York cocktail parties. She could not give the Zumba gang high marks in the taste department. Two of the dancers drank canned beer—*honestly*—and even Lainie, who acted as if she should know better, sipped wine of a rude pink color that looked suspiciously like white zinfandel. Thank goodness she'd specified BYOB.

What would Edward make of this? He'd be gobsmacked to see her mingling with this crowd; although, of course, Edward hadn't much cared to mingle with anyone. One on one, though, he was a stimulating partner – smart, curious, and intellectually engaged. Margy got her bookishness from him. Thinking about it, Gwendolyn knew her late husband would have adored Charlie. Gregarious Henry was more *her* cup of tea.

•   •   •

The gatherings became a regular event. Though aware she was slumming it, Gwendolyn's craving for social contact – combined with the mellow buzz from the wine on the warm afternoons – made it easy to lose track of time, and happy hour sometimes stretched out to seven o'clock. She'd missed Sam dreadfully ever since their falling-out. But at least she needn't rush home for Zoom calls anymore.

It was Gwendolyn's turn to host the group. She'd known this would be challenging, but she developed an ingenious plan. The guesthouse currently occupied by Sunny stood at the end of the driveway, attached to the garage. Next to this structure was a triangle of lawn abutting the edge of the property. It had sufficient space for the small group to gather without being seen from the main house.

When her friends arrived and parked out on the street, Gwendolyn noticed that Charlie's car was gone. Good. And Sunny must still be at the spa. Margy would be at work in the house, and for once Gwendolyn was glad that her daughter found her job so absorbing.

The group strutted up the driveway to the side yard, toting lawn chairs they had brought at Gwendolyn's request. Fred also carried a folding card table. "I thought we'd play a little poker," he said.

Though Gwendolyn wasn't sure she remembered the game, the others were so enthusiastic that she went along with it. They passed the next hour or so drinking and playing cards. She surprised herself by becoming so absorbed that she lost track of time. Then Fred announced, "I need to take a leak. Actually, *leak* doesn't describe it. More like a torrent."

"Thanks for sharing," said Lainie, sticking out her tongue to show disgust. Fred guffawed.

"You can use the guesthouse," Gwendolyn said, fairly certain the front door was unlocked. Sure enough, the door swung open, and she pointed out the loo to Fred, retreating to the side yard to rejoin the others.

A few minutes later – a woman's scream. Gwendolyn recognized Sunny's voice. *Busted.* She trotted toward the sound of the scream, cursing the gods for bad timing. She saw Sunny fleeing the guesthouse, shouting, "There's a stranger in here!"

Margy emerged from the main house and made a beeline for her friend. "Sunny, are you okay?"

"Omigod. I walked inside and saw him coming out of the bathroom, zipping his fly. How did he get in my house?"

"I'll call the police." Margy swiped her cellphone.

Gwendolyn said, "No! No police. He's with me." At that moment, Fred emerged from the guesthouse, bad teeth exposed in a sheepish grin.

Margy looked at Fred and then turned to face her mother, jaw gaping. "He's with *you?*"

Gwendolyn launched into smooth introductions as if nothing had happened. "This is my friend Fred, from Zumba. Fred, this is my daughter Margy, and her friend Sunny."

"Sorry to give you a scare, young lady," said Fred to Sunny. Gwendolyn thought he looked more amused than apologetic.

"We've been enjoying our Zumba happy hour. I'm sure you'd love to meet our other lovely dancers," Gwendolyn said, as if they were all part of some distinguished troupe. Margy and Sunny followed her around to the side yard to the table scattered with poker chips and playing cards.

"Your mother's a gutsy player, but she just lost a big hand to me." Fred crinkled his weathered cheeks in a broad grin. "Gwendolyn, you owe me three hundred bucks."

"It's ridiculous that a flush should beat a straight. That can't be right," she responded.

"You lost three hundred dollars *gambling?*" So accusatory was Margy's tone, one might think she'd discovered Gwendolyn running a sex trafficking cartel. "Party's over, everyone." The guests departed at once, mumbling awkward goodbyes.

Gwendolyn watched Sunny disappear into the guesthouse, then shook her head at Margy. "Did you have to make such a scene? There was no need to embarrass me in front of my friends."

Her daughter glared back. "Sometimes I can't believe your gall."

"What are you all in a snit over?"

"Let's see, where to begin?" Margy dripped with sarcasm. "For starters, you might've had the decency to ask Charlie or me if this was okay. Instead you tried to keep it under the radar screen, hiding everyone over in the side yard. And you scared Sunny half to death, letting that man into the guesthouse."

"But I *did* ask." Gwendolyn looked injured by Margy's allegations. "I called from Zumba class. You didn't pick up the phone, so I left a detailed voicemail, saying we'd stay as far as possible from the house. You never responded."

"You left a voicemail?" Margy scrolled through her phone. "What time?"

Gwendolyn replied without missing a bit. "Around four."

Margy scowled at the cell. "There's no message from you. Goddamn this stupid phone." She sighed. "Look, Mum, don't do this again. Unless you get permission from Charlie or me first."

"Absolutely, Margy darling." Margy disappeared into the house, while Gwendolyn retrieved her chair and wine glass from the side yard. Once her daughter was out of sight, she smiled at having gotten away with this little deception. Thank heavens Margy's cell had been dropping calls and losing messages. Gwendolyn could pin it on the unreliable phone, and no one would be any the wiser.

But her smile quickly faded. Margy was always on her case about one thing or another, and although Charlie avoided lecturing or criticizing, he still sided with her daughter. And the loneliness – she felt so ignored. Everyone in the household was working all the time, and Henry couldn't seem to find a free moment for his Gwen-Gwen. The only time they included her in their plans was on Sundays, when Charlie manned the grill and they all dined at the massive outdoor patio table.

Gwendolyn knew her transgressions were having a cumulative effect. The more she fibbed and sneaked around, the more Margy and Charlie distrusted her. The little white lies were leaving a big dark stain. *I'll log onto Nordstrom.com and buy them gifts to show how much I appreciate them. Perhaps a couple of nice sweaters for the chilly coastal evenings. Cotton cashmere.* She thought of seeing a doctor, but what would she say? "I'm pissing everyone off and I can't stop myself. Can you help?" She didn't suppose there was a pill for that.

But maybe there was another remedy. She phoned Sam to apologize for her behavior and nearly cried with relief when he answered at once, whispering, "My sweetheart." They talked for a solid hour, warmly and lovingly, without blame or recriminations. By the time they wrapped up the call, everything had been settled.

Gwendolyn was going home to New York.

CHAPTER 17

"Charlie—can you take over story-time with Benny?" Margaret called down to him from the upstairs hallway. "I just got a text from Robert. He wants to talk."

"At this hour?" asked Charlie as he strode up the stairs to tend to their young guest. "It's nearly eleven o'clock in New York."

"You know what a night owl he is." It wasn't unusual for Margaret's boss to contact her in the evenings. "I shouldn't be long." She kissed him on the cheek and handed him a well-worn copy of *Winnie-the-Pooh.*

Charlie sank down onto his king-sized bed and scooched over next to Benny, who was propped against two enormous throw pillows. "GrandMar read me the one about Eeyore losing his tail. Can I pick the next story?" Charlie handed Benny the book and the boy thumbed through the pages, finally stopping at one of the later chapters. "Read me the one about Piglet."

Charlie glanced at the chapter heading. "How about Eeyore's birthday party instead?"

"No, this one," Benny repeated, insistent.

Unfortunately, the chapter described teeming rain that didn't let up for days. Piglet, who was alone and couldn't swim, required a dramatic rescue after becoming surrounded by water.

This heightened Benny's eco-anxiety to the point of tears by the chapter's end.

Charlie put down the book to give Benny a comforting hug. "It's okay."

"No, it isn't," said the boy, inconsolable. He snuffled and gave Charlie a doleful look. Climate change had even reached the Hundred Acre Wood.

"What I mean is, it all worked out okay," Charlie said. "Piglet was rescued and he was fine. They were all fine, and their houses were too."

Benny brightened up a little. "Even Eeyore?"

"Even Eeyore."

"But Eeyore's never really fine," the boy said. Charlie smiled. "Why is Eeyore always sad?" Benny asked, and then answered his own question. "I guess that's the way some donkeys are."

"I believe you're right."

"And people too?"

"Some people, yes." Charlie hoped Benny's own Eeyore-like tendencies would diminish with age.

With the guest quarters fully occupied, Margaret had arranged a futon at the foot of their bed for Benny to sleep on. Fortunately, night terrors weren't an issue. The boy was quiet and peaceful in repose, not disturbing them. Nor could they be concerned with him cramping their style in the bedroom – since, at the moment, he and Margaret had no style to cramp.

After they tucked Benny into bed with a plush version of Pooh, they went downstairs to join Gwendolyn for a nightcap. "I was afraid that story would set Benny off," Charlie said, relating the incident to the two women.

"The complicating part is that his fears are real," Margaret said. "I mean, it's not like he's worried about some bogeyman leaping out of a dark closet. Climate change scares the crap out of me too." Charlie nodded.

"Have they thought about getting professional help?" Gwendolyn asked.

"Heather found a family therapist, and they're going to start visits next week. Even more to her credit, she got Michael to agree with the plan." Margaret swirled her wine glass, took a sip, and leaned forward in her chair. "I feel horrible saying this about my own son, but Michael is so overprotective, sometimes I think his anxiety makes Benny more afraid."

"Michael doesn't wear his stress well," Gwendolyn agreed. "Have you noticed? He looks very puffy, like he's putting on weight – which that young man can ill afford." She gave her own trim waistline an absentminded pat. "Unlike his father. I can't believe how Henry has slimmed down since Alice died."

"That's true," said Margaret, "but we're not running a weight control clinic here."

"Darling, you know me, I can't help but notice these things. I must say, grief becomes Henry. He hasn't looked this good in years."

Charlie gulped down the remaining wine in his glass. Margaret joined him. Later, after Gwendolyn had gone upstairs, he said, "Remind me when your mother is leaving?"

"Ten days."

He sighed. "Why so long?"

"Sam's gone to Virginia to meet his first great-grandchild, and Mum's waiting until he's back. But don't despair, love. She's making noises about a getaway somewhere before flying home. We can only hope."

The next day, as Charlie blinked open his eyes, he could tell by the quality of the light that the hour was early. He rolled toward Margaret's side of the bed, hoping for a warm snuggle, but she was already up.

Looking down at the sleeping child on the futon, his hair mussed and his breathing soft, Charlie felt both moved and inspired. He continued to gaze at Benny, wondering whether this might be the day when his writer's brain would start firing and the elusive idea would at long last arrive.

And today, it did.

The big idea was not about Nomi, or her son, or any characters from his previous novels. In fact, it had nothing to do with his accustomed craft of adult literary fiction. Charlie wanted to write a children's story. A story for Benny.

As a childless man who'd never read nighttime stories to youngsters – let alone *written* anything for them – he was startled by his own epiphany. This was a radical departure. But during the boy's brief visit, his bouts with anxiety had stirred tender-hearted feelings in Charlie; and the idea struck him to address Benny's fears in an imaginative story, an upbeat lesson that might provide solace. Only later did he realize he was addressing another problem at the same time – the writer's block.

After noodling the idea for a few days, Charlie shared his plans with Margaret and Gwendolyn. "My story would center on a little boy who's worried about climate change. His father is a scientist who develops a wand that can control the weather, and he recruits Benny to help. I'm not sure exactly how it will play out, but in time he learns to get his fear under control."

"Would the boy in the story actually be Benny?" asked Margaret.

"More or less. I mean, I'd give him a similar name. Maybe . . . I don't know . . . Barney?"

"Like Barney the purple dinosaur?" Margaret said.

Charlie wrinkled his nose. "Oh, right, I guess that name is taken. I'll look for something else. And the boy would have some distinguishing feature that resembles Benny, like that cute cowlick in the middle of his forehead."

"So this would be, like, a story with illustrations?"

Charlie nodded. "Yes. For children around Benny's age."

Gwendolyn sprang from her chair. "I've got an idea for you, darling. Little Benny could have a sword fight with a monster that looked like a big dark cloud. He would kill the cloud monster with his sword and save the world from climate change."

Margaret fanned the fingers of one hand over her lips to hide what Charlie suspected was a cynical smile. He willed himself not to smirk. "Hmmm, that's an interesting idea, Gwendolyn. But you know how we writers are. We have to stick with our own personal vision." Gwendolyn gave a comprehending nod, as if she knew only too well the challenges of maintaining creative integrity.

Margaret asked, "Do you hope to publish this?"

"I haven't gotten that far yet. Initially it would be a gift to Benny."

"What a wonderful idea," said Margaret. "But where will you find the time, as busy as you are with the novel?"

Charlie flinched and hoped Margaret didn't notice. "I—I'll make time for it. It'll be fine."

She smiled. "You'll bounce this idea off Kathleen, right?"

"Kathleen?" Gwendolyn asked. "Who's that?"

"My agent." Charlie shrugged. "I'm not sure."

"But why wouldn't you get her feedback on it?" Margaret asked.

Because my self-confidence is in the toilet, and I've been avoiding my agent for weeks. Because I don't want to face her questions about why my new book hasn't progressed past page one. But Charlie knew Margaret was right. He said, "I'll talk to Kathleen. She's had some prior experience with children's publishing. But I need a clearer idea of my story before I pitch it to her."

•　　　•　　　•

He did some research to figure out what category of children's literature the book should target. His would be a picture book, hovering in complexity between the simple board books for toddlers and the chapter books for older children. After mapping out the storyline, he called Kathleen.

As they exchanged greetings, Charlie braced himself for the conversation that would follow. Sure enough, Kathleen wasted no time. "I emailed you last week to ask how the new book is coming, and you didn't respond."

"I apologize. I should have been in touch sooner," he said. "To be honest, I'm dragging on it. Bit of a dry spell. But I'll snap out of it. I actually called to talk to you about something else I'm working on."

"Something else? Okay, you've piqued my interest," said Kathleen, but she sounded grudging.

"I've written a one-page summary. Should I email it to you?"

"Yes, but paraphrase it for me now." Her tone remained curt.

"It's about a little boy named Bernie who's terrified of the extreme weather happening all over the world. His father is part of a group of scientists who've invented a wand that can control the weather. But they can't agree on the best way to use it. They spend months talking about it, but one day while they're busy debating, wicked storm troopers invade and steal the wand."

"Keep going," she said.

"They use the wand for evil purposes, to wreak havoc with the climate. The weather is worse than ever: blizzards, hurricanes, wildfires, tornados. Something must be done. Bernie's father breaks in one night to the fortress where the wand is hidden and recaptures it. I—I haven't quite worked out the ending," Charlie said to Kathleen. "But the scientist dad will recognize that a single wand won't save the planet, it will take thousands, with trusted people to operate them. He'll appoint Bernie as his first deputy, and they'll begin the process of fixing the problem. That's it. Still a little rough, but—you get the idea." He inhaled, nervous to hear his agent's response.

"Okay, well . . . I'll admit I'm having trouble picturing you as a children's author. But your idea has possibilities."

"It does?" He could feel the beginning of an adrenaline rush.

"It's certainly timely. Email me the synopsis and I'll give you some notes. In the meantime, a couple of suggestions. Don't give us too many examples of weather disasters. You'll find that you have to self-edit to keep to the required word count, anyway."

"Okay, good. Anything else?"

"Yes, and this is important. When things seem like they can't get any worse, Bernie has to be the one turn it around – not the father."

"So I should make Bernie the problem-solver. The hero."

"Right," said Kathleen.

"And you think you could sell this to Scranton? Or another publisher?"

"Look, I can't make promises about a book that isn't even written yet. But there's a long tradition of well-known fiction authors who crossed over into children's literature. Even Tolstoy did it." Charlie hadn't realized this. "Publishers adore this sort of thing – much easier for them to market a familiar name than an unknown writer," she continued.

The next step, simply stated, was for Charlie to write the book. "Picture books are so short, the folks at Scranton will want to see the copy, not a synopsis," Kathleen said. "And think visually. Write short descriptions of the illustrations as you envision them. They might not use your ideas, but it will help develop the story."

"What about the actual artwork?"

"Let the publisher worry about that. Get a good draft under your belt and then . . . "

"And then?" Charlie asked.

"Finish your goddamn *grownup* book."

•   •   •

How hard could it be to toss off a children's story of six hundred words or so? Pretty fucking hard.

This was the length Kathleen recommended in a follow-up email in which she encouraged Charlie to proceed with the idea as fast as possible. A thousand words was the absolute top limit, she advised him – the shorter, the better. This was a drastic departure for Charlie. "I can't believe something this short can be this difficult," he said to Margaret before bedtime. She was snuggled up against him, an arm slung across his waist.

"I'm not surprised," she said. "Did I ever tell you I interned at an ad agency?"

"I don't think I knew that."

"I was trying to decide whether to go into advertising or editorial work after college. Anyway, I wrote a lot of ads that summer. Everything had to be so brief and punchy. It was exponentially harder to write fifty words than to write five hundred."

Charlie nodded in agreement. "Less is more, huh?"

Margaret smiled. "You seem—I don't know—*happier,* I guess, since you started working on this. More enthusiastic." She wound both arms around his neck and massaged the back of his head with a gentle hand. "I wondered why you'd been on edge. I thought maybe you hit a few bumps revising the novel?"

Tell her now. Tell her the truth. But all he said was, "A bump or two, but it'll be okay. Just a little slower than I'd like."

"I'm still concerned that the Bernie story might distract you from the main event. The revisions." Charlie pulled away, not wanting Margaret to feel his body tensing up.

"It—it'll be fine," he said again. He kissed her goodnight, turned out the reading light above his side of the bed, and rolled over to go to sleep.

CHAPTER 18

Sunny had never seen a woman bat her eyes at a man, not literally. But here was Gwendolyn, fluttering her eyelashes at Henry like some brazen young flirt instead of — what? A woman nearly twice Sunny's age.

Though tempted to blame it on the insane amount of alcohol they'd consumed at dinner, Sunny knew better. Since living here, she noticed that whenever they all assembled, Gwendolyn directed her comments to Charlie or Henry, rarely glancing at her or Margaret. It seemed that Gwendolyn regarded herself as a rival for the men's attention.

Henry had received another fancy wine club shipment and brought several choice bottles to the Sunday barbecue. The red wines went down easily, providing the extra warmth Sunny needed on this chilly night. After dinner she said, "It feels like rain to me."

Gwendolyn countered, "Nonsense. This is California. Even if it is a bit gloomy tonight, I'll miss the weather here." Over dinner, Gwendolyn had announced that Sam bought her a JetBlue Mint ticket and she'd be leaving for New York in a little over a week. Sunny had stared down at her plate, not wanting anyone to see the look of relief that washed over her.

She turned away when Margaret and Charlie stood and embraced before retiring indoors, citing the heaviness of the

"May Gray" weather. She wondered if they'd had enough of Mum's flirting too.

Maybe it was better to have a youthful self-image like Gwendolyn than to be old before one's time. Lilly Ericsson had seemed ancient, even before the Alzheimer's diagnosis. Sunny pushed away this unhappy memory as Henry and Gwendolyn launched into a humorous discussion on awkward social situations. First Gwendolyn told a story about how she'd attended the wrong wedding at a multi-event venue and had to pretend she knew everyone.

"By the time I caught the bride's bouquet, I was having such a fabulous time, I'd completely forgotten these people were strangers. Everyone said they couldn't wait to come to *my* wedding, since I'd be next in line."

"Funny, Gwen-Gwen," said Henry. "Listen to this one. I invited an important client to an exclusive French restaurant in Santa Monica. You need to reserve a month ahead, and even then, you need to know someone to get a table. Trouble is, I forgot to book." Not until they showed up at the restaurant did Henry realize his mistake. "When we got to the maître d's station, of course he had no record of the reservation. I made quite a scene, accusing them of incompetence."

"Did they kick you out?" asked Sunny.

"On the contrary, they groveled at my feet with apologies." Henry laughed. "They seated us right away. At a good table." Gwendolyn leaned in toward Henry, lashes fluttering, and giggled. "That's not all," Henry said. "The next people seated were Tom Hanks and his wife. When they walked by our table, Hanks said, 'You may be a better actor than I am. Nice bullshitting.'"

Sunny suspected Henry was bullshitting them right now, but she couldn't help smiling. She liked Henry. He had an inexplicable charm. The term *je ne sais quoi* came to mind.

Gwendolyn acted confident of her own appeal too. Though Sunny used to think she was fun, as Henry clearly did, her opinion had changed. Margaret's mother was always out for herself, blind to the concerns of others. How did Charlie put up with her? Sunny supposed he did it out of love for Margaret – a thought that made her feel sad, then jealous, then guilty.

"Your turn," said Henry, smiling at Sunny.

"I'm too tired to think of anything." Sunny felt socially awkward all the time but found nothing funny about it.

Gwendolyn stood and stretched her arms over her head. "I think I'll watch something silly on TV. Night, all. Kiss, kiss." She blew air kisses, then went into the house.

"Did you feel raindrops?" Sunny asked.

Henry glanced up. "I don't think so."

"Anyway, I'm beat. Think I'll call it a night as well."

Henry smiled again. "I'm gonna finish my wine and be on my way."

Sunny retired to the guesthouse. She was deciding whether to watch TV like Gwendolyn, or crawl into bed and read, when she noticed a pile of dirty dishes in the sink. She scrubbed them clean and loaded them into the dish rack to drain. After finishing, she turned around and jumped at the unexpected sight of – Henry. He stood behind her, only a couple of feet back, holding two empty wine glasses.

"You surprised me, Henry. With the faucet on, I didn't hear you."

He flashed an apologetic smile. "The heavens opened up, so I ran in for cover."

"It's raining?" Sure enough, raindrops glistened in his dark hair, and the shoulders of his jacket were damp. They were both quiet for a moment, and now Sunny could hear the rain beating on the roof.

"I'm sorry," said Henry. "I'll go."

"No, it's okay. Why don't you stay till it lets up?"

"If you're sure—that would be great. I'm afraid I don't have any more wine, though."

"Oh, I've had enough wine," said Sunny. Buzzed didn't even begin to describe how she felt. Then she worried she was being ungracious. "I'd be embarrassed to serve you the wines I keep around here, but let's see what I can rustle up." She poked her head in the fridge but couldn't find so much as a container of dip. Then she had an idea. "What about a little recreational pot? Edibles."

Henry hesitated. "I haven't done that in a long time, but— why not."

"I have CBD gummies and brownies," she said.

"Are they your famous brownies?" Henry asked, his eyes shining with amusement. He had deep-set, nearly black eyes that dominated his face – even more so since the weight loss that had drained the former puffiness from his cheeks.

"No, I'm afraid these are from my trusty local dispensary. This kitchen only has a stovetop, so my baking days are over for now." Though Sunny had never received an avalanche of praise for her culinary skills, her brownies were popular. Not always, though. She thought back to the Valentine's Day when she was twelve and had baked a pan of brownies for Mother and Far. Her father took one bite and spat it into a napkin, pronouncing it dry as dust. *"How did you manage to overcook these so much?"*

"I'll take a brownie," Henry said, bringing her back to the present. Sunny poured two glasses of water from the fridge. Standing in the kitchen, she and Henry munched on their edibles and washed them down with sips of water.

"Shall we watch TV? I want to relax and chill out." Sunny knew she wasn't capable of sustained conversation.

"Sure."

She cracked a window to let in the fresh air, enjoying the rhythmic sound of the rain as it pounded on the gutters. She and Henry sat on the couch, a couple of feet apart; and as she started channel-surfing with the remote, he picked up her sketchbook from the coffee table.

"Okay if I look?" He flipped through the sketches. "These are terrific, Sunny. You're a talented gal."

She grinned, then paused the TV on an old World War II movie. "Let's try this."

"I don't feel any different," said Henry after a few minutes.

"The edibles take a while." They turned their attention back to the movie. Set in England, it shifted between the separate stories of a war widow and a soldier who'd returned from the front and couldn't find any trace of his wife. Sunny followed the parallel tracks of their lonely lives, knowing the man and woman would cross paths at some point and become romantically involved. About halfway through the film, as the cannabis heightened her emotions, she started feeling deeply for these people. How tragic to survive the horrors of war, only to end up so lonesome and desolate. Then she stole a glance at Henry, who'd been forced to endure tragedy too. Tears rolled down her cheeks and she gave a loud sniff.

"What's wrong?" Henry's expression darkened with concern.

"It's just — everything is — so sad." She didn't want to tell him she felt sorry for him.

"Oh, Sunny. Poor Sunny. I heard you were in a relationship that ended too." All at once he slid over on the couch and wrapped her in an embrace. He'd misunderstood her sorrow, thinking she was crying for herself. Torn between prudence and giving in to her need for the physical touch of a man, she decided, what could be the harm?

The next thing she knew, he was kissing her. Henry had a large mouth that jutted out – *pouty lips*, Margaret had called them – but it turned out to be an excellent mouth for kissing. His lips felt soft, moist, sensuous. And yet . . .

Shit. This really isn't a smart idea.

"I think I'm feeling the effects of that brownie." Henry gave a lopsided grin and blinked at her. His pupils looked dilated.

"Maybe we shouldn't be doing this," she said, though the protest was half-hearted.

Henry stroked her hair. "I know." But those soft lips covered hers once again in a deep kiss. The cannabis having kicked in, the rest was a blur. She didn't remember what happened next or how they moved from the couch to the bed. Apart from the kissing, another detail that stuck in her brain involved Henry's hands. He had large, paw-like hands with thick fingers. His were not soft hands, but they were gentle and experienced, and she liked the feeling of them exploring her body as they made love and eventually drifted off to sleep.

•   •   •

The next morning, when Sunny opened the door to see Henry out, Margaret stood on the patio of the main house with a mug of coffee while Petey tended to business. Sunny cringed but waved at Margaret, who was watching Henry hurry toward his car in yesterday's rumpled clothing. Margaret didn't hide her surprise.

"Well, well," she said after Henry had gone. "This is certainly weird."

Sunny blushed. "I—I know it is, so soon after Alice d—"

"I was actually more focused on the weirdness of my ex-husband and my best friend hooking up."

Oh dear – how did Sunny not realize this? "Are you . . . upset with me?"

"Upset?" Margaret seemed to consider the question. "No." She shrugged. "Charlie is the only man I love."

Sunny knew this, though it hurt to hear it. "I'm relieved you're not mad."

"But as for Mum – that could be another story when she finds out." Margaret gave an exaggerated wink.

"She sure gets possessive about Henry." Sunny flinched as she imagined Gwendolyn glaring at her with displeasure. Then her thoughts turned back to Charlie. How would he react? How did she *want* him to react?

Margaret grew more serious as well. "But Sunny, what does this mean? You and Henry?"

"I have no idea. It just . . . happened."

"You know Henry's history – the good, the bad, and the ugly. I won't preach to you about that." Margaret glanced at her phone. "Jeez, it's later than I realized. My Monday staff meeting starts in a few minutes."

As Sunny drove to work, she reflected on Margaret's question. What *did* last night mean? All she knew was that she planned to do nothing. She'd wait for Henry to make the next move. If there was to be one.

He called the spa later that afternoon. "Sorry to bother you at work. I should've asked for your cell number before I left." His voice sounded deeper on the phone. Kind of sexy.

"That's okay. I'm not busy."

He asked how she was doing and then launched into what she suspected was a prepared speech. "Sunny, I could say I don't really remember last night. Or I could say it was wonderful, but let's pretend it never happened. Or I could come up with any number of reasons it's not wise for us to pursue this, right after being in other serious relationships." He paused.

"So . . . which of those things are you saying?" Sunny asked.

"None of them. Because the truth is, I think you're beautiful and special and gifted. I want to see you again, and soon. I hope I can convince you."

Normally, she'd never take up with a man who'd lost his partner so recently. Especially when that man was her best friend's ex-husband. A husband who had dabbled with infidelity frequently during the marriage before leaving her for another woman. But Henry thought Sunny was beautiful. Special. Gifted. When had a man ever heaped that kind of praise on her? "You don't need to convince me," she said. "I want to see you too."

CHAPTER 19

It was a cloudless weekend afternoon when Sunny first visited Henry's house. She couldn't decide which was more impressive – the ultra-modern interior or the sparkling expanse of the Santa Monica Bay below, the coastal land curving around the water like an enormous horseshoe with Malibu at the opposite end.

"The view is even better at night." Henry smiled with pride as they looked out at the Los Angeles basin. "It's like a crescent of twinkling lights. The real estate agents call it the queen's necklace view."

"It's amazing," said Sunny. "My little condo had a sliver of water view from the balcony, but you had to hang over the railing to see it." He chuckled. "Margaret's place – the one she rented before moving into Charlie's – that had a nice harbor view, but nothing to compare with this. And the apartment was tiny." She regretted the words as soon as they slipped out, wondering if Henry might think she was critical that he'd emerged from the divorce with the superior piece of property.

"Tiny would not be the operative word for this place," he said. "But my last house was at least as large. Margaret could've stayed there, but she chose to move." Sunny had heard as much from her friend. "I'll show you around. We can take the elevator."

The place had a fricking *elevator?* Sunny was decidedly out of her depth. She stepped to the corner of the room where two enormous glass windows converged into a V shape. She felt like a bird perched high in a tree, gazing down at tiny sailboats gliding through the blue water below. Tilting her head back to look to the top of the large open atrium, she could see a hallway above that led to two separate wings. They rode the elevator to this upper hall.

"Here's the master suite," Henry said as they strolled around the top level. It was equipped with his-and-hers walk-in closets and an extravagant master bath nearly the size of Sunny's former studio. She noticed that one of the closets was empty except for a few cardboard boxes. Henry, or someone appointed to the task, must have cleaned out Alice's clothes.

The other wing had two more bedrooms, each with its own bath, and a smaller room that Henry described as Alice's hobby room. He closed the door softly after Sunny caught a brief glimpse of a sewing machine, a worktable cluttered with glittery knickknacks, and shelves crammed with magazines and oversized books.

As they descended in the small elevator compartment, Sunny's gaze was level with the open neck of Henry's light blue golf shirt. The shirt hung loosely over his navy shorts, and his stomach swelled out above the waistline, but the paunch wasn't too bad overall. Sunny noted, though, that his body had a slackness to it, like a man whose sole exercise was swinging a golf club. It might do him some good to take the stairs.

"This is my favorite part of the house," Henry said proudly. They stepped out into a large room with a pool table, oversized leather couches and armchairs, a massive wall-mounted TV, and a sunken wet bar with four stools facing the bay.

"Oh, what a great rec room," said Sunny.

"Rec room?" Henry laughed. "That's a term I haven't heard in a long while." Sunny blushed, uncomfortable at choosing words that would better describe a tacky room in a tract house basement.

Again, Henry didn't seem bothered that she'd misspoken. He poured a French rosé brut into slender champagne flutes, and the two of them sank into one of the deep couches. Halfway through the second glass, Sunny felt deliciously buzzed from the combined effects of the effervescent wine, the sun-kissed afternoon, and the buttery leather seat. So when Henry wrapped his arms around her and nuzzled her neck, she welcomed the overture.

He gently lifted off her top and then her camisole. Sunny arched her chest toward him. When they first started sleeping together, she'd feared that her small breasts would seem a paltry offering after Alice's generous bosom. But he'd said, "They're like two perfect little buds – incredibly sexy" – as if she'd presented him with something worth making a fuss over.

He kissed those perfect little buds, and they made love there in the rec room, game room, entertainment center, or whatever the term might be. It didn't matter that she'd misdescribed the room. Verbal gaffes and social unease faded to the background for Sunny when she and Henry got physical. As long as she had enough wine or weed to smooth the way, she found the sex enjoyable enough. But she was never transported by it.

She returned home a little after six, declining Henry's offer to take her to dinner. She would devote the evening to laundry, cleaning, bill-paying, and catching up with Julia. Sunny was trying to stay in more frequent touch with her sister, and they were due for a chat.

As she walked toward the guesthouse, she saw Charlie on a yoga mat near the pool deck, in a forearm plank pose. She debated whether to speak to him, then decided it would be rude not to. She strode across the lawn to Charlie. His clenched smile betrayed the exertion of holding the difficult plank position. "Sorry to disturb you."

"It's refreshing to hear an apology," said Charlie. His limbs quivered a little from maintaining the pose. "Gwendolyn seems to think I enjoy her constant interruptions."

Sunny admired Charlie's long, muscular legs. He was shirtless, and his upper arms and torso looked lean and chiseled. No belly fat pooching out on this man. Here she was, ogling Margaret's boyfriend . . . and only a short time after having sex with her friend's ex-husband, no less. She averted her gaze. *What is happening to me?* Sunny felt like her behavior disrespected all three of them. Grateful that Charlie couldn't read her mind, she said, "I thought you liked practicing yoga in your studio upstairs."

"I do. But it's such a beautiful evening, I came outside instead." Charlie lowered his knees, leaned back on his haunches, and then sat, extending his legs in front. "You weren't at the spa this late, were you?" he asked.

"No, our last appointment today was at two o'clock. I went over to Henry's."

"How's he doing?"

"Fine." She felt her cheeks redden, then blushed even more with embarrassment at being embarrassed. *It's probably a dead giveaway what I've been up to.* "How's the writing going?" she asked, changing the subject. Charlie told her about a children's story he was working on, and she asked if there would be illustrations.

"Yes. My agent said it might help me develop the story if I jot down ideas for the visuals. That's not my strong suit, but I'm giving it a shot."

"Well, I'll leave you to your yoga," Sunny said. "I've got a million things I need to get done." Hurrying toward the guesthouse, she mulled over Charlie's new writing endeavor. Talking about the illustrations made her realize how much she missed drawing. She'd dived into her art after moving here, then slacked off once she started seeing Henry. She hoped she'd soon be able to pick up where she left off. Maybe she should offer to help Charlie with his project.

•   •   •

Three days later, Sunny received an early morning call from the property manager of the Village Canyon Day Spa. A pipe had burst in the building, flooding the lobby, the little kitchen area, and an adjacent treatment room.

She drove immediately to the spa, panic-stricken, imagining the worst – equipment and furnishings damaged beyond repair, her beloved Laurel Canyon mural a soggy mess. When the property manager ushered her inside, it wasn't as bad as she'd feared. The water had already been pumped out, and fans and dehumidifiers were running to dry everything out before mold could form. A couple of walls had suffered damage, but fortunately not the mural itself.

He'd already spoken to Eleanor since the protocol was to notify the business owner directly in an emergency. "She asked you to call her right away." Sunny nodded. She'd also have to phone the staff and tell them the spa was closing temporarily. And, of course, the few customers who had booked treatments.

Her fingers shook when she picked up the landline to call her cousin. "It doesn't look too serious. The manager said everything should be totally back to normal in a week, ten days at most, if they can get a crew out quickly." Sunny heard Eleanor heave a deep sigh – a sigh that sent chills through her.

"I've given it a lot of thought." From the coolness of Eleanor's tone, Sunny could tell her cousin had made an irrevocable decision. "The way business has been going, I can't afford to keep both facilities afloat. I need to focus on the flagship location here in Mill Valley." Eleanor explained that she was losing too much money on the southern California spa, especially since

Salon DHQ had opened. Today's flood closure was the final nail in the coffin.

"I see." Sunny's brow furrowed.

"I'm sorry. No one ever dreamed we'd have such a formidable competitor right down the block. It's no reflection on you."

Sunny wasn't so sure. Last week, she was walking into the Seaside Fitness locker room when she'd heard Judith's unmistakable nasal twang. "I had another treatment at Salon DHQ," she said. "The place is freaking amazing."

"I feel bad for Sunny. Tough break for her spa," another woman said.

"That's show biz," said Judith. "Anyway, who wants to fucking listen to Joni Mitchell while you're having a relaxation massage?" Sunny had taken it personally. She'd tiptoed backward from the locker room and fled to her car, not wanting anyone to know she'd overheard.

"Sunny? Are you there?"

"Yes, sorry." She refocused on the call.

"You and the staff should file for unemployment," Eleanor said. "The lease runs out in a few months. When the time comes, I'll get movers in." She promised to set up a plan that would pay for continuing health insurance coverage, so at least Sunny had that. If there was a chance Eleanor might offer Sunny her old job back managing the Mill Valley spa, this would be the moment for that conversation to take place. But it never came up.

Sunny started crying as soon as the call ended. What next? She couldn't even imagine where she'd look for another job. Her cell buzzed. She debated whether to answer but then picked up. "Hi, Henry." She gave a loud sniffle.

"Sunny. Are you all right?"

"Not really." She gave him a condensed version of events.

"Come over."

Sunny wasn't sure she'd be fit company for anyone in her current state, but the desire for comfort won out. "I need to make some calls, but I can be there in an hour or so," she said.

On the drive to Henry's, she played one of her Laurel Canyon mixes through Bluetooth. "I Saw Her Again," a favorite tune by the Mamas and the Papas, came on. Sunny sang aloud with this song about a man who kept faking love for a woman he didn't really care about. Switching off the car audio, she all at once felt uncomfortable – unsettled – by something more than the job loss, but she wasn't sure what. Then an unwelcome memory surfaced. When her luck had gone sour before, Todd had turned his back on her – not once, but twice. What if Henry reacted the same way, spurning her because she was unemployed?

But when she arrived at his house, he greeted her with a hug and said, "I've got an idea for you." His tone was cheerful. But then, Henry's tone was usually cheerful.

"Let's hear it."

"In time, in time. Let me get you a drink. I can pour us both a glass of wine, or mix a pitcher of mimosas. What's your pleasure?" He led her downstairs to the lower level as they talked.

"Thanks, but no alcohol for me. Not a good idea when I'm feeling this weepy," said Sunny. "Sparkling water, if you've got it."

"Lemon or lime?"

"Lemon, please." She sank down into one of the soft leather armchairs, avoiding the couch where they'd made love a few days earlier.

"Why don't you tell me what happened?" he asked as he handed her the sparkling water and sat on the end of the sofa closest to her chair. He took a swig from a bottle of craft beer.

Sunny recounted the conversation with Eleanor in more detail. "Bottom line, it's over," she said in conclusion.

Henry leaned in and leveled his dark gaze at her. "Come work for me."

"For you?" She wasn't expecting this.

"Business has been great," he said. "A few weeks ago I hired a couple of new gals to work in our inside sales department."

"You hired two new people, and you still have openings?" Sunny asked.

"Well, no. I'd have to let one of the girls go."

Sunny took a sip of water, frowning into the glass as she responded. "I'd feel awful, causing someone else to lose their job like that."

Henry brushed her concern aside. "You'll be terrific. You've got a pleasant manner with people. Hell, after handling a bunch of pampered spa customers, this'll be a cakewalk for you."

"That's nice of you to say, but—I don't know—me going to work for you? Maybe that's not such a good idea."

"Why not?" Henry looked bewildered. "Alice worked for me." Oh, right. Sunny also remembered Margaret telling her that, during their marriage, he'd lobbied long and hard for her to quit her editorial job and become marketing director at Schuyler Enterprises.

"I've always thought it was risky to mix business with personal relationships," Sunny said.

Apparently Henry had no issues with it. He shrugged. "It might solve a problem for us both."

"What's the problem on your side?"

"Oh, um . . . you know . . . if one of the new gals quits, or it doesn't work out." It sounded like he'd pulled this excuse out of a hat.

"I—I just don't feel comfortable with the idea," she said, looking down at her lap. "I'm sorry."

Henry reached out to her with one hand and patted his lap with the other. "Come here, Sunny One." He'd taken to calling her by that nickname. She wasn't crazy about it, though she supposed it was an improvement over *Babe*.

She settled on Henry's lap, and he encircled her in his arms. He gave her a probing look that made her feel they weren't done discussing this subject. She felt comforted yet constrained at the same time, like an infant whose swaddling was too tight. "Everything will be okay," he whispered, increasing his hold on her. "We'll get you back on your feet in no time."

Margaret's voice rang out in her head like a warning bell. "Henry tries to buy people, the same way he buys luxury cars and expensive wines," she'd said more than once. Was the job offer an attempt to take ownership?

She buried her face in his shoulder, trying to shake off a lingering sense of disquiet. But when he kissed her and reached under her blouse, she pulled away. "I—I'm too upset," she said, apologetic. "Sorry to be a Debbie Downer."

Henry winked. "I was hoping I could help you escape your troubles, but I get it."

As eager as she'd been for his company, now she was antsy to be alone. When she got up to leave, she apologized again. "Thanks for understanding, Henry."

"I'll talk to you soon." He gave her a light kiss on the lips and showed her to the front door.

On the way home, she turned the music back on to "I Saw Her Again." The guilty refrain revealed that the singer kept leading this woman on, dishonestly, because he was lonely and found it comforting to know she wouldn't leave him. Then Sunny realized why she'd felt unsettled on the drive over. If you swapped out the pronouns, the song reflected her own feelings about Henry. In fact, it described them to a tee.

CHAPTER 20

As Gwendolyn's departure date for New York approached, tensions in the house intensified – though she wasn't sure why. Clearly they all needed a break. She floated her idea for a getaway. "I'm thinking of going up to the Santa Ynez wine valley for a few days. When I get back, I'll shop and pack for my trip home."

Margy said, "Good idea, Mum." At least they agreed on something.

"Henry can give you recommendations," said Charlie. "He took Sunny there last week to pick up a wine club order."

Gwendolyn's face scrunched up as if she'd been assaulted by an unpleasant smell. "He took Sunny?"

"I'd be happy to speak to him."

She shook her head. "I'll call him myself."

"There's a great B&B where I've stayed several times. I know the manager. I'll make a reservation for you," Margaret said.

They all got to planning. First on Gwendolyn's list was the call to Henry. "Gwen-Gwen!" His cheerful voice boomed over the phone. After she explained why she'd called, he said, "I'll contact my favorite wineries and make appointments for you. I'm sure they'll waive the tasting charges for my guest." Gwendolyn grinned into her cellphone, pleased to have Henry back in her court.

Margaret reported to her on the inn reservation. "I went over everything with the manager. They've booked you into a nice room with its own patio."

"Margy, how lovely." Gwendolyn couldn't see the need for a private patio, since she'd rather mingle with the other guests, but there was no point arguing over it. She'd learned to choose her battles.

Gwendolyn asked to borrow a carry-on roller bag for the short trip. Wheeling in the suitcase, Margy looked at the items laid out on the bed. "You're not taking those shoes, are you?" She picked up Gwendolyn's dress sandals, the ones with the tall ankle strap heels. "You'll break your neck."

You'll break your neck? You'd think the girl was scolding an errant child for reckless maneuvers on a skateboard. "Don't be a fusspot, Margy. I'll be fine."

"Mum, *please.* Those heels are so spiky. I don't want to stress over this the whole time you're away."

"You stress over everything. But all *right* . . . if it will stop the bellyaching." Later, after Margy left the room, she sneaked her sandals back into the bag.

•   •   •

Cruising up the 101 freeway toward Santa Barbara County, Gwendolyn smiled like a girl who'd been let out of school. Why hadn't she done this sooner?

The inn was a stately Victorian building, freshly painted, with a welcoming wraparound porch. But when the manager on duty showed Gwendolyn to her ground floor accommodation in the back, her lighthearted mood evaporated. A large oak tree blocked most of the light from the tastefully furnished but modest-sized room, and the shady patio had two uncomfortable-looking metal chairs flanking a tiny table. "Do you have anything else?" Gwendolyn asked.

"We only have one vacancy. It's a nice room if you don't mind being upstairs. There's no elevator here," the manager said.

They walked up the main staircase to a high-ceilinged, sunlit corner room with a four-poster bed. It looked twice the size of the other room. "This will be perfect."

"Glad you like it, Mrs. Meyer. Shall we bring breakfast to your room tomorrow?"

Gwendolyn waved her hand. "No, I'll come to the dining room. How about nine o'clock?"

"Very good. Is this your only luggage?"

"Yes."

"Enjoy your stay. We have a complimentary wine and cheese hour in the side garden, starting at five o'clock."

At happy hour, the server led Gwendolyn to a patio table in the middle of a Victorian-style formal garden. The uneven brick pavers were a bit of a challenge in the high strappy sandals – but her balance was excellent, thanks to all the Zumba. She smiled, thinking herself lucky her daughter hadn't inspected her luggage. Apparently, even General Margy let something fall through the cracks now and then.

Two women were seated at the adjacent table. They looked alike – sisters, no doubt. One had lovely silver hair styled much like Gwendolyn's, in a sleek cut that fell nearly to the shoulders. Her companion was a little heavier, with a rounder face and short, layered blond hair. Though they were attractive – at least, the slimmer one was – their long boxy skirts, cotton shells, and low-heeled pumps looked preppy and unflattering. But Gwendolyn envied them the comfort only a sensible pair of shoes could deliver. Her own feet already ached like the dickens after the walk down from her room.

The server brought her a small plate of brie and crackers, and a glass of salmon-colored rosé from one of the local wineries.

"Delightful," she said, and the women started chatting with her at once.

"I'm Rebecca, and this is my twin sister, Peg," said the blonde. "We're celebrating our seventieth birthday."

"Good for you. I'm Gwendolyn. Seventy isn't so terrible, I promise. I celebrated that milestone recently myself." Okay, maybe nine years wasn't so recent, but the birthday girls would be none the wiser.

"My, you don't look seventy," Peg said. Gwendolyn beamed.

She returned the compliment – falsely, because in fact she thought they *did* look their age and more. "Is that Peg as in Margaret? That's my daughter's name."

The woman nodded. "How old is your daughter?"

Gwendolyn had to stop herself from blurting fifty-two. That would've made her a mother at eighteen. Unacceptable. She didn't want the twins thinking she was trailer trash. "I'm under strict orders not to broadcast her age," she said, winking. They chatted until the end of happy hour, when Rebecca invited her to dinner at a restaurant two blocks away. "That's awfully sweet, but I couldn't intrude on your celebration," said Gwendolyn.

"You wouldn't be intruding," said Peg. "Our actual birthday dinner is tomorrow. Please join us. It'll be fun."

She did, and it was. Peg was not only better-looking but also more amusing. Gwendolyn felt sorry for Rebecca, having to go through life in her sister's shadow. But as the evening progressed, she found Rebecca had greater depth. The less attractive twin had spent twenty years in Manhattan and been active in the arts. "I was involved with a performance space on West 42nd Street. We raised money to build four theaters there, one of them for student performances. It's still going strong."

"Were you a volunteer?" asked Gwendolyn.

"I was their development director," Rebecca said. "I have a professional background in fundraising."

"My goodness." Gwendolyn was impressed. "I did similar work for a small museum downtown, but strictly as an amateur."

After retiring, Rebecca said, she helped organize the student performance programs as a volunteer. "The kids were my passion. I miss that project. I miss the city." She looked wistful.

Gwendolyn sighed. "So do I." Talking to Rebecca about New York somehow brought Gwendolyn back to herself – the self that had been slipping away during the boozy gatherings with the lowbrow Zumba contingent. She was thrilled to feel the old familiar Gwendolyn re-emerging, thrilled at the reminder of her imminent return to Manhattan. Yet she chastised herself for pre-judging Rebecca as the inferior twin simply because her sister was a tad prettier and wittier.

•   •   •

The two tastings on the following day, arranged by dear Henry, were spectacular. The first was at a large-production winery on a lovely farm. The wine-tasting tables sat under sprawling shade trees on an expansive lawn next to a lavender field. Gwendolyn stopped at the gift shop on the way out to purchase lavender body lotion for Margy and a ceramic bottle stopper emblazoned with the winery logo for Charlie. As the salesgirl was ringing up her order, she spotted a basket of lavender sachets and picked up two as birthday favors for the twins, inhaling their soothing aroma.

The second winery, about half an hour west, was in an unlikely location at the rear of an industrial park. The tasting room was a bright, high-ceilinged space with a wall that displayed paintings by local artists. Gwendolyn sat at a communal tasting table where she enjoyed a pleasant conversation with a charming young couple from San Francisco. The wines were magnificent. She bought two bottles for Margy and Charlie, and a third special wine for Henry, a private selection Syrah.

Later she went to wine and cheese hour at the bed-and-breakfast, wearing her dressy sandals, light gray slacks, and a long silky blouse with a dolphin motif that resembled a watercolor painting. The dolphin made her think of Benny, and she realized with a twinge of guilt that she hadn't thought to buy him a present. She'd find something tomorrow.

Rebecca and Peg waved and signaled for her to join them. "We've ordered a bottle of French champagne to celebrate," Peg said, smiling. "Please share it with us. Look, there's already a glass for you."

"You're much too kind," Gwendolyn said as the server stopped by to fill her champagne flute. They raised their glasses. "To the next seventy years," she said, taking an appreciative sip before giving her new friends the sachets.

The twins had to leave twenty minutes later. "I just got a text, our driver is out front," said Peg.

"We're going to a Spanish restaurant up the road for a tapas dinner. Eight courses. No breakfast for me tomorrow." Rebecca patted her substantial tummy and laughed.

Gwendolyn finished the rest of the champagne, followed by a glass of sauvignon blanc. She'd skipped lunch and hadn't cared for the hard cheeses on offer tonight, so when she stood, it wasn't surprising she felt a little unsteady. She waited to regain her equilibrium, then threaded her way out of the garden. But as she entered the inn through the French doors, she stumbled on the raised threshold, twisting her right foot. "Damn! Stupid bloody floor," Gwendolyn cried out. She was sprawled out, lying on one hip, when the manager rushed over with an alarmed, oh-shit look in her eyes.

"Are you all right?" The manager squatted by her side.

Gwendolyn stifled the impulse to fire back a sarcastic response. Reaching one hand to her ankle, she winced and then stayed still, trying to catch her breath. "Just help me back to my room."

The manager helped her stand with considerable difficulty, then summoned two of her burlier employees. "Do you think you can make it up the stairs together?" she asked. "I'll call for an ambulance if it feels like you've broken something."

"Of course I haven't broken anything," Gwendolyn said irritably. *Except my right shoe heel.* Through her pain she reflected, *I hope it's fixable. Those sandals cost a fortune.*

The two inn employees helped Gwendolyn remove the strappy sandals. The laborious trek upstairs was an exercise in humiliation. They half-carried, half-supported her to the second floor room and positioned her on the bed. The manager arrived at the room moments later with an ice pack. She propped pillows behind Gwendolyn's head and asked if there was anything else she needed.

"Can you bring me a sandwich or something?"

"Of course, Mrs. Meyer. I recommend the California club. And perhaps a small frisée salad with that?"

Gwendolyn nodded. "No mayonnaise. And a large glass of red wine."

"Absolutely. Dinner is on the house. We have three different local pinots by the glass, or if you prefer a more full-bodied —"

Gwendolyn gave an impatient wave. "I don't care." She shifted her position, grimacing as she tried to get comfortable.

"Are you sure you don't want the paramedics to have a look?"

"Yes, I'm sure. It isn't serious." Gwendolyn had nearly screamed when she tried to put weight on the foot. But she wasn't one to let a silly ankle ruin her holiday. With ice, rest, and Advil, it would be better tomorrow.

Sure enough, she felt somewhat improved the next morning. Henry had scheduled her first tasting for eleven-thirty. The winery was in a rustic setting, with picnic tables spaced along the edge of a small pond. It was a long walk from the parking lot, and Gwendolyn had to haul her throbbing foot onto the picnic bench, stuffing a folded sweater underneath to cushion the tender ankle. She sipped her flight of rosés, the specialty of the winery, and watched the ducks gliding across the pond as she pretended the injury was only a tiny inconvenience.

By the time she reached her car, Gwendolyn knew she needed to rest. She reluctantly canceled her second tasting and returned to the inn, spending the remainder of the afternoon icing the foot. Determined not to miss her final happy hour, she limped downstairs at five o'clock with the aid of a cane provided by the manager. It was mortifying to see the twins' concerned expressions as she hobbled across the brick pavers.

"Prop up your foot on this," said Rebecca, sliding over a low end table and covering it with a pillow from the back of her chair. She arranged Gwendolyn's leg on the pillow with gentle hands. The twins suggested driving to a nearby sushi place for dinner.

"Maybe the restaurant has a wheelchair they can lend us," said Peg.

As if. That decided it. She would dine in her room again.

•   •   •

The morning of her departure, pain shot up her leg as she pressed on the gas pedal to merge onto the freeway. She thought about the twins. Ironic that she'd felt sorry for Rebecca, and then she herself ended up as the object of pity. The ankle was worse, not better, and it would be impossible to hide her injury as she'd hoped. Still, Margy and Charlie didn't need to know everything.

"It was a freak accident." Gwendolyn described the alternate reality she'd invented on the excruciating drive home, a drive made forty minutes longer by a few wrong turns after exiting the freeway. "I was headed to my car after the tasting in that industrial park, and a man walking the other way lurched into me, knocking me off balance. He was a large man – Henry's size, I'd say, but a good fifty pounds heavier."

"That's terrible. Did he help you up?" asked Charlie.

"No, can you believe it?" Gwendolyn sounded indignant. "He kept right on as if nothing had happened. He must've been drunk."

Margy said, "What were you wearing?"

"My turquoise capris and the dolphin blouse."

"I meant what *shoes*."

"Oh." Gwendolyn gave her an innocent look. "My flat walking sandals."

Later that day, when Margy came up to deliver a glass of sparkling water and a fresh ice pack, she said, "Let me empty your suitcase while I'm here."

"No, don't!" Gwendolyn could imagine the accusations, the finger-pointing, the I-told-you-so's when Margy discovered the telltale broken sandal. "I—I already took my cosmetic bag out. There's nothing else I need in there. Just leave it. I know how busy you are with work."

Her daughter sighed and sat at the foot of the bed. "That's for sure. I wish I could spend more time with you, Mum. I'm sorry you're hurting. Poor you."

Hot tears stabbed Gwendolyn's eyes. She took a deep breath and willed them away. "Why *are* you so busy, still? I thought the editor on medical leave came back to work."

"Yes, he did. But my managing editor had the bad manners to get pregnant, and she's having health difficulties, so her doctor ordered her to rest. She was like my right arm. It's been one step forward, two steps back."

It was Gwendolyn's turn to cluck in sympathy. "Poor *you*."

The next day, when Margy saw how swollen and bruised the ankle looked, she insisted on making a doctor's appointment. They waited together in the lobby, and the receptionist brought

Gwendolyn a clipboard with a pile of forms to fill out. She grumbled as she completed the paperwork. "I don't know why they ask all these stupid questions. Is it relevant that I had a cyst on my right breast twenty years ago?"

Her daughter squeezed her hand. Gone was Bossy Margy – she'd been gentle and caring ever since Gwendolyn limped into the house. She didn't even argue when Gwendolyn said she wanted to see the doctor alone.

After the exam, she told her daughter, "They took an x-ray. The doctor said it's a moderate sprain. I'm supposed to stay off it, take Advil, and do that RICE thing for several days."

"Rest, ice, compress, elevate."

"Yes. He gave me a compression bandage and this walking boot. He wants to see me again in two weeks. Ankle sprains can take a long time, he told me. Four weeks. I—I can't fly back to New York until it's better."

Margy gave her a peck on the cheek. "We'll take good care of you. Charlie says you should stay as long as you need to."

Once again, that momentary stabbing of tears. She bit down on her upper lip and said, "I probably made it worse by walking on it too much after I fell. That's what the doctor thinks."

Margy looked surprised by this admission of careless judgment. "I'd better get back to work. And Petey and I have our rounds at the nursing home later."

Amazing, the way her daughter wore so many hats: editor, volunteer, dog owner, grandmother, fitness enthusiast. And now, caregiver. While her job used to be the sole focus, Margy had spread her wings, expanded her repertoire.

Is it too late to expand my repertoire? Gwendolyn wasn't optimistic. Her own world seemed to be contracting. "If it isn't too much trouble, can I have dinner in my room tonight?" Her tone was uncommonly meek. "I'd rather stay off my feet." There was another reason she didn't share. Henry was coming, and as much as she wanted to see him, she felt like a fifth wheel since he and Sunny had become a couple.

Nor could she bear to Zoom with Sam and watch him fuss over her pathetic foot. When they spoke by phone instead, he said, "Promise me you'll take it easy. If you don't, it will only get worse." Gwendolyn knew he was right. She'd follow his advice if that's what it took. But it seemed impossibly depressing to contemplate that she, the invincible Gwendolyn Meyer, should be reduced to this pitiful state.

CHAPTER 21

The librarian leaned across the counter to pass Sunny her library card and checked-out items. "Enjoy your books, Ms. Ericsson. These are due in fourteen days."

She'd been despondent after closing the spa. But when she had the idea to visit the library for art books, Sunny's outlook improved. She devoured everything she could get her hands on: volumes about art movements and individual artists, drawing and painting technique, fundamentals of website and graphic design. Between her art studies and her sketching, Sunny felt focused and productive again. She had a plan.

She ran into Margaret and Petey as she toted the latest stack of books to the guesthouse. "We're going for a short walk. Join us?" asked Margaret.

Petey's "short" walks took at least forty minutes. "Thanks, but I want to dive into the reading."

"You sure are dedicated. How do you get through all these?"

"A lot of times, I'm leafing through more than reading. And I'm previewing the textbooks to see which ones are best. I've already ordered two online."

"Before you go, look at this adorable picture of Benny that Heather texted me," Margaret gushed. "I'll forward it to you." As she did this, the dog issued an impatient woof. "All right,

Petey, we're going. Sunny, I meant to ask – did Charlie give you a copy of his story?"

"*Bernie and the Weather Wand*. Yes, he did. I'm planning to look at that today as well." Sunny couldn't wait to read it. She hoped her impatience wasn't showing.

"It's a sweet story," said Margaret. "I hope it helps Benny. In any case, I think he'll be thrilled to have a book written specially about him."

•   •   •

Sunny immersed herself in Charlie's book. Then she re-read it, twice. Though she was no expert on children's literature, she could visualize the story through her artist's eye, jotting notes on the manuscript as the images flooded her brain.

Inspired, Sunny pulled out her phone and studied Benny's photo. The cowlick over his forehead was a defining feature, the other being a deep dimple in the center of his chin. She took out her sketchpad and started making drawings from the photo. The stack of library books sat on the table, untouched, as she spent the next few hours sketching the boy in various scenes. When she'd finished, Sunny shot Charlie a text.

Sunny
Read your story. Can I stop by your office to chat?

She felt a flutter of nerves after texting him, but she attributed it to insecurity over how he'd react to her comments.

•   •   •

Charlie looked through the notes Sunny had scrawled on the short manuscript. "I think the illustrations should be cartoonish, but not like what you'd find in action comics. The style needs to be softer, gentler," Sunny said. Charlie nodded. "And where you've got Bernie in the middle of a blizzard, and then fighting a fire – I'd change that," she said.

"Change it how?"

"Keep the disasters way in the background with Bernie upfront, distanced. You don't want those scenes to be too threatening."

Charlie tugged on his beard. "Maybe. I'll see what Margaret thinks."

"And on the page where Bernie first gets the wand, he should look strong and happy. He could even wear a cape, like a superhero." She continued to explain her scribblings.

"This is really useful, Sunny."

He's warming up to my ideas.

"It helps to get the perspective of a visual person," he said. "Margaret's been great with the dialogue. She has a good feel for the way kids talk. But she's a writer like me, not an artist. I'm going to tweak some of my copy based on your notes."

"Um, before I go, one other thing. I—I hope you don't mind, but I made some sketches of the Bernie character. Margaret sent me a new picture of Benny this morning, and it kinda gave me the idea. Maybe I—I should have asked you first?" *Stop apologizing, Sunny.*

As Charlie flipped through the sketchbook, she felt her heart rate quicken the way it did whenever she'd confronted a dissatisfied customer at the spa. "These are good. They're excellent, in fact," he said.

"This is the illustration style I was talking about. But I could make Bernie look more realistic if that's what you want."

"I like the way you've done it here. With the cowlick and the dimple, anyone who knows Benny would recognize him in this character," said Charlie. "Yet you've given Bernie his own look, his own personality."

"Do you really think so?" Sunny beamed.

"I do. Look. I think I mentioned this before, but when I talked to my agent about this project, she brushed off my question about the illustrations."

"I remember that." Sunny's cheeks reddened.

Charlie wrinkled his brow. "I'll be honest. If I ask Kathleen whether you can be a candidate for illustrator, I'm not sure how she'll react. I don't think the author has much say about the artwork."

"Okay, but – suppose I were only doing the drawings for Benny? And to repay you for all your kindness? And—and Margaret too, of course," she stammered.

"You don't need to repay us," said Charlie. "But a book with pictures will be a lot more meaningful for Benny than words alone." He paused as if reconsidering the options. "Hell, I have no idea if this will ever sell to a publisher. So our homegrown version might be the only one that ever comes to fruition."

Sunny glowed at Charlie's use of the words "*our* homegrown version." But she needed to make sure he was on the same wavelength. "Then I can work with you on the illustrations?"

Charlie raised both hands in a double thumbs-up. The collaboration was a go.

•   •   •

She was eating a late dinner with Henry at a French place in the harbor area, facing the window to gaze out on . . . a wall of fog.

"Great table, but not much of a view tonight," said Henry. "Though the view from where I'm sitting is pretty damn nice. That dress is great."

He'd bought Sunny a clothing gift and asked her to wear it on their date, even though the red silk cocktail dress was not appropriate for dinner. She had a feeling he was praising himself for the purchase more than admiring her, but she accepted the compliment.

Sunny looked out the window. "I love the fog." Even as a young girl, she'd liked the way it felt to shelter indoors, shrouded in an impenetrable gray mist. Her father wrote it off as another of her peculiarities. Far couldn't even stand her taste in weather. Pushing this thought aside, she took a bite of her fish and smiled at the distant blare of a foghorn. "The sole meunière is delicious."

"Good. So are the lamb chops." He wielded his steak knife and fork to carve out every morsel of the tender red meat.

Henry had insisted on ordering two pricey bottles of wine – a hearty cabernet for himself and a Sancerre for her. Even the sommelier had looked surprised. Sunny tried saying, "I'll be fine with whatever you're having," but Henry wouldn't hear of her pairing a full-bodied red with such a delicate fish.

First, they chatted about business at Schuyler Enterprises, which had settled into a more manageable rhythm since they'd added staff. "How about you? Having a busy week?" he asked.

"Yes, I've been doing a lot of studying and sketching," she said, keeping her answer vague. When she'd informed him of her work on the *Bernie* book, his response had been chilly. After she'd rebuffed his job offer, perhaps it displeased him to see her partnering on a project with Charlie. A project for Henry's own grandson, no less.

She took another sip of wine, enjoying the citrusy taste and the warm glow it created as she sat at the table, safely cocooned from the fog outside. Feeling a twinge of guilt toward Henry, she smiled at him, and he grinned back. His steady dark gaze and full smiling lips reflected calm self-assurance. She wondered if his wealth had given him that.

Sunny couldn't deny it. The idea of being cared for – the prospect of never, ever having to worry about money again – was seductive. She'd felt the same way when he took her to Santa Ynez and she saw how the winery people fawned over him. "I think I've reached a decision about my future." Sunny smoothed down the full red skirt of her dress with one palm.

Henry looked at her with interest. "That sounds . . . important."

"It is," she said with a nod. "I'm going back to school to get a degree in graphic and web design."

"Interesting. Online or in person?" he asked.

"Online."

"What made you decide this?"

"I love it, and I think I'm good at it. And there are job openings."

"Then you should do it," he said.

"I'm going to. I already have a list of places where I plan to apply." She set down her empty wine glass, and the vigilant server rushed to the table to refill it. "I'm sorting through the applications and loan documents."

"You're borrowing money?" Henry asked, touching the dinner napkin to his lips.

"Yeah, you know, mostly to cover school tuition and expenses."

"Mostly? What else?"

Sunny hesitated. "I—I need to finish paying off a few debts I ran up a couple of years ago when my mother was sick." She took a sip of her wine and tried to change the subject. "I'm glad you talked me out of red wine with the sole."

Her strategy didn't work. "How much money?" he asked.

"Oh, it's not important."

"Come on, Sunny One, how much do you need?"'

She took a healthier gulp of the wine. "A little over twenty thousand dollars. But I—"

"I'll give you the money." Henry waved his napkin in a flippant gesture, as if suggesting the sum was inconsequential.

Her mouth gaped open. "Gosh, I hope you didn't think I was telling you this so you'd—I couldn't accept that kind of money from you, Henry, I just couldn't."

"Sure you could."

She shook her head.

"That money would make life a whole lot easier for you – and it's nothing to me." He flashed a smile. You'd think he was trying to slip her a twenty-dollar bill, not twenty grand.

"I don't know. It doesn't feel right."

Henry closed his mouth, his lips forming a hard line. His dark eyes flashed with a momentary look of . . . annoyance? Resentment? "Tell me why you feel that way," he said, his gaze challenging her.

Sunny found herself tongue-tied. "I—it's hard to explain."

"First you won't accept a job – that offer still holds, by the way. Then you won't accept a gift." His voice had grown louder and carried an unmistakable rasp of irritation.

This dress was a gift. What next? She forced a smile, trying to placate him. "Henry, don't think I'm ungrateful. It's an extremely generous offer."

"Then take it." He furrowed his brow.

"I wish it were that simple, but—"

"It *is* that simple. You're the one who's making it complicated. Your money problem won't solve itself." He refilled his own wine glass and slammed the bottle down on the table, causing the server to hurry over as the couple at the next table shot them an uncomfortable glance.

Sunny looked down and twirled her thumbs. The coziness she'd felt moments ago was disintegrating as the cautionary refrain from the Mamas and the Papas song echoed in her head. This wasn't the first time she'd seesawed back and forth between conflicting emotions about Henry. "I know it won't solve itself," she said, her voice little more than a whisper.

"Then promise me you'll think about it."

Sunny squirmed a little in her seat. "Okay. I will."

"Good, good." He snapped back into his usual jovial demeanor. "I'm sure you'll come around to seeing it the way I do."

•   •   •

Back at Henry's, they went to the lower level to watch TV. After about an hour, Sunny said, "I'm dead tired. Do you mind if we go to bed?"

"You go ahead. I think I'll stay down here a while longer and catch some news and sports."

She rose and stretched her arms, relieved that Henry was not going upstairs with her. She supposed he was no more in the mood for sex than she was after their tense discussion at the restaurant. She tossed and turned for much of the night, falling into a fitful sleep a couple of hours before dawn. After awakening to use the bathroom, she crawled back into bed and Henry flung a sleepy arm across her. He snuggled up, spooning himself against her backside. Maybe he'd forgotten about last night. She willed herself to conjure up that cozy sense of safety and security.

But then he whispered into her ear, "How are we feeling this morning about — you know — what we discussed? A new day, a new perspective, I hope." Sunny's stomach did a little flip-flop. It dismayed her that Henry was already resuming his pressure campaign. He kissed her cheek. "Fair warning, I'm not giving up on this until you see the light."

Chafing at the false levity in his voice, Sunny realized she hadn't merely been agonizing over Henry's cash offer. She'd been agonizing over what to do about the relationship. And suddenly she knew. She stood up, hastily grabbing the dress she'd draped over the bedside chair last night. She hurried back into the bathroom and shut the door behind her. Standing in front of the sink, she could hear Henry's muffled voice calling out to her.

"Sunny?"

"I—I'll be out in a minute." Trying to compose herself, she turned on the tap with trembling fingers and splashed her face with cool water. Her hands a little steadier, she put on the dress and returned to the bedroom. Henry had slipped on a bathrobe and perched himself at the edge of the bed, his arms close to his sides, back rigid and shoulders hunched. She scooped up her purse from the chair and slung the strap over her shoulder.

"You're leaving?" he said. "What the hell?"

"Henry, I—I can't do it. I just can't." She felt ridiculous, breaking up in a red cocktail dress at seven-thirty in the morning.

"Is this about the money? I don't get why you're being so stubborn."

"You're a very generous man. But if I take the twenty thousand, I wonder if there'd be a *quid pro quo*. And if so, what would you want in exchange?"

He gave an innocent shrug. "I don't know why you think I have some evil motive here. Why not say yes since the amount means so little to me?"

"To me, it's a fortune, and I couldn't accept such a large gift without feeling like I was compromising myself, or—or worse."

"Aren't you being a little melodramatic?"

Sunny shook her head. "I can't take the money. And I can't see you anymore."

He squeezed his eyes shut. "I was afraid of this. She's poisoned the well, hasn't she? I knew it."

"Who? What well?"

"Margaret. This is exactly how she reacted to my largesse while we were married. When I offered her a terrific job opportunity at Schuyler or a beautiful BMW to replace that old clunker she was so attached to - she behaved like I'd fucking *insulted* her." Henry scowled. "It's plain as day, she's been influencing you."

"That's not how it is. Really. We hardly even talk about you." Apparently, Henry didn't care for this response either because he scowled even harder. Then, to Sunny's immense discomfort, he choked on a sob and his shoulders sagged. "I'm sorry – I didn't think you'd be this upset." Remorseful over hurting him, she leaned in to stroke his arm.

Henry watched her as if trying to interpret the gesture, then buried his face in both hands. "Oh, God. Alice . . . Alice . . ." For a moment she thought he was calling *her* Alice.

"What about Alice?"

"Whenever I did something nice for her, she'd tell me how much she loved me. How wonderful I was," he said. "She was the only woman who appreciated me."

Was this a genuine expression of grief? Or was Henry the one acting melodramatic? Sunny wondered if she was being played. "It was a terrible loss for you. Again, I'm sorry. But I can never be Alice."

"You sure as hell can't," he said, hands still covering his face.

The revelation that he was mourning a different woman smarted a little. At least it would make it easier to take her leave. The skirt of her red dress flouncing, Sunny fled down the stairs and out of the house, forever closing the door on any chance of a comfortable life with Henry Schuyler.

CHAPTER 22

Charlie delivered a bottle of mineral water to Gwendolyn's room while she nursed her ankle. He found her seated in the corner chair and staring out the window, her leg propped on a footstool. "Thank you," she said, barely glancing at him.

It unnerved him to see her so subdued. "I know you're a reader, Gwendolyn, and I've got quite a library in my office. If you tell me what you like, I'll bring up a basketful of books."

She flashed a grateful smile but didn't answer right away, as if pondering his offer. "I'd like to read your newest book, *Second Chance*. But first, I think I should re-read *Bicoastal*. It's been years, and I want to refresh my memory before jumping into the sequel." Flattered by her request, Charlie went straight to the garage and rummaged through boxes in the storage area to retrieve author copies of the two novels. He inscribed the first one:

To Gwendolyn. You've become a bicoastal resident yourself since joining our household. Happy reading.
Charlie

On the title page of the sequel, he wrote:

To Gwendolyn. May all of us have second chances in life.

When he presented her with the books that evening, Gwendolyn read the inscriptions and said, "How lovely." She smiled with a warmth Charlie had seldom seen in her. Long ago, he'd published a story about a crusty old man who was softened by illness. Was the ankle injury having the same effect on Margaret's mother?

By the end of the following week, since Gwendolyn could now manage the stairs, Charlie suggested they meet in the living room for a book discussion. Though it was a warm, sunny day, she drank hot tea like a true Brit. "What are your thoughts about the new book?" he asked.

"Oh, uh, lovely, dear. Excellent sequel," she said vaguely, without elaborating. She dodged another question and focused instead on what it was like to be an author. "It must be marvelous to enjoy such success – to have thousands of adoring fans. What a special gift," she said.

"Sometimes it feels like more of a curse." Lately, he was under the constant spell of this curse, unable to break free. "Success is great while it lasts. But when you fall short, when you don't clear the bar, the whole world knows it," said Charlie.

"Ah. So it's the public humiliation that you fear?"

"In part." He couldn't bring himself to speak about the other part – the *private* humiliation he'd experienced during these barren weeks. And not just humiliation – deep-seated dread about what the future held in store. Gwendolyn didn't question him further, so he veered to a different topic. "Sunny mentioned she's going to the library tomorrow. If you'd like to check out some books online, she'll pick them up for you."

She wrinkled her nose at the mention of Sunny. "Tell her thanks, but no thanks. I think I'll catch up on magazines for now." Charlie didn't respond, but he had the strangest feeling Gwendolyn hadn't finished the books he gave her. If she'd even read them at all.

•　　•　　•

A few days later, he examined Sunny's latest drawings on the worktable in his office. He noticed that, ever since the breakup with Henry, she'd become so laser-focused on the Bernie project she spoke of little else. "I revised the picture for the second spread," she said. "What do you think?"

"Looks good. And this one is the artwork Margaret suggested?"

Sunny nodded. Margaret had purchased a light-up plastic wand that she'd found online. "Draw the wand to look like this, and we'll present Benny with the toy wand the same time we introduce him to the book. That way, the real-life Benny will have the same wand as the fictional Bernie."

"That'll help him engage with the story even more," Charlie had said. He turned away from the computer to watch Gwendolyn hobbling past them outside, her black walking boot strapped over her right foot. Her ankle on the mend, she took short daily strolls around the yard.

"Hi, Gwendolyn. Looks like you're walking a little better every day," said Sunny through the open French door.

Gwendolyn stopped in her tracks, made a face at Sunny, and said, "At it again, are you?" Then she mumbled something that sounded like *humph* and stumbled away. So much for Gwendolyn softening.

Sunny heaved a sigh. "That woman does not like me."

"Gwendolyn isn't herself these days," he said, trying to make Sunny feel better. "She's super-quiet or she's super-cranky."

Sunny shook her head. "I think she has it in for me."

"I wouldn't spend too much time trying to analyze it." Though he thought Sunny was right, Charlie didn't want to make things worse. His cellphone buzzed. "Hi, Henry."

"That's my cue to leave," whispered Sunny, gathering up her sketchbook. He gave her a thumbs up as she departed.

"Charlie, my man. You available for a round of golf tomorrow?"

"I appreciate the offer, but not this week. I'm finishing up this book project for your grandson. In fact, I'll be reading it to him on Zoom at seven tomorrow night. Join us?"

After a pause, Henry said, "Thanks, but I'd better pass."

"Let's have a drink soon, at least," Charlie suggested.

"Sure – but not at your place, for obvious reasons."

"Right. How are you doing?"

Henry coughed into the phone. "You mean since Sunny gave me the old heave-ho?"

"If that's what you call it—yes."

"At first, I had high hopes for me and the Sunny One." Henry sighed. "But ever since the spa closed down . . . I dunno. Sometimes that gal likes to wallow in misery. There's no making her happy."

"I'm sorry it didn't work out." Charlie wished he could find something less trite to say.

"Yeah, well . . . I realize, I was never in love with Sunny. I guess I got involved with her to—to move on after Alice."

"I can understand that."

"Anyway, I'll be fine. There's this gal in the women's golf league, a divorcee, who's been acting friendly. Think I'll have lunch with her at the club this week, see if I can get something started."

"That's the spirit," Charlie replied.

When he reported this conversation to Margaret later, she said, "Sounds like Henry, all right. Any port in a storm."

•   •   •

The following evening, Charlie was ready for the family launch of *Bernie and the Weather Wand.* Or as ready as he could be. The conclusion of the story wasn't up to snuff. In the rewrite, Bernie was the one who recaptured the wand, following the agent's suggestion to make him the hero. But Charlie knew the ending could be better, and it nagged at him.

He marveled at how much he wanted this project to succeed. It had started as a fun way to help Benny while stimulating his own creativity. But then the seasoned professional in him had taken over, giving the book as much importance as if he were penning the great American novel.

Sunny didn't make a full set of illustrations for the book, but she produced artwork for the cover, as well as four spreads that were interspersed through the pages – enough to provide a good visual sense of the story. She plugged everything into a layout template to give the project a polished look. Margaret had delivered the toy wand to Michael's house, where they hid it in the closet until the big reveal.

For the debut of the book, they agreed to meet on Zoom so everyone could preview the pages at the same time. Though Charlie had encouraged Sunny to join them, she declined, saying, "I think you should keep it in the family." Charlie led the session from his office, Margaret seated by his side. Gwendolyn logged in from the den on the iPad. He saw that Michael, Heather, and Benny had gathered in their kitchen.

Benny appeared fidgety at first, but as soon as Charlie shared the document and the cover popped up on screen, he grew still. "That boy looks like me." Charlie began to read aloud. "Is that me? Am I that boy?" asked Benny. Heather touched one finger to her son's lips in a gentle shushing motion.

"He's a boy very much like you," Charlie said. "Just listen and you'll find out more."

He continued to read. Now and then Benny exclaimed "wow" or "cool" but he no longer interrupted. By the end of the story, he was all smiles.

"Did you like the story?" asked Charlie.

"It was good," the boy said. "But at the end, after Bernie captures the wand, I think he should keep it and only work with other kids to help the planet."

"Why can't the adults help too?" asked Margaret.

"*Because*," said Benny, in a tone that implied the answer should be obvious to all, "the grownups were arguing all the time and not getting anything done. Kids will do a better job. Besides, kids are the ones who'll be around in the future."

As Charlie reached over to squeeze Margaret's hand, her lips curved into a broad smile – one that mirrored his own. "From the mouths of babes," she said.

To which Charlie replied, "I think I found my ending. I'll make that change first thing tomorrow."

Michael, who'd been silent, said, "Charlie, I hope you plan to give Benny a co-author credit. We can negotiate terms later." They all laughed.

Benny clapped when Heather presented him with a wand just like the one in the story. "There isn't really a wand to fix the weather, is there?" he asked.

"Not yet," said Michael. "But they're working on it."

"And when they build it, I can help?"

"Of course you can," said Heather.

After the meeting, Margaret turned to him and said, "I don't think that could've gone any better, do you?"

That couldn't have gone any better was the exact phrase Bet had used when they'd exited the Hollywood premiere of the film version of *Bicoastal*. Charlie thought back to the standing ovation and the streams of admirers that night, congratulating him and asking for autographs. Now his fan base had been reduced to a five-year-old boy and his girlfriend's immediate family.

But he shook off this thought when he saw Margaret's eyes sparkling with pleasure and, it seemed to him, pride. He pulled her in for a steamy kiss, the kind they hadn't shared in far too long. She responded with a low moan, winding her arms around his neck. Charlie's phone pinged, interrupting them. Pulling the cell from his pocket, he saw a text from Sunny.

Sunny
How did it go?

He felt bad that Sunny hadn't been there to witness Benny's reaction first-hand. She would've loved to see him exclaiming over her drawings. He gave Margaret a light kiss on the nose. And then he broke away from the embrace to respond to Sunny's text.

CHAPTER 23

Gwendolyn's bloody awful day started with the follow-up visit to the doctor. After the exam, she tromped out to the reception area with her mouth pulled into a frown. "What's wrong?" Margy asked as she helped her to the car.

"The doctor said I'm doing much better."

"But Mum, that's great news." Margy pulled out of the parking lot and began the short drive home.

"He refused to prescribe therapy for me."

"I'm still not understanding."

"I *so* wanted a physical therapist to come work with me. But the doctor said I don't need PT, and he gave me a list of boring exercises instead. If I do them every day I can probably drive in a week or two."

"I'll help you with the exercises," said Margy. Gwendolyn rolled her eyes to signal her lack of enthusiasm. A good therapist might have relieved her boredom, and maybe treated her to a nice back and shoulder rub. If only she could get a damned massage. She knew Margy would arrange it if she asked, but her daughter was already working day and night.

Back home, Gwendolyn announced she'd like to relax on a lounge chair by the pool. "Can I get you a pillow for your neck? Or a cold drink?" Margy spoke in soothing tones as she helped her into the chair.

Gwendolyn narrowed her eyes into slits. "Am I dying or something?"

"What?"

"It's just that – you and Charlie have been so indefatigably *nice*." It made Gwendolyn blush with shame to recall how she'd treated Edward after he lost his independence. She'd gone about her own social schedule, leaving all the hard work to the paid caregivers. "I thought the doctor told you I have some fatal affliction that showed up in my x-rays, and everyone's feeling sorry for me."

Margy chuckled. "I doubt a fatal affliction would turn up in an x-ray of your right foot."

Gwendolyn grimaced, as if her daughter had delivered a searing insult. "I'd adore an iced tea. With lemon if you don't mind." She tilted her head upward to catch the warmth of the summer sun. She knew this would age her skin, so she only allowed herself to bask for a minute before shielding her face beneath a wide-brimmed straw hat. Come to think of it, she could use a good rejuvenating facial even more than a massage.

Moments later, she saw Sunny walking to the guesthouse. Gwendolyn summoned her over. "I wonder if I could ask a small favor?"

"Sure."

"I thought I'd book myself a massage and facial. Would you mind driving me?"

Sunny fidgeted with the bottom of her shirt. "Where?"

"You know – that lovely place over in the Village. Salon DQ or whatever it's called."

Sunny gave her a stricken look. "I can't believe this," she said.

"Can't believe what?" asked Margy, who was crossing the patio with a frosty glass of tea.

"Nothing, dear. Nothing at all. *Forget it.*" Gwendolyn spat out these last words, directing a frigid glare at Sunny, who hurried off like a frightened rabbit. *I should have known better than to ask her.*

"What was that all about? Sunny looked like she was about to cry," said Margy.

Gwendolyn slammed a hand down on the arm of the lounge chair. "Sunny is perpetually about to cry. One wonders how her parents ever named her Sunny at all."

"What did she do to set you off like this?"

Gwendolyn slapped the armrest again. "I asked for a simple favor, and she became all unglued. I don't know what the big deal is. It's not like she has anything else to do."

"Lower your voice."

"Why? The guesthouse is all the way across the yard."

"I don't care. You're practically shouting, Mum." She pulled up a chair.

"The fact is, that girl isn't good enough for you. Not just *you.* Charlie too, and Henry of course."

"Why would you say such a thing?"

"Because she's forty-something and still taking charity from her friends. What kind of woman does that?"

"Sunny offered to pay rent on the guesthouse, but we agreed she'd share household expenses instead," said Margy. "And she stopped seeing Henry because she felt uncomfortable that he was pressing her to accept a large gift of money. She didn't want to be beholden to him. I don't see how that makes her a charity case."

Gwendolyn shrugged. "Maybe not – but you can't deny, her life's a wreck. She seems to lurch from one crisis to another. And when she does, it's 'poor little me,' always blaming her troubles on some misstep she made in a past life a hundred years ago. It's ridiculous." She kept her voice down but didn't hide her annoyance.

"I understand how you feel, but Sunny has been through a lot. Maybe when you're not so down in the dumps yourself, you'll be a little kinder toward her."

"She was a fool to break up with Henry."

Margy leaned in, still exhibiting a patience that Gwendolyn found exasperating. "You didn't like it when Sunny was seeing Henry, and now you're upset with her for breaking it off with him."

Gwendolyn waved an angry arm, as though her daughter were being the contrarian. "It's Sunny's fault that Henry won't come around anymore. He doesn't want to run into her, and who can blame him? I've had the worst cabin fever with this stupid ankle, and it would be such a solace to visit with dear Henry."

Margy took Gwendolyn's hand. "I know, Mum. I'm so sorry you've had to go through this. Damn that horrible drunk man."

She looked at her daughter, confused. "Henry?"

"No, the man who plowed into you and made you fall."

"What on earth are you talking about?" Then Gwendolyn vaguely remembered fabricating some story about her injury. She couldn't recall the details, however; and so rattled was she by this, she never voiced the real reason for her displeasure with Sunny. *If I were you, Margy, I'd watch out for that girl. She wants what you have.* But what was the point in saying it? Margy would only stick up for her friend.

Later in the bloody awful day, Margy had a dental appointment. On her way, she dropped Gwendolyn at the Zumba studio, stationing her in a comfortable chair so she could watch the class and visit with her old friends. But this too failed to improve her mood.

When Margy returned, she asked, "How was the class?"

"A crashing bore. I had no idea how ludicrous it looks for a bunch of old people to klutz around like that. When you're dancing yourself, you don't realize the absurdity of it. Zumba may be forever ruined for me."

"I doubt that. Wasn't it fun to see the old crowd again?"

"Not really. I was hoping there'd be a happy hour after class, but it seems all the social activities crashed and burned after I left."

"You always were the life of the party," Margy said.

But Gwendolyn remained disconsolate. "Take me home . . . please. I need to see Sam. I need to see him more than anything."

With his lively manner, dry wit, and twinkling eyes, Sam could usually be counted on to lift Gwendolyn's spirits. But on their Zoom call that evening, she soon learned that Sam was also having a bloody awful day.

"Hello, my dear." He looked at her across cyberspace and smiled, but he looked sad. "How has your day been?"

"Dreadful," said Gwendolyn, though she wasn't sure why. "I think the main problem is that I miss you."

"Same here. I've been thinking about our birthdays in August."

She blinked at him. "You have? That's ages from now." Was it?

"I know, it's not even July yet, but this'll be a milestone for us both. I don't want to celebrate our eightieth birthdays apart."

She raised her hands in prayer position. "Oh, Sammy . . . Sammy," she whispered. She had never spoken the diminutive form of his name, but suddenly one syllable didn't seem like enough. "You won't. I'm coming home."

"When?"

"This stupid ankle . . . I'm still not walking well," she said. "But as soon as I'm stable on two feet, I'll fly back. In time for our birthdays. I promise."

•   •   •

Cheered by this new plan, Gwendolyn smiled at her reflection in the mirror as she flossed her teeth that night. It would be marvelous to be back in New York, even in the heat of summer. She massaged her gums methodically with the string of minty floss. Upper right, upper left . . . but when she got to the lower left quadrant, she hesitated. *Did I do the top gums yet?* Better to start over and be sure.

In bed, she tried again to dive into *Second Chance*. She was embarrassed she hadn't read it for her tea with Charlie, though she'd covered her tracks well enough. Maybe new reading glasses would help. She'd had to cancel her annual eye exam when she extended her stay in California. Yes, she concluded, squinting at the pages until she snapped the book shut. It must be my eyes.

Then she sat up at attention, thinking of something else. She'd forgotten to floss.

•   •   •

Sunny completed two more illustrations for the *Weather Wand* book. She knew Charlie had already sent her artwork samples over to his agent along with the manuscript, "just to let her have a look," he'd said noncommittally; but she felt compelled to continue the work. She walked the drawings across to Charlie's office and showed him her latest efforts.

"These are good, but you understand I can't submit them, right? Kathleen has already forwarded everything to the publisher. It was nice of her to send them your work along with mine, since that's not the way it's normally done."

"I'm grateful for that. But I wanted to do these."

"Sunny, I've said it before, but this is a real long shot. Rejection is a way of life in the publishing business."

"Maybe for some people, but not for you."

Charlie shook his head. "Trust me, I don't have the Midas touch. *Second Chance* was flying high for a couple of months but then drifted down like a leaky balloon. And one of my earlier books, *Newlyn Nights,* was a commercial disaster."

Sunny could feel her hopes deflating like Charlie's figurative balloon. "But both those novels received national attention," she said. "Most writers would be thrilled to get that far. And illustrators too." She looked at Charlie with pleading eyes, as if it were up to him to publish her drawings.

Charlie sighed. "Those books were disappointments compared to my other work." He lifted a ballpoint pen and clicked the top in a repetitive motion. Why was he so fidgety all of a sudden? "But my latest novel won't even see the light of day. The publisher turned it down. She flat out rejected it, to use my agent's words." As he said this, he didn't look at Sunny but kept his gaze on the pen, as if it were an object of fascination.

"She did?" Sunny asked. She loved that he'd bared his thoughts and exposed his vulnerable side, but she took care to contain her joy. "Oh, Charlie, I had no idea. I'm sorry to hear that."

"Yes. Well." He dropped the pen on his desk. "The point is, it's a tough business. Don't get your hopes up."

"I won't," she said. "I promise you, I have zero expectations."

This was untrue, though Sunny couldn't admit it even to herself. Despite Charlie's heavy dose of reality, she still indulged in the giddy fantasy of becoming a *real* artist – a published illustrator sharing a by-line with renowned author Charles Kittredge. Maybe it wouldn't be a fantasy after all. "The Bernie drawings will be helpful when I apply to art schools," she said, to justify completing the illustrations.

"True, but think about diversifying your portfolio. You're good at still life, nature drawings, animals, even caricatures. Show them your breadth." She knew Charlie's advice was sound. The admissions people didn't need to see a dozen pictures of Bernie with his wand.

"You're right. Can I show you the portfolio when it's done, to see if there's a good balance?"

"Sure," he said with a reassuring grin. She liked the wrinkle lines that formed around his eyes when he smiled.

On her way to the guesthouse, an idea surfaced. She would follow Charlie's recommendations about the portfolio, but she'd finish illustrating *Bernie and the Weather Wand* as well. She was determined to wrap up what she'd begun. It wasn't merely the desire for completion. The truth was, Sunny didn't want to let go of her partnership with Charlie. Every time they'd experienced a breakthrough in the project – the successful tweaking of a difficult drawing or the crisp rewrite of a dialogue exchange – they celebrated together. She'd relished every moment, even when he spoke of the setbacks in his career.

But of course, they were no longer collaborating. Sunny missed their daily meetings, she missed being immersed in the project as a team. Continuing the work on her own was a poor substitute, but it made her feel closer to Charlie, nevertheless. It would have to do.

CHAPTER 24

Charlie yawned, stretched his long legs, and reached for the yellow pad on his bedside table. Where he'd been hopelessly blocked before, ideas poured from him during his first moments of wakefulness. Today he scribbled page after page of notes for nearly an hour. No doubt about it – the Bernie project had gotten his creative juices flowing again.

Reading through the notes, he recognized he still hadn't come up with *the* idea, the single spark that would ignite his imagination and propel him forward into his next great novel. But he wasn't discouraged. No, the ideas resembled little seedlings. If he tended to them, if he watered and fertilized them long enough, one of them would sprout into a flourishing tree. It was only a matter of time.

Meanwhile, Charlie sometimes worried how he'd respond if Margaret renewed her inquiries on his non-existent revisions. But she hadn't asked lately. He knew she must be distracted, given how busy things were with *Powder World* and the new magazine. When he finished his morning notes, he found her sipping coffee as she ended a business call, her tone measured and professional.

Margaret gave him a weary smile. "We're finalizing our promotional materials for next year. So I'm juggling extra planning meetings and production deadlines on top of the usual stuff. Can you take care of Petey's walks today?"

"Sure. Any improvements with the staffing situation?"

"I wish." Margaret sighed. "I have approval to hire a new editor, but searches are time-consuming, and I haven't had a spare moment to get the ball rolling. I need to make it a priority."

"Anything I can do to help?" asked Charlie.

"Yeah. Can you write me a feature on current trends in the pneumatic conveying equipment market?"

Charlie laughed. "No problem. I'll have it to you by lunchtime."

Margaret smiled and reached out for a hug. "You *are* helping me with Petey. And thank God, Mum is more independent again. That relieves some of the pressure."

Even with her hectic schedule, Margaret somehow found time to give Gwendolyn extra attention. The ankle sprain had triggered a subtle yet perceptible shift in the mother-daughter relationship. Margaret seemed more tolerant of Gwendolyn's mood swings, which were substantial. "Mum" was alternately spewing venom or withdrawing into a saddened, muted, almost watered-down version of her once feisty self. By the end of the day, though, Margaret's crushing schedule would catch up with her. She'd retire apologetically to the bedroom, exhausted, sometimes hours before Charlie was ready to turn in.

•   •   •

Though he felt encouraged to be noodling ideas for a book, Charlie knew Kathleen was waiting for pages. How much longer would her patience hold out? That night, he said to Margaret, "I'm thinking of going away for a couple of weeks by myself. On a writer's retreat." They were alone on the patio, Petey at their feet.

"Really? I thought you told me it was self-indulgent when writers went off on retreats to nurture their creativity."

He smiled. "You got me. I've often said in interviews that any author worth his salt should have the discipline to work from a home or office. But I need something to help my productivity."

"Where will you go?"

"To a cabin in northern California, or maybe along the Central Coast. Depends on what's available."

Margaret had been using a paper cocktail napkin as a coaster under her wine glass, but she started shredding it into little strips. "For how long?"

"A couple of weeks," Charlie said. "I think the isolation will be helpful. I need to get away from things for a while."

"Things? Or people?" Margaret examined the napkin shreds as if they contained important secret codes.

"Okay, people too." She looked up, stricken. "I can't help feeling like my space has been invaded, and it's difficult for me to concentrate," said Charlie. "But it's not you, Margaret. I swear it."

"Even so, it's *because* of me. Mum and Sunny and the others have only been around because I brought them into the household."

True. But Charlie didn't say this. "I won't go if it makes you unhappy."

Margaret looked at him, her expression inscrutable. "If it's important to your work, you should do it."

"You're sure about this."

"Yes. I'm sad – but also relieved."

His eyebrows shot up. "In what way?"

"I've been so busy, between the magazine and Mum . . . I feel like I've been giving you short shrift. Maybe this'll be good for us both." Though Charlie had worried about wounding Margaret's feelings, now he feared she was too sanguine about him leaving. But then she reached over and ran her palm down his beard from ear to chin in one long, smooth stroke. "I'll miss you."

"Not as much as I'll miss you," he said.

Did they speak these words to reassure one another? Or to reassure themselves? Compared to the passionate partners they'd once been, lately he and Margaret seemed more like a couple of roommates, distracted in turn, sexually out of sync.

When he tiptoed into the bedroom that night, Margaret was snoozing on her side, one arm slung over the pillow, a strand of hair across her cheek. Her unruly curls were always falling into her face like that. He didn't begrudge her the sleep, given her relentless schedule, but as he looked at her, he felt a bittersweet ache of desire.

Charlie leaned over to brush the hair back from her face. If she woke up, he'd take her in his arms and kiss her, then make love if she responded. With his late wife, this gentle awakening technique had served him well. Despite her fragility and her ailments, Bet could emerge from a sound sleep ready for sex. But when he touched his finger to Margaret's skin, tenderly pushing the stray lock off her cheek, she pawed the air with one arm as if shooing away a mosquito. And she kept on sleeping.

•   •   •

"What does a writer do when he *retreats*?" asked Gwendolyn.

Charlie had reportedly leased a wretched cabin somewhere in the mountains and planned to depart early tomorrow on a two-week leave. The goal was to be unplugged while he inhabited these primitive digs – no social interaction, no phone service, no internet. It sounded appalling, and she was trying to understand the point of it.

"With any luck, the writer writes," Charlie said.

"Can't he just as easily write at home?" She gave him a coy look.

"In theory, yes. But I need to pick up the pace. I'm hoping fourteen days of solitude will boost my creative output."

Gwendolyn was reviewing her notes for the Fourth of July party as Charlie pulled cold cuts out of the fridge to make a sandwich. "Darling, don't eat too much," she said. "There'll be enough food tonight to feed a small municipality." She'd organized a patio party for the group. It would be an Independence Day celebration, a send-off for Charlie, and—well, she had another surprise up her sleeve.

She'd ordered tonight's menu from the best Italian restaurant in the area, wines from a Manhattan Beach merchant, and wildflower arrangements from the local florist, all being delivered this afternoon. "Why so much fuss and fanfare?" Charlie asked. "It's only the four of us."

Gwendolyn adored fuss and fanfare, even for four. She was in her element talking to caterers and florists. When Edward lived, she always overdid their little family celebrations. It was one of the unspoken compromises that made their marriage work – she could indulge her party-planning appetite without subjecting Edward to the large gatherings he detested.

Anyway, it should've been five people for dinner instead of four, she thought grudgingly. Such a pity Henry had to be left out—*thank you, Sunny, for that.* Surely she could find some angle to lure him to the party. Yes, she'd phone him when Margy was out of earshot and convince him to come.

"Michael and Heather are bringing Benny over early for a swim," said Gwendolyn. "Michael insists they're not eating with us, but we'll see about that."

"Benny's afraid of fireworks. Michael wants to get him home and indoors early, before all the noise begins." Charlie slathered Dijon on two slices of bread.

"I *know* he'll change his mind once they get into the spirit of the day." She said this as if Michael were the sort to throw caution to the wind.

"I'll eat this in my office," said Charlie, plating his sandwich and grabbing a napkin. "I need to organize my laptop for the trip tomorrow. Unless I can help with anything for the party?"

"Oh, no thank you, darling. You're the guest of honor. I don't want you to lift a finger." She flashed him her most charming smile as he left the room.

Gwendolyn placed a call to the restaurant to request a couple of final tweaks to the order.

Smiling to herself, she imagined the perfect evening ahead: raising a glass to Charlie in a toast, explaining the various dishes on offer, sipping fine wines she'd paired with the Italian cuisine. As guest of honor, Charlie might be the star of the evening, but Gwendolyn would enjoy being the sun around whom everyone would orbit.

These pleasant musings were interrupted when Petey walked into the kitchen, toenails clicking on the Saltillo tile floor. He parked himself in front of her and cocked his head. Petey's sweet brown eyes focused on her with that imploring look every intelligent dog had mastered – the look that said, *I will die of starvation if you don't feed me this second.*

"I know what *you* want." She smiled and went to the pantry for Petey's liver treats. She was under strict orders not to feed him these – Margy said they were meant as an obedience tool. Gwendolyn slipped three of the forbidden morsels to Petey, who swished his tail and woofed in gratitude. "Don't tell Margy," she said, wagging an admonishing finger at the terrier. She kissed the top of his shaggy head. "This will be our secret."

She heard Margy's voice from behind. "You're big on secrets, aren't you?"

Gwendolyn turned toward her, giggling. "Oh, come now, you're not seriously upset that I gave Petey a wee snack." Then she glanced down and saw what her daughter was holding. It was her strappy dress sandal. The one with the broken heel, which dangled by a precarious thread as Margy thrust it toward her.

Dammit to hell. Busted . . . again.

"How on earth—" she said, unprepared for this confrontation.

"Charlie needed a suitcase for his trip, and I remembered my bag was still in your room."

Margy's tone was so icy, a shiver pulsed up Gwendolyn's spine. "I was emptying the bag when I found *this*," her daughter continued, waving the mangled shoe. "So, Mother, I have to ask. After you sprained your ankle, did you only lie to me about which shoes you were wearing? Or did you make up the entire sad story of how you hurt yourself?"

Gwendolyn stalled for time. "What story?"

"The one about the man who tripped and fell in the lobby of the inn and pulled you down with him."

Gwendolyn huffed. "I don't know why you'd question that."

"Really? I guess I'm questioning it because that wasn't the story you told me."

Gwendolyn blinked hard and said, "I can't believe you would trick me this way."

"*I* tricked *you*? Give me a break. Here I've been feeling sorry for you all these weeks, believing you were an innocent victim of some freak accident."

"You think I sprained my ankle on purpose?" Gwendolyn assumed a posture of outrage and hurt.

"Of course it was an accident – a preventable one. If only you hadn't worn those outrageous spiky heels. But no, you always want to look like the youngest, most fashionable woman in the room."

"Darling, can't we save this discussion for later? I've got so much to do before the party."

"If you're hoping I'll forget all about it, you're wrong. I don't know which is more infuriating – that you had the stupid accident or that you lied about it." Just then, Margy's phone buzzed. "I need to take this call. You win, we'll talk about it later. But we *will* talk." She left the kitchen.

Well, thank goodness for the interruption. Maybe Margy would cool down by the time they resumed their chat, hopefully long after the party. Gwendolyn didn't want anything to interfere with her well-orchestrated plans. But another shiver ran through her as she went over her lists one more time. Their argument did not bode well for the evening ahead. No, it didn't bode well at all.

CHAPTER 25

Late that afternoon, Sunny sat in Charlie's office, perched on a stool by the open French doors. Charlie was at his desk scrolling through the personal statement Sunny had written for her school applications. She jotted down notes as he gave her his critique.

Across the yard she could hear Benny's happy cries punctuated by splashing noises as he played in the swimming pool. Michael's deep voice carried across the yard. "Come on, Benny. Last call. Time to get out of the pool."

Charlie peered at the wall clock. Sunny followed his gaze. "Yikes, I didn't realize it had gotten so late," she said.

"Yes, we'd better wrap this up. I think we're finished, anyway. This is a good draft, and I like the way you've personalized your story. But try to keep it more positive."

She nodded. "Okay, I'll change those parts that sound too . . . self-pitying. Can I send the revision back to you for another quick look?"

"Afraid not. I'll be unplugged up at the cabin – no Wi-Fi or cell service."

"I keep forgetting," said Sunny.

"The owner of the cabin has a landline you all can use as an emergency number."

Charlie's cellphone buzzed. "Kathleen, hi. I'm in my office with Sunny Ericsson, the illustrator."

Sunny's heart rate quickened. Charlie's agent must have news for them. "Yes . . . uh-huh." Charlie turned away from Sunny to continue the conversation. "What else did they say?"

She tried to read Charlie's body language. Why had he turned his back and hunched his shoulders, as if he were trying to conceal the phone? She strained to hear Kathleen's voice but couldn't make out the words. She wondered why he didn't put the agent on speaker phone. Sunny clasped her hands together so hard it left nail marks in the skin. "Tell me," she said as soon as he ended the call.

"Scranton wants to publish the book, and they're going to fast-track it because the story is so timely," Charlie said. "But—"

She clapped her hands and bounced on tiptoes. "That's amazing! The way you were speaking in hushed tones, I thought for sure—"

"Sunny, listen. They're not using your illustrations. Kathleen said they have a stable of professional artists under contract. They've already assigned the book to someone."

Sunny came down off her toes. "Did Kathleen say if they—if they disliked the work?" She struggled to maintain composure.

"The work wasn't the issue. It's the way they do things."

"But if they'd *loved* my drawings, couldn't they make an exception and—"

"Don't do this to yourself. Your drawings are great. Trust me, this wasn't a personal failure. It was a couple of corporate publishing executives playing by the rules."

Sunny tried to will away the tears of disappointment pooling in her eyes. "I should never have gotten my hopes up," she whispered.

"I'm sorry."

"It's not your fault. You kept warning me it was a long shot, but I—I got so swept up in the dream, I didn't listen." The tears intensified into a flood. Charlie put a tentative arm around her and patted her on the back. She threw her arms around his neck and squeezed tightly. She felt Charlie's back stiffen in her embrace.

Sunny heard the click of a door. Charlie pulled back from her grasp. "What was that noise?" she asked.

"I left the door open a little, and the breeze must've caught it. Are you okay?"

"I guess so." She swiped one hand over her eyes to brush away the tears.

A moment later, a knock. "Charlie?" It was Gwendolyn. "Are you in there?"

"Yes." Charlie backed up further. "Come in."

She opened the door and poked her head in. "Why aren't you at the party? The food has arrived, the bar is open, and everybody's waiting for the star of the show."

"Didn't mean to keep you waiting," said Charlie. "We'll be right out."

"Very well," Gwendolyn said, casting a suspicious gaze in Sunny's direction. "I'll see you on the patio."

A few minutes and several tissues later, Sunny sucked in her breath to compose herself as she followed Charlie out the French doors into the warmth of the afternoon sun. Dejected as she was about the publisher's decision, she mustn't cast a pall over the festivities. But as they walked toward the patio, when she saw Gwendolyn eyeing her again with that contemptuous sneer, Sunny's spirits plummeted further.

•   •   •

Gwendolyn admired the patio table, determined to banish Sunny from her thoughts and focus on her own handiwork. The tasteful arrangement of wildflowers, which looked casual yet elegant at the same time, made a charming centerpiece. The white tablecloth supplied a crisp contrast to the heavy Mexican ceramic dishware, the special occasion ones from Charlie's pantry. Margy wanted to use paper and plastic, and serve good old American Fourth of July fare, but Gwendolyn had drawn a line in the sand. "Hot dogs and disposables have no place at a party of mine."

An open bottle of champagne nestled in an icy glass bucket on the small table Gwendolyn had earmarked as a bar. Michael and Heather raised half-empty flutes to Charlie. "I know it's bad manners to drink in advance of a toast, but we're leaving soon, and we wanted to savor a glass. This is much too nice to chug," said Michael.

"I assured them you wouldn't mind," Margy told Charlie.

"Of course," Charlie agreed.

"Margy, why don't you pour glasses for the rest of us, and you and your friend can distribute them." Gwendolyn gave Sunny a condescending look when she said *your friend*, then turned away from her to focus on Michael's family. "Please stay for dinner, darlings. What's the harm? I set places for the three of you, praying you might reconsider."

Michael shuffled his feet and fidgeted. "I—I told you we couldn't stay. Benny gets freaked out by the noise."

"Oh, honestly," said Gwendolyn with an exasperated sigh. She turned toward her great-grandson, who squatted at the edge of the pool, splashing one hand in the water. "Benny, I have a glass of cold lemonade for you," she called to him. His back to her, he continued to splash. "Benny—lemonade," she repeated.

"He doesn't hear you with those earplugs he uses for swimming. We're leaving them in until we get home."

Ignoring Michael, she walked over to Benny and crouched down, handing him the lemonade. "I'm so sad you have to go." She planted a kiss on his cowlick and pulled out the earplugs before enveloping him in a hug. "Tell Mommy and Daddy you want to stay for dinner and—"

At that moment, a deafening noise resembling a gunshot startled them all. Someone had set off firecrackers in a neighboring yard. Benny let out a scream and began sobbing.

"What are you doing?" Michael said to Gwendolyn. He hurried toward them, but Heather got there first. She snatched Benny out of his great-grandmother's arms as though rescuing him from an abductor.

Gwendolyn went rigid. "This is ridiculous. Benny's not an infant. He needs to learn to tolerate a little noise on the Fourth of July."

Margy intervened. "That's not your decision to make. You had no business taking out his earplugs."

"Mom's right." Michael looked like he was ready to explode, his face the color of raw beefsteak. "I can't believe you did that."

Heather held Benny closer, trying to comfort him as he squirmed and wailed in her arms.

"See the trouble you've caused?" Margy said to her mother. "You're incapable of respecting anyone's boundaries."

They were all determined to gang up on her. Gwendolyn shifted the path of the argument. "Well, if we'd started earlier, *as I'd wanted*, at least Michael and Heather and Benny could have had more time with us. As things stand, they're leaving when the party's scarcely begun, and it's very hurtful to me." With that comment, Gwendolyn once again trained the evil eye on Sunny.

"I'm afraid the late start is my doing," said Sunny. "I asked Charlie to review an application I'm working on, and we lost track of time. I—I'm so sorry if I held anything up."

"Sunny, this isn't your fault," said Margy. "*You* . . ." she pointed a finger at Gwendolyn, "have done nothing but cause problems. You're always making bad choices without considering anyone but yourself." Gwendolyn gave her daughter the pained expression of a woman wrongly accused.

Margy continued the tirade. "I'll bet Charlie and I don't know the half of what you've done. God knows how many things you've lied about to indulge your whims or your vanity. I'll wager that tale about how you sprained your ankle was only the tip of the iceberg. And stupid me, I knocked myself out to play nursemaid. I can't believe I felt so sorry for you."

While Margy unleashed her wrath, Gwendolyn watched Michael and Heather gather up Benny's pool toys. As the three of them trotted across the yard toward the street, eager to escape, Benny cried out in his excited little-boy voice, "Grandpop!"

Crossing the lawn in the opposite direction, wine bag in hand, was Henry – wearing a *what-did-I-walk-into* expression as he surveyed the unhappy group. "Darling, how marvelous to see you," said Gwendolyn, gloating that her call to him this morning had worked. A pity he had to choose the worst possible moment to arrive.

"Dad?" said Michael, perplexed.

"Henry? What are you doing here?" asked Margy.

Gwendolyn saw Sunny and Henry lock eyes for one uber-awkward moment. She wasn't sure whose face went redder.

"I thought you wouldn't be here," Henry said to Sunny.

"Right now, I wish I weren't," Sunny replied.

That makes two of us, Gwendolyn wanted to say.

"What's going on?" asked Margy.

"Well, I—it didn't seem right for dear Henry not to be part of this. I thought we could all put our differences aside to celebrate." Gwendolyn flashed the group a strained smile.

"You invited Henry and told him Sunny had other plans, to manipulate him into coming?" Margy said.

"I—I wasn't sure about Sunny's plans," said Gwendolyn. Suddenly, that seemed true.

"You just wanted everybody here for *your* party," said Margy.

Michael cleared his throat. "We'd better go. I'll talk to you soon, Mom."

Gwendolyn gave her grandson a regretful smile, but he wouldn't even look in her direction. Instead, he turned to Henry. "Dad, why don't you follow us back to our place? We've got wine and beer and hot dogs."

Honestly. After all she'd done to get Henry there. "Look what's happened—you've driven everyone away, Margy," Gwendolyn fumed. "I've planned this party for days, and it's been a dismal flop, right from our late start."

"I'm sorry again about—about that," said Sunny.

"Sunny, darling." Gwendolyn spoke with mock sweetness. "I can't imagine why you're feeling sorry over our little family gathering, considering all the other trouble you've caused."

"Trouble?" Sunny's question came out as a mouselike squeak.

"You seem to make a sport of chasing after everyone else's men." Gwendolyn glowered at her. "First you had a go at Henry, but you tired of him in a few weeks. She gave Henry an apologetic shrug. "Sorry, darling."

"Your sympathy is misplaced, Gwen-Gwen." Henry's tone was easygoing, but his body language was not. "I'm already dating someone."

"Bravo, good for you." She pivoted back to Sunny. "Ever since finishing with Henry, you've been monopolizing Charlie instead. Why don't you fly to New York and make a run for my Sam? Then you'll have covered all the bases."

Predictably, Margy came forward in Sunny's defense. "Don't talk to Sunny that way."

"I'm only trying to protect you, Margy," Gwendolyn said, unperturbed.

"From what?"

"From what I witnessed with my own eyes. Before the party, when they were in Charlie's office, she was throwing herself at him. The door was open and I could see into the room," Gwendolyn explained.

Sunny dropped her head, staring down at the patio pavers. A guilty response if ever Gwendolyn had seen one. "It's not the way it looked," said Sunny.

"It never is, darling." Gwendolyn gave her a bitchy smile.

"Charlie was comforting me."

He nodded in affirmation. "That's true."

"Comforting you? Why?" asked Margy.

"My agent called. They're not using Sunny's illustrations," Charlie said.

"Yes. I started crying when I heard the news, and he felt sorry for me," Sunny babbled. "Charlie has been very understanding of my feelings, since he knows what it's like to experience professional rejection."

Margy went to Charlie and touched his arm. "Oh, no. They turned down *Bernie and the Weather Wand*? I'm so sorry. But I'm sure Kathleen can—"

Charlie stopped her. "No, they've accepted the book. Scranton has made me a nice offer, in fact. But they've assigned one of their contract artists instead of using Sunny's drawings."

So, their unholy collaboration was coming to an end. Gwendolyn hid her smirk.

"I wasn't talking about them rejecting the *Bernie* book—I meant Charlie's new novel," said Sunny. Was Gwendolyn misinterpreting, or did Charlie throw Sunny a desperate glance?

Margy disengaged her hand from Charlie's arm. "What are you talking about? Charlie, I thought the editor gave you revision notes."

"That's what I thought too," said Gwendolyn.

Charlie shook his head, slowly, and blinked hard. "Actually, my novel was rejected awhile back." Margy's face contorted with pain, as if she'd suffered a physical blow.

Sunny clapped one hand over her mouth. "Oh shit." She gave Charlie a remorseful look. It was clear to Gwendolyn they were in on some secret, and Sunny had spilled the beans.

Margy spoke through gritted teeth, as if trying to contain an explosion. "What. The. Fuck. Where am I living, the House of Lies?"

"Oh, Margaret." Charlie's voice sounded heavy with regret. He reached out to her, but she recoiled.

"Yes, House of Lies sums it up." Then she turned toward Gwendolyn, opening her mouth as if to admonish her again—but instead, Margy shrugged and walked briskly toward the house.

Henry deposited his gift bag on the bar table and joined Michael and his family. "Well, crap. This is awkward, huh?" He waved to Charlie. "Sorry, buddy. I hope things go well up at the cabin. You'll understand if I don't hang around for this super-fun holiday bash. I'm out of here."

"There's no need for you to run off, Henry," said Sunny. "*I'm going.*" Gwendolyn watched her bolt for the guesthouse, slamming the door behind her.

CHAPTER 26

As Charlie expected, Henry did not stay, accepting Michael's invitation instead. Charlie carried two plates of food indoors and handed one to Margaret, who accepted it silently. Gwendolyn came into the house toting her own plate – half a marsala chicken breast and a parsimonious spoonful of julienne vegetables. The three of them took their dinners to separate rooms, like cruise ship passengers confined to their cabins during rough seas.

After eating, Charlie carried the foil catering pans in from the patio and stashed the leftovers in the fridge. An eerie silence hung over the house. He went upstairs and found Margaret in the bedroom, sitting cross-legged on the bed, looking at her laptop. Petey had stationed himself on the floor close by, as if to guard her.

"Can we talk about this?" Charlie asked, his voice subdued.

Margaret glanced up from her laptop and shook her head. "Not ready." Her eyes looked red and puffy.

He stood near the door, not daring to sit on the bed beside her. "Why don't I postpone my trip to the cabin? I'll stay home tomorrow. We can talk all day if that's what it takes."

Margaret sighed as she closed the cover of her laptop. "That's the last thing I feel like doing. You should go ahead with your plan."

He tried to read her expression to figure out if this was what she wanted. "Are you sure?"

"Yes." She gave a weary nod. In this same situation, Bet would be screaming at him, wailing, oozing emotion. He and Margaret didn't often have disagreements, but when they did, her inscrutability was like uncharted waters to him. Her measured self-control seemed more ominous, harder to navigate than Bet's tantrums had been.

"Okay. I'm going downstairs for a while," Charlie said, picking up the dinner plate Margaret had left on the bedside table, most of the food untouched. "I have a few more items from the office to pack."

Returning upstairs later, he expected to find Margaret asleep as usual at this hour. But she was lying in bed, her back propped up against a stack of fluffy pillows, reading on her Kindle.

"You have the emergency phone number, right?" he asked as he stuffed socks into the roller bag.

"Yes, I saved it in my phone and my computer. And I taped a copy on the fridge."

"Great." He felt encouraged by this detailed response, as if Margaret had cracked the door open enough for him to stick in one foot. He pulled out an armchair from the corner of the room, plunked himself down, and spoke.

"This whole thing with the writer's block . . . it wasn't because of you. It was the living situation here in the house. But keeping the truth from you was a mistake. It's been hanging over my head, causing a rift between us. I've known that all along. And today, I shamed myself and humiliated you in front of the people you most care about. I'm sorrier than I can say."

Finally, Margaret unleashed her fury with the power of a dam bursting under pressure. "How *could* you?" She grabbed a throw pillow and hurled it across the room. Though she didn't aim it at him, this was—for Margaret—a dramatic gesture.

Charlie retrieved the pillow from the floor and smoothed it across his lap. He had to make sure the only thing she suspected him of was the deceit concerning the book. "I swear, I've never been unfaithful to you. You believe me, don't you?"

"I'd like to believe you, but I don't know, Charlie. This was still a betrayal." Margaret closed her eyes. "How long has Sunny known about your book rejection?"

"Not long. A week, maybe ten days."

"And how long have *you* known?"

Charlie wished he could shrink to the size of an ant and scurry from the room. "About four months."

"Four *months?* You kept it from me all this time, but you confided in Sunny – why?" The hurt in her eyes made him wince.

"I knew her drawings would likely be rejected, and I was trying to prepare her by sharing the story of my own rejection. I thought it might cushion the blow. She's a lost soul, and a kind soul as well." There was something else he didn't say. Sunny gave him something that Margaret couldn't – her undivided attention. She was always available and eager to work with him, bolstering his ego as they collaborated.

Margaret surveyed the bed as if looking for something else to throw. "So, this was like the emotional equivalent of . . . a pity fuck?" She spat out the words.

Charlie flinched. "I wish you wouldn't think of it that way."

"How am I supposed to think of it?" asked Margaret, her voice trembling. "You still haven't explained why you felt the need to lie to me."

How could he convince her he'd never intentionally hurt her? "I didn't mean to lie. The day Kathleen called to say the book had been rejected, I was going to tell you then and there. But you and your mother were so excited, so sure the news was good . . . it caught me off-guard. I was too embarrassed to say anything. And from there, the lie snowballed and spun out of control. The longer I postponed telling you the truth, the more impossible it became."

"Were you honestly afraid I'd think less of you because your book was turned down?" Margaret asked, her expression still pained. "Do you think I expect you to be perfect – or that I would even want that?"

"Sometimes I think *you're* just about perfect at your job. You never seem to falter."

"Hah." Margaret gave a humorless laugh. "Things aren't always what they seem. Since I moved in with you, work has been more challenging than any time in my career. It's overwhelming. Some days I question everything I do."

This was unexpected. "Really? Why haven't we talked about this?"

She sighed. "I felt like, if I verbalized it, that would make it real. It seemed better just to tough it out." Then she told him something else. "Around the time when we first met, I quit my job at *Powder World* on impulse after an argument with Robert."

Charlie was astonished. "I can't believe you two had a falling-out. Robert thinks you walk on water. What happened?"

"Let's just say it was a foolish, foolish move on my part," she said. "But I got lucky. Robert offered me my job back a few weeks later. If he hadn't, I can't imagine where I would be today. My career might've been tanked by an impetuous mistake."

Charlie scratched his beard. "Wait a minute – I remember something that happened around the time we were first hanging out together at Seaside Fitness. Do I have the timing right?" Margaret nodded. Charlie described his recollection. "You got a phone call, and after the call, you looked elated. You said you'd solved a problem."

"Yes, that was the day I got my job back."

"Why didn't you tell me the real story?"

Margaret was quiet for so long, Charlie thought she wouldn't answer. But she said, "Like you, I — I was afraid you'd think less of me."

•   •   •

When he slipped into bed an hour later, Margaret switched off her reading light and rolled over to face away from him, as if raising an invisible barrier between them. Not necessary, since the six-foot-wide king bed already created a chasm of space. "Did you pack a warm jacket?" she asked, unexpectedly.

"I did, thanks." He tried to take heart in her concern. "Margaret. You always seem so self-assured, I didn't realize you've struggled as well." His tone was soft, regretful. "While I've been stalled in neutral with my writing, I kept comparing you to a high-speed train hurtling down the track. I felt like I couldn't keep up with that train."

It was too dark to make out her expression, but she sighed and responded in a voice pierced with sadness. "But Charlie . . . this was never a contest. It was never a race."

In the middle of the night, he woke to the sound of muffled weeping. He slid across the bed to Margaret, wrapping one arm around her. "Don't cry, my love. Please don't cry," he whispered in her ear, wanting to cry himself. "Before your mother came, we had such a beautiful year together. Can we try to get back to that? I want it more than anything."

"Me too. But it's not that simple."

She didn't resist when he snuggled up to her and planted gentle kisses along her neck and her wet cheek. But when his touch became more sexual, he felt her tense up. "No, Charlie. I'm still . . . "

"Shhh. I understand." He moved his hand back to safer territory. They lay in silence for a few minutes, until her breathing finally lost its ragged edge. "I'm not going to the cabin," he said. "I can't leave you like this."

"No, don't cancel," said Margaret. "You need this retreat to get on track with your writing."

He kissed her hair just above the ear. "Why don't you come with me? Get away from this craziness."

"You know that's impossible. Anyway, I need time to process things. Time to figure out if I still trust you. Two weeks apart will be good for us."

It was clear Margaret wouldn't budge on this. "You know how to get a message to me," he said. "If you want me home, I'll come back in a heartbeat."

Before sunrise, Margaret appeared to be stirring as Charlie got ready to leave. That lock of curly hair had strayed across her face again. He leaned in to brush it aside with one fingertip and kiss the side of her mouth. But before he could do this, she turned onto her stomach and burrowed her face in the pillow, muttering something unintelligible.

Sighing, he tiptoed from the room.

•   •   •

Sunny had no plan for where she might go. She only knew she couldn't spend one more day in Charlie's guesthouse.

Last night after fleeing the party, she'd thrown herself miserably on the bed, sobbing. She wished she could undo everything that had happened. She wished she could undo her whole life. No matter what she did, she made the wrong choices. Hugging Charlie had been the least of it. She'd ruined the party and upset every person on the patio – most of all Margaret, who'd been her best friend ever.

During the restless night that followed, Sunny had reached the inescapable conclusion – it was time to leave. She'd endured more than her fill of Gwendolyn's antagonistic taunts, and she knew it wasn't good for her own emotional health to be in close daily contact with a man she wanted but could never have.

Why had Charlie shared his innermost feelings about the book rejection with *her* but not with Margaret? Perhaps . . . Hope flamed up in her chest at the thought that maybe Charlie reciprocated her feelings after all, that he nursed a hidden attraction he'd been keeping under wraps. For a moment, Sunny allowed herself to imagine Charlie's arms holding her in an embrace born of passion rather than compassion, a coming together rooted in desire rather than friendly affection. But no, she mustn't tumble down that slippery slope. Even if Charlie *were* interested, how could she betray Margaret?

The morning sky was overcast when Sunny threw her belongings into the back of the Corolla, praying she wouldn't run into anyone from the household. Though she'd enjoyed some happy times here, and the guesthouse had been a generous gift from her friends, it had become a prison from which she couldn't escape fast enough.

CHAPTER 27

By nine o'clock that morning, Gwendolyn wondered why there'd been no sign of Margy. Usually her daughter was in the kitchen long before this hour, drinking coffee, fingers flying on the laptop keys as she caught up with her morning correspondence. She must've been here at some point. The green light was illuminated on the coffee maker, the glass pot half empty but still warm.

No sign of Charlie, so Gwendolyn assumed he'd left at dawn to drive up to that god-awful cabin. She knew her daughter was furious. Which version of her would emerge today? Sad Margy? Cold Shoulder Margy? Margy on the Warpath?

Better to have the inevitable confrontation sooner rather than later. Besides, Gwendolyn had other important news to disclose. The news nobody gave her a chance to announce at the party. Perhaps Margy had taken her coffee out on the back patio with Petey? Unlikely, since it was an overcast morning with a chilly-looking mist hanging in the air. Still, she'd take a peek.

She opened the back door, noting Petey's leash hanging from the doorknob. She strolled out a few paces, far enough to see across the pool area and the yard beyond. No sign of daughter or dog. When she turned to go back in, she found a note taped to the outside of the door, printed in block letters on a piece of scratch paper.

MARGARET, I'M SO SORRY ABOUT EVERYTHING.
LOVE, SUNNY

Gwendolyn took the note into the house and started calling for her daughter. "Margy? Where are you?" She tried shouting from the kitchen, the bottom of the stairs, the hallway.

"In here," Margy called from Charlie's office. Gwendolyn walked down the hall, gave a tentative knock, and entered only after her daughter grunted approval through the closed door. She was at Charlie's desk with Petey curled up in the corner on his doggie bed.

Margy looked up with weary eyes. When she spoke, her tone was listless. "What do you want?" She turned back to the computer to signal that she didn't wish to engage.

"I thought you should see this," Gwendolyn said. "It was taped to the back door." She handed her Sunny's note.

Margy read the brief message, furrowing her brow. "Where is she? Did she leave?"

"I didn't notice."

Margy stood. "Let's go look."

Sunny's Toyota was gone, and there was no answer when they knocked on her door. Gwendolyn followed her daughter into the guesthouse. Everything was neat and tidy, as if the place had been cleaned up to make way for a new guest. Margy opened the door to the small closet. "Her clothes are gone."

"Where could she be?"

"I have no idea. This is your fault."

"Of course. Everything is my fault." Gwendolyn snorted. "Well, we can safely presume she's not at Henry's." Noticing something on the coffee table, Gwendolyn walked over to see what it was. "It looks like she forgot her sketchbook."

"Hmm," said Margy. They sat side by side on the couch. Gwendolyn started leafing through the pages, poring over the sketchbook as though it might shed light on Sunny's whereabouts.

The first pages had drawings of little Bernie, Bernie's parents, and various storm scenes.

"These must have been early sketches for the book," Gwendolyn said. She continued thumbing through. There was a picture of Petey, a few drawings of people they didn't recognize, a sketch of the patio table laden with food and wine.

"She really is quite talented," said Margy. Gwendolyn gave a grudging nod.

Then a sketch of Charlie seated at his computer.

Charlie leaning over the worktable, reviewing an illustration as Sunny smiled at him.

Charlie on the yoga mat with his legs crossed.

Charlie on the lawn in a forearm plank pose, his torso bared.

Charlie. Charlie. Charlie.

•   •   •

"Would it be too early to drink?" Margy asked as they walked back to the kitchen.

"Not if we were in London." Gwendolyn's tongue clucked in displeasure. "I knew I was right to be wary of that girl."

"Oh, God, do you suppose she and Charlie . . . "

"She and Charlie what?"

"You know — went off together. Seems a bit too coincidental, both of them leaving on the same morning, don't you think?"

"I *think* you are adding two plus two and arriving at an incorrect sum, darling." Gwendolyn reflected further. "Although, I wouldn't put it past Sunny to follow him up to the cabin."

"How would Sunny know the way to the cabin?" said Margy. "Unless . . . unless . . . "

"Unless Charlie invited her?" When Gwendolyn saw the panicked look in her daughter's eyes, she regretted floating this possibility. "Nonsense. Call her and find out where she's gone. Sunny has her flaws, but I don't think she's a liar."

"I don't want to."

"Call Charlie then."

"No cell service, remember?"

Gwendolyn raised an index finger in a gesture that said *problem solved.* "Use that emergency number he gave us."

"Oh, sure. I'll call the owner and say, 'Would you mind popping over to the cabin to see if Charlie has a tall blond woman with him?' I don't think so." Margy sighed. "Anyway, I can't call him. I can't." To Gwendolyn's dismay, her daughter started crying.

"You need to get a grip, dear. Sit down and I'll fix you some cinnamon toast, just the way you liked it when you were a girl." Gwendolyn assumed a reassuring maternal tone, as if a few bites of toast would fix everything.

Margy sat, obedient, but she continued her soft weeping. "I can't seem to turn off the waterworks. When Henry cheated on me—"

"With Alice?"

"Before that. I told you he had a series of one-night stands on his business trips." Gwendolyn didn't recall that, but she nodded.

"When that happened, I—I didn't care," said Margy. Then she corrected herself. "I mean, of course I *cared.* I didn't like what he was doing, but I didn't feel broken inside."

Gwendolyn pulled a slice of whole wheat bread from the cellophane package and popped it into the toaster. "I know you didn't."

"But if—if Charlie were to do something like that—" Margy started crying harder and dabbed a tissue to her eyes. "I want to trust him, but . . ."

"But after Henry, it's hard not to be suspicious."

Her daughter gave a vigorous nod. "Yes. I love Charlie so much. If he were to cheat on me, it *would* break my heart. I don't think I could go on."

"Of course you'd go on. Hearts don't really break, darling, they bruise a little, and eventually they heal. You would take solace in Petey and your family and friends. You would do your job without allowing the work to suffer. You would get through it."

"Do you think so?" asked Margy.

"I'm certain of it. I didn't raise you to be a blubbering crybaby. I taught you to be strong." Margy wadded up the tissue and hid it inside her fist, as if to conceal any evidence of sniveling behavior. Clearly, the girl needed more reassurance. "Listen," said Gwendolyn. She transferred the toasted bread to a small plate, topped it with butter and cinnamon-sugar powder, and handed it to Margy. "I may not trust Sunny, but I do trust Charlie. I've been living in this house with the two of you for three months. Can you believe it?"

Margy groaned. "Four months, actually, but who's counting?"

"I've watched the way he looks at you – the way he treats you. That man adores you. He's not running off with Sunny or any other woman. You have my word."

Margy shrugged, looking down at her plate, and said, "You really think so?"

"I know so."

Her daughter took a bite of the toast. "God, I'd forgotten how good this tastes."

"Did you and Charlie talk last night?"

"A little. He said we had a beautiful year before you—" She stopped. "He wants us to get back to how things used to be."

"There it is, then. Charlie made a mistake. But he's not Henry. Hiding a book rejection isn't the same as concealing affairs."

Margy stopped chewing, as if to concentrate all her attention on this notion. Gwendolyn leaned forward, napkin in hand, and wiped away a buttery toast crumb lodged on her daughter's chin. "I'm sure he's sorry. Forgive him and move on. Can you do that?"

Margy swallowed her food. "I don't know. He's repentant, but it doesn't take away the pain."

Gwendolyn paused before continuing to speak. "Margy. I'm sorry about how things escalated last night. I admit I sometimes tend to over-stir the pot when I should leave it to simmer. But that Sunny gets so under my skin that I—well, this time, I let things boil over. I won't deny, I'm glad she's gone. But I never meant for you to get hurt." Her daughter cast her another distraught look. "I'll try to behave better in the future, but I don't always live up to my intentions."

Margy dropped her toast on the plate. Her gaze hardened. "Well, that's convenient, isn't it?"

"What?"

"If you're not responsible for your own actions, you can keep on hurting people no matter what the consequences. Do you have any idea how much trouble you've caused? My best friend has disappeared, and my future with a man I love deeply is in doubt."

"Darling, I'm sure this will all work out before—"

Margy shook her head violently, having none of it. "And to assuage your conscience – if you have one – you'll try to buy me off with a bottle of wine or a cashmere sweater or . . . cinnamon toast." She pushed the plate away. "I can't believe I still fall for that crap. Henry was always bribing Michael and me with expensive presents and trips. I swear, you and my ex are cut from the same bolt of cloth."

"Oh, Margy." She thought she'd made headway, but now the girl was hopping mad.

"Don't 'oh Margy' me, like you're all contrite. I'm onto your tricks, Mother. Leave me alone, all right? I—I need time to myself to think."

"You'll have plenty of time to yourself when I'm gone." She blurted out her announcement. "I'm leaving. I'm flying back to New York."

Margy eyed her with skepticism. "Are you being dramatic? Because I said I wanted to be alone?"

"No, I've been planning it for days. Sam booked me on a noon flight Thursday."

"When were you going to let me in on this?"

"I meant to announce it at the party last night, before all hell broke loose."

"And then you'll move in with Sam?"

Gwendolyn nodded. "There'll be red tape with the homeowners' board where Sam lives, but he is very adept at that sort of thing." Sam was adept at many things. Once Gwendolyn had decided to return home, she could hardly wait to reunite with him.

Margy looked her in the eye. "That's good. You need to leave, after everything that's happened. Your presence here is toxic."

"Toxic?" That sounded harsh.

"Yes, Mother. Toxic."

She wondered whether Margy had sworn off calling her *Mum* for good. "I'm sorry you feel that way. But I believe things will be fine with you and Charlie. Better than fine."

"How do I know you even mean that? What you said about Charlie adoring me, and that you're sure of his love for me . . . It sounds like a calculated strategy to win me back to your side." Margy's shoulders slumped forward. "Like the cinnamon toast."

Gwendolyn, who abhorred gratuitous displays of emotion, found her own eyes awash with tears. "God knows I deserve your doubt, after the way I've behaved. But I mean every word, Margy." She studied her daughter's face, hopeful these last words would have a softening effect. But Margy's expression remained hard, unyielding. The girl was often irritated with her, but this was something different. Something that went deeper. No question, they both had their work cut out for them. Margy must learn how to find forgiveness. And Gwendolyn must learn how to earn it.

CHAPTER 28

Slipping away from Charlie's like a criminal on the run, Sunny drove aimlessly for an hour before stopping for a long trail walk by the ocean. The water was calm today, a sheet of silver glass, and the distant horizon merged monochromatically with the cloudy sky above.

After she walked a couple of miles, the clouds began to break. By the time Sunny returned to her car, both sea and sky had warmed to a brilliant blue. She drove to a quiet nearby park with shaded picnic tables, figuring it would be a good place to work on her sketches. She rummaged through the cardboard boxes and shopping bags in the trunk in search of her art supplies. Her colored pencils and charcoal were buried at the bottom of a bag, but the sketchbook was nowhere to be found. *Damn.*

She drove to CVS to purchase a drawing pad, bottled water, and peanut butter crackers, and then returned to the park. For the next few hours, she drew soothing seascapes and trees. How wonderful it was to pass the time escaping into her work and forgetting her problems.

Stopping by her favorite vegetarian restaurant, Sunny ordered a tofu veggie bowl to go. She drove to the beach and sat on a park bench, eating slowly, and gazing out for the second time today at the ocean, dotted with whitecaps as the afternoon breeze kicked up. Time to face reality. Where would she go tonight, and all the nights that followed?

Two and a half years ago, after her mother's care had plunged her into debt, Sunny had to give up her apartment. It seemed unbelievable at the time to accept that she'd become a *homeless* person. When she thought back on her life during the six trying months that ended with her move to northern California, it still seemed unreal. Until today. Because it was happening all over again.

As Sunny savored her final bites of tofu and veggies, she reviewed that earlier period of homelessness, mulling over how the experience might benefit her now. She used to sleep in her car, in the back of the employee parking lot at Seaside Fitness. After the gym opened in the early morning hours, she would go inside to shower, relax in the women's lounge, and enjoy endless cups of free coffee and snacks on the outdoor water view deck. But when she was laid off from the spa, she canceled her health club membership to save on expenses; and even if she still belonged, Seaside Fitness would be off limits given Margaret and Charlie's regular presence.

Sunny's other favorite home away from homelessness, as she'd called it, was the library. She used to settle into a study cubicle and use her laptop or read books and newspapers for hours on end. The library might be a good place to work on her art school applications, but it didn't solve the problem of where to sleep or shower.

A growing sense of dread gnawed at her insides. Sunny focused on taking slow, deep breaths and counting the inhales and exhales to keep her anxiety at bay. She couldn't go back to sleeping in her car. But what was the alternative? Most of the people in her social circle were more acquaintances than close friends. She could hardly turn up on Judith's doorstep and ask to be taken in. And she was reluctant to squander her severance pay on a hotel room.

When Sunny had been in such dire straits before, Eleanor helped turn her life around. She'd given her a job at her spa in Mill Valley and invited Sunny to live rent-free in her guest apartment over the garage. That gave her another idea. Scrolling through the Favorites in her phone, she tapped Eleanor's number. She wouldn't beg her cousin for a place to stay, she'd simply scope out the situation.

Eleanor answered on the second ring. "Sunny, hello. It's been too long. You okay?"

"Yes, fine. How about you?"

Eleanor groaned. "We're healthy, but what a time we've had up here. Between the smoke and heat and smog . . . "

"I—I'm embarrassed to say I'd forgotten about the fires around the Bay Area," said Sunny. "Are you in any danger?"

"No direct fire danger, but it's miserable here, especially with no A/C in the house. I had to buy a portable unit for the tenant, though."

"What tenant?"

Eleanor explained that she'd rented out the garage apartment to bring in a little extra monthly income. "Money's been tight, as you know."

"Oh, right." Sunny's hopes deflated. There went her safety net.

They chatted a few more minutes and then Eleanor said, "I almost forgot to mention. The spa lease runs out August 31st. During the second half of August, I'll need you to help coordinate the move. I'll pay you cash under the table for your time so you can still collect unemployment. Sound okay?"

"Sure, that'll be great."

"Of course, maybe you'll have a new job by then," said Eleanor. "If you're too busy to handle this when the time comes, don't worry. I'll find someone. I wanted to give you the heads-up."

After they exchanged goodbyes, Sunny dropped her phone on the passenger seat and gave herself a literal smack on the forehead. It seemed so obvious. How could she have racked her brains all day and not realized she had the perfect place to stay?

•   •   •

Thanks to Charlie's early departure, the trip to the cabin on the Central Coast had been uneventful. He made the six-hour drive without turning on music or news to keep him company. The silence allowed him to think, uninterrupted.

Mostly, he'd thought about how much he already missed Margaret. It was hard to fathom what the next two weeks would be like – alone, unable to talk to her, unable to email or text. He should've delayed his trip to stay and smooth things over. As it was, everything felt unsettled, unresolved, and he ached for her already.

He tried to focus on reassuring thoughts. Last night, as upset as Margaret was, she remained sensible and steady, never growing hysterical or unreasonable. He recalled the poignant moments when they'd reconnected through their pain. The softness of her tear-stained cheek. The warmth that radiated as he held her. He hoped she was remembering it too. But his mood seesawed from hope to despair when he recalled something she'd said. *"I need time . . . to figure out if I still trust you."*

As the drive up the coast progressed, he'd thought of the others as well. And to his surprise, he found he also missed this bunch of misfits who were incapable of a relaxed, conflict-free gathering. How was this even possible? *We're a fucked-up family, no question about it.* Actually, they weren't a family at all. But these were his people now. And if he were to lose them, it would mean losing the woman he so dearly loved. They were all bound together.

And then it dawned on him. *Family isn't always who you're related to by bloodline or marriage. It can be defined by who you are **with**. It's the men and women in your world who keep you up laughing with their stories until late in the night, then turn around and ruin your holiday party the next day. It's the people who embrace and infuriate you, who reward and punish you, who make you smile and scream all in the same minute. Sometimes that's where you find your true family – with the people who start out as unexpected guests and end up changing your life.*

Then Charlie thought of those other unexpected guests – the ones that came to lodge not in your home but in your head. The fears that invaded your psyche and refused to leave, ill-mannered visitors all. The anxieties that held you with their paralyzing force. Charlie had been in their grip for many weeks now. Sunny had too, and young Benny, and he suspected even Gwendolyn.

With a lightning-bolt flash of perception, Charlie envisioned a story about a quirky family that wasn't a family, trying their best to support one another as they faced their demons. Suddenly he knew the book he wanted to write. The characters were already filling his head: the outrageously behaved older woman, the flashy ex-husband, the artistic friend, the sensitive little boy. And the strong, intelligent woman who was the steadying presence in their intersecting lives. He could hardly wait to get started.

Consulting the directions, Charlie found the landlord's house and stopped to pick up the key. From there he proceeded down the final stretch of dirt road to the rental. Nestled in a grove of towering spruce trees, the log cabin resembled a film set for *Grizzly Adams*. He waded through an ankle-deep sea of pine needles to reach the door.

The living area had a stone fireplace flanked by a loveseat, easy chair, and rocker that looked like they'd been ordered from an early twentieth century Sears and Roebuck catalog. Charlie smiled at this. An area with a two-burner gas stove, an old refrigerator, and a stained porcelain sink would make do as a kitchen. In another corner was a rolltop desk below a high window where shards of daylight filtered down from between the trees. A fine workspace. No internet – but as long as the electricity worked, he'd be good.

A trundle bed with handsewn quilts and an antique trunk more or less filled the bedroom. Charlie walked across the braided rug and inspected the cramped bathroom with a shower stall so tiny he'd have to duck to avoid hitting his head. But overall, the surroundings were warm and inviting, and he'd be comfortable here, if not for missing Margaret.

He took out his cellphone and saw the "No Service" message. He'd seen that same message for several miles along the rutted roads he'd driven while experiencing the revelation about his ad hoc family. Now he had a second revelation, about him and Margaret. It was something he must share with her. Right away, before he went off the grid.

He drove the forty minutes back to the nearest town and turned into the unpaved parking lot of a general store. His tires kicked up dust as he pulled into a space. Not wanting to risk getting tongue-tied or sidetracked, he typed his message into the notepad app on his cellphone so he could read it to Margaret the moment she answered the phone. Charlie needed to not mess this up.

He dialed her number and waited, drumming his fingers on the dashboard. After several rings he hung up without leaving a message. Glancing again at the notepad, he made a few tweaks to what he'd written, wanting the words to be perfect. He tried three more times to reach Margaret. No answer.

Shit.

Taking a break to do his shopping, Charlie worried she was not answering on purpose. He mulled over the possibilities as he maneuvered his cart up and down the unfamiliar aisles, grabbing hot dogs, bacon, a can of beef stew. Maybe she was preoccupied with something else, like an unpleasant confrontation with her mother or Sunny. He put two dozen eggs, bread, and milk in the cart, then couldn't resist adding a quart of chocolate chip ice cream. What if Margaret had decided she wanted nothing to do with him? Self-doubt set in and, by the time he loaded his groceries into the back of the car, he'd lost the nerve to call her again.

Charlie was pulling out of the parking area as a speeding black pickup truck turned into the lot. The driver lost control and the truck skidded on the dirt. When Charlie swerved to avoid him, the pickup continued on in a cloud of dust, missing the driver's side door of Charlie's SUV by a few inches at most. Heart thundering in his chest, Charlie backed up slowly and brought the car to a stop. The other driver screeched to a halt. "Why the hell don't you watch where you're going?" the man shouted out the window.

Incredulous, Charlie opened his own window. "You're the one who was driving like a bat out of —"

The pickup driver jumped out of the truck. He had to be six inches taller than Charlie and twenty years younger, with a barrel-chested physique. His face contorting into a murderous expression, he shouted obscenities, as if the near miss had been all Charlie's fault. Charlie snapped his mouth shut and raised both palms in a gesture of surrender. But the man started toward him in long strides, waving an angry fist.

A woman's voice called out from the pickup. "Bobby, for Chrissake, just buy the friggin' beer so we can get to my sister's house. We're already late." The man veered away and trudged into the general store.

Charlie let out a long, low exhale. *I could've been seriously injured by this maniac. Fuck, I could've been killed.* If Alice's death had taught Charlie anything, it was the fragility and uncertainty of life. Maybe if he waited two more weeks to tell Margaret how much she meant to him, it would be too late. Maybe tomorrow would be too late.

This time, when she didn't answer his call, he left a message. "Hey, it's me, just wanted to let you know I arrived safely. The owner wasn't kidding. There is zero cell signal within miles of the cabin. I'm calling from town before I settle into the writing. I miss you already, and I love you more than you could know. And there's something I'd like you to think about while I'm away. Remember when I compared you to a train that I couldn't keep up with? You told me, it was never a race. Well, you were right. It's not a race, it's a journey. And if I haven't pissed you off irreparably, it's a journey I want us to take together, the two of us. As husband and wife. Can we do that? Please, my love, can we do that?"

When Charlie put down the phone, his whole body pulsated with nervous excitement at what he'd just done. He let out a whoop, sucked in a cleansing breath, and hightailed it out of the parking lot before Bobby the surly pickup owner could emerge from the store and beat the crap out of him.

•   •   •

Sunny waited until the dentist's office and other adjacent businesses had closed for the day before arriving at the Village Canyon Day Spa, parking the Toyota in the tenant parking space at the rear of the building. At the door, her hand wobbled so much it took a few tries before she could insert her key in the lock. Her heart was pumping as if she'd run a half-Marathon.

Why am I so nervous? I'm not breaking any laws. Sunny reminded herself that as former spa director and current leaseholder, she had every right to enter the premises. If anyone questioned her presence, she'd say she was there to tie up loose ends and check on the repair work performed after the burst pipe.

The door opened smoothly – why shouldn't it? There was no reason to suspect the landlord had changed the lock. Once inside, Sunny proceeded with an excess of caution, afraid she might find something that would derail her plan.

She flipped a switch, and the lobby light came on. *Electricity!* She walked over to the front desk, picked up the telephone receiver, and heard the hum of the dial tone. She reached to fire up the desktop computer but remembered it was networked into Eleanor's, and she mustn't risk discovery. Pulling the laptop from her backpack, Sunny plugged it in. Since she'd used it before at the spa, it connected to Wi-Fi at once and she opened the web browser with a single click. *Internet!*

The place was warm and musty, but it was clean and she found no trace of the previous damage. She walked around, cracked a few windows open, and turned on the ceiling fan in the lobby and portable fans in the other rooms. In this coastal location, where temperatures were moderate, she would be comfortable enough without A/C.

After bringing her belongings inside, Sunny moved her car to a residential street several blocks away. Back in the spa, she turned on the audio system, keeping the volume low, and selected one of her Laurel Canyon playlists. A Carole King song played through the speakers. *Music!*

She strolled around evaluating the facility in a new light, not as a spa but as a temporary residence. The treatment rooms had blackout drapes, so she could spend the night, even with lights on, and escape detection. A massage bed was harder and narrower than a standard sleeping mattress, but it was infinitely more comfortable than the back seat of the small Toyota sedan. Plus, the place was equipped with fresh linens, blankets, and towels.

She walked into the bathroom and ran the tap. *Hot water!* She could enjoy long showers, wash out her clothes by hand when she needed to, and use the adjacent changing room to dress and undress. What more could any woman need? True, there wasn't much in the way of a kitchen – just an under-counter refrigerator and tabletop microwave in an alcove off the rear of the lobby. She'd make do.

The more she looked around, the more possibilities she uncovered. Sunny felt a surge of confidence in her own resourcefulness. And to think she'd been on the brink of desperation only a few hours ago. Then, when she believed it couldn't get any better – rummaging through the front desk, she found two of her old vape pens wedged in the back of the bottom drawer. *Jackpot!* The discovery couldn't have come at a better time. The Village Canyon Day Spa was already proving to be the Ritz Carlton of homeless shelters. Relieved at how the day had turned out, Sunny sent a text message to Margaret.

Sunny

I have a safe place to stay. Don't worry about me, I'll be fine. Again, I'm so sorry for any pain I might have caused. I hope you can forgive me.

Love, Sunny

But her newfound euphoria vanished in an instant when she thought of something.

The sketchbook. It all came back to her – this morning she'd set it on the coffee table while fumbling for her car key. Since she'd searched every inch of the Toyota, it must still be on the table.

Sunny's heart raced. In her mind she saw the pages and pages of Charlie in her book: at his desk, on the patio, his chest naked . . . She put her head between her knees, her breath coming hard and fast. Anyone could see the passion expressed in those drawings. Margaret would find the sketchbook, and then what? What would her friend think of her now? She picked up her cellphone with a knee-jerk instinct to text Margaret again. But the damage was done. Would Margaret even believe anything she might say?

Sunny reached for the vape pen.

CHAPTER 29

Charlie made a few more edits to the manuscript and leaned back in his desk chair to take a breather. Fingers interlaced, he stretched both arms over his head, then straight in front of him, to work out the kinks in his neck and shoulders. Hunching over the computer was a professional hazard, but he'd learned how to mitigate the aches and pains.

He reviewed his pages from the previous day while downing a cup of coffee, a huge bowl of cereal, and a banana. Quick to fix, easy to eat. By the time he finished the breakfast and the editing, conditions outside the cabin were ideal for a long walk. The early morning chill was gone from the air, but the afternoon heat had not yet descended.

Charlie hiked for more than an hour and a half on the dusty trails that wound through the neighboring woods, thinking about what he wanted to write. He wasn't sure how the repetitive rhythm of walking aided the thought process, but it did. By the end of the walk, Charlie had a detailed mental roadmap of the day's chapters. He wolfed down a peanut butter sandwich with a second cup of coffee, then returned to work.

Page sixty-eight. Hard to believe he'd made this much progress in six days. Charlie normally spent weeks outlining a new novel, but this time he leaped into the story. From the time he typed the words "Chapter One," the page count accumulated with astonishing speed. The knowledge that he was writing about Margaret – or at least, a fictionalized version of her – excited him and stimulated his creativity. He worked late into the evenings, eager to capture every detail as fast as he could.

The absence of internet service proved to be a boon. He didn't realize how much time he'd spent pausing the writing to look online for synonyms (*Is "frou frou" the right descriptive for that French poodle?*), or to research facts (*Do you make shepherd's pie with ground beef or lamb?*). He would tend to these details later.

The ideas kept flowing, despite the apprehension about Margaret that constantly simmered close to the surface. Every day he was tempted to drive back into town and call her again or at least check his phone for messages; but he reined himself in, remembering that she'd asked for time apart to process things. He didn't want to pressure her.

When the day's work was done, Charlie poured red table wine into a glass – one of those ancient Welch's jelly glasses. Most of the furnishings and kitchen items in the cabin were retro, and Charlie wondered whether they were original equipment or if they'd been added later as an affectation.

Should he fix himself a plate of hot dogs and beans for supper or open up a can of beef stew? Gwendolyn would be scandalized by his hillbilly diet. Here at the cabin, food was simply the fuel that kept the engine running. Gourmet dinners and vintage wines were a pleasure reserved for special evenings with Margaret. Maybe she and Gwendolyn were enjoying grilled fish and veggies tonight or salads from their favorite local takeout. That is, if they were enjoying *anything* together. They might've torn each other to pieces by now.

He missed Margaret terribly. What had her reaction been when she listened to his marriage proposal? He liked to imagine her tearing up, smiling wide. Replaying the message over and over. Then again, it's possible she'd frowned and deleted it. Dark thoughts took over, and he feared he might have pushed

Margaret over a precipice. What if she didn't trust him anymore? What if, when finally face-to-face, Margaret said no? He ran through the options endlessly, trying to prepare himself. It was all speculation until he spoke to her.

•   •   •

Next morning, Charlie jumped into the car and drove to town. Surely it was okay to check in with Margaret after a week apart?

Pulling into the general store parking lot, he scrolled through all his emails and texts once, then twice, praying for an impassioned response from her. Nothing. Then he played back his voicemail messages, but they were all spam. He tried calling Margaret twice, but she still didn't answer and he left no message this time. What could he say? Clearly her silence was a form of response. She hadn't forgiven him. Perhaps she'd even stopped loving him. He returned to the cabin, dejected.

By the time he got out for his walk, the day had grown uncomfortably hot. Instead of following one of the usual trails, he headed down the dirt road to the owner's house and knocked. The owner opened the door seconds later. "Morning," he said. "Everything okay?"

"Fine," said Charlie. "I just stopped by to see if you have any messages for me?"

"I sure don't." The man sounded cheerful, as if he were delivering welcome news. Doubly dejected, Charlie thanked him and walked back to his cabin. He managed to solve a thorny plot problem that afternoon, which distracted him from the thorny Margaret problem. At least the writing was going well. Maybe even well enough to propel him to his goal – returning to the pinnacle of success he'd enjoyed with *Bicoastal.*

Charlie drove to town again the next day to check voicemail and email. Still no word. *Fuck.* He sped back up the mountain; at the fork, he swerved away from the cabin and headed to the owner's house. Margaret had to have left him a message by now. The landlord's manner was brusque this time. "No need to keep stopping by. I'll let you know first thing if anyone calls."

•   •   •

Sunny listened to the melancholy refrain of *California Dreamin'*. Though she loved the song, it only intensified her sadness right now. Turning off the Mamas and the Papas, she smoothed the covers over the massage bed in the room she'd designated for sleeping. It was a little early for bed, but once inside the spa there wasn't much to do.

Loud voices from outside broke through the silence, startling her. They sounded so close. Her heart rate quickening, Sunny pinned herself against the wall and glanced at the blackout drapes, making sure they were drawn all the way. She'd chosen the smallest room, in the most tucked-away location, as her bedroom. The voices faded into the distance.

Within a week, Sunny's initial elation over solving her homeless problem had turned to anxiety. If she were a rule-breaker like Gwendolyn, she could spend her days and nights in contentment, untroubled by scruples. But Sunny was no Gwendolyn.

She was violating the lease by sleeping here, and she lived in perpetual fear of discovery. Even with the drapes closed, she might be caught coming or going. Maybe the management company would notice someone was using water and electricity at night. Could they monitor that? As new ways to be discovered surfaced in Sunny's mind, her worry increased.

The next day began like every other. After rising early, Sunny drank a cup of instant espresso, made her bed, and had a quick shower. She walked on a coastal trail for her morning exercise, then shopped at a distant neighborhood where she wouldn't run into Margaret or Gwendolyn. From there she went to one of her regular spots, a little park tucked behind a real estate development close to the shoreline.

She spent the afternoon creating a watercolor of birds flying over the seashore. Looking at her work, Sunny could see she'd failed to convey a sense of motion – the birds looked more like cardboard cutouts pasted on the sky. Her skills were no longer improving. She needed professional instruction to keep growing her talent. Tonight she'd put the finishing touches on the last of her school applications. Thank goodness she had backup photos of the drawings in her lost sketchbook to include with her submittals. If only Charlie was there to give her essay one final read . . .

She missed the group dinners on Charlie's patio – the laughter and the camaraderie. She missed her friendship with Margaret, who had never texted her back. And as shameful as it was, she missed Charlie most of all. She wondered how he was faring at the cabin. Had Margaret forgiven him? She'd seemed so upset the night of the party, perhaps not. If the rift was permanent, Charlie would be free again, and then—*no*. Sunny mustn't allow such hopes to enter her head.

Julia called that night. "I haven't heard from you in a long time. Any news on that book you and Charlie collaborated on?"

Not wanting her sister's pity, Sunny sugarcoated the truth. "The publisher accepted the book, but it's their policy to use staff illustrators. They said they wished they could've used my drawings." Sunny said nothing about her living circumstances. When she'd been homeless two years before, she kept it from her sister, not wanting Julia thinking she was a hopeless loser. Come to think of it, she hadn't told Julia a lot of things. Well, Julia didn't need to know the truth back then, and she didn't need to know it now.

•   •   •

The bad dreams had begun a few days into her stay and now haunted her nightly. Most of them involved her father.

In one dream, she was a girl again, and Far was punishing her because she'd sneaked into Julia's room and tried on her big sister's lipstick. Before the spanking began, he used the lipstick to draw an "X" across each of her butt cheeks – "so I'll have a target," he said in the dream. She awoke terrified and ashamed. It seemed so real. Would she, *could* she, ever know if it was?

Another dream took place in the present-day world. She and Far went to a movie, but when they walked into the darkened theater, Sunny realized they had no tickets. An usher escorted them out as fellow moviegoers yelled at them for the disturbance. Far was furious, saying it was Sunny's fault for losing their tickets. During his rant, the scolding parent morphed from Far into Gwendolyn.

The dreams frightened Sunny, but she yearned to understand them. She tried to calm herself with vaping. That helped, but only a little, and she finished off both vape pens in no time. She forced herself to stay awake, fearful of what frights her unconscious mind might unleash. Eventually, she drifted off to sleep, exhausted, but the nightmares still came.

She'd set her phone alarm for an early wake-up so she could leave before business hours to avoid arousing suspicion. Her exhaustion worsened. Months ago, her doctor had prescribed a tranquilizer to help her sleep. The pills made her dopey and sluggish so she'd stopped taking them, afraid she might be late for work or make a careless mistake. Time to reconsider.

That evening, a little after dusk, she heard an insistent pounding at the front door. Had the police come to kick her out? Her heart crashing in her chest, Sunny raced down the hall to the back treatment room where she cowered, lights out, drapes closed, for as long as the knocking persisted. A man was yelling but she couldn't understand the words. She covered her ears as if she were still a child.

When Sunny was a little girl, Far would pound on her bedroom door with the same ferocity. It was always the prelude to a punishment, usually a spanking. She would crouch in the corner covering her ears until he came in. She never understood why he bothered knocking since there was no lock on her door. If Far did it to torment her, it worked.

When the noise at last abated, Sunny peeked out the window, the pounding of her heart as loud and insistent as the knocking had been. A man retreated from the front door and shuffled down the block. Recognizing him as a homeless guy who hung out in the neighborhood, she gave a nervous laugh. But even though she knew this man was no threat, the incident had unraveled what was left of her already frayed nerves. The laughter turned to tears, then to violent sobs.

She turned on the audio system to drown out the knocking noise that still reverberated in her head. A Joni Mitchell song came on, something about a battered wife who died by suicide. The song gave her the creeps, especially one phrase describing how the husband abused her because he despised her frailty. Far had despised Sunny for her weakness and her inability to live up to his ideal. Maybe Gwendolyn saw her the same way. Why else would Margaret's mother treat her with such disdain?

This was not the best song for improving Sunny's mood. She paused the track to search for something less upsetting. After the complaint from Mrs. Darling, she'd added a couple of conventional spa playlists. The gentle harp strains would be mindless and soothing tonight. Maybe they'd take her mind off not only her nightmares but also her waking terrors. The terrors of the present: How would she pass the lonely hours without going crazy? What if someone discovered her? And the terrors of the future: Where would she go from here? How could she climb out of this pit of homelessness and joblessness and isolation?

Then she remembered the tranquilizers. She found the bottle and held it up to the light, looking at the tiny white pills. Since she'd only taken a couple, the bottle was still full.

Sunny had long believed in reincarnation. She felt certain she'd lived many past lives, with more to come in the future. The present one wasn't panning out too well. Was this to be her destiny? To claw her way out of that dreaded pit, only to fall back down again? What if there were another way? Sunny shook the pill bottle that she still grasped in her hand. What if she could short-circuit the process and leapfrog into the next life? A life with greater potential – and less pain.

What if?

Though Sunny didn't usually bathe in the evenings, she took a long shower where she lathered both head and body, and then rubbed a rich shea butter cream on her limbs and chest after toweling off. She dried her long hair and tied it back into a ponytail. Next she went to her suitcase and found her one elegant item of sleepwear, a long, blush-colored silk nightgown. It felt soft against her skin as she slipped it over her head and pulled it down across her slender hips.

Sunny poured white wine into a glass and sipped on it as she continued her preparations. She brushed her teeth, dabbed moisturizer on her face, and put on a glossy pale pink lipstick that matched her nightie. She thought she looked rather nice.

She drained the last of the wine, rinsed the glass, and returned it to the cupboard. She walked down the hall to the treatment room that had served as her bedroom for these past weeks and switched on the countertop diffuser that released lavender oil into the air. Within a few minutes, the soothing fragrance permeated the room. Why hadn't she thought of this before? She dimmed the recessed overhead lights to the lowest setting, so they gave off a faint glow of soft orange illumination.

Reclining on the massage bed, Sunny pulled the top sheet and lightweight blanket up to her chin. She closed her eyes and allowed her breathing to become shallow and regular, inhaling the lavender scent and letting the harp music lull her into a sense of calm.

Turning onto her side, she reached for the bottle of tranquilizers, opened the cap, and shook some of the pills into her palm. She rolled them around in her hand, examining them like a jeweler appraising a collection of gems. After swallowing a single pill with water, she poured the rest back into the bottle. As the medication pulled her down into a deep slumber, all the usual thoughts and fears emptied from Sunny's head. It was blissful.

•   •   •

After a nine-hour sleep, she thought about the events of last night. It might've been nice to fast-forward out of her unsatisfactory existence into something more rewarding. But what if the next life turned out to be no better – or even worse? Or if reincarnation didn't exist, and there would be no life after this one?

What if?

As Margaret once quipped, the prospect of eternal nothingness was singularly unappealing. So it seemed safer, all things considered, to stay with the life she had. Sunny felt thankful to have a second chance and comforted to know she had the power to control the ending this way. She'd played out her impromptu drama with dignity and flair. Everything but the final scene.

CHAPTER 30

During breakfast on the eleventh day of his retreat, Charlie heard a knock. Through the window he saw the landlord, and his heart soared. Surely this must be a message from Margaret. Swinging the door open, Charlie wanted to hug the man.

"My next renter canceled," the landlord said. "If you wanna stay a third week, I'll only charge you a hundred and fifty bucks, cash. You know, to cover expenses."

Swallowing his disappointment over Margaret's continued silence, Charlie considered the offer. Ten more days of nonstop writing sounded tempting. At the rate he was going, he could be halfway through a draft by then. No, more than that. As itchy as he was to reconnect with his love, there was no denying his productivity had skyrocketed since they'd been apart. "Can I let you know by tomorrow?" he asked. The landlord nodded.

Charlie couldn't recall when he'd last felt so self-assured about his work. Most of his previous novels had been sweeping in scope, set in multiple locations and spanning years or even decades. But this entire story took place over a single weekend, centering on a Fourth of July party where a lot more than fireworks exploded. With the book's focused setting and ensemble cast, he could already envision a TV movie or mini-series adaptation. Possibly even a stage play. He hadn't written a play since college, but he must still be capable of it. He felt capable of anything right now.

Charlie's mind leapt to the future, to a chilly evening in Times Square. He imagined himself striding into a Broadway theater with Margaret on his arm, cameras flashing as they arrived for the opening night of Charlie's play. Though he knew this was far-fetched, he didn't care.

Whatever was going on with Margaret, would another week make any difference? He thought again of how much he could accomplish with this extra gift of time. Maybe he should stay.

When he set out to write after rinsing the breakfast dishes, Charlie conjured up the Broadway scenario again to stoke his creativity. But this time he entered the theater alone – no Margaret. He chuckled at the absurd notion that Margaret could seize control of his fantasy and change the outcome. Then, when he tried to focus on the writing, anguished memories of recent events re-surfaced. Charlie thought of Margaret's wrath and disappointment as she'd hurled the pillow across the room. He thought of her weeping in their bed later that night. Of her silence when he'd tried to reach out to her.

In the next hour he only produced a single puny paragraph. What had he been thinking? Was he so obsessed with the work that he'd forgotten what truly mattered? He needed to see Margaret, to talk things through, to close the cavernous space between them. He mustn't wait ten days, or even ten minutes. He must go to her now.

Without taking time to shower, he yanked open the suitcase and stuffed his clothes in. The possibility of holding Margaret in his arms this very evening – and he recognized, it was only a possibility – propelled him into action. He fixed himself a sandwich for the road and stopped at the main house. The owner cracked the door open a few inches and said, "Did you decide to stay?"

Charlie handed the key through the narrow opening. "Sorry, no. Change of plans. Something urgent came up, and I need to leave right now."

He tried phoning Margaret from the car to alert her. As usual she didn't pick up. The whole way back, he fretted like an anxious teenager. When he pulled into the driveway, the Prius was parked outside the garage. No sign of Sunny's Corolla or Gwendolyn's rental car. Excellent. If Margaret was the only one home, they'd have an intimate reunion.

Sure enough, when Charlie walked through the back door, she sat on her customary stool at the kitchen island sifting through papers. But as he started toward her, arms outstretched, she looked both startled and wary. Dropping his arms and shoving his hands into his pockets, he stopped cold. When Petey ran to him with tail wagging, only then did Charlie extricate one hand to pet the dog.

"Charlie? What are you doing home?"

"I thought I'd come back a few days early to surprise you."

"Well – surprise me, you did."

This was not how he'd envisioned his homecoming. He looked around. "Anyone else home?"

"No, I'm alone." Then her gaze hardened. "Are you?"

"Who would I be with?" Charlie asked.

"Oh, maybe, uh, Sunny? To pick a name out of a hat."

"I don't understand."

She squeezed her eyes shut and raised both hands to her temples, as if plagued by a searing headache. "Sunny left here the same morning as you. She hasn't been back since."

"Shit." Charlie cringed at the implication of the two of them vanishing at the same time. "Margaret, I haven't seen or heard from Sunny since the Fourth of July."

She opened her eyes and blinked hard. "I was so afraid she'd gone with you to the cabin. And when I never heard from you during all this time . . . I thought you'd at least call from the landlord's to tell me you'd arrived safely. I waited and waited for days, but . . . *nothing*." He could see the pain in her eyes.

"But I did call you the day I arrived. I tried several times and left a message."

She gave him a sad look. "But you never called again?" It came out more as a statement than a question.

"I tried a couple of times again, a week later, but I didn't leave another message."

She seemed borderline angry. "*One* message? That's it?"

"I didn't want to pester you. You said you needed time alone."

"I never said, don't call or text!" she shot back – definitely angry now, and irrational to boot. There were further volleys, with Margaret admitting that her iPhone seven was still losing calls, then directing the blame back at Charlie for failing to try her business line. Every time he tried to make amends, she struck back with a stinging retort.

Then Charlie thought back to that evening, long ago, when Margaret had invited him to the romantic dinner at her apartment. They'd been wary of each other that night too, afraid to voice their feelings, leaving important words unsaid. That night, he'd gone with a plan to end their relationship. Today, his intent was the opposite – not to sever ties, but to forge a bond that would unite them for life. Yet the hotshot novelist was undergoing another crisis of communication. If he failed to find the right words this time, he might blow it for good. So he changed course. "Margaret. I know you're upset. But please hear me out, and then you can yell at me all you like."

She breathed in, then said, "All right. But Petey hasn't been out since morning. Let's talk on the patio."

They walked outdoors. Margaret gestured for Charlie to sit as the dog scampered off toward his favorite peeing location, tail trembling. Charlie cleared his throat. "First off, you need to know that I haven't been with Sunny, not at the cabin or anyplace else, not ever. I think of her as a friend and nothing more."

To his immense relief, Margaret nodded. "Okay. I believe you. Wherever she is, I hope she's safe."

"Maybe she's trying to distance herself from us after what happened," he said. But all he could think about was how Sunny's mysterious departure had amplified Margaret's pain.

"My mother tried to convince me you two hadn't run off together. For once I should've listened to her."

"Gwendolyn? But she was the one who stirred up the pot to begin with."

Margaret sighed. "Yeah, well . . . that's my darling Mum. Oh, she's gone too. She flew to New York three days after you left."

Gwendolyn, gone? Surely this was for the best. But he just said, "I'm sorry you've had to deal with all this."

"It's kind of ironic," she said.

"What is?"

"You rented the cabin to get away from everybody, and then they all jumped ship."

They were both quiet. Charlie leaned forward in his chair. "Getting back to the message I left . . . the one you apparently never received?"

She scrolled through her phone to double-check. "Nope, didn't get it." She shrugged. "That was the message to tell me you'd arrived?"

"Yes. But I said some other things too." Charlie inhaled deeply. This was his chance to do it right. "The night before I left, I compared you to a train that I couldn't keep up with. Do you remember what you said?"

Her eyes looked sad. "I said it was never a race."

He nodded. "You were right. It's not a race, it's a journey."

"Okay, a journey."

"If I haven't pissed you off irreparably . . . "

She knitted her brow.

How to do this? Without overthinking it, Charlie dropped to the ground on one knee. "It's a journey I want us to take together. The two of us." There he was, a scruffy and unwashed man down on one knee with no ring, proposing marriage to his beloved. "As husband and wife." He wasn't sure if she started to laugh, cry, or both. She flapped her hands wordlessly to signal that she couldn't speak. Charlie looked at her with imploring eyes as he asked, "Can we do that? Please, my love, can we do that?"

"Fucking iPhone seven," she said through a choked sob.

Charlie cocked his head to one side, hoping this angled perspective would allow a clearer window into Margaret's mind. "Is that a yes?"

She gave an emphatic nod and clutched both hands to her chest, then traced a heart shape with her fingers. "That's a yes."

They sprang up at the same time, Charlie from the ground and Margaret from her chair, launching bodies and mouths together with an intensity that caused Petey to run back, barking. The terrier wriggled between their legs, trying to push them apart like a referee separating two prizefighters in the ring.

They laughed and pulled the dog into their embrace.

•   •   •

"I know it isn't cocktail hour, but this calls for a glass of something," said Margaret when she and Charlie finally came up for air. Petey, bored with the make-out session, had resumed sniffing bushes. She returned with two chardonnays, apologizing for not having anything bubbly on ice. They toasted each other and sipped the wine. Charlie caressed her arm across the table, but then Margaret grew serious and said, "There's something else we need to discuss."

He tensed and pulled back his hand. Was there still a trust issue between them?

"While you were away," said Margaret, "I realized something about myself. I've been slipping back into a bad habit from my marriage to Henry – burying myself in work to avoid dealing with other problems."

"I thought work *was* the problem. You've been so overwhelmed and short-staffed. What else?" he asked, still anxious.

"Well, Mum, for one. She and I could never get along for four days, let alone four months. Also, you and I – we kind of lost the beat somewhere along the way. I hated that, but I didn't know how to confront it. I kept hoping it would resolve itself."

"Yeah, same here."

"Also, Charlie . . . while I was buried with work, I failed to give you something you needed from me. So you got it from Sunny instead."

Though this was true, Charlie was in no position to point the finger at Margaret. "I've learned something important too. When I first got blocked, I blamed it on you for breaking up with me. Then I blamed all the guests who invaded my space: Gwendolyn, Sunny, Henry, even Benny. I see now, outside distractions aren't my problem. *I'm* my problem. I've been putting way too much pressure on myself – not only to write, but to write a blockbuster. I'm chasing an unachievable goal."

"How can you be sure it's unachievable?" she asked.

"Maybe *unrealistic* is a better word. But I need to change the goal."

Margaret gave him a penetrating look. "Maybe this is more about changing your outlook than moving the goalpost."

Charlie immediately recognized the wisdom of these words. He needed to redefine what being a successful author meant. Not just redefine it, but accept and embrace a more pragmatic self-image. "You're right, Margaret. If I don't mend my ways, I could lose everything – including you. I nearly lost you already."

Her brown eyes filled with tears. "We nearly lost each other."

The idea hurt like a physical slap. "How do we make sure that never happens?"

"Suppose we were characters in one of your novels?" Margaret asked. "What would you have us do?"

"Ah, my characters are better at sorting out their problems than I am."

"Couldn't we learn from them, then?" Margaret said.

"It doesn't work like that. Even though we'd like to believe otherwise, life doesn't really imitate art. Rarely, anyway."

"I love you, husband-to-be. We haven't solved everything, have we?"

"Not yet," he said, awash in a sea of emotions: love, sorrow, joy, vulnerability, hope. "But this is a good start." He reached over and gently brushed away her tears, then whispered, "What's on deck for the rest of the day?"

"I have an important meeting in thirty minutes. It could be a long one."

Happiness turned to frustration. He pictured Margaret on a late Zoom call with Robert and the staff, mapping out plans for the next issue. *She's doing it again . . . burying herself in the work.* "Who is your meeting with?" he asked, masking his disappointment.

She grinned. "With you."

Charlie's heart skipped a beat. "Where is this meeting taking place?"

Margaret let out a throaty laugh. "On the yoga mat."

If he hurried, half an hour should be enough time to take a hot shower, shave off his beard, and splash on the citrus and musk aftershave she liked. He raced through these tasks and padded out to the yoga alcove in his robe. Margaret lay waiting for him there. The soft curve of her breasts swelled above the top edge of the sand-colored blanket draped over her. She lifted her bare shoulders and extended her arms.

Charlie stepped out of his robe, slipped under the covers, and commenced the meeting.

CHAPTER 31

Walking the short distance from her car to the front door, Sunny could already feel sweat trickling down her brow. Her sister answered her knock and squinted into the bright daylight. "Sunny?" Julia's mouth dropped open in astonishment.

"Surprise," said Sunny with a nervous titter.

"What—what brings you here? Why didn't you call?"

Sunny gave an apologetic shrug. *I was afraid you might tell me not to come.*

The morning after she'd taken the tranquilizer, Sunny's first instinct had been to flee the spa as quickly as she could. The lease wouldn't run out for another six weeks, but no way could she last that long. Nor did she want to be on the run again, like when she'd made her hasty escape from Charlie's. She willed herself to stay put until she figured out her next step. While she waited, the pills helped with sleep, though she cut back to half the prescribed dose. Five days later, after reaching a decision, she exited the spa for the last time and drove to Phoenix.

"I needed to see you," she told her sister. "Is it okay if I come in?"

Julia rolled her eyes. "It's a hundred and twelve degrees. Get in here before all this nice air conditioning leaks out the door. Do you have luggage?"

"Yeah, but you're sure this is okay? What about Ross?"

"He's in Tucson helping his mom."

Thank God for that, at least.

"She fell and broke her arm," Julia continued. "His mother lives alone, so he'll need to stay with her for a few weeks. You can keep me company." Julia showed her to the upstairs den, which had a convertible couch, dresser, small desk, and wall-mounted television. All the comforts. Sunny dropped her bag on the floor.

She'd never been here before, but nothing about the house surprised her. A cookie-cutter southwestern tract home, it wasn't more than twenty years old but it had a worn, dated look. Julia and Ross had bought it new, not long after Sunny finished college.

Following her sister to the kitchen, Sunny saw a trio of cactus paintings resembling wall decorations in a Marriott resort villa. The furnishings and southwestern fabrics gave the same impression. The only personal touches were family photos scattered on end tables and mounted on one wall. A framed portrait of Julia, Ross, and their two children dominated the grouping, surrounded by older pictures from family reunions. Several of the relatives had shiny auburn hair, the same color as Far's – that rich reddish brown that had somehow eluded Sunny.

Julia brushed a lock of hair off her face with one palm and raised her left eyebrow. It had always been a signature expression of hers. "Why are you here? Did something happen?"

"I—can I have something to drink?" asked Sunny. "I could use fortification."

"There's white wine in the fridge and liquor in that top cabinet over there. Help yourself. I'll take a glass of wine while you're at it."

Sunny wasn't enthralled with the open jug of cheap Chablis, but she poured two glasses and handed one to her sister. She noticed that Julia's wavy auburn hair was muted by an abundance of gray. Though her face was still pretty, she'd developed a bulge around the stomach and hips. It hadn't been visible in their Zoom sessions.

Julia pulled an assortment of raw veggies from the fridge and placed a salad bowl, chopping board, and chef's knife on the countertop. "You can make salad. I'll sauté leftover chicken with mushrooms and rice." Sunny took a tentative sip of white wine and stifled a pucker. All those weeks with Henry, Charlie, and that crowd had spoiled her. "Tell me already," said Julia. "I can't take the suspense any longer."

"In a nutshell . . . I lost my job, broke up with two boyfriends in short order, and had a kind of complicated disagreement with the people I'd been staying with, so I have no place to live. And my book illustrations were rejected, but you heard that on our last call."

"Is that all?" said Julia. "You had me worried it was something serious." They chuckled together and raised their wine glasses.

Chopping and dicing usually had a therapeutic effect. But today it didn't cut the tension dammed up inside Sunny as she gave Julia the details about the last few tumultuous months and her recent traumatic memories of their father. "Far was different with you. I—I bet he never hit you, right?"

Julia was spooning their dinner onto two plates but stopped to look at Sunny, her left brow curving upward again. "No, why?"

The dam broke, and everything Sunny had been keeping inside poured out in a relentless stream. "He used to spank me and make fun of my butt, even while he was smacking me. And before the punishments, he would pound on my door until I prayed he'd just come in and get it over with."

"The spankings – did they happen often?" Julia looked distressed, but not shocked.

"Often enough. He did other things too, but we don't need to talk about that." Sunny had thought it would be cathartic to tell

Julia her story. Instead, it stung like a fresh beating. The heart-pounding fear and the wretched sense of humiliation came back as if Far had just finished spanking her.

"Okay, you're scaring me. What other things?" Sunny could see growing alarm in her sister's eyes. But she shook her head, not wanting to go on. Julia said, "You drove all the way from Los Angeles to talk. And that's what we need to do."

Sunny nodded and said, "One day I came home with a C on a spelling test. Far got mad and hurled a dictionary into my chest." She gave a bitter laugh. "He literally threw the book at me. Another time, I dropped a fork and left it on the floor. He picked it up and—" She swung her forearm in a jabbing motion.

"Oh, dear God." Julia flinched as if she herself had been threatened. Although her sister looked horrified, Sunny had the oddest feeling Julia knew something she wasn't saying. Sunny gulped down the rest of the wine, no longer caring how it tasted, and topped up their glasses.

"The food's getting cold," said Julia. They took their seats. "Was there anything else you wanted to tell me?" Her voice was kind. Sunny shook her head and gripped the edge of the kitchen table, trying to calm her racing heart. "Far started a business a couple of years before you were born," Julia said. "Industrial supplies."

"I didn't know that." The chicken dish smelled greasy and looked like it was drenched in cooking oil. Sunny fought off a wave of nausea.

"He lost his shirt on that company. It put him into debt."

"So when Mother got pregnant with me, the timing wasn't so good?"

"Exactly. They were in financial trouble. They were old and tired. Far was angry and upset."

"I didn't know they had money problems," Sunny said.

"You were too young to remember. Their finances improved, but not for a long time."

"Sometimes I thought he was mad at me because I wasn't a boy," said Sunny. "Other times I thought it was because I wasn't like you. I never measured up."

"He was mad at the world."

"He never had a kind word for Mother either. You seemed to be the only one he spared." Sunny pushed the food around the plate with her fork, forming it into neat little mounds. "I was afraid if I told you how he treated me, that you'd take his side. That you'd hate me like he did."

"I don't think he hated you," Julia said. "But having a baby at their age must've added to his problems. And you were a kid – an easy target." Julia grabbed the salt and sprinkled it on her chicken dish. "Shouldn't you eat something?"

"My appetite's gone." They fell silent until Julia finished her meal. "It's bothered me to keep these secrets," said Sunny. "I've felt so alone. I knew I needed to open up, but it's hard."

Julia cleared their dinner plates, and on the way back to the table she stopped to rub Sunny's back. "I'm sorry we didn't talk about this sooner." Sunny jumped at the touch, then gave herself over to the soothing back rub and tried to relax. She squinted against the setting sun streaming into the kitchen. "I'm glad you came to see me," Julia said. "You should plan to stay awhile. So these people you fell out with – you left their place and drove straight here?"

"No, I moved out a few weeks ago." Sunny made a mental note to text Margaret that she'd be living with her sister in Phoenix for now. Even if Margaret despised her, she wanted her friend to know where she was. "Luckily, I was able to camp out at the spa. At first, it was okay. But then I got paranoid about being discovered, and every day I felt more on edge." Sunny noticed the sun's orange glow made it look like the cactus paintings were on fire. "Here I was in this place of serenity, but I was nervous and exhausted. Then yesterday, I listened to a song about suicide by Joni Mitchell, and it really depressed me. I kinda fell apart."

Julia straightened in her chair. "What do you mean, fell apart?"

Sunny recounted last night's scenario in the spa – the cleansing ritual, the preparations in the bedchamber, the bottle of tranquilizers. "You should've seen me, lying there in my fancy silk nightie, burning lavender oil with the spa music playing . . . It was surreal." Sunny laughed.

Julia's eyes widened. "Have you done anything like this before?"

"No," Sunny said.

"But how — why — this sounds creepy."

"You're making too big a deal." Sunny lightened her tone. "I was like an actor in a play, rehearsing a scene."

"Rehearsing for *what?*"

"Now I'm sorry I brought it up." Sunny's skin prickled with irritation.

"Don't take this the wrong way, but . . . maybe you should talk to a therapist," said Julia, her voice low.

"What?" Sunny was not expecting this. "So you think I'm a hot mess?"

"I'm worried that you might try to harm yourself. What you did last night – it's called suicidal ideation."

Sunny bristled. "You're a shrink now? Did you get your license?"

"Of course not," Julia said, "but I learned something about this from a friend."

Sunny's voice sharpened. "You're taking it way too seriously." She rose from the table and bolted for the stairs, Julia following close behind. Sunny ran upstairs to the den and slammed the door. She heard a soft knock.

"Sunny, don't be mad. I'm concerned about you."

"I keep telling you, I was never going to take those pills."

"Even if you weren't in real danger of overdosing, the fact you were even thinking about it might be a warning sign."

"Julia, let it go."

Another polite knock. "Please open the door so we can talk."

"No."

"I need to tell you something about Far."

Sunny called through the door. "You told me he was angry and depressed – not because I was a disappointment, but because of his own problems. I understand everything now."

Julia said, "Actually, you don't."

"But you told me —"

"I lied."

•   •   •

Sunny cracked open the door gingerly, as if afraid that flames from the fiery cactus paintings might leap across the threshold and singe her hair. She peeked out at her sister. "Lied about what?"

Julia jerked her head and pointed at the stairs. "Coffee."

"You lied about coffee?"

"No, I need to put on a pot of coffee. Then I'll explain." Sunny followed her sister to the kitchen. Julia grabbed a bag of coffee beans and then promptly stuck it back in the cupboard. "Fuck coffee." She reached up to the liquor cabinet and pulled out a bottle of scotch, took two glasses, and plunked everything on the table.

Sunny scrunched her nose. "Can I have something else?" The nausea had subsided, but she still felt fragile and trembly.

"Help yourself." Julia gestured toward the cabinet.

Not a fan of hard liquor, Sunny went for the Bailey's Irish Cream. Pouring a few ounces into her glass, she took a gulp and faced her sister. "The story you told me about Far losing the business, and being depressed and all . . . it's not true?"

"Oh, it's true. But there's more that I—I neglected to tell you." Julia took a large swig of whiskey. "Mother was having an affair."

Sunny's heart rate sped up. "An affair?" Her parents had a lousy marriage – even so, she never pictured Mother as the unfaithful type.

"When Far had all those problems with the business, things between the two of them got strained. Mother moved into the spare bedroom and some days they didn't even speak. So when she got pregnant, Far was madder at her than I'd ever seen him . . . and I suspected something."

"Wait, you were how old?"

"Twelve. Old enough to know babies didn't come from any stork."

"What the hell, Julia? Are you saying Far wasn't my real father?" asked Sunny. She rubbed her palms together. They were slick with perspiration.

"Yes."

"Did they tell you that?"

"No. At the time, I didn't know what to think." Julia swallowed more scotch.

"So you were assuming." Was Julia right? Did Sunny *want* her to be right? She was too stunned to decide.

"At first, yes," said Julia. "I didn't find out the truth until I was in college. When you were around six, I came home from school on winter break. One day they thought I was out, but I was actually studying in my room when I heard Far shouting at Mother."

"What about?"

"He said, 'Maybe Sunny's real father is a slob like her. She didn't get it from me.' And then from other comments he made, I gathered that your birth father was someone from the school where Mother taught."

"I can't believe this. Another Madison High teacher?" Sunny's hands were so slimy with sweat, she could barely hold her glass.

"I suppose. Anyway, that appears to be how you were conceived."

"But . . ." Sunny racked her brain, trying to find holes in Julia's story. "Accusing Mother of being unfaithful doesn't make it true."

Julia sipped her whiskey. "Far said to her, 'I should have thrown you and your brat out of the house years ago.' Then I heard Mother say, 'We both know why you didn't. It was my paycheck that paid the bills.'"

Sunny shivered. "I don't remember Mother standing up to him like that."

"You're right, it was unusual. Far claimed it wasn't about money and said he didn't want to bring dishonor to the family by letting the world know Mother had another man's baby. Apparently, he made her agree never to tell anyone who your real father was."

"*Who was he?* Julia, did they say? I need to know."

Her sister shook her head. "No idea. I'm sorry." Sunny's face clenched with disappointment. "While they argued that day," Julia continued, "Far asked Mother if she'd broken their pledge of secrecy."

Sunny shook her head in disbelief. "Pledge of secrecy? He fucking said that? Jesus." She squeezed her eyes shut and pressed both thumbs against her temples, as if trying to stop her head from exploding. "So why did they stay together? Was it money or the crap about honor?"

"I think they each believed their own version of the truth."

"And why were they arguing about this six years later? I don't get that."

Julia sighed. "You hadn't picked up your toys, and when Far came home from work, he tripped on one of your dolls and banged up his knee. He went ballistic. That's when he started hollering about your real father."

Sunny's body went cold, and she pulled her sweater around her. "Oh God. I remember."

"You remember him saying that?"

Sunny shook her head. "No, I remember him tripping on the doll in the front hall. He yelled and then smacked me with the doll, hard enough that—that her head broke off." Sunny rubbed her arms, trying to stimulate warmth. "It was my favorite doll."

"Shit. I'm sorry," said Julia.

"I guess this explains the hair. I always wondered why I was the only one in the family who didn't inherit Far's red hair," Sunny said.

"Well, now you know."

Sunny gripped her glass tightly. Though the sweet, creamy alcohol was making her queasy again, maybe it would neutralize the shock. But her hands shook so much, the liqueur splashed out. She found a sponge to wipe off the tabletop, surprised at how rubbery her legs felt. "Know what? I'm relieved to find out I wasn't Far's daughter. Maybe my *real* father was a kind man."

"I should've told you about this sooner."

"But you didn't." Sunny wanted to shriek. To learn after all this time that she had a different father – only to find out Julia had zero information. How would she search for him? Was that even possible after forty years?

"It's hard to explain, but I felt like I should respect their decision to keep it a secret. And I figured what you didn't know wouldn't hurt you. But then you described your suicide fantasy."

Resentment pricked at Sunny. "You're making too much of that. I told you it had nothing to do with suicide."

"Maybe not, but you scared the hell out of me. I just want you to be safe." Sunny could see the worry in her sister's eyes. "We know nothing about your birth father. Far accused him of being a slob. But what if he had more serious problems, like a family history of suicide or mental illness? Suppose you've inherited some terrible gene that puts you at high risk?"

"Gee, thanks for that," said Sunny, sarcastic. "Do you have any more helpful thoughts?"

"Look, this is way outside my wheelhouse," Julia said. "Yours too. That's why I hope you'll consider talking to someone."

Sunny drained her glass and put it in the dishwasher, slamming the door shut. "I'm going to bed. My head is spinning from all this."

"You're okay, though? I know it's a lot to take in."

"I'm not planning to kill myself, if that's what you're worried about."

"That's not what I meant." Julia sighed. "You're my sister. I love you, and I'm concerned for you. Is that so wrong? You've had a shock tonight."

Sunny went upstairs. As she lay on the lumpy sofa bed, her anger boiled over and settled into a long, low simmer. She seethed at the triple betrayal. Far had abused her even though she was a young child and an innocent victim. Mother had stood by and allowed it to happen. And Julia had played God, deciding what her younger sister should or shouldn't know.

•　　　•　　　•

Sunny woke to a nasty hangover and more bad news – her first art school rejection. The email contained one of those form letters. "*Unfortunately, we have more qualified applicants than we are able to accept . . .*" Tears of disappointment stabbed her eyes over the quick and bureaucratic dismissal. Of course they must have thousands of younger, more talented applicants. She was a woman in her forties with nothing beyond a few sketches to recommend her. Who was she kidding? She felt herself plunging back down into the dreaded dark pit – the pit from which it became harder to escape each time. She could hear Far saying "I told you so" in that mocking voice of his. He'd always said her art was a waste of time.

Fuck Far. Fuck all of them! She opened her mouth in a silent scream, wanting to shout at the top of her lungs till she no longer had a voice. But if she did, Julia would freak out and ratchet up the pressure for Sunny to seek help. She snapped her mouth shut.

Then she realized Julia was right. Maybe with someone to throw her a rope, Sunny would find a way out of the pit. She picked up her cell and dialed her doctor in Los Angeles.

CHAPTER 32

A gravel-voiced man crossing the street shouted obscenities at a driver who'd honked at him. An NYPD squad car raced by, siren screaming, and drowned out his rant. Even after a month of sticky summer weather, Gwendolyn was still so thrilled to be back in her favorite city that the jarring urban cacophony delighted her ears.

"Shall we ask to move inside where it's quieter?" Sam asked.

They were at a sidewalk café a few blocks from Parkside Gardens. "No, darling. Living in California gave me an appreciation for outdoor dining." She reached over and held Sam's hand.

"Your presence is a tonic to me, you know."

She felt a clench of anxiety. "What did you say?" She heard the echo of Margy's words. *Your presence is toxic.*

"You're a tonic. You make me feel better."

"Oh, thank you, darling." She turned away so he wouldn't see the tears blurring her vision.

"If someone told me two months ago we'd be living together before the end of August, I wouldn't have believed it," said Sam.

Gwendolyn held up her wine glass to let the server know she'd appreciate a top-up. "I'm sure you believe it now, after I filled your poor apartment with all my moving boxes."

Sam pulled a face. "It was daunting at first, but I think we've done a good job blending households."

"We have Amanda to thank for that." Amanda, Sam's granddaughter, had helped Gwendolyn with the move. A sophomore at Columbia, she was a bright young woman who worked as a sports reporter for the *Spectator*, the university's daily newspaper. She'd organized all of Gwendolyn's possessions and recruited friends from the football team to do the literal heavy lifting.

"Yes, hats off to Amanda." Sam smiled. "And to JetBlue for bringing you back. For a time there, I thought you'd never make it home. Do you miss California?"

"Ask me in January." Gwendolyn smiled back. "Of course, it was terrible being stuck out there, but we had our cozy little family group in Charlie's lovely yard. We could relax by the pool in the daytime and dine alfresco every evening."

"Sounds too good to be true," said Sam.

Her smile faded. The thing about Sam was, he could see right through her BS. "Truth be told, I was naughty at times—even difficult—while I was living there." She and Sam had been so preoccupied with the move, they'd never really discussed what happened in California. But the day of reckoning had come. "I'm afraid I may have burned some bridges."

"Who with?"

She considered this. "With . . . everyone."

"Are you serious?"

"That girl Sunny, for sure. I was much too hard on her, and I regret some things I said toward the end." No need to tell Sam that her actions had effectively driven Sunny off the property to God only knows where. "I feel like I should do something. Maybe send a nice gift? I used to love giving massage certificates. That was my go-to present."

"Not appropriate for a woman who lost her spa," Sam said.

For one mad moment, Gwendolyn thought she might cry again. Why this sudden rush of sympathy for Sunny? "Perhaps I should just, I don't know . . . apologize?" She choked a little on the word, as if she'd chomped down on a piece of gristle in her *coq au vin*.

"Excellent idea. But you said you'd burned bridges with everyone. Who else?"

"Margy wasn't too tickled with me," she said. "Nor was Charlie, come to think of it. And by the time July Fourth rolled around, Michael and Heather were probably happy to see the backside of me."

"My, that really is everyone. But I don't understand. Surely Margaret isn't angry – you said the two of you talk and text all the time."

"I might have fibbed a teeny bit about that." Gwendolyn squirmed in her chair.

"To what purpose?" To her dismay, she heard disapproval in Sam's voice. "Are you trying to convince me everything's fine – or convince yourself?"

"You read me too well, darling." Yes, he was definitely onto her BS. And his mild reprimand caused her to tear up, for the third time now, and they hadn't even ordered dessert. This weepy behavior was becoming a most unattractive habit.

"Gwendolyn, what's the trouble?" Sam handed her a tissue and she dabbed her eyes. "You don't seem yourself tonight."

She blew her nose and sniffed loudly. "I'm not myself, Sammy. And that's exactly what the trouble is."

Sam ordered an herbal tea for her and a decaf espresso for himself. As they sipped their hot beverages, she confessed that the unkindness to Sunny was a mere page in the catalog of her misdeeds. She related her unaccountable actions during the stay in California. The unlikely friendships. The reckless outings. The bizarre purchases. The lies and cover-ups. The hours of anxious navigating in the rental car when she'd lost her way.

Sam listened calmly and quietly, stroking his chin with one hand between sips of coffee. "Since she helped you with the move into my place, Amanda's been saying, 'How's Gwendolyn doing? Better, I hope.' Did something happen?"

Gwendolyn shrugged. "Sometimes she'd ask a simple question, like what did I want to do with a box of kitchen items, and I'd get so rattled I had to sit down to calm myself. She was such a dear, she'd say, 'Don't worry, never mind, I'll figure it out.'"

Sam reached for her hand. "Moving is one of the most stressful things a person can do. I'm sure that was part of it, Gwendolyn. But there's a doctor I'd like you to see, just to check everything out. Are you okay with that?"

She nodded again. "Of course."

This was another thing about Sam. He had a way of making Gwendolyn see what was right – and more important, a way of making her *do* what was right.

•   •   •

At first, Sunny didn't like the new therapist assigned by her LA doctor.

"When I told Dr. Lee that my karma wasn't good, she kind of dismissed my beliefs," she told Julia after her introductory Zoom with the psychologist in early September. "Maybe she's not the best fit for me. I wonder if the doc could refer me to someone else."

"You need to give it a chance," her sister said.

Sure enough, on their next virtual visit, they sorted things out. "All I meant was that we should leave karma out of the discussion for now," Dr. Lee said. "We're trying to confront the issues that brought you here. If we write everything off to karma, that's not really confronting."

Sunny nodded. "I might've taken your comments too personally last week."

"Does that happen often?"

"Hah," Sunny snorted. "All the time."

"Can you give me an example?" Dr. Lee asked.

Sunny didn't have to think for long. "My brother-in-law Ross came home a few weeks ago, and he takes pleasure in needling me. Ross is – well, his views are a lot more conservative than mine. Whenever he makes dick comments to me, I get flustered and upset. Sometimes I even burst into tears."

"I'm going to give you an assignment, Sunny. Next time Ross does that, tell yourself, *don't take this personally*. Take a deep breath and try to let it go. Then keep a journal of your reactions. Are you tearful? Angry? Indifferent? Make notes while it's fresh in your mind."

She'd have to get used to taking direction from this slender Asian-American who looked like a college freshman. In reality, Dr. Lee probably wasn't much younger than Sunny.

"The journaling part – can I sketch my feelings instead of writing?"

"Absolutely. If you're more comfortable expressing yourself visually, that's a terrific idea," the therapist said.

Sunny said Ross reminded her a little of her own father.

"They say some women marry their fathers. Do you think Julia's done that?" Dr. Lee asked.

"I don't know," said Sunny. "There's so much I don't understand about — about Far. And Julia."

"I know. That's the journey we've begun, but we won't get there all at once. Think baby steps."

"Baby steps," Sunny repeated. Near the end of the session, she told the therapist, "There's one thing I'm confused about. You said I should confront things. But if I ignore Ross when he baits me, isn't that more like retreating?"

Dr. Lee pressed her hands together. "Great question. You need to confront the unresolved issues in your life, for sure. But don't waste your psychic energy getting into a verbal clash with every jerk who offends you with—what did you call it?—dick comments. The challenge is to know when to confront . . . and when not to."

The next day, Sunny applied this strategy for the first time. She was watching a movie on TV when Ross came in during a scene of two women kissing.

"Does that turn you on?" he asked Sunny.

"No, but I'm enjoying the film," she said neutrally.

"I thought maybe you—ya know, batted for the other team."

"I don't know why you'd think that." Sunny kept her voice calm and her eyes fixed on the screen. *Don't take it personally.*

"Well, you've never been married and you're, like, almost fifty?" Ross's tone sharpened, perhaps from annoyance that he'd failed to provoke her.

Ross knew she was much younger than that, but she just shrugged and said, "Whatever." The quick sketch she drew after this encounter showed a blasé Sunny with shoulders raised in a shrug. A pity she hadn't known this trick while she was living with Gwendolyn.

But when she and Dr. Lee discussed Sunny's childhood recollections of Far, those sketches came out dark, scary. It would be a long journey indeed.

•　　•　　•

After three tough art school rejections, Sunny received two simultaneous acceptances. She resisted the temptation to text Charlie to give him the news and ask his opinion on the schools. She chose the one that would allow her to nurture her illustration talent along with the more practical computer skills needed to compete.

Though she should've been flying high, her emotions were a little flat. That happened now and then with the antidepressant her LA doctor had prescribed in a telehealth appointment back in July. He'd also advised her to steer clear of cannabis while on the meds, so that was an adjustment as well.

This same week brought another important piece of news. A DNA test report on Sunny and Julia confirmed they were not full sisters. Ironically, this loosening of their genetic ties only strengthened the emotional bond between them. Closer than ever, the half-sisters had long conversations now, especially when Ross was at work or out with his drinking buddies.

"You were always Mother's favorite," said Julia. "Maybe because you were her love child."

"I think she was compensating for Far's coldness toward me," said Sunny. "And we *were* kindred spirits. She was always lost in thought about whatever book she was reading or teaching. She'd get totally absorbed, like me with my art."

"Far hated that," said Julia. "He'd crack mean jokes at her expense, sometimes at yours. I'm sorry to say I used to humor him. I—I'm so ashamed."

"It felt like the family was split into two teams, you and Far versus Mother and me. But our team always lost," said Sunny, bitter. "We were the ones who were abused. You weren't." Sunny noticed Ross wasn't abusive to Julia either, only to her. In that way, he reminded her of the man who raised her. "I thought after Far died, Mother and I would be happier. But then she got sick." Sunny opened up about the financial difficulties she'd faced because of Lilly's dementia, and the long stretch of homelessness after she'd died.

"All our phone calls," Julia said. "Why did you keep this a secret? I had no idea you were in such awful straits back then. I could've helped. I *would've* helped."

"I was too ashamed. I felt like it confirmed what Far believed – that I was the loser, the daughter who screwed up."

Though Sunny had always been the fragile one, the emotional sister, this time it was Julia who wept.

•　　•　　•

Sunny turned down an invitation to Julia's book club meeting. "I haven't read the book," she said to her sister. "And besides, I need to study the school catalog and decide on my classes." Ross was going to a poker game, so the house would be quiet.

Around nine-thirty, Sunny took an ice cream break. As she rinsed her bowl in the sink, a noise startled her so badly she fumbled the spray nozzle, drenching the front of her thin t-shirt with hot water. It was Ross. He had crashed into the kitchen, slammed the door shut, and literally fallen into a chair.

"Jesus, Ross, you scared me. I didn't hear your car."

"Uber. The guys made me Uber back to the housh," said Ross, slurring, beyond drunk. His eyes traveled downward from Sunny's face and he roared with laughter. "Will you check out that nipple action?" he said. "I didn't even know if there was anything going on with that flat chest of yours."

She looked down, horror-stricken, to see her erect nipples straining against the soaked fabric of her shirt. Ross stumbled over to her. "Let me help you dry off," he said, reaching out his hands and rubbing them against her breasts.

She backed away. "What the hell, Ross? I don't believe this."

"Hey, I got a great idea. You wanna cop a feel in exchange? Just be my guesht." He pointed at his crotch. "Call it tit for tat. Or tit for *cock,* more like." He laughed louder at this last remark, which definitely qualified as a dick comment.

"I got a great idea too," said Sunny. "Never touch me again." She shoved him so hard he fell back on the floor, landing on his tailbone and cursing from the pain. She turned away – confronting and retreating all at once – and walked straight into Julia.

It was time to move on.

•   •   •

"Where will you go?" her sister asked the next morning as she helped Sunny carry her bags to the Toyota.

"Back to LA. But not where I used to live. The South Bay isn't a great area for a single woman. I'm thinking Venice or Culver City."

"Where will you stay when you get there?"

Good question. "I'll get by. I always do."

Julia thrust an envelope into her hand. "This will help." Sunny opened it and gaped at the check inside. It was an enormous amount of money, nearly twice the sum Henry had once tried to win her favor with. Bribe her with, more like. Which made her wonder . . .

"Julia. Are you, like, paying me off?" She thought of her sister's expression last night as she took in the scene before them, Ross on the floor in pain, Sunny with a look of disgust on her face.

"I'm paying you *back,*" said her sister. "All that time you spent dealing with Mother, all that money for her caregivers . . . I owe you big time for that."

"But how do you even have this kind of money to give me? Ross will be furious."

"Ross doesn't know about it. When Far became ill," Julia said, "he established an investment account in my name and funded it generously. He fed me a load of crap about how he wanted me to have this money because I was his special girl, his *only* girl. I bought into it at the time, but now I see the malicious intent behind it. He didn't want you or Mother to get your hands on the money."

"Because I wasn't his – and she wasn't either, in her heart," said Sunny.

"But I was."

"His special girl," Sunny echoed. "In all these years, you never spent the inheritance?"

"Sure, I spent quite a bit. But the money was well invested, so the account grew. At this point it's roughly equal to the original amount, and I'm giving you half. Which is rightly yours," Julia said.

•   •   •

The sketch Sunny drew for Dr. Lee this week was more detailed. It showed Sunny in the driver's seat of her Corolla – the car packed with luggage and art supplies, Sunny smiling triumphantly at the wheel. Next to the car was a caricature of Ross on the ground, leaning back awkwardly on his tailbone . . . hands gripping his crotch, features contorted in a pained grimace.

Next to Ross, a road sign. *Los Angeles – 370 miles.*

CHAPTER 33

Charlie's new novel, *Unexpected Guests,* was less than half the length of his previous books, drafted in a fraction of the time. Kathleen was excited about it and wanted to send the manuscript to Scranton right away. Charlie was uncertain.

"I've never submitted an early draft before," he told Margaret. "I'm not sure it's ready yet. And if Scranton turns me down this time, it will be exponentially worse than the first rejection. There may not be a path forward."

"But Charlie, Kathleen's right – the book is wonderful."

He felt buoyed by the conviction in Margaret's tone, the enthusiasm that lit up her face. She'd given him valuable feedback and pitch-perfect line edits. It astounded him how well her skills as a technical editor translated to this radically different genre. He respected her instincts about character nuance too. With her help, he'd made important improvements to Madeleine, the protagonist loosely based on Margaret herself. "Okay – you've convinced me," he said. "I'll tell Kathleen to send Debra the manuscript."

Margaret clasped her hands and flashed an encouraging smile. "Great. While you're doing that, I need to catch up on some work."

Emerging from her office an hour later, Margaret looked serious, distracted even. "Anything wrong?" Charlie asked.

"I've had an email from Sam."

Why was Sam contacting Margaret, Charlie wondered? He knew relations with her mother were tense. During the three months since Gwendolyn had left, Margaret checked in dutifully once a week, usually by text, to make sure all was well. In August, they'd sent flowers and a card for her eightieth birthday. But he could see the interactions between mother and daughter remained cool and impersonal.

"Yes. He wanted me — wanted *us* – to know that Mum's been struggling with some 'issues' since she left California."

"Issues? Like a health problem?"

"I'm not sure what else it could be." Margaret looked at her phone. "I'll read you the rest of the email. 'No need to panic, but it would be helpful if we could meet in person to share information and end the long period of strained avoidance.' It doesn't sound like she's deathly ill, at least," she said, looking more hopeful. "I need to get to New York, Charlie."

"I'll come too," he said at once.

He talked through the details with her. They'd travel in a week to ten days, depending on when they could meet with their respective publishers, who were both in Manhattan. Margaret was due for an in-person meeting with Robert, she told him; and who knew, maybe Debra would be finished reading by then. This wasn't *War and Peace,* after all.

Margaret positioned the visit to Gwendolyn solely as a business trip. They both knew this explanation would sit better with her mother than an emergency house call.

•   •   •

Gwendolyn thought Margy and Charlie both looked fidgety when they first arrived at Parkside Gardens, as though they were awaiting a dental extraction and wanted to get it over with. Margy had called last week to say they had business in New

York – would it be convenient for them to come for cocktails, say around five-thirty? They had another dinner engagement that night, but Margy suggested lunch the following day. It was the first time Gwendolyn had spoken with her daughter since California. How fortunate work had brought Margy here at a time when she most needed her . . . as much as she hated to admit it.

Sam broke the ice by suggesting a tour of the condo. "It's spectacular," said Margy after viewing the spacious living area, Carrara marble kitchen, lavish bedroom suite, and den. "To be honest, I thought the apartments in senior housing were minuscule."

Gwendolyn rolled her eyes. "*Senior housing* sounds like some gloomy subsidized project in the Bronx. Parkside Gardens is one of the best residential buildings in Manhattan."

"There are assisted living units in one wing of the building, and they're smaller," said Sam. "Perhaps you were thinking of those."

"I guess I was," Margy said.

"So this is an independent living community?" asked Charlie.

"Of course," said Gwendolyn. "It's not as though Sam and I need help with toileting. At least not yet." She shot Sam a meaningful glance, but he looked away.

They took seats in the living room on the super-comfy sofas. Gwendolyn leaned back into the silky olive-green, gold-threaded fabric and plush accent pillows. Sam went to the kitchen, returning with an open bottle of red wine on a silver tray with four stemmed glasses.

"No martini for you?" Margy asked Gwendolyn.

"No, I—I've switched to pinot noir," she said. "So much more appropriate for the cooler weather."

"Charlie, tell us what's happening with your writing," said Sam. He poured wine into all four glasses but gave Gwendolyn a lesser amount. *This is my future*, she thought, looking glumly at the stingy pour.

Charlie nodded. "My agent and I met with the marketing team today for *Bernie and the Weather Wand*."

"It's launching before the holidays," said Margy proudly, "and the publisher plans to do a lot of promotion. Charlie's agent thinks it could be a top seller in its category."

"How exciting." Gwendolyn applauded with fluttery little claps. "And to think we were in on the first reading ever."

"And I had a good meeting with my editor and agent today on my new novel," Charlie added.

"Am I in it?" Gwendolyn batted her eyelashes.

Charlie laughed. "Do you want to be?"

She considered the question. "Only if I get approval rights."

"Then I'm afraid not," said Charlie. They laughed.

"Margaret, how is your job at the magazine?" asked Sam. "Your mother has often talked about how hard you work."

"It's going better. I hired a new editor who's nearly up to speed. I'm finally getting my life back," said Margy. "And I don't feel like I'm neglecting Charlie anymore."

He gave her an affectionate kiss on the cheek. "To the contrary. She's taking excellent care of me." Margy rubbed Charlie's arm and leaned her head on his shoulder. Whatever problems they'd had during Gwendolyn's stay seemed to have been resolved. She hadn't seen them so happy since — well, *ever*, come to think of it.

"What's up with you two?" Gwendolyn asked.

"I don't know what you mean, Mum." Surely Margy was just being coy. But she'd called her "Mum" for the first time in God knows how long. Yes, something was going on for sure. Those two were acting much too lovey-dovey.

Charlie said, "We're getting married."

Gwendolyn and Sam clapped their hands at the same time and made joyful exclamations.

"How long have you known?" Sam asked, smiling broadly.

"Charlie proposed in July, right after he got back from the cabin," said Margy. "But we haven't told anyone till now."

"Well, that is wonderful." Sam's smile faded. "Perhaps you should know I proposed to Gwendolyn as well."

Margy's eyes widened. "That's fantastic."

"A double wedding, maybe?" said Charlie with a wink.

"I'm afraid not," said Sam. "She turned me down."

Gwendolyn hadn't meant to introduce the subject of her diagnosis in this manner – but really, what difference did it make? There was no good way to deliver bad news.

"Why don't you want to get married, Mum? If you're worried about combining families at this stage in life, prenups are the perfect way to—"

"It's not that." Gwendolyn took a healthy sip of wine, smoothed down her skirt, and assumed an erect posture on the sofa. "I have Alzheimer's."

Sam looked at her and turned quickly to Margy and Charlie. "She doesn't. Gwendolyn, we don't know that."

Margy's mouth hung open in surprise. "What's going on?"

"Sam took me to a doctor who ran some tests."

"He diagnosed your mother with mild cognitive impairment. MCI—" said Sam.

"Which is usually a precursor to Alzheimer's Disease," Gwendolyn said.

"Not usually. Sometimes," Sam corrected her. "It can lead to other dementias too. And sometimes it doesn't lead to anything at all. The patient can remain stable indefinitely."

"*The patient*. That's what I've been reduced to," said Gwendolyn with a signature groan. Margy hurried to her side and grasped her hand. "Is all this drama necessary, Margy? I'm not on my deathbed."

"I know, but I'm confused. How did you conclude that you might or might not have Alzheimer's? If you call that a conclusion."

"I told you, Sam took me to a doctor. We were concerned about some of my actions and agreed it would be a useful precaution."

"What actions?" her daughter asked.

"Darling, Sam convinced me you needed to know about this, but I'm in no mood to go through a tedious recounting of the details. The whole thing is a crashing bore. But if it's any comfort to you, I haven't been getting lost in my own home or stashing my purse in the freezer."

"I'm sure you haven't," said Margy. "But what—"

Gwendolyn cut her off in a stern voice. "Enough. I mean it. Also, this news stays right here, inside this apartment. Only the four of us need to know."

Margy withdrew her hand and nodded silently. "All right. But this is the reason you're not getting married?"

"I want to take care of your mother," Sam said. "I know I can help her stay on an even keel. We can mitigate the problem together and possibly delay the onset of . . . whatever is coming." He cast Gwendolyn an imploring glance. "You know we can."

"And you know my decision." She turned to the others. "Sam took care of his wife after her cancer diagnosis. I don't want him to become a two-time caregiver. Given the short while we've known each other, this shouldn't be his cross to bear."

Sam gave a helpless shrug. "I'm not giving up." Damn the man, he was every bit as stubborn as she was.

"What happens next?" Charlie asked.

"The doctor wants to see Gwendolyn in three months. At that point he'll do another assessment and likely order more tests. A brain scan, for one."

Gwendolyn scowled. "Nobody is going to look inside my brain. What's the point? It's not as though they can cure whatever this is. Let's get back to a cheerier subject – the wedding. Have you set a date?"

"No, but sometime next April," said Charlie.

"You know, darlings, the popular wedding venues book months ahead, sometimes years," Gwendolyn said, donning her event planner hat.

"We've decided on a home wedding," Margaret said.

Gwendolyn nodded. "That's nice too. Large or small? Cocktail fare or full dinner service?"

Margaret squirmed a little in her seat. "I don't know. We haven't gotten that far." It was clear to Gwendolyn, she and Sam had upstaged Charlie and Margy's news with their own. Though she'd hoped to turn the conversation back to the wedding, she could see that she'd knocked the wind right out of their spinnaker.

When they got up to leave, Margy handed Sam a piece of notepaper. "We made a lunch reservation for twelve-thirty tomorrow at Bar Boulud over by Lincoln Center. Here's the information. Mum used to love the Café Boulud when she lived on the East Side, and this is the same restaurant group."

Gwendolyn clucked at her daughter. "Honestly, Margy, I'd appreciate it if you wouldn't talk about me as though I were in a different room. I'm not that out of it yet." Margy mouthed "sorry" and gave her a stricken look. Yes, Gwendolyn was right to keep her diagnosis under wraps. This was exactly the sort of reaction she wanted to avoid.

•   •   •

When Charlie woke during the night, he experienced that *"Where am I?"* confusion that made him wonder, if only for a split second, whether he was channeling Gwendolyn. A glow emanated from the far corner of the dark room and then he remembered. They were in their Upper West Side hotel, and

Margaret sat at the desk hunched over her laptop. He must've fallen asleep reading in bed, without telling Margaret about the meeting with Scranton. It was nearly three a.m.

He walked across the room, kissed the top of her head, and gently kneaded her shoulders. "Have you slept at all?"

She shook her head. "I've been doing some research."

"On mild cognitive impairment?"

"That, and early stage Alzheimer's." When she looked up, he could see the dark smudges of sleep deprivation beneath her eyes. "Charlie, I'm the worst person in the world."

"Of course you're not. Don't even think it, my love."

She shook her head again, more fiercely. "Listen to this." She picked up a hotel memo pad covered with scribbled notes. "They say someone with Mum's diagnosis can exhibit one or more of these symptoms: *personality changes, mood swings, irritability and aggression, losing one's way, showing poor judgment, saying or doing inappropriate things, engaging with strangers, losing the thread of conversations, books or movies . . .*"

Charlie thought back to his "book club" with Gwendolyn, when he suspected she was only pretending she'd read his novels. It hadn't occurred to him that a cognitive issue might be the culprit. He'd thought this was simply Gwendolyn being her usual sneaky self.

"I've been such a bitch," said Margaret. "Every time she was rude or mean-spirited or just plain wacky, I lectured her for acting selfish and inconsiderate. I thought she was just – I don't know – a rebel without a cause. I should've known something else was going on."

He sighed. "I didn't see it either."

"A couple of years ago, I went to visit an old neighbor of mine, Nancy Ostrowski. I recognized almost immediately that she was having cognitive problems. But my own mother lived with us for months, Charlie, and I was blind to it. Did I need someone to post her picture next to the symptom list?"

"Look, you told me she's always been difficult and self-absorbed. Eccentric, even. Her intelligence and verbal skills are intact, so anyone could miss the warning signs. Even the people closest to her."

"Maybe so. But I still feel like a total shit." She closed the laptop. "Do you think Mum has any idea that Sam engineered our trip to New York?"

"I doubt it," said Charlie.

"Good."

"What's your schedule tomorrow?" he asked, then corrected himself. "I guess I should say *today*."

"Hopefully, I can catch up on sleep in the morning before lunch with Mum and Sam. I don't have to go to the office until mid-afternoon."

"Come to bed, love. It's so late."

"I will, but Charlie – first tell me what happened at Scranton. You only said it was a good meeting."

How best to explain this? He'd start on a positive note. "They want to publish *Guests*."

Margaret's eyes widened. "That's terrific. Why didn't you tell Sam and my mother?"

"The situation is—complicated."

"I don't understand."

"They made me an offer, but not for the premier Scranton division that publishes all the blockbusters," said Charlie. "They launched a boutique imprint a couple of years ago for 'quieter' books with family and domestic themes. That's where my book will go. Kathleen tried to spin it as something new and exciting, but I could see what was happening."

Margaret tilted her head in a questioning posture.

"I'm like last year's star pitcher who can't get the ball over the plate any longer. They're sending me back to the minor leagues."

"I can't believe—"

"Okay, I exaggerate. But it's still a demotion."

She appeared to be studying his face as she asked, "How —how do you feel about that?"

He paused. "Relieved, Margaret. And a little surprised at my relief." Placing his hands on her shoulders, he stared into her eyes. "I told you about all the pressure weighing me down from chasing that unrealistic goal? Well, once I got over my initial disappointment today, I realized the pressure's gone. It feels . . . liberating. Like I'm finally free to enjoy my life with you, while I continue to write – and maybe do other things too, like working with young writers." He squeezed her shoulders. "You nailed it – moving the goalpost wasn't the solution, I had to change from within. Today was a kind of attitude test. And I think I passed." He studied Margaret, trying to gage her reaction. "Are you disappointed about the book?"

Margaret wrapped her arms around his neck. "Of course not. Charlie, I am so proud of you." Then she kissed him so deeply that his limbs tingled with a pleasurable weakness. He reminded himself of a swooning maiden in some cheeseball time travel romance. This image made him laugh out loud.

"My kiss was laughable?" Margaret asked, teasing.

"Only because you make me so happy."

"Even when we're dealing with all this heavy crap?"

"Especially when we're dealing with all this heavy crap."

She sighed. "We need to meet with Sam and Mum about her healthcare directive." Last night, as Sam showed them out of Parkside Gardens, he told them Gwendolyn had signed a directive permitting him to communicate with her doctors. Not wanting to usurp Margaret's authority as next of kin, he suggested meeting to review how this would work. "I want to coordinate with them on decisions. Mum won't like it, but—"

"Shhh. Not now, love." It was his turn to kiss her, and passionately. "You need to get some sleep." He kissed her again. "But maybe not quite yet." With that, he led her back to bed.

CHAPTER 34

This was the crazy thing. Since Gwendolyn had received her diagnosis – or her *pre*-diagnosis as she preferred to call it, given its preliminary nature – she actually felt better in some ways. It was an enormous relief to have the unpredictable goings-on of the last six months explained, and to know her perverse behavior hadn't been intentional. And though the doctor couldn't yet give her condition a label, she preferred his assessment to Margy's "running amok."

With Sam by her side, directing their social life and overseeing her appointments, Gwendolyn wasn't as confused or uncertain as she'd been in California. Oh, that unwelcome fog still descended some days; and now that she recognized it as a possible sign of dementia, it frightened her all the more when it happened. She tried to live in the moment, to embrace the good things about her life.

It was a cloudy and dark afternoon, and as she glanced out the window at the view of Central Park, giant raindrops splattered across the glass and blurred her view. Brown, rust, and yellow leaves swirled in the blustery air and drifted to the sidewalk. It was only November and she already missed the LA weather.

She picked up her phone and scrolled through her photos of California. The pictures of her family, the Zumba group, and other activities were interspersed with images she'd snapped to keep herself from growing disoriented. Photos of the rental car to remind her where she'd parked. Photos of street signs to keep her from losing her way on a walk. Photos of menus to document restaurants she'd visited. Maybe she'd been more tuned into the cognitive problem than she'd realized.

She swiped through pictures of one of the group's Sunday dinners and paused at an image of Sunny passing a cheese plate, her straight blond hair hanging in a shimmering curtain. Gwendolyn flushed with guilt. Her cruelty to Sunny may have been out of her control, but that still didn't excuse it. Time to mend fences with the girl.

How did people generally begin an apology? With a pleasantry? The weather was a popular topic. Settling at the computer desk in the den, Gwendolyn pecked on the keyboard. It took minutes just to write the words, *Dear Sunny.* Lately she struggled with writing – it was another cognitive thing the doctor had talked about. "Sam, can you help me?" she called.

When he joined her in the den, she proposed a collaboration. She would express her thoughts, and Sam would put them into writing. "I'd like to begin by saying it's a gloomy autumn day in New York, but maybe she's enjoying better conditions wherever she may be."

"Are you sure that's how you want to start?" asked Sam, taking a seat at the computer.

Gwendolyn pondered this. "Maybe not. It sounds rather shallow, doesn't it?" He nodded.

"What if I begin by complimenting her talent? *'I went to an art exhibit yesterday and one of the sketches reminded me of yours. I hope you've been nurturing your gift . . . '* Or something like that."

Sam began typing, but she immediately said, "That's no good either. It sounds like I'm kissing up to her." Framing a simple apology was more difficult than she'd expected. No wonder Charlie had to retreat to a dusty little cabin to bang out a few chapters. It was a miracle anyone managed to write anything at all.

"It needs to come from the heart," said Sam.

"You're right, darling." This time, she let the ideas flow without straining to be clever. Sam typed a sentence or two at a time and read it back. This continued until they finished the draft. After they'd smoothed over the rough spots, Gwendolyn asked Sam to read it again, rocking back and forth on her heels as he did so. She pictured Sunny reading the message and hoped the words would resonate, that the girl would know she meant them.

> *Dear Sunny,*
>
> *I apologize for the way I treated you at Charlie and Margy's. I'm referring not only to the appalling Fourth of July party, but my general behavior toward you while we were both living there. It was unfair as well as unkind.*
>
> *I can't even offer a good explanation. I will only say that I was unhappy and frustrated at the time – at being marooned three thousand miles from home, at being laid up by a foolish and avoidable accident, and at feeling forever left out and put-upon, even though everyone was trying their hardest to indulge me. Somehow I used you — inexcusably — as a scapegoat.*
>
> *Wherever you are now, I hope you're staying well and keeping up with your art.*
>
> *With sincere regret and best wishes,*
> *Gwendolyn Meyer*

Sam smiled. "Well done."

She leaned down to give him a kiss. "Are you sure it isn't too . . . too . . ."

"It's perfect. Let's send it before you change your mind." He clicked on the mouse and then stood.

"Darling, do you have a few more minutes?" she asked.

"Of course." Sam had cut back on his volunteer commitments to be more available to her, sweet man. "What can I help you with?"

"Before the day is out, I have more apologies to send."

•   •   •

Sunny squinted against the sunlight streaming through the windows, loving how bright and cheery her new apartment was, even in late November. A third-floor walkup in Culver City, the cozy place radiated Victorian charm, with ornate ceilings, warm wood paneling, and cute little nooks and crannies that Sunny wanted to fill with antique teddy bears and dolls. But she knew she shouldn't squander her inheritance on anything so frivolous.

Scooping up her car keys and grabbing a sweater, Sunny went through her mental to-do list as she hurried down the two long flights of stairs. Dr. Lee at eleven – their first in-person session. Work at the agency all afternoon. Online classes in the evening. She hoped she had something in the freezer to heat for dinner.

As she drove through downtown Culver City en route to the 405 freeway, she thought about how smart she'd been to move to this town with its hip, young vibe. Through the placement office at her art school, she'd landed a part-time job at a boutique advertising agency, miraculously located just three miles from her apartment. Her demanding work-study schedule left her with little free time, but she had made friends at the job, and her days were productive and purposeful.

•   •   •

"I can't believe I've been back in LA for two months and this is the first time I've come here." Sunny looked around her therapist's small South Bay office, in a medical building with a distant view of the Palos Verdes Peninsula rising to the south. "I never asked if it was okay to keep meeting on Zoom."

"How does that old saying go? 'It's easier to ask for forgiveness than permission.'" Dr. Lee smiled. "It's fine, Sunny. I realize it would take you at least half an hour each way to commute down here. You're a busy lady, and Zoom is very efficient."

"Thanks," said Sunny. "It is a long drive, but I wanted to see your office . . . and visit my old stomping grounds." This was Sunny's first time in the area since the morning last July when she'd vacated the Village Canyon Day Spa for good. It seemed like a hundred years ago.

"How does it feel to be back?"

"Weird. Sad, I guess. Margaret, Charlie, that whole crowd – my life revolved around them a few months ago. Now I don't know if I'll ever see them again. I've been thinking about it a lot since – *this*." Sunny extracted a piece of paper from her purse, unfolded it, and handed it to Dr. Lee. "Gwendolyn emailed me this. I was shocked. She's not the type to apologize. Though I admit it sounds sincere."

Dr. Lee read the letter silently. "Yes, it does. Did you respond?"

Sunny shook her head. "Here's the thing. I think I've put that episode of my life behind me – but if I write to forgive Gwendolyn, I'll feel like I'm re-engaging with her. Frankly, I'd rather steer clear of the woman. So I'll probably do nothing. Am I being a coward?"

"Doing nothing doesn't make you cowardly or indecisive. Sometimes, it's a choice."

Okay, then. She'd chosen.

"You mentioned Charlie – how do you feel about the possibility you'll never see him again.?"

Sunny winced. "I—I try not to think about him. Luckily, I'm so busy between school and work that I don't have time to dwell on it. My life is going pretty well right now. Oh, and you'll be glad to hear I've taken steps to find my biological father."

Ever since Sunny had learned she and Julia were half-sisters, Dr. Lee had encouraged her to look for her birth father. Unfortunately, with everything going on in her life since leaving Phoenix, that activity had taken a back seat. But Sunny finally made time to subscribe to two of the leading ancestry websites and post on their message boards. She explained this to Dr. Lee. "If I can locate my real father, I feel it will open a door, you know? Like it will unlock the secrets that have troubled me for so long."

"Secrets about Far?"

"About my mother, more like," said Sunny. "I blame Far for everything because he was the cruel one, but she's the real mystery. How could she stay with him all those years? Who was the man she really loved? Why didn't she try to protect me?" Sunny sighed. "But maybe I'll never get to open that door. Maybe there *is* no door."

"If not, over time you'll adjust to that, and you'll develop coping strategies. But let's not go there yet. You've just started searching in earnest." Dr. Lee was right. For now, there was nothing to do but wait.

CHAPTER 35

Dear Sunny E.,

I just received my ancestry report, and it looks like you and I share almost 25 percent of our DNA. I have no idea how that's possible but thought I'd reach out to you since we seem to be closely related.

Paul G.

It was the most exciting news Sunny had heard in a long while, but her emotions were flatlining again. The antidepressant. She reread what Paul G. had posted on the ancestry website, eager to show it to Dr. Lee. She'd been hoping for this lead since September of last year, and she couldn't believe it was already March . . . six months! She looked at Paul's profile picture a hundred times. There was something familiar about his nose and his smile and the shape of his head. But the real telltale sign – the big green eyes. Sunny kept her response ambiguous.

Sharing a quarter of our DNA could mean I'm your aunt, or your niece, or your half-sister. Sunny

Though she was pretty darned sure which one it was, Sunny didn't want to play all her cards at once. For two anxious days, she heard nothing more from Paul and had to fight off the urge to call Dr. Lee in a panic. Paul finally sent another message. They traded cell numbers and agreed to speak late the next day.

When the time approached, Sunny practiced her yoga breathing in the living room. She sat in shadows, grateful for the darkness that would allow her to focus on the conversation without distractions.

Paul did most of the talking at first, and Sunny was content to listen. She learned that he'd lived in northern California since he was a young boy and taught mathematics at UC Santa Cruz. He played three instruments, but only as a hobby. He was six months younger than Sunny and had a partner named Cameron, who convinced him to do the DNA test "out of curiosity."

Sunny warmed to Paul's voice, which sounded clear, crisp, and intelligent over the phone. A math professor – of course he was intelligent.

When Paul was three, his parents divorced, and he and his mother moved to the Bay Area from Los Angeles. Sunny mentioned she was also from LA, but she grew up in the Valley while Paul spent his early childhood in Brentwood. "Where do you live now?" he asked.

"Culver City." She described her apartment, her job, her studies. "Tell me more about your parents," she said.

"My mom was the star of the family. She was a violinist with the LA Phil, a prodigy, really – the youngest string player in the orchestra. Dad was a high school teacher."

Sunny's pulse quickened. "What did he teach?"

"Art."

She felt a grin split her face. This was too good to be true. "No kidding. At what school?" She tried to sound casual.

"Madison High."

This time her emotions kicked in. She jumped out of the chair and bonked her head on the floor lamp, not seeing it in the dusky light. Rubbing the side of her head, she said, "My mother taught English at Madison."

A pause. "So, they were both . . . your mom . . . my dad . . . " Paul stammered. The silence that followed was so gaping, Sunny feared he'd hung up on her.

"Paul?"

"I'm here."

"I'm pretty sure you and I have the same father," she said.

Another silence. "I'm sorry. I need time to process this."

This time he hung up for real, and Sunny collapsed in the chair, disappointment overtaking her. Then she remembered how she'd reacted when Julia disclosed the news about her parentage – the feelings of shock, then denial, then betrayal. This couldn't be easy for Paul. She must give him time.

The next night he called again. "What are the chances the test results are wrong?"

Sunny had done her homework. "Less than one in a thousand."

Bit by bit, they pieced it together. Paul's mother and father never got along – he'd learned this from both parents, being too young at the time to understand their relationship. "I think they had me to try and save the marriage. The classic mistake," he said.

She did the math. Paul's mom must've gotten pregnant a few months before Sunny's birth. Is that when the affair ended? Did Paul's dad know he also fathered Sunny, or did Mother keep the secret even from her lover? She wouldn't share these musings with Paul. Not yet. She confined herself to Julia's story of their parents' estrangement, the surprise pregnancy, and the later discovery of Mother's affair with an unnamed man from the high school.

Another interesting fact Sunny learned from Paul was that her birth father was almost ten years younger than Mother. And the most important news of all – he was still alive.

In the days that followed, Sunny struggled to rein in her impatience. She couldn't wait to meet her father and brother, to probe the hundred unanswered questions with them. At least Paul had agreed to talk on FaceTime now. His hair looked darker on the video calls, but the emerald eyes matched hers. He remained hesitant. "Look, I'm still reeling from this news, and I'm trying to decide the best way to broach it with Dad. I need to do this in person, and it may be a few weeks before I have time to drive down and see him."

Drive *down*? Perhaps her father was still in Southern California, maybe right here in LA. But Paul wouldn't reveal where he lived or much else about him. "I want to respect his privacy until I talk to him."

"I get that," she said, "but can you tell me if he's in good health?"

A pause. "I guess I can since the answer is yes. Dad's always been a pretty healthy guy – physically and mentally." Sunny recalled the terrible gene Julia once speculated about. It had weighed on her ever since. Now Sunny's shoulders seemed to lighten, as if that onerous weight had lifted with Paul's brief reply.

•   •   •

"I'm so excited to meet my half-brother – and my father, of course. Maybe I'll get to meet other relatives too. I wonder if we'll all gather for the holidays." Sunny chattered enthusiastically to her therapist during their weekly session, this time on Zoom.

"Whoa, let's slow down a little." Dr. Lee raised her hand. "This is a road filled with potential landmines. We should take things cautiously, one step at a time, the same way we've been uncovering your memories of Far."

Sunny knew she was right. "Gotcha. I need to take baby steps in approaching my new family."

"Baby steps. Good."

At the following week's in-person session, after two more FaceTime chats with Paul, she told the therapist, "I figured out I've been building a fantasy about my new family – same way I fantasized about Charlie."

"How is it similar?"

"Charlie was kind, thoughtful, and encouraging about my work. Everything I always wanted in a father but never got. Maybe that's why I dreamed of a relationship with him."

"That's an important discovery. What about your biological father?"

"I'm imagining us going to museums together, talking about art, having this wonderful closeness. But in reality, he might not even accept me. Or we might not like each other. A lot could go wrong, and I'm trying to prepare for that. I don't want to set myself up for disappointment like I did with the book illustrations."

Dr. Lee nodded. "Sounds like you're in a good place about this."

"I've been feeling more in control, and I'm wondering about going off the antidepressant."

"We'd need to talk to your family care physician first."

"But what do *you* think of the idea?" asked Sunny.

"Well, you're dealing with some heavy issues right now. You might meet your birth father soon, and learn about your family history."

"So this might not be the best time to go off the meds?"

Dr. Lee nodded. "There's an adjustment period involved, and it's better not to go through that while you're confronting potentially traumatic news. You're doing very well, but I'd advise you to hold off a little while."

"A little while is okay, but I don't want to stay on this drug long term."

Dr. Lee dipped her chin in another nod. "By the way, Sunny, I noticed you haven't drawn me any sketches in some time."

Sunny reddened. "I know. With my crazy schedule, I haven't had time for art therapy."

"I suspected that was the reason. It's okay. We're making good progress without it."

After the appointment, Sunny made the short drive to Seaside Fitness to see Margaret for the first time since returning to LA. Though she was ready to reconnect with her friend, her stomach did somersaults when she walked in.

The club had opened a café and sandwich shop where Margaret suggested meeting. Located inside the main entrance, it was a small but airy space with white walls, a polished light wood floor, and large windows open to the sea breeze. The wall behind the coffee bar was painted a warm tomato red.

Margaret was already seated with a tall glass of iced coffee. She wore geometric print leggings with a gray top and looked like she'd just finished a workout. They hugged. By the time Sunny ordered tea and brought it back to the table, the fluttery feeling in her stomach was gone. Being with Margaret already felt familiar, comfortable.

"What happened to the free coffee in the lobby?" Sunny asked.

"Gone, along with the snack baskets. Oh, for the good old days," Margaret said.

Sunny rested both elbows on the table and leaned forward, chin propped on her hands. "I—I felt so relieved when you emailed me a couple of months ago. So much time had passed with no word from you, I was sure you wanted nothing to do with me."

"I thought the same thing about you," said Margaret. "But I was so worried, I had to contact you, no matter how you felt."

The two women had exchanged several emails since Margaret first reached out, and Sunny had written about her job and her studies.

"I'm glad we're back in touch." Sunny glanced around the café and the adjacent lobby. "Does Charlie still go to yoga classes here?" As comfortable as she felt with Margaret, she wasn't ready to face Charlie.

"Yes, but he has a Zoom with his agent today." Sunny almost said "Good" but nodded instead. "How's your sister?" Margaret asked.

"Julia's fine. I mean – we've always had our differences, but she's been making amends." She explained the unexpected windfall.

"That's amazing."

"She also feels bad about . . . about keeping some secrets from me since we were kids." She gave Margaret an abbreviated account of her mother's affair, the DNA testing, and her newfound half-brother.

"Wow, you've had a lot to deal with," said Margaret. "I can see why Julia wanted your forgiveness."

"Speaking of forgiveness, I got an email from Gwendolyn last fall. She sent me a heartfelt apology, very genuine. I'm afraid I never responded."

"Really," said Margaret. She started shredding her napkin into a little pile on the tabletop. "Sunny, when your mother first showed signs of dementia, what were the symptoms?"

"Forgetfulness, mostly. The dangerous kind, like leaving the stove burner on. Why?"

"It's just that my — it's nothing. I was asking on behalf of a friend."

Sunny looked at her. "It's not one size fits all, you know. Everyone is different."

"Yeah, I've heard that."

Margaret glanced at her watch, causing Sunny to say, "Sorry, I've been gabbing for the past hour. You've barely gotten a word in."

"Next time I'll do the gabbing. Right now I need to get home for a phone conference." As Margaret rose, she handed Sunny a shopping bag. When Sunny peeked inside, she felt herself flush. *I must resemble that tomato-colored wall.* Her old sketchbook.

"Have you looked through it?" she asked, thinking of the endless drawings of Charlie.

"Yes." Margaret's gaze was direct, but she didn't look confrontational.

"Are you—did you—" Sunny couldn't even form a sentence.

"Sunny, listen. It was a stressful time for all of us back then. We don't have to revisit the past unless you feel the need to talk about it. Do you?"

She let out a long exhale. "No. I've moved on too."

They hugged again. Then Sunny noticed something else in the bag, a fancy-looking envelope addressed to her. "What's this?"

Margaret grinned. "Open it when you get home."

•   •   •

After several agonizing days passed with no further news from Paul, he phoned her with the schedule. "I'm seeing my—sorry, *our*—father in three weeks. Saturday the sixteenth." The date sounded familiar. "I plan to spend the night at Dad's place." *Dad's place.* A house? Apartment? Senior living facility? Paul was still playing it close to the vest.

"Did you tell him why you're coming?" asked Sunny.

"I said we're overdue for a visit. But I gave him fair warning that I plan to revisit some ancient history. To get him thinking about things."

"That's exciting – and scary. Are you nervous about this, too?"

"Oh yeah. I don't know whether he'll even admit to having an affair. He might be defensive. If he chooses not to meet you, I can't force him."

As much as she'd tried to brace herself for this possibility, the idea seemed intolerable. "That would be really disappointing."

"I know. But whatever happens, *I* want to meet you soon, and I'll share as much information about the family as I can. I want us to be part of each other's lives." Paul's promise enveloped Sunny like a huge, warm hug. Her eyes got misty.

"I feel the same way, Paul. I'm glad we found each other."

"Me too. I'll call you as soon as Dad and I have our talk."

"The sixteenth."

"Yes."

After the call, Sunny looked at her cellphone. Glancing at the calendar entry for that date, she thought about the envelope from Margaret. How could she have forgotten?

CHAPTER 36

"Over here!" Gwendolyn waved an arm at Margy and Charlie to flag them down at the LAX baggage claim terminal. They threaded through the crowd to join her and Sam at the carousel.

After everyone hugged, Margy stepped back to look her up and down. "Mum, your hair."

"Yes, I finally let it go."

"I love it. The silver looks so close to your old color, I couldn't tell the difference on our Zoom calls."

Gwendolyn basked in the compliment. "My stylist thinks the natural hair color works better with my skin tone than the ash blonde." Charlie's hair looked a tad grayer these days as well, but she didn't mention that.

Sam pointed at a blue hard-shell bag that dwarfed every other piece of luggage in sight. "Charlie, can you manage that?" Charlie pulled the gargantuan suitcase off the belt, staggering a little under the weight.

"Are you planning another four-month visit?" Margy looked apprehensive.

Gwendolyn smiled. "After my last stay, I've learned it's best to come prepared. Anyway, I've got a wedding to go to, so I wanted to pack lots of nice things."

"Including sensible shoes, I hope."

Gwendolyn rolled her eyes. "Starting already, are we?"

Sam laughed as if to defuse the tension. "Stop it, you two. Let's get to the hotel. I can't wait to see the place."

On the drive to the waterfront hotel, Charlie commented on their choice of accommodations. "It's a great location, but this is an older hotel and it's small and unassuming," he said. "It doesn't have the bells and whistles you'll find at the resorts on the hill."

"That's okay with me – preferable, in fact," said Sam. "It looked perfect in the website photos."

"And it's only ten minutes from our house," Charlie said. "I feel bad that we aren't hosting you."

"I wish we could've put you up in the guesthouse, Mum, but it's become a staging area for the party planner and caterer," Margy added.

"Nonsense," Gwendolyn said. "You two are getting ready for your wedding. Don't worry about us."

"Besides," Sam chimed in, "it's more exciting being in a hotel. Perfect for a pair of geezers living in sin." He gave Gwendolyn a light smack on the behind. She adored it when he acted naughty like that.

•   •   •

Charlie and Margy returned to the hotel later as their dinner guests. The aroma of salt air filled Gwendolyn's nostrils as they took seats at their harborside table. A sea lion barked in the distance.

"You can't beat this location," said Sam, gesturing at the sailboats docked a stone's throw away. "Our room is cozy, but it's fantastic. I said to Gwendolyn, we're so close to the sea, I hope we won't be underwater at high tide."

Charlie told him, "Now that you bring it up, this hotel has flooded during storms. One winter the access road was submerged, and they had to airlift the guests out by helicopter."

"Good heavens, should I worry?" asked Gwendolyn.

"I think you'll be safe," said Charlie. "Your main weather risk is getting sunburned on your balcony."

Digging into the salad course of their leisurely *prix fixe* dinner, Margy said, "This will be our last chance to relax until after Saturday. I can't believe how much work a home wedding is."

"You're getting married at the house?" Gwendolyn asked. She saw them give her horrified looks before quickly rearranging their faces. "Oh, right, I knew that." After dinner, she presented a slender gift-wrapped package to the couple. "Something from Sam and me to commemorate your wedding."

"But Mum," said Margy, "I thought we agreed, no gifts. We specified that to all the wedding guests."

"I didn't say it was a gift, I said it was a — a — "

"Commemoration," said Sam.

"Thank you, dear," Gwendolyn said. "Charlie, you open it." Charlie unwrapped the white-and-gold paper and pulled out a large envelope. Inside was a letter, which he read to himself.

Gwendolyn thought Charlie might be tearing up, but he recovered and flashed a warm smile at her and Sam. "This is wonderful, absolutely wonderful." He passed the letter to Margy. "Gwendolyn and Sam have ordered five hundred copies of *Bernie and the Weather Wand*. They're donating them to children's hospitals and school libraries around the country."

"Yes, and a charitable organization specializing in this sort of thing will handle the distribution. This," Gwendolyn motioned to the letter, "is a thank you from the director of the charity."

"Mum, what an amazing thing to do." Margy leaned over and hugged Gwendolyn, planting a kiss on her cheek with uncharacteristic emotion.

"Sam deserves most of the credit. He found the charity."

"But you came up with the idea," Sam reminded her.

"This is very generous," said Charlie. "I want to donate my profits from this purchase back to the same organization."

Gwendolyn clapped her hands. "That's a lovely idea. I'm sure the director can work out the details with you."

Sam, who was fidgeting in his seat, said, "I'd like to stretch my legs."

"I'll give you a walking tour of the harbor," said Charlie. "Anyone else?"

Gwendolyn said, "I could use a cup of tea right now. I'll stay here and chat with Margy."

When the men had departed, her daughter leaned across the table and said, "How are you, Mum? No bullshit."

"How do I seem to you?"

"Good, I think," said Margy. "Maybe a little lapse here and there. But mostly the same as you were in New York six months ago."

"Excellent. I don't want people to know what's going on with me for as long as I can hide my condition."

"Your *condition?*"

"I know, I sound like a pregnant sixteen-year-old. But I mean it, Margy. My brain health is not a topic for public debate."

Margy looked perplexed by this. "What about your old friends? You've told them, haven't you?"

"I most certainly have not."

Her daughter was clearly unhappy to learn this. "Mum, this isn't the nineteen-fifties. People talk about these things now."

"Not the residents of Parkside Gardens."

"But so many people are going through the same thing. People who understand your feelings and want to help. There's a lot of support for what you're dealing with."

"I don't need support from strangers," said Gwendolyn. She gave Margy a harsh glare that said *back off* and hoped her daughter had received the message. "Sam is all the support I need. Can you believe we're both eighty now?" Like a dog shaking water off her coat, Gwendolyn shuddered as if trying to shed a few years. "He's smart and considerate and good at keeping me in line. I'm blessed to have him." She pulled a compact from her purse, regarded herself in the mirror, and applied a fresh coat of lipstick.

Margy nodded. "I agree."

Gwendolyn cleared her throat. "I've made a decision."

Margy sat up in her chair. "You're going to marry Sam?"

"Oh, no, dear. Really, what's the point? He's taking good care of me regardless, and he will for as long as he's able. And when he isn't – who knows? A marriage license at our age may sound romantic and sweet, but in time it will be an unnecessary complication." Noting Margy's silence, Gwendolyn assumed her daughter agreed.

"Then what's your decision?"

"When I see the doctor for my next appointment, I'm going to ask him to order those tests. You know, the brain scan and the . . . whatever. I've been putting it off, but it's time."

"And you decided this because . . . ?"

Gwendolyn sighed. "When I first learned about the cognitive trouble, I was in denial, Margy. I just wanted my life to go on as before. And perhaps it will, for a while longer. But I've been doing my research. There are marvelous resources in the city, very nice memory care facilities where they treat you like their own family. That's where I want to go when the time comes."

"*If* it comes to that," said Margy.

"You sound like Sam. Ever the optimist." Gwendolyn made a face.

"There are other options too. You've got Charlie and me."

Gwendolyn pressed her lips together, wondering how Charlie would feel about that. "Thank you, darling." She ran a brush through her shiny silver hair, snapped the compact shut, and stuffed everything back in her purse. "Yes, when I first got the MCI diagnosis, I was nowhere near ready to face the truth. Now . . . "she smiled sadly, "I think perhaps I'm ready."

•   •   •

"We've been over the seating plan a hundred times, love. If it's not perfect, too late to do anything about it. The guests will be here in a few hours." As soon as he spoke the words, Charlie realized this was the wrong thing to say. Margaret burst into tears.

"Remember the last time this group got together?" she said, releasing nervous little puffs of air. "There are too many explosive combinations. I don't want a repeat of the Independence Day party from hell." With fond amusement, Charlie listened as she recited the list of explosive combinations.

He took her hand. "Listen, my love, today is our wedding. Our friends and relatives are gathering to celebrate and share our happiness. Everyone will be on best behavior."

Margaret appeared to consider this. "Except, well, Petey is a dog, so he doesn't really get it, does he? I wonder if it was smart to make him the ring-bearer. Suppose he spots a squirrel and bolts when he's halfway down the aisle? Our rings could end up in a flowerbed, or at the bottom of the pool."

Here we go again. "He never misbehaves when he wears his therapy harness. Petey will be fine."

"And Benny as the flower boy . . . what if he gets stage fright and refuses to participate? You know how fearful he can be." Though Benny was still an anxious child, most of his fears didn't seem deep-rooted. He'd shed one phobia and move on to another, like a growing child advancing to the next clothing size. Climate change, though inescapable, was no longer hysteria-inducing, and the boy had forgotten his terror of loud noises.

Now it was cars. After seeing a wreck on the shoulder of the 110 freeway, Benny fretted over automotive disasters. He refused to ride on the interstate, citing personal preference rather than fear. When Michael had suggested that Charlie address the problem by writing another *Bernie* book, it seemed he was only half joking. No, Margaret wasn't wrong to worry about Benny ditching his ceremonial duties. But all Charlie said was, "I'm sure Heather will deal with it."

"Were we right to let Mum give a speech? You know she has trouble reading now."

"She's only planning to talk for a couple of minutes," he said.

"But Charlie, what if she bungles it? I've been urging her to be more open about her cognitive issues, but I don't want her to embarrass herself in front of fifty guests."

He knew how frustrating Margaret found her mother's stiff-upper-lip, go-it-alone stoicism. "She's a Brit through and through. Pointless trying to change her." Then he waited for Margaret to complain about her ex.

"And Henry . . . It will feel odd, having my first husband attend my second wedding."

"Henry is the father of your child and he's become a close friend. And it was so generous of him to supply the champagne for tonight."

"Generous? Hah." Margaret snorted. "He was buying himself a guaranteed spot on the guest list."

Charlie laughed. "Let's not worry about Henry. Let's not worry about *anything*." His voice sounded too cheery even to himself. "This is our day, and we should savor every moment." He gathered Margaret in his arms. As he tried to placate the nervous bride with a warm embrace, he looked over her head to the patio outside, where the wedding planner and her assistant were arranging the tables. He felt a raging tide of emotions inside him, a tide that swelled all the way to his throat and threatened to overwhelm him with its power. In truth, he was every bit as jittery as Margaret. Though fairly confident the guests wouldn't end up in a fistfight, he was sweating all the details and didn't want Margaret to know. Should they have eloped?

Then, he reminded himself for the umpteenth time that Margaret neither wanted nor expected him to be an unwavering tower of strength. "That assistant has been staring into her phone for the past hour," he said. "I'd better go make sure she's not screwing up the place cards."

Margaret pulled away and gazed into his eyes. "You're scared too, aren't you?"

"Out of my wits." And off he hurried.

•   •   •

Sunny nearly didn't go to the wedding.

When it was time to get ready, she pulled out the silk skirt and jacket that served as her go-to outfit for special occasions. The soft aqua color reminded her of Charlie's pool, conjuring up painful memories. Then she noticed the red dress, the gift from Henry that she wore when she broke up with him. That one certainly wouldn't do. She should've given it away long ago. Maybe her floral print with the low-cut gathered bust? But she saw this one through Gwendolyn's eyes and imagined her saying, "Sunny looks like a milkmaid in that dress."

Facing Gwendolyn was even scarier than a potential run-in with Charlie or Henry. She must be peeved with Sunny for failing to accept the olive branch after her contrite apology. The woman could be so vindictive . . . and so insightful at seeing into Sunny's heart.

I could solve everything by not going. But she knew that would be unfair to the bride and groom. Besides, this was a time to confront and not retreat. It had taken a professional to make Sunny realize how often she ran away from anything or anyone who made her uncomfortable. Her phone buzzed. *Paul.* She flung the milkmaid outfit on the bed and rushed to answer.

"Sunny, hi. I just finished talking to Dad."

"Is it like we thought?" Sunny's pulse quickened. "Did he acknowledge being my father?"

"At first he didn't say a word."

"Oh, shit." Her heart sank.

"No, no, that's the way Dad is. He asked if I had a picture."

She squeezed her eyes shut. "Then what happened?"

"I showed him your profile photo," said Paul. "He looked at it and still didn't speak. But he buried his face in his hands, and I could see him shaking."

"Oh my God. Then what?"

"He got up and went to his bedroom. I thought he didn't want to talk. But after a few minutes he came back out and handed me a picture of your mother."

"He still has a picture of her?" Sunny hadn't considered this possibility. She started to weep – not tears of sorrow, but of overpowering emotion.

"He agreed to meet you. Tonight."

Tonight. The temptation to ditch the wedding came back stronger this time. But it still wouldn't be right. "I've got that wedding." Sunny said, her voice tight with unhappiness. "Why not tomorrow?"

Something had come up at Paul's house and he had to rush back to Santa Cruz early tomorrow. "I'll be leaving Torrance first thing."

"Our father lives in Torrance? That's close to where my friends are getting married." Together they worked out a plan. Paul would pick up Sunny at Charlie's house at 8:45. That way, she'd only miss the final hour or so of the reception. He'd drive her to Dad's apartment for an introductory visit. Since their father was absorbing the news, it was hard to predict how things might go. Sunny shouldn't expect too much all at once. "Baby steps," she said.

In the end, she selected a floor-length slinky yellow-gold number that set off her blondness. After the extended call with her brother, she barely had time to pull her long hair into a tight ponytail and brush on a little mascara and peach lip gloss. She spent too long looking for her favorite dangle earrings, then gave up the search and popped in pearl studs and a matching bracelet.

Crawling through the airport traffic crush in her Uber ride, Sunny wondered if she should clear her early departure plan with Margaret. Then she remembered the expression Dr. Lee had used. *It's easier to ask forgiveness than permission.* Sunny had already told her friend that she'd soon be meeting her half-brother and possibly her birth father. Margaret would understand.

•   •   •

When Sunny arrived at the wedding and checked in for her seating assignment, her heart swelled upon seeing a sketch she'd drawn of Charlie and Margaret, inspired by a photo of them on their patio. He had one arm around her, and her head rested on his shoulder, fond smiles on both their faces. Sunny was proud of the drawing, pleased with how successfully she'd captured their love.

Today, the framed sketch was displayed at the check-in table for the guests to admire, flanked by a note. *With thanks to our dear friend, artist Sunny Ericsson.* She was grateful she hadn't followed her earlier instincts and been a no-show, after they'd honored her this way. Coming tonight was the right decision.

She proceeded to a tented dining area where propane heaters were already turned on in anticipation of a clear but chilly April evening. Sunny stopped to deposit her sweater and purse at the table and was joined by a mother-daughter team seated to her left. "My mom and Margaret have been friends since college," said the daughter, a diminutive brunette named Isabel who looked around thirty. As they chatted, two men joined them, and the older gentleman introduced himself.

Sunny recognized Robert's name. "You're Margaret's boss, aren't you?" He nodded.

The younger man at the seat next to Sunny's said, "I'm Jeffrey. Robert's my boss too. I'm the regional advertising manager. I came up from Orange County for the wedding." She wondered if seating Jeffrey next to her was a fix-up scheme on Margaret's part. That wouldn't be half-bad. He had a fresh-faced, immature look about him, but his black-rimmed eyeglasses gave him an appealing bookishness.

"You're the artist who did that portrait of the newlyweds?" asked Margaret's college friend.

"Yes, that's mine."

"I love it," she said. "Is that what you do for a living?"

"I wish," Sunny said. "For now I'm working at an ad agency to pay the bills while I finish my degree in graphic design."

"I'm a partner in an advertising agency." The woman handed over her business card with the name of a well-known firm in Sherman Oaks. "We do our design work in-house. Give me a call when you're finished with school. I can't promise we'll have an opening, but we're always on the lookout for new talent."

Well, if Jeffrey wasn't a fix-up, this woman was for sure.

When the guests were summoned to the patio area for the ceremony, Sunny took a seat to the far left. She knew Margaret and her mother would walk down the center aisle together, and the last thing she wanted was to make eye contact with Gwendolyn. Jeffrey sat near the center aisle next to Robert, one row ahead of her. When he glanced back with a dimpled smile, she had to admit he was kind of cute.

Charlie looked as handsome as she'd remembered, standing tall in a fitted, slate-gray suit, his eyes warm with feeling and his thick hair brushing the top of his jacket collar. Sunny braced herself for a wave of emotion, but it was merely a trickle. Her feelings for Charlie had faded, thankfully, like an old wound that no longer throbbed but was still a little tender to the touch.

CHAPTER 37

Charlie watched with trepidation as Margaret and Gwendolyn, the matron of honor, walked down the aisle together. A few hours before, Margaret had gasped, "Oh God, will you look at Mum's shoes?" Charlie thought they weren't as bad as the notorious strappy sandals, but Margaret pointed out that the cone heels were more precarious than prudent. Somehow, mother and daughter made it down the aisle unscathed.

Margaret wore a cocktail dress she'd described as jacquard tulle, in a sort of floral pattern in pale rose over a silky, cream-colored backing. Below the wide V neckline, the dress clung tantalizingly to her bosom and waist, then flared out at the skirt. The fabric was soft and richly textured to the touch. Charlie thought it was perfect.

They were followed by Benny and Heather, and then by Petey, with Michael holding his leash. Charlie's cousin from San Luis Obispo officiated. His brief yet eloquent remarks were followed by original marriage vows that Charlie and Margaret hadn't revealed even to each other before this moment.

A respectful hush fell over the audience. Even the birds seemed to stop chirping. Charlie heard the silence, broken only by the occasional sniffles of guests struggling to contain their emotions. He felt the moistness of his palms, smelled the delicate fragrance of the flowers that lined the aisle. As they exchanged short but ardent vows, it seemed as if all the sights and sounds and scents were paying homage to his love for Margaret, their love for each other.

His cousin concluded the short ceremony by saying, "Ladies and gentlemen, for the first time, I bring you . . . Charlie and Margaret Kittredge." Petey lightened the mood with an exuberant *woof* as Charlie kissed the bride.

"Let's mingle," he said. They strolled around, champagne flutes in hand, greeting the guests. The champagne tasted exquisitely dry – no surprise given the source.

Charlie stole glances at his wife, admiring how the dark curls fell around her smooth shoulders. Two days ago, he'd witnessed a kerfuffle between mother and daughter on the question of hairstyle. Gwendolyn lobbied for the bride to do something spectacular with her hair, but Margaret insisted on wearing it down in her natural everyday manner. In the interest of compromise, the bride agreed to let Gwendolyn hire a professional makeup artist. The result was that Margaret looked like a stage actress version of herself – more glamorous, more dramatic. He rather liked the change, but only for this special day. Charlie wore a lightweight suit that Margaret had helped pick out. "I like how the gray sets off the color of your eyes," she'd said when he tried it on.

A relative of Margaret's approached them with her congratulations and inquired about Charlie's writing. "How's the novel biz? I heard you have another book coming out," said the cousin.

"Yes, in around six months," said Charlie. "It's called *Unexpected Guests.*"

"I'll look forward to reading. What then?"

"Starting next fall, I'll be leading a graduate seminar in creative writing at UCLA. Depending how that goes, the novel biz may become more of a sideline." He grinned at Margaret, who gave him an affirming nod.

•   •   •

He and Margaret shared the head table with Gwendolyn and Sam, and Charlie's cousin and his wife. Michael's family sat separately with Henry. In an abundance of caution, they placed Sunny as far as possible from Henry's table.

After a gourmet meal of endive salad, bay scallops, black rice, and grilled vegetables, Charlie asked the guests for a few minutes of attention. "My wife, Margaret Kittredge — doesn't that have a beautiful ring to it?" There was a smattering of applause. "My wife said she didn't want to bore people with endless speeches, so we promise to make this as painless as possible." He thanked everyone for joining them, making special mention of the guests who'd traveled from far away. He singled out those who took part in the ceremony and introduced Gwendolyn as the next speaker.

She stood up, and Charlie saw her hand shake a little as she squinted at her notes. "Good evening, everyone. I'm here because my Mar — my daughter Margy — " She dropped her notes on the table. Margaret made rapid twirling motions with her thumbs, as if the gesture would free Gwendolyn from her tongue-tied state. "Never mind," said Gwendolyn. "I hate prepared remarks. I'll just say whatever pops into my head. I'm sure that has my daughter filled with apprehension."

"You can say that again," Margaret said to Charlie under her breath.

Gwendolyn surveyed the crowd. "I don't know if anyone here is old enough to remember *The Man Who Came to Dinner*?" Someone applauded in acknowledgement.

"It was a stage play, a classic comedy about an arrogant celebrity who went to dine at the home of a well-to-do family," Gwendolyn said. "He slipped and hurt himself, and the poor family was stuck with their injured guest for days on end. The celebrity—his name, what was his name? Oh, I don't suppose it matters. Anyway, he wreaked havoc, screaming at people all the time and—and—meddling in everyone's affairs." Gwendolyn smiled at the newlyweds. "That pretty much describes my stay in California. Except in the play, it was hilarious. In real life, not so much."

Charlie heard a familiar guffaw. Henry.

Gwendolyn continued. "Charlie and Margy tolerated my spoiled behavior for weeks – no, I guess it was longer than that. Three months? Four? I—I don't suppose that matters either. During that time, I witnessed the strength of their bond and the—the —depth of their commitment to one another. If these two lovely people could survive the man—I mean, the *woman* who came to dinner, their marriage can survive anything." Now Charlie heard a mingling of laughter, sniffles, and applause.

"Finally, I'd like to say—tonight I—oh, dear . . . " She's lost her way, Charlie thought. But Sam came to the rescue. Standing and taking Gwendolyn's arm, he said, "I'm not a scheduled speaker tonight, but as a former litigation attorney, I can't resist an opportunity to make my case before a crowd." Laughter. "Don't worry—I won't speak for more than forty-five minutes." More laughter.

He turned to Gwendolyn. "All I want to say is, I hope that Charlie and Margaret find their relationship as rewarding as mine and Gwendolyn's. I'm confident they'll be every bit as happy, even when they are octogenarians like the two of us."

Charlie hoped the guests didn't see the distress on Margaret's face. She leaned toward him and said, *sotto voce,* "World War Three is about to erupt. Sam has revealed Mum's age to the entire wedding party." But when they looked over at Gwendolyn, she rewarded Sam with a benevolent smile and a fond kiss. This time, Margaret whispered, "My, my, who would have believed it? Now if only Mum would stop thinking she has a dark secret to hide from the world."

Charlie ran a finger down the line of her chin. "Your mother stopped coloring her hair. She stopped lying about her age. She'll stop covering up the dark secret as well. Give her time, my love. She'll get there."

•   •   •

With the dinner and speeches concluded, the dancing began. The deejay introduced a rap song by Drake, causing Margaret to bounce out of her seat and haul Charlie to the center of the dance floor.

"I hate it when people our age get married and only play oldies at the reception," Margaret had said when they met with the deejay. After all her classes at Seaside Fitness, she knew her music and had her funky moves down.

As they brushed past Henry, who was dancing with that college friend of Margaret's, Henry spoke into Charlie's ear. "I can't believe Margaret is taking your name. The Schuyler name was never good enough for her." His full lips jutted into a pout.

"Look at us," Benny called out to them. He was "dancing" with Petey, who rested his paws on the boy's shoulders.

Charlie saw Heather drag Michael to the dance floor. She laughed and gyrated, but Michael's movements were stiffer, his arms close to the body. He looked at his mother and Charlie with a smile that radiated warmth and good feelings.

As Gwendolyn and Sam joined the dancers, Charlie grinned affectionately and said, "Your speeches were perfect. Magnificent, in fact." They smiled back. Even though a Stones song was playing, the older couple danced in the traditional manner, the fingertips of Sam's right hand resting lightly on Gwendolyn's back to guide her around the floor. Then Charlie saw Sunny approach the dance floor with the advertising rep from *Powder World*. Margaret had said their friend was finding her way to a happier life, and he hoped it was true.

•   •   •

As Jeffrey led Sunny out to dance, she nearly had a brush with Gwendolyn. Henry saved the day by calling "Gwen-Gwen" in the nick of time, allowing Sunny to escape Gwendolyn's notice. She'd dodged her nemesis once again.

She and Jeffrey danced to a Michael Jackson song. Suddenly he was channeling MJ, slinking across the floor with confident moves that rivaled Margaret's expertise. He was definitely growing on her, even if he looked awfully young.

All evening Sunny had felt happy, wistful, and teary all at once. She tried to keep envy out of the equation. Now that she'd outgrown her fantasy about Charlie, she accepted he belonged with Margaret. Maybe someday she would meet her own version of Charlie, someone who belonged with her. They returned to their table after two more songs. "That was fun," Sunny said.

"I know. Last time I danced was at my twenty-fifth high school reunion last fall." This put Jeffrey in her age group – not so young after all. Good. His chief interests, he told her, were chess, classical music, and soccer, none of them topics on which she had much knowledge. But she said, "Very cool," and he flashed her that adorable, dimpled grin again, as if she'd heaped praise on him. She felt an odd mix of awkwardness and attraction.

"I understand this party shuts down at ten o'clock," he said.

"Yeah, the neighborhood has a residential noise ordinance."

"Maybe we could go someplace for a drink afterwards?"

"I—I can't. There's someplace I have to be later."

"A date?" The corners of his mouth turned down a little, which touched her.

Sunny shook her head. "Nothing like that."

Robert tapped Jeffrey on the shoulder to talk, and Sunny picked up a conversation with Isabel about school and work. Isabel sighed. "You're so lucky." Sunny glanced over her shoulder, wondering whether the girl was addressing somebody else.

"Lucky? Me?" She didn't associate herself with good fortune.

"Well, yeah. For one thing, you've got an amazing artistic gift, something you're passionate about. I have a dead-end job I can't stand at a local cable company. All day long customers gripe about how crappy and expensive the service is. They're right, but I'm not allowed to agree with them. I'm supposed to read from a stupid script defending the company."

Sunny gave her a sympathetic smile. "Look, I didn't have a plan for the future when I was your age. When I was ten years older than you I was still in professional limbo. Don't be too hard on yourself."

Isabel shrugged. "Maybe so. I still say you're lucky to have so much going for you."

They were interrupted when a man stopped by the table to speak with Isabel and her mother.

Sunny turned back to Jeffrey. He tilted his head down and peered at her from over his glasses. "I'm in LA every couple of weeks to visit clients, and I'd love to take you to dinner. If that sounds good, text me your number and I'll call next time I'm in town." He handed her his card.

"I will." She stashed the card in her purse and checked the time. Eight-thirty. Almost time to meet Paul. She felt a surge of anticipation, then reminded herself to set the bar low. *He'll drive me to Dad's place. We'll shake hands, drink a cup of coffee or something, and make polite conversation for an hour. It will be awkward, but we'll get through it. Baby steps.*

Sunny looked around and found no sign of Gwendolyn, though Sam was in his seat. Perhaps she'd gone off to the loo, as she called it. This would be an opportune time for Sunny to say her goodbyes. She wove through the small crowd. Margaret and Charlie were standing at the far end of the dance floor, close to the head table, speaking to Michael and Heather. Sunny approached them. "It's a beautiful wedding," she said. "I'm sorry I need to leave early. Something important came up."

"Oh, Sunny, is this what you told me about?" Margaret asked.

"I—I hope so," she replied, her voice choking with sudden emotion.

Charlie gave them both a searching look, then said, "We received lots of compliments on your portrait. You may get a couple of commissions out of this."

Sunny dipped her chin. "That would be amazing." She saw Gwendolyn emerging from the house and started to turn away but changed her mind. She walked straight to the older woman with confident strides – her heart thump-thumping in her chest, but determined to stay the course. "Gwendolyn. I didn't want to leave without speaking to you."

Margaret's mother broke into a smile that was, by all appearances, genuine. "Sunny, you look stunning in that dress. It sets your coloring off beautifully."

"Thank you." Sunny moved in a little closer. There was a subtle difference in Gwendolyn – her hair, now silver instead of blond. But there was something else too. Sunny couldn't put her finger on it. "Last year, you apologized to me in an email," Sunny said. "I should have responded, but at the time, I wasn't sure what to say. I was still very hurt over what happened."

"I understand, dear. I hope you took my apology to heart. Now, you must meet Sam." She steered Sunny over to the head table.

"You're that talented artist," said Sam amiably. "Gwendolyn has spoken of you often. And if memory serves, you ran a spa that she said was delightful, right down to the unusual music selections."

Gwendolyn has spoken of you often? Really? But Sam's comments were specific enough that he must know her history. Sunny was shocked by this. What was Gwendolyn's word? Gobsmacked. Yes, Sunny was gobsmacked. They chatted for a few more minutes. Gwendolyn remained gracious, and Sam seemed like the perfect gentleman, charming and pleasant. Gwendolyn had done well for herself.

Feeling a chill in the air, Sunny slipped on her sweater and floated into the house to freshen up before meeting Paul. She felt like she was, in her forties, enjoying her fifteen minutes of fame. The guests made a fuss over her art. She met a new man who showed interest. The young woman seated next to her hailed her as a role model. Even the much-feared Gwendolyn treated her as a person worthy of respect, a person one discussed with one's partner.

Freeing her long hair from the ponytail tie and shaking it loose, she reflected on Isabel's comments about how lucky she was.

But Isabel had it wrong. The things happening to Sunny were not luck or fate or karma. Despite what she used to believe, the developments in her life weren't inevitable rewards or punishments for past actions. They resulted from thoughtful choices. Like the choice to start over in a new community. To return to school. To find a job that wasn't just a paycheck but a stepping-stone. To pursue her art. Most of all, the choice not to let life overwhelm her.

She walked outside to meet her brother.

•   •   •

Only the established couples remained on the floor as the deejay played mostly slow tracks. Charlie had been working the crowd with his bride, but now he wanted only to dance with her.

He hooked his thumbs under the cap sleeves of Margaret's dress, and when he pulled her close, she wound her arms around his waist. He closed his eyes as they danced to the slow music with their bodies touching. He took in the light tropical scent of her shampoo and felt the softness of her curls. He kissed her warm cheek. He blinked his eyes open and observed the other couples on the dance floor, everyone looking relaxed and happy.

In the periphery of his vision, Charlie noticed two men across the lawn. Strangers. The older of the two was tall and angular, with thinning whitish-blond hair; the younger man was shorter, broader, dark-headed.

And then he saw Sunny. Sunny, streaking across the grass with the lightness and speed of a girl . . . hurtling herself toward the older man who stood with arms outstretched, as if waiting to catch someone dear to him in a fond embrace. "Look at that," he whispered.

Margaret beamed at the sight of Sunny and the elderly man hugging. "Charlie, it really happened," she said in his ear.

"What happened?"

"Sunny just got the one thing she wanted most in life."

He pulled her in close. "So did I, my love." The tension drained from Charlie's body like a receding tide as he guided Margaret across the dance floor. "So did I."

THE END

ACKNOWLEDGEMENTS

I wrote the first draft of this novel in the spring of 2020. Since I was I lockdown with nothing else to do, the work progressed quickly. In no time at all I was typing "The End" – pleased with myself for completing a 90,000+ word manuscript in record time. As so often happens with fiction writing, The End was only the beginning of this book's journey.

The Unexpected Guests wasn't just conceived during Covid, it was *about* Covid – written in real time and focusing on an ensemble of characters suffering together through the early days of the pandemic. I showed it to several guinea pigs (sometimes referred to as beta readers) who gave me encouraging feedback. Alas, by the time I started peddling it to agents and publishers, these industry gurus informed me that the reading public had grown weary of all things Covid. Nobody wanted to read about fictional middle-aged men and women wiping down their groceries or arguing over masking etiquette.

So, it was back to the drawing board. Writers can't bear to kill their darlings – a term used to describe the deletion of favorite lines or scenes from a text. I'm sorry to report, dear readers, that in this rewrite the carnage was horrific. Eighteen months and hundreds of dead darlings later, I finally had a Covid-free manuscript I considered worthy of publishing. Fortunately, the acquisitions team at Black Rose Writing agreed.

To be clear, I didn't follow this winding road as a solo journeyer. Far from it. In thanking my fellow travelers I'll begin, as usual, with Mary Todd, who remains my close friend and personal editor extraordinaire. Not only did she apply her customary reading and editing wisdom to the project – this time she also functioned as cheerleader and coach when I nearly abandoned the revisions, doubting whether I was up to meeting the challenge. Mary believed in me when I didn't believe in myself, convincing me to see it through.

I'm also indebted to my fellow critique group members who spent countless hours poring over every page of the early drafts: Julie Mayerson Brown, Kelly Flowers, Mary Jo Hazard, and Tricia Hopper Zacher. Every time I re-read these pages, even now, I hear your individual voices echoing in many of my favorite scenes. Mary Jo performed double duty, later donning her therapist's hat to help me understand Sunny's mental health issues. Special thanks, as well, to Dr. Harriet Wilburne, who applied her professional knowledge of psychiatry to the same task; and to Tim Paulson, who educated me on ancestry websites.

In the final stages of the writing process, as I struggled with the remaining holes in my manuscript, I was fortunate to connect with Pamela Taylor. A professional editor and successful historical fiction author, Pam showed an uncanny ability to cut to the chase and show me what was needed to fix the problems. It was her expert hand that pulled me across the finish line.

Heartfelt thanks to my many beta readers along the way for their encouragement and feedback: Tish Andrewartha, Hedy Carpenter, Marsha Jacobson, Daisy (Nancy) Kalina, Erica Karlin, Mary McKinney, Winifred Morice, Susan Paxton, S.M. Stevens, and Cam Torrens. Thanks also to Gayle Taylor and her book club members, Joanne Deldotto, Mary Jane Dellafiora, Myrna Everhart, Debbi Gelbart, Cheryl Graue, and (again) Mary Todd.

To Reagan Rothe and the rest of the team at Black Rose Writing, I am so grateful to you for believing in my work enough to publish both this book and the prequel, *My Year of Casual Acquaintances*. It's a delight to work with you all and to be part of your wonderful community of authors.

"I Saw Her Again" (1966) was co-written by the Mamas and the Papas band members John Phillips and Denny Doherty. The song about suicide that upset Sunny while she was hiding at the spa is "Not to Blame," written and recorded by Joni Mitchell (1994).

To my fellow AlzAuthors, Renegades, Black Rose authors, and the many other writers I've had the pleasure to meet, thank you for your camaraderie and support.

To my husband David and the rest of my family and friends, I am so thankful for your steadying presence during my roller-coaster publishing ride of the past couple of years.

Last in these acknowledgements but first in this writer's heart—my readers. I can't thank you enough for inspiring, motivating, and rewarding me in so many ways.

ABOUT THE AUTHOR

Ruth F. Stevens likes to create stories that will make readers laugh and cry. A former public relations executive in New York and Los Angeles, she is a produced playwright and author of two previous novels, Stage Seven and My Year of Casual Acquaintances. Ruth is a proud member of the Women's Fiction Writers Association and the Dramatists Guild of America and serves as a volunteer and acquisitions editor for AlzAuthors.

Ruth lives in Torrance, California, with her husband. In her spare time, she enjoys travel, hiking, hip-hop and fitness classes, yoga, Broadway musicals, wine tasting, leading a book club, and visiting her grandsons in NYC.

Visit Ruth at www.ruthfstevens.com and consider signing up for her monthly newsletter to receive publishing updates, book reviews, and special offers.

OTHER TITLES BY RUTH F. STEVENS

NOTE FROM RUTH F. STEVENS

Word-of-mouth is crucial for any author to succeed. If you enjoyed *The Unexpected Guests*, please leave a review online — anywhere you are able. Even if it's just a sentence or two. It would make all the difference and would be very much appreciated.

Thanks!
Ruth F. Stevens

We hope you enjoyed reading this title from:

www.blackrosewriting.com

Subscribe to our mailing list – *The Rosevine* – and receive **FREE** books, daily deals, and stay current with news about upcoming releases and our hottest authors.
Scan the QR code below to sign up.

Already a subscriber? Please accept a sincere thank you for being a fan of Black Rose Writing authors.

View other Black Rose Writing titles at www.blackrosewriting.com/books and use promo code **PRINT** to receive a **20% discount** when purchasing.

9 781685 135348